JUSTICE
4 ALL

DONNELL HARRIS

authorHOUSE®

AuthorHouse™
1663 Liberty Drive
Bloomington, IN 47403
www.authorhouse.com
Phone: 833-262-8899

Published by AuthorHouse   04/10/2023

ISBN: 979-8-8230-0575-3 (sc)
ISBN: 979-8-8230-0574-6 (e)

Print information available on the last page.

This book is printed on acid-free paper.

CONTENTS

INTRODUCTION

Afrika has always been known as a loner initially while attending Powell Elementary School. Being a loner, certain individuals, like the neighborhood bullies, would perceive him to be an easy target for their extortion scheme, but he have learned, everybody can form their own opinions about anything, even about a person. He wasn't going to hide his money in his shoes, socks or behind his belt buckle. Giving his money to some girl then obtaining it once inside the cafeteria wasn't happening either like the other male students attending Powell Elementary up at 10th and Penn Street. He was from the DMZ, and they had a motto. "Fight or take Flight." He wasn't taking flight from anyone especially Rhine Boy and his little crew. They were posted up as usual "strong arming" (extorting) the male students at the cafeteria door. When he was trying to walk pass, Rhine Boy decided to tap his pockets to see if he had any change and he heard the light jiggling. Instead of having a long nonproductive conversation, he hit Rhine boy with a three-piece combination that the left hook damn near decapitated his head. His act was so sudden that his crew didn't know how to react, and he was deep in another guy butt also. He was handling his business until they realized that it was safer and more beneficial to "bum rush" him. Just as fast as their weight came down on him, their weight dissipated just as quickly as he scurried to his feet with his hands in a fight position. Those that came to his assistance were Bear, Tek9, Kimba and Black. Guys that also lived in the DMZ with him. From this little incident, they would become inseparable for life.

JUSTICE 4 ALL

AFRIKA MUHAMMAD WAS born, raised, and educated in the streets of Camden, New Jersey. For those of y'all who don't know where Camden is located, it is in South Jersey. Their closest neighbor is right across the Ben Franklin Bridge, and they are separated by the murky waters of the Delaware River. Philly, the alleged City of Brotherly Love. From those living in Camden, their name should be referred to the City of Brotherly Blood. As a child playing by the polluted water of the Delaware, he was sure he would be able to throw a stone from his bank to the bank of Philly when he became a teenager, but he wasn't able even when he was a young adult. He did have to swim it twice out of necessity. The alleged city of Brotherly Love wasn't displaying any love on those two occasions. Do you know there are some cities that actually lived by their slogans. Like, New York being the city that never sleeps or like Chi-Town, Chicago being the Windy City. Both cities emulate their slogan to a T. Philly is consider the city of brotherly love but don't check the annual murder rate or how Baltimore is supposed to be the City that Reads but don't research the illiteracy rate or dropout rate especially among young black males teenagers. In reference to Camden, News Week asked a very provocative question in the early nineties; "Who could live here?"

Camden and Philly back in the day was like oil to water. They just did not mix. Way before his time, Philly use to venture into Camden every Friday and Saturday night to party with their neighbor while some would travel over into Philly until a violent incident in Camden severed their unspoken contract. Now, Afrika had heard several stories over the years as to what initiated this "beef." Although the story varied like the people telling it, two things remained evident and constant. First, a gun was involved and secondly, someone got murder. Who is at fault doesn't matter. After that incident, the partying that existed between the two neighbors ceased completely. So, the street laws and etiquettes concerning Philly was establish long before he was able to leave the porch and run through the broken bottles, urine smelling, rat infested allies in Camden at the age of eight.

Afrika lived in the North side of Camden. The land of the Kackalacks as they were known throughout the city and people did not just venture into their set. Although a rare few guys from out of North went where ever they wanted in the city, they gave respect and demanded it back. Walking into North without an invitation, strolling through like it was a Sunday or cruising through like it was Parkside or Lawnside could be detrimental to the health of your body or the property that you might possess. Stumble down into 3rd Street will without a doubt get you touched. Known in North as Viet Nam, and that shines a bright light on those boys down there. I can only advise you to run if you foolishly stroll on their set and being an out of state guest, your family should have told you to the possible horrors going down beyond 4th Street. 3rd Street was known to even have "beefs" among themselves. Now, how psychotic is that? There are people that lives in North that did not go or like venturing down into that hell hole.

The elementary school that he had to attend was Powell Elementary up on 10th and Penn Street. instead of Cooper Point down on 3rd Street and State Street. Just because he live on a specific side of 6th Street, he was forced to migrate up to 10th Street. For the first couple of years, he flew under everyone's radar of the bullies, but he could feel a change in the air. So-called tough guys were starting to patch up and "strong armed" (extort) the weaker students or those perceived as an easy target. He constantly had his eyes on Ape Man and Tick Tack including the bitch ass antic they took the other students through. Since it did not have anything to do with him, he would turn a blind eye to their intimidating antics. In fourth grade, he started peeking on the bullies peeking at him. How you handle your antagonist dictates the respect you receive or the living hell you will endure. how everybody, including those bullies in standing in the shadows, will perceive you. North has a slogan, "Fight or take flight." Afrika wasn't taking flight from anyone, no matter what the numbers.

His life altering decision materialized one day as he was preparing to go to lunch. He had just placed his books inside his locker and was proceeding towards the cafeteria when he spotted Rhine Boy with his six goons standing at the door hitting the male students up for coins. He was not going to hide his money in his shoes, in his socks or behind his belt buckle. And he definitely wasn't going to give his money to some girl to hold for him until he was inside the cafeteria. Na, he was holding his own money. Rhine Boy had been peeking on him for a minute but never tried his hand. He knew Afrika was a loner, but Afrika also knew, he would be thinking like that. Today, he was nudging Top Cat and nodding in his direction. Just as he was about to walk through the door without being harassed again, Rhine Boy decided to tap his pocket to see if he had any change and he did. Big mistake on his part. Afrika was never about a lengthy conversation especially when the plot was already laid out. So, instead of a long nonproductive conversation, he leaped deep into Rhine Boy's ass before his goon knew what was happening. When Top Cat step up, he hit him with a five-piece combination and a left hook that damn near decapitated his head. As they came at him staggered, he was hitting them with three and four-piece combinations and rocking their world. He was handling his business until they realized it would be healthier to "bum-rush" him altogether. Just as quickly as their weight came upon him. He felt their weight dissipating just as quickly. Scurrying to his feet with his hands up, he recognized the guys that came to his assistance were Bear, Tek9, Kimba, Black and Murk. They also lived in the DMZ Zone where he lived. They finish tearing the fur off of Rhine Boy and his goons then out their feet up in their assess for good measure as they were leaving.

"What did I tell you!?" Bear said laughing then winking over at him. "I told y'all he was going to get up in their assess."

"I wouldn't have believed it if I hadn't witness it myself" admitted Tek9, staring him in amazement. "Man, they should call you Scrappy."

"I told y'all was sleeping on that boy" Bear chuckles were more like a low roar. "You can't tell every book by its cover, but a man's eyes will reveal all you need to know.

"Damn man, you are nice as hell with hands" complimented Black smiling over at him.

"Thanks man" he replied wiping the blood from his nose while glaring at Rhine Boy, friends assisted him to his feet.

"You can't tell every book by its cover, but a man's eyes will tell you everything that you need to know" replied Murk staring in his eyes with a slight grin. "I like him fellas" he said never averting his eyes.

"You don't like anybody!" they chimed together then burst out laughing.

"Well, there is a first time for everything, motherfuckers" he replied trying to contain his smile while staring over at Afrika.

This simple incident solidified their friendship. They were together every day. If you saw four of them, the other two weren't far behind. Their final two years at Powell were a growing process for them. Afrika was constantly up in bullies assess if he caught one strong arming another student. Eventually, all the bullies went hiding in the shadows because of the beat downs that Afrika was admonishing, but that didn't prevent them for paying some form of retribution as they would seek them out in those shadows and brought drama straight to them. Almost every week they were pressing up on them. Kimba would create a fabricated lie that was cosigned by one, and another bully would be educated on what eventually comes to all bullies. Guys that wouldn't defend themselves or refused to fight didn't have to hide their money anymore or give it a girl to hold for them. The last two years at Powell could have elevated their status but they weren't looking or desired to be popular, especially Afrika. They used their combine status to curtail the violence and other antics against other students. Noncombative or humble students enjoyed their last two years of elementary from the steady harassments from bullies, not tough guys. Graduating sixth grade was their first accomplishment, and they were flying high.

During the summer months, Afrika was spending three hours a day at the library down town on Broadway while his partners were doing little mischievous things around the community or crossing 10th Street bridge to walk pass Abbott Village as they made their way towards East Camden. Although they teased him regularly, he tried to ignore the slick things filtering pass their lips but some the things they said were funny as hell. Yet, they never deterred him from his academics. He became intrigued with the library quite by accident. He was still a loner then and walked into the library to escape a sudden summer shower. He walked towards the literary department and started fingering the books. Although he was only eight years old at the time, he became interested in the book covers of Donald Goines especially "Black Girl Lost." This was the first book he actually read. Although he would constantly stop to reflect on what the writer was saying or describing, his young eyes would stare around his community seeing the same things that were being written. Two liquor stores on opposite sides of the street and this scene was played out all around the Black communities he walked through in his city. When he tried to initiate a conversation on the things that had materialized in his young mind, his partners would call him a geek and actually tried calling him School Boy, but he shut that right down. He liked his Afrocentric name and denounced any and all nick names.

Entering Pyne Poynt Junior High School at 7th and Erie Street, the culture of the school will transform tremendously. Those guys up at 10th Street were forced to attend the Poynt and intermingle with the guys from 3rd Street. Their separate elementary school kept them apart, but at the age of twelve, that luxury was gone now. The only solace that they had was where the school was located, in the DMZ Zone. With the park, the community center, the swimming pool, and basketball courts all in the Zone, this will be a safe haven for the children growing up. If a rare fight occurred, one on one is the established rule and those breaking the rules that were established before we were a thought in their father's nut sack, will pay dearly for their indiscretion's once the OG's find out and they will find out.

Another transformation at the junior high, level was the daily forced infiltration of guys and girls from South Camden and East Camden especially those living in Abbott Village, Monday through Friday. Abbott Village did have an option, other than crossing 10th Street which was the much closer school. Those that did come would take 9th Street to the school because it was basically out of sight and took them towards the track and field. They were fortunate that the guys living up around 10th Street were more obliging than those living down on 3rd Street. South siders had three ways to enter North if they decide to keep their bus fare and walk. Taking 7th Street Bridge would give you a straight shot to Pyne Poynt with minimum obstacles or take the Underground Tunnel down 6th Street. The Underground runs under the traffic heading and coming off the Ben Franklin Bridge from Philly. This is one of the safest routes because it is located where the MTA Police usually congregated and more importantly, the main vein into the DMZ. One thing about the South side, they need to humble themselves instead of always ready to reveal their canines. Why would you go stomping through 3rd Street like you don't know the reputation of those psychotic acting guys. By simply taking the Tunnel or 7th Street Bridge, the drama would cease, but not y'all hard heads. Flexing while deep in Viet Nam, those boys didn't have a problem in reaching out and viciously touching your dumb assess. What an asinine way to start your morning. But 3rd Street must always remember, what goes around comes around. When 3rd Street venture down town to buy new clothes, records or just to sight-see and peek on the girls by the harbor, their heads had better be on a swivel. They are in the heart of South Camden, and they will seek revenge for any previous indiscretions. Do you blame South side for seeking restitution because most of the guys in North don't. You weep what you sow, right?

As the fellas grew older, they did do things that knucklehead little boys would do. Like, they would be walking down the stairway then looking up to get a peek under the young ladies dresses and skirts. Yeah, they were manifesting into nasty little boys, but they weren't delinquents. They would always debate the dumbest things like who is the ugliest girl in the school like students weren't whispering about how dusty they looked because they were definitely dusty. They would also debate which bully they would taunt next and laugh until tears were coming out of their eyes from some imaginary bullshit that one of them would create. Although very mischievous and the product of their environment, there were a lot of things that Afrika just was not down for. He was not going to throw eggs or tomatoes at anyone and especially five-o. He could make a meal out of them. He was not going to tease wine-o's. Some have given him some essential information about life through some clever jokes although their fee is usually the coins in his pockets. He absolutely was not snatching any woman's purse because he did not want anybody snatching his mother's purse although all they would get is practice because she didn't have any money. Even still, he would hunt them down personally. Stealing hub caps off of cars or car batteries then selling them to the chop shop were not happening either. The pay was not worth the risk he constantly told them especially after dividing the money by six. How ironic it was for them that he would be the one to introduce then to their next adventure that will sustain then. The impish smile he had on his face one day while they sitting on their corner at 6th and York is what tickled their curiosity, especially Murk but he won't reveal his thought until they were organized.

When he finally revealed his hand, they were openly shocked but couldn't contained their laughter. Like most geeks, he did his research on interstate auto and the charges they would face as juveniles if caught. They were just starting to turn fifteen when they ventured into his very lucrative business especially living in New Jersey. By the time they were sixteen, they were the best dress teenagers in the city and known for keeping a little cash. You know when you are flourishing and your popularity also when chop shops started calling their burners (pay phones) and placing special orders.

They usually would put on a suit with their small brim hats and casually walk out of North under wondering eyes. People knew they were doing something, but did not know what? It was apparent that they weren't selling drugs, or it would have hit the grapevine. Whatever they were secretly doing they were still flying well under the radar. They would last be seen descending the Underground steps or descending the stairs at one of the speedline entrances that took them to Philly, but their truly destination would still go unknown especially when they did not surface at 8th and Market Street as most people from Camden usually do. They would transfer over to the Blue Line instead then take the Amtrak from 30th Street Station to New York to search the parking garages near and around Madison Square Garden. Once an order was filled, the person would cross the Hudson River out of New York through the Holland Tunnel and wait in Jersey at a designated rendezvous location. Once all orders were filled or a substantial substitute in a reasonable time, they would all take 95S to get back home and staying out of the fourth lane until they change lead cars. If you are smart, you will stay the fuck off of the New Jersey Turnpike. The time you enter the turnpike is stamped on the card you received and could cause you unwanted grief when you are getting off. If you are exiting faster than the initial time limits allow, you are speeding, and a State Police will be right there to hear another ridiculous explanation or lie. You cannot argue against time while factoring in speed when it comes to math. Only a fool would stay persistent. Afrika did have them agree on one specific agreement before they had even ventured into this lucrative business. If any one of them gets pop, they would cease their expeditions to the Big Apple and shut down their lucrative operation. They maintained their operation throughout junior high.

The summer before attending high school Bear got a proposition that took them down a completely new illegal path. They were chilling inside Pyne Poynt Park watching the fellas playing basketball. They were all casually dressed in leisure sets with their small brim hats. They were trying to decide what type of mischievousness they can get into. Tek9 and Kimba was always ready to invade Parkside or any other set where there were vibrant young ladies looking to get into some mischief. They swear the ladies love the brothers from out of North. They counter that they were the only ones from out of North that travel around the city like they owned it and have not seen this love they were talking about especially from Centerville. Granted, they have received love from several parties that they have attended around the city, but they never attended an after party, they were not that naïve. What most of them wanted to do was explore the Forbidden Garden over in Philly. Guys were always asking them why would they willingly subject themselves to the possible bullshit seeking the Forbidden Garden? And they always responded with the same question, have you ever talked and socialized with the women who lives in Philly? The expression that came to their faces always made them burst out laughing.

While they were still trying to make up their mind, they spotted Thunder's sky-blue Bentley Continental pulling up on the 7th Street side of the horse shoe causing the fellas to cease their antics and peek at one another. He was definitely out of his lane. He does not venture into the DMZ unless he was conducting business. Those who knew his car stared at it intensely as two immaculately dressed bodyguards stepped out and open the back driver's side door. Thunder stepped out wearing a blue four-button Louis Vuitton with matching derby and alligator shoes. He stood there long enough for everybody to take notice of him and the Havana cigar he was smoking before heading inside the park as all eyes followed him. Standing a mere five feet eight and well over three-hundred pounds, the mid-fifty gentleman did not look the part of a Kingpin. He gave the appearance of a pimp but not a Kingpin. He has been controlling the drug scene in the city with a strict and unforgiving fist for well over twenty years. A nickel bag of dope being sold up in Centerville or down on 6th and Berkley Street was his shit. You can cut it or mix it with someone else shit, but it was still his shit, initially. To set up shop on his streets, you will pay a property tax if you are trying to make money in Camden. His quiet assassin was a guy name Lights-Out, but he was presently doing three years at Rahway State for a parole violation of all things.

"Which one of y'all is Bear?" he asked staring over at them.

"I am, O.G" he replied as they got to their feet.

"Is this your little clique?"

"They are my partners, O.G" he replied returning his stare.

"What is this shit I'm hearing about y'all have been cutting through different sets for years? Is this true?"

"We walk in peace, O.G" he replied still returning his stare.

"For someone walking in peace, y'all seem to be reaching out and touching a lot of people" he shared with a slight grin.

"Only when someone is trying to impede us or touch us" he replied slightly hardening his eyes. "What's this about O.G?"

"I have a proposition for you and your crew."

"Partners" Afrika corrected him catching his eyes.

He instantly returned his stare checking him out from head to toe very slowly then, focusing on his eyes. "You must be Afrika" he mentioned slightly grinning.

"Yes, O.G" he replied never averting his eyes.

"Like, I was saying Bear" he said then returning his eyes on him. "I have a proposition for you and your partners. I'm talking about Big Boy shut if y'all are down."

"What is it?"

"There is money to be made near the Inner Harbor and I want it" he shared staring over at him then at his partners, but they all had blank expressions on their faces. "Do y'all want to get paid?"

"We do our own thing, O.G."

"Yeah, I have heard" he informed them, but no expression came to their faces again causing him to slightly smile at how cool they were remaining. "Y'all have been doing y'all thing for a couple years and without getting caught up. That is extremely impressive to me for someone y'all ages. I have never pressed up on y'all about my taxes over the years" he stressed staring in their eyes individually. "Y'all could easily make ten G's a day once you get started with the clientele, I have prepared for y'all" he shared revealing a coy smile that perked their interest.

"Why us, O.G?"

"Because y'all don't seek recognition and that is what I need. Besides, what teenagers do you know dress like y'all?" he asked lightly chuckling. "Do y'all want to get this money or what?"

"Can I have a quick conversation with my partners?" Bear requested already knowing the answer.

"Sure, time is just money" he replied pulling from his cigar then stared at the basketball game that was being played. "I hear I have lost a lot of money betting against these boys on the basketball court especially the Golden Streaks."

"In their age bracket, even stack teams can't beat those boys, Thunder. They are down her isolated beating up on one another then enter the basketball season demolishing all teams."

"I'm through betting against them" he replied watching a guy floating towards the rim and slamming it.

The fellas walked a short distance to the pavilion and took seats.

"Well?" Bear asked staring over at them.

"You know it was only a matter of time before someone pulled us up" mention Tek9 with a smirk.

"What I'm curious about is who put us on blast?" mention Afrika hardening his eyes.

"Yeah, so would I" cosigned Black slightly snarling.

"No use in getting mad" replied Kimba smiling. "We have been under cover for a minute. You must admit that" he shared peeking over at Thunder while snickering.

"That we have" cosigned Murk snickering while tapping his knuckles.

"If we don't get this money, somebody else will and I personally want to attend college" mention Afrika.

"You book worm ass don't have to worry about that" mentioned Bear causing them to burst out laughing then peek over at Thunder already peeking at them.

"Do y'all understand what we are contemplating" asked Black staring around at them. He has always been the rational one when Afrika logic wasn't enough.

"If you aren't down, we aren't down" Afrika told him returning his stare.

"No, brothers" he said smiling at them. "I'm not insinuating that I'm not down. We cannot be a mule for no man. If we are going to jump into this game, we need our own product" he voiced his opinion.

"I'm cosigning that" Tek9 said. "Do you think Thunder will go for it?"

"I don't know" replied Bear as they stared out at him still watching the basketball game.

"If he wants that money, he will go for it and don't forget brothers, he came seeking us out. He said we are exactually what he needed" Afrika said slightly smiling at them. "If he don't accept our counter proposition, he will be seeking his back taxes and we will have to shut it down because I am not paying a motherfucker shit weekly" he said with conviction forcing more snickers from his sincerity.

"No doubt he will be seeking those back taxes" Black cosigned snickering again.

"You know we have never consider jumping into the drug game but if he has it laid out for us, we need to get that money" Kimba shared his thoughts.

"I agree" Bear replied. "There is nothing for us to do but lay our cards on the table."

"Let's see if he bites our hype" replied Tek9 grinning.

"Let's" replied Bear as they got to their feet. They left the pavilion and strolled casually back towards him under the watchful eyes of his two bodyguards.

"So, what is y'all decisions" he asked trying to get a hint

from their posture or expression, but none was given. They all stood erect and had nonchalant expressions on their faces.

"We appreciate your offer, O.G but we can't be a mule for another man" Bear told watching him closely. "Now, I am not saying that we do not want that money, but we will grind for only ourselves. How about you selling us your product, but we grind for ourselves?"

"That is not what I am looking for" he replied snarling at their suggestion.

"We understand that O.G" he replied returning his stare.

"O.G" interjected Afrika, catching his eyes. "You initially said that you had a proposition for us not a demand. We heard your lucrative offer, and it is intriguing to us. We are simply making a counter offer or proposition. Getting that money is all we are trying to do for you."

He stood there staring up at Afrika. Everybody that he talked to informed him that Afrika might not be out front, but his words holds a lot of weight especially with his partners. There is not another crew in North that carried it like they did, nonchalantly. When he found out that they had been doing interstate auto and for three years, he was actually shocked and that doesn't happen very often. They had stayed that low beneath the radar and not flashing their success showed their maturity. He wanted the money he had sitting up on the shelf for three months and the only crew that could get it for him was the young men standing in front of him. He has only one whole card to play and how they answer the question will dictate who wins. So, he asked.

"Suppose I can't accept your counter proposition" he inquired staring directly at Afrika.

"Then we will shut our business down and pay you your back taxes" he replied never averting his eyes.

"I hear y'all business is extremely lucrative. Y'all would shut it down?"

"Definitely!" they replied together while staring over into his eyes.

A faint grin came to his lips. "I will have to get back with y'all."

"Okay, O.G" replied Bear as Thunder suddenly turned walking away with his bodyguards close behind. They sat on bench watching his climbing back into the back seat then closed the door. His men climbed inside and started up the engine. They sat there for about five minutes before gently pulling away and going around the horse shoe doing about five miles per hour. Their eyes followed the car taking their eyes off of it when they were obstructed by the old radio station and peeked at one another. Coming back up 6th Street, his Bentley suddenly pulled over then one of his men climbed out then started approaching them.

"Come to this location tomorrow at noon" he instructed extending a card to him. "Bring your money if you are trying to get jump started" he told them then turned and walked away.

"Hell, yeah!" boasted Bear smiling from ear to ear. "Are y'all ready to get this money, brothers" he asked tapping Kimba's knuckles.

"Or time" mention Afrika watching their expressions changing.

"Not funny, Afrika" replied Black causing the others to burst out laughing and easing their apprehensions.

"How much money do we have?" Tek9 asked. "I got eight G's."

"I have eleven" mentioned Black.

"I have seven" shared Kimba.

"I'm sitting on twenty-five" mention Afrika shocking them all.

"Twenty-five!" mentioned Tek9 staring at him surprised. "How in the hell do you have that much?"

"By staying the hell out of Parkside, the East side and Lawnside sniffing after those young ladies that you and Kimba like chasing after" he replied causing them to burst out laughing except him and Kimba. All they could do is just smile.

The next morning, they were hitting their stash places in their parents houses then hooked up at 6th and York at eleven o'clock before catching the bus down town. They exited at the main Speedline (subway station) on Broadway then brought round trip tickets. They found seats then laid back taking in the changing scenery. Twenty minutes later, they were arriving in Moorestown. They exited the train then came down the escalator and departed the terminal under flirting and curious eyes. County guys and girls were everywhere. Was this their private hang out spot? They spent their time waiting on their ride flirting with the adventurous, but vulnerable or naïve county girls and young ladies. This was the spot where the majority of their parents was going to pick them up or connect to their next bus they found out as a black Escalade pulled up with two riders inside then the passenger window lower.

"North?" the passenger asked staring out at them.

"Yeah" replied Bear.

"Hop in" he instructed then wined the window back up while unlocking the doors.

They climbed inside amazed at the space and third row seats. As they rode up Rt.130, they took in the serenity of the environment as they weaved through clean and pristine streets. Ten minutes later, they were pulling up on a horseshoe parking pad in front of a gorgeous single-family home. Exiting the SUV, one of the men lead the way towards the house. Parked beside Thunder's Ghost was a Bentley Flying Spur and a motherfucking McLaren 650S. The fellas just peeked at one another while slightly shaking their heads and smiling as they walked pass. Walking through the front door, light oak floors extended throughout the first floor. The sounds of Lockjaw Johnson saxophone floated to their ears as they walked towards the music. In the family room, Thunder was sitting around with three other impeccably dressed men.

"Good afternoon, gentlemen" he greeted, admiring the suits that they were wearing.

"Good afternoon, O.G" they replied together taking in the scene while removing their hats.

"Make yourself, comfortable" he offered watching them fanning out before taking a seat. "Do y'all want a drink?"

"Na, we don't drink, O.G" replied Bear.

"Okay, this is how I want this shit to run" he told them staring at them individually. "There numerous of white boys at Rutgers University trying to get their groove on and they desire strictly cocaine. I will make the initial introduction and y'all will be working with him exclusively. Is that okay with y'all?"

"Are you saying our clients will be only the students at Rutgers?" inquired Bear slightly grinning.

"Them and those that they will be introducing to y'all" he informed them with a slight snarling smile. "I am going to sell them especially those snow bunnies the purest cocaine those rich white kids have ever sniff. Y'all won't be selling dimes or twenties, but quarter to ounces. I am talking some Big Boy shit soldiers and not any corner boy money. Just because of y'all nature way of dressing and demeanor, they will feel relaxed without worrying about that thuggish bullshit kids are portraying today" he snarled. "But with y'all" he slightly smiled. "They will get a different presentation like the shit Afrika kicks out" he told them openly smiling at them. He have heard how Afrika could captivate people's attention with his intellect and subtle charm. Numerous of young ladies were highly disappointed to find out that he was still "jail bait" but could not wait to see how he continued to mature.

"True" admitted Tek9. "But he does have a slick tongue when he has to use it" he shared lightly snickering as he stared over at him.

"So, who is this initial connection?" inquired Afrika.

"Barry Wilcox is his name. He is a sophomore right now" he informed them slightly smiling. "We have the next two years to drain as much money from his or their parents personal accounts including his associates. All I need to know is how much coke do you want?"

"What are your prices?" inquired Afrika.

"I have ounces going for sixteen hundred and eight hundred for half an ounce if you are coming out slow" he told them smiling.

"How much for a key?"

"I will hit y'all off for twelve a key" he replied. "If you don't have the full amount, you can pay me after y'all have acuminated the difference" he informed them staring in Bear and Afrika eyes specifically.

"We will take five key" Bear informed him while returning his stare.

"Five?" he replied surprise as Tek9 stepped forwards then pulled out three stacks and counted out an additional ten G's then sliding it across the table at him. "Damn!" he chuckled staring over at his three associates. "What did I tell y'all" he asked smiling at them. "Big Tony, go get these gentlemen their five bricks" he instructed one of his men. If his hunch was right about them and he was on point already, they are about to get paid and so was he. They were doing interstate auto for over three years before anyone caught wind of them. They never flash their wealth but remained fashionably dress. He wonder what they would do if they knew that Two Fingers and his crew was the ones that dropped the dime on them. The thought caused him to lightly chuckle and catch stares from those around him.

"Here you go gentlemen" Big Tony informed them extending the bag towards them.

"I got that" Kimba informed him taking possession of their package.

"Y'all are two short this afternoon" mentioned Thunder.

"They are taking care of business" Bear replied. "Is there anything else, O.G?"

"Give Barry a call when y'all are ready to open up shop" he said extending a card to Bear.

"Sure will" he assured him getting to his feet with the others and placing their hats back on their heads "Gentlemen" he addressed as they tipped their hats to O.G and his quiet partners. Bear lead the way as Afrika brought up the rear admiring what wealth can get accomplished. As they walked out the front door, the driver of the Escalade was waiting on them. Dropping them back at the speedline, they stood on the platform waiting on their train.

"We need wheels" mentioned Kimba.

"Bear and Tek are the only ones old enough to drive" Murk reminded them.

"Na, it's quicker and safer taking the train" Afrika counter.

"Plus, I'm not trying to explain a damn thing to my abusive alcoholic father on how I obtained a vehicle" Bear said as they stared at the train approaching from around the bend. They climbed on board and found seats. They exit at 4th and Cooper Street stop then ascended the stairs. They enter the lobby of Mid-Town hotel under the watchful eyes of the manager and tenants that lived in the building then took the elevator to the 7th floor. They knocked on 721 and heard footsteps of someone approaching.

"Yeah?" called Murk.

"Salaam" replied Bear.

He open the door tapping their knuckles as they walked pass before securing the door with the two by four between the two L-brackets. Sitting at the table was Black with things spread out on the table. Two stainless-steel shifters, two scales, packaging material, baby laxative and face masks. With the radio set on WDAS, they got to work breaking down the first two bricks. They would be bagging quarter ounces for four hundred dollars; halves were eight hundred dollars, but ounces were going for eighteen hundred. They grind for four straight hours before taking a break. While Kimba placed their stash at their second location on the 8th floor in the heating duct in the bathroom, they gather up what they have bagged then place their product in two leather book bags. They will initially take about twenty quarters, forty half ounces and thirty ounces just in case.

Tek9 took possession of the bookbag with Kimba watching his back as Bear reached out to Barry using the burner (pre-paid cell cell) they brought for all communications. They agreed to meet near 3rd and Cooper Street. One block from the sororities housing and three block from Rutgers University. Bear was standing near the corner with Afrika as a small group of white boys came strolling up the street. You could tell by their sudden change in their disposition and the way they were staring at them that they were wondering if they were the guys they were supposed to meet? They did not dress or possess the persona of drug dealers. So, Bear stepped up.

"Barry?" he asked staring at them while removing his retro sunglasses.

"Yeah, I'm Barry" a freckled face thin built white guy answer. "Are you Bear?"

"Yes, I am" he replied extending his hand and shaking his hand. "So, what can I do for you?"

"We are looking for a half ounce if you have it" he replied staring up at him then over at Afrika.

"No, problem. The price is eight hundred dollars."

"I got it right here" he replied reaching in his pocket and counting out eight Franklins then started to extend it to Bear.

"Na, have one of your friends give it to one of the guys across the street" he pointed to Kimba, Murk, Tek9 and Black. One of his boys went to Murk and gave him the money as

Kimba gave him the product. "If you need anything else, hit me up. I will be in the area."

"I might be coming right back" he told him stuffing the coke in his jacket breast pocket.

"We will be near those benches under the trees."

"Okay" he slightly smiled then retracing his route back to his sorority house with his partners.

A half hour later they were flooded with requests. Barry escorted and introduced several fresh faces to them. They couldn't believe how the money was flowing. In the first hour, they made easily five thousand dollars with clients steadily coming. Murk went back to their stash and grabbed about everything that they had bagged. When the sun finally descended and under the cover of darkness, the young addicts came out of the walls like roaches with requests for halves and ounces. They had to sell them two halves instead of the full ounce on their initial night, but they will rectify that small indiscretion. By the end of the first week, their faces were known around campus by those seeking their services. Individuals were approaching them with friendly dispositions and conversing freely. Within the first month, they were staggered by the money they were making weekly especially on the weekends. They could pull in well over forty thousand dollars and a hell of a lot more when one of the sorority houses were having a party. Their second re-up with Thunder was for ten keys. Their next flip was for twenty keys. They had flipped their money three times without buying themselves nothing extravagant.

With the money Afrika was making and stashing, he found himself staring in the mirror one morning. He was about to make a big decision concerning his life because he knew that selling drugs was not going to be his profession and hopefully, not his down fall. If he had a relationship with his mother or father, he would not be contemplating the things that he was. He did not have the traditional family according to America's standards, but America's standards were never intended for him or those looking like him with their systematic exclusion policies. His father was one of several Black men that found the responsibilities of being a father and provider too demanding then bail out when on him when he was three, but you better not challenge their manhood for such a cowardly and self-serving act, or the outcome could become extremely violent. According to his mother, he had such potential coming out of school until the seductive whispers of the streets started calling to him.

His mother was taking him downtown when he was about nine to the second-hand store to buy some clothes for the coming school year. When she pointed him out to him sitting across from the main speedline terminal on Broadway, she said. "Be anything but nothing like him" she said slightly hardening her eyes. At the age of nine, he understood what he was staring at. Although his cloths were preserved and his outward appearance acceptable, he knew his father was one of several junkies that plagued the streets of Camden and most hoods. He found himself creeping out of North regularly to spy on his father. He appears to be constantly on the lookout for something. As people flooded out of the terminal to catch their buses that would take them home, he watched his father deliberate movements as he approached different people. He would charm some of those hard-working people out of their hard-earned money then thank them with a smile similar to his. After about two hours, he would sit by himself and count the money he had acuminated. He transformed the coins into dollars then headed down towards S. 3rd and Benson Street near Downtown Liquors. He watched him approached a guy barely fifteen to purchase his drug of choice, heroin. He would usually go to a shooting gallery at 6th and Berkley Street out of convince. He would knock on the door and a woman would answer. He would give her three dollars and she would allow him to enter. He would usually stay inside for about two hours before reemerging high as a motherfucker and retracing his route back to Broadway to start his hustling all over again. He had walked around him, sat around him, and linger around him on several occasions. He have even stared him in his eyes hoping to be recognized. Either his father couldn't recognize him or choose to ignore his presence. Either were hurtful.

His mother was dealing with her own private demons associated with someone trying to kick their habit on their own. She would go weeks ignoring the whispers of her demons until she finally conceded and pull out her spike then injecting the deadly and highly addictive drug into her bloodstream. The affects were almost instantly as her concerns slowly dissipated like the dew on the morning grass, but they were not gone, they were simply being ignored. Through glossy eyes, she was not naïve to the things that her only child was doing. She just did not know what he was about or when he got started. What is a fifteen-year-old doing to be able to place a thousand dollars in her hand? Imagine placing a thousand dollars in a recovering addicts hands, what did he think she was going to do with the extra money? With the money, she found herself losing days being consumed by her nodding and abundance of heroin.

She would creep into his bedroom occasionally while he was in school and stare around. How was he able to purchase a forty-five-inch flat screen television and sneak it pass her? Why was a fifty-inch leaning against one of his walls still in its box? Where in the hell did, he get that X-Box and all of those video games? Coming out of a nod one afternoon, she awoke to find the fifty-inch on a stand in front of her with the remote on the coffee table. How did he know she had invaded his bedroom? On another occasion, she open his closet and stared at the many fashionable cloths he possessed, but how did he get them past her? Opening his desk draw, she found all of his report cards since he was in third grade. As she inspected them, he maintained the honor roll every semester of every year with a maximum of seven days absence in a school year. Opening one of the folders, she was amazed at all the awards and certificates of achievement he had acuminated. Initially, she was very skeptical about his new-found friends, but they appear not to hinder his academic. Several Black universities were already extending their hands to him with academic scholarships if he persisted on the path he was traveling, and he was just entering high school. He definitely got his style of dress and academic abilities from his worthless ass father.

Although his mother did not keep a lot of company, their house never felt like a home and that is what he have been privately craving. A home. At sixteen, he was standing six feet two and steadily growing towards his father's height of six feet six. On this particular morning, he found himself wearing a light brown three-button suit he brought from 3rd Street Suit Corner in Philly with a pair of soft bottom brown wingtip shoes and his matching small brim hat. As he descended the stairs, he heard his mother talking to her best friend Ms. Candy. They stared at the attire he was wearing but neither women asked where he was going with his leather bookbag. He stepped outside adjusting his brim slightly then proceeded towards State Street. He caught a hack (people using their car as a taxi) to the Cramer Hill Apartments. Entering the office, all the young ladies eyes feel upon him.

"May I help you?" a mid-thirty white woman asked admiring his attire.

"Hopefully" he replied suddenly smiling at her and causing her to slightly smile. "I'm starting college and was wondering do you give students discounts?" he inquired still staring into her eyes.

"You are a college student?"

"Freshman year" he lied flashing all thirty-two teeth.

"I'm sorry but we don't offer college students discounts" she finally replied. "But we do have reasonable prices. What are you looking for?"

"A two-bedroom with a balcony."

"We have several available. Would you like to see a couple?"

"Definitely" he replied, as she got one of the young assistance to walk with him. Twenty minutes later, he found the perfect apartment. Sitting out on the balcony, he could stare into the forestry with his binoculars and watching the wildlife drink from the stream. He was back in the office filling out paper work then swiped his debit card and keys were placed in his hand. He warned them that his friends will probably be visiting them next week if they don't find a deal. Once outside and out of their eyesight, he revealed his jubilation. "Yes!"

Standing on River Road, he convinced a cab to allow him to rent him for four hours or less for two-hundred-dollar and he leaped on the deal. His first stop was to IKEA. He brought five rice paper floor lamps. Three to illuminate the front room and the other ones in the bedrooms. He also brought some unusual styles of plates, bowls, utensils and other little nick-nacks including an entertainment stand. From there, he went to Value City to buy the queen size beds and a high stand kitchen set with a guaranteed delivery in two days. He brought his towels, face clothes and several bamboo baskets from Five Below. On his way to his apartment, he made a detour to Wal-Mart. He purchase a stainless-steel toaster, a microwave, six goose feather pillows and an Infinity sound system. He dropped everything off at his apartment before cutting the guy loose downtown at the main terminal. Stepping out of the cab, the guy handed him his cell number on a piece of paper before pulling away. He stared across the street to find his father nodding on one of the many benches. He entered the terminal slightly shaking his head at his father and brought an all-day pass. He descended the steps and waited on the platform for his train to arrive. Five minutes later, the squealing of its wheels could be heard coming from the tunnel before pausing in front of him. He took a seat near the window, so he could stare down on the murky water of the Delaware River as the train climbed the Ben Franklin Bridge. Less than five minutes later, he was getting off at the first stop at 8th and Market Street then walking down to 3rd Street. When he first enter 3rd Street Jazz and climbed the stairs, he had no intentions of salivating. He was not ready for the rows and rows of music in the open floor plan. Buy three, get one free.

By twenty and get eight free. From buying albums that wasn't on CD to the numerous of jazz musician picture he brought, he did not realize that he spent two hours in the spot. He dropped almost three-thousand dollars on music but possessed a broad smile when he left carrying three crates. He caught a cab then lean back as the cabbie climbed the Ben Franklin Bridge.

By the time he reached his apartment, he was worn out. He don't even remember falling asleep on the carpet floor until the morning sun creeping through his balcony door woke him up. Looking around from the floor, he was slightly disorientated at first then a broad smile came to his face. Glancing at his watch it was eight-thirty, he had an hour and a half before the first delivery. He took the time to assemble the entertainment center then his Infinity stereo system. The first song he played was by Indigo Jam Unit "Roots." The clarity of the sound had him lightly laughing then took one of the crates and sat out on the balcony enjoying the slight breeze. The truck from Value City arrived actually at ten o'clock. He instructed which bedroom the bed should go and where to place the front room set. Once they left, he stared constructing the beds and throwing two traditional pillows on the bed with two goose-feather pillow. He had four goose feather pillows. Around noon, IKEA came and dropped of the things he brought especially his balcony set. Checking his watch, it was already three o'clock and he haven't eaten a thing. He called his cabby to pick him up. When he arrived a half hour later, he had him taken to Marlton's Tropical Fish where he brought several diverse fish and a hundred-gallon fish tank with little items to place inside. His next stop was to Rite Aid to get a couple of pictures taken from his cell phone and several frames from the Dollar Store. His last stop was to African Traditions to buy several artifacts and books. He returned home to clean the tank before placing the fish inside. He walked through his apartment admiring the transformation. He called Bear informing him to bring everybody to the address he was going to text him when they closed up shop. He had gotten low on them, and he knew their curiosity was eating them up.

Around six o'clock that evening, he was entering is mother's house. She had a couple of people over to celebrate Candy's birthday and they were doing their usual including the scent of marijuana and alcohol consuming the air.

"Hi, everybody" he greeted causing his mother to look up.

"Hey, Afrika" most of them greeted him.

"Mom, let me holla at you" he requested surprising her never breaking his stride. He never waited for a response. He entered his bedroom and grabbed an over-sized carrying bag.

"Hey, where are you going?" she asked staring up at him.

"I have to go Mom" he replied. "Here is some money for you and a number you can reach me at" he informed her extending both to her. She accepted the envelop but sorrow was in her eyes as tear suddenly formed. "Don't cry Mom. I will be okay and safe" he tried to assure her. "I have some contemporary furniture arriving tomorrow at ten o'clock. Have them discard that filthy thing out there. If you need anything, give me a call" he said, ignoring her silent plea in her eyes as he stepped around her and retraced his steps out of the house. He would be officially moved in two days.

Around twelve-twenty, there was a light knocking on the front door.

"What's up fellas?" he greeted them wearing a broad smile and tapping their knuckles as they walked pass.

"Whoa!" stated Murk looking around. "What girl around here are you macking?"

"You know I don't play the young ladies."

"What is that picture of us doing on that wall?" inquired Tek9 smiling up at the poster size of them when they were ten years old and looking dusty as a motherfucker.

"Who place is this Afrika?" Kimba asked holding another picture of them in Camden High Park when they were fifteen.

"Mine's" he replied nonchalantly.

"Yours!" they chimed together then walking freely throughout the apartment.

"Oh, we are about to party our assess off" Tek declared smiling from ear to ear.

"Not here, y'all won't" he informed him bursting his bubble. "This is my place of tranquility and not y'all's whore motel. I told management that y'all will be coming and she informed me to tell y'all to ask for her personally. So, if you want a whore motel or a place to call home, get with her" he informed them as broad smiles consumed their faces.

In the days that followed, he introduced them to Ms. Taylor, and they all acquired their own apartment except Tek9 and Kimba. They were partners inside of their partnership and road dogs like Afrika and Bear.

"Hey, fellas" Bunny greeted them one Saturday night with three of her girlfriends. She had been peeking on Bear since their initial introduction by Barry several months previously.

"Hey, Bunny" they greeted her returning her smile.

"My friend and I have been wondering about something" she mentioned with a coy smile.

"What's that?" Bear asked staring into her greenish eyes then at her full breast.

"How old are y'all?"

"Old enough to do what we want" he replied returning her stare.

"Does y'all have girlfriends?"

"Na, y'all are too expensive and time consuming" he replied causing the fellas to lightly snicker and them to giggle.

"We aren't that expensive" she countered grinning. "What do y'all do when y'all close up shop?"

"Try to get in trouble" interjected Tek9 returning one of her girlfriends stare. "Are y'all trying to get in some trouble?"

"I don't know" she replied returning his stare then looking over at her girlfriends. "Are y'all trying to get in some trouble, ladies?"

"Only if they are willing to come to my place" Susan mentioned staring directly at Afrika. "Do you have a problem with that, Afrika?"

"I'm sure they don't" he replied staring into her blue eyes and natural blonde hair.

"Good, how about y'all coming to my apartment around one o'clock" she suggested extending a piece of paper to Afrika with her information on it. "Just give me a call when y'all are in the area, okay?"

"Okay" he replied smiling down into her eyes while placing the paper in his front pocket.

"Then we will see y'all later, Bear" Bunny stated staring up into Bear's eyes.

"We will be there" he told her slightly shaking his head at the impish smile on her face.

"Okay, later fellas" she said turning and walking away with her girlfriends giggling.

"It appears they have intentions brothers" Bear mentioned grinning.

"They don't have the vaguest idea what is about to jump off" Kimba said tapping Tek9's knuckles and snickering.

"Not the vaguest" Tek9 cosigned snickering.

"Put your dicks away and think with your other head" Afrika told them. "We can easily fuck up our money and I'm not trying to do that."

"We won't be fucking up our money, Afrika" Tek insisted.

"We will once jealousy raise its ugly head. We got into this business for the money and not to be fucking some curious ass white girls. If y'all break those naïve girls backs in bed, do you know the type of trouble they can cause us especially with them being white?"

"I'm cosigning Afrika" Black said returning their stares.

"What's wrong with having a little fun" Tek asked with an impish grin.

"Nothing unless it has the potential to fuck up our money or get us incarcerated for what we are doing" Afrika reiterated staring over at him and Kimba.

"Why do you always have to make sense?" Tek slightly hardening his eyes but grinning.

"Because you and Kimba are quick to think with your lower head" he replied grinning. "If y'all are going to hook up with them, go ahead but please, don't fuck them partners" he stressed returning their stares.

"We hear you Afrika" Bear told him. "No fucking our clients, gentlemen."

"Damn" Murk smiled. "Susan fine ass is all up in your face, Afrika and you are not going to exploit that?"

"Not worth the possible drama, Murk" he replied returning his stare.

"Not even once, Bear" persisted Kimba.

"Is it that fucking important?" he asked staring in his eyes, and he shut it down because he knew, no piece of pussy is worth their freedom. If he or any of them was pressed about fucking a white girl, stroll up Broadway to Kaighn Avenue and you can pick out one trying to make that money turning tricks.

They did keep the appointment but not Afrika. He had noticed an Egyptian pharaoh pendant Susan was wearing around her neck from Arianne and the Mark Loren ankle bracelet. Both items together could easily cost ten G's. He did not know if she was flaunting her jewelry or hoping that no one knew their value. One thing was certain; she or her family definitely had money. Winston, a prominent pimp had told him if a woman is willing to spend her money on you, getting her pussy wouldn't be shit, but it will separate you from the money you could have obtained. Continue to get that money until she boxes you in a corner then you slay her ass and wait for the next installment.

When he hooked up with the fellas the next day at the room, they were sharing their experiences of the previous night while wearing broad smiles and laughing their assess off. They were there a good hour before Bunny stared getting frisky with Bear from the cocaine that she and her girlfriends were snorting up like a vacuum cleaner while Susan was disappointed that Afrika didn't show up. Their conversation of course evolved into an erotic theme as they asked questions concerning a Black man. Do y'all have a big dicks? Have y'all ever experience a menage trios? When did you lose your virginity and other intrusive questions. Of course, they eventually wanted to dance and grind up against them while getting excited by what they were feeling pressing up against their pelvic and assess. Although very alluring and explicit with their body movements, they held fast to their promise. If they had told those girls to get comfortable, they would have gladly complied except maybe, Susan, but she was still getting her freak on while sharing dances with the fellas except Bear. Bunny have claimed him. They said they stayed at Susan beautiful apartment until four o'clock in the morning. They were constantly trying to get them to stay longer, but they remembered their last conversation. "Don't fuck up our money over some damn pussy."

Starting high school at Camden High, the castle on the hill, they strolled through the halls with that North Camden swag. Ignoring the slick things coming out of guys mouths for not attending Woodrow Wilson High as they were supposed to coming from out of North, but nobody tried impeding them and damn sure didn't put their hands on them. Although the young ladies were intrigued by them attending the High, they also knew about the reputation the ladies in North had about another bitch sniffing after their men. Being one of the best dressed freshmen, upper-class young ladies admired their style of dress and quiet disposition. Their first year went pass relatively quickly. Although his partners were constantly trying to hooky school and take some of the adventurous young ladies to their apartments, Afrika was the voice of reason that kept them in school and on their academics. Passing into the eleventh grade, Afrika was the only honor roll student among them, and they rode him bare back for days while laughing. During the school year, they would open shop at six p.m. and closed by eleven o'clock except for the weekends. They would close up shop at one o'clock in the morning especially if a sorority house were having a party.

When class was officially over, they would be posted up at 3rd and Cooper by noon playing chess or a game called Twix's. It was on a Thursday afternoon when Barry showed up with his partner Steve. They wanted to inform them that they had some friends in Philly attending Temple, Drexel and La Salle Universities that were looking for a new connection. The connections they had in Philly was becoming overly aggressive and disrespectful with some if the things they were saying to the fellas and the young ladies specifically. They were willing to pay a slightly higher price if they were willing to deliver their product. They told Barry that it wouldn't be a problem, but they weren't going to run away in Philly with the abundance of drug they would have on them. They would have to meet them. Afrika suggested Franklin Square between N 6th and 7th Street in Center City. The meeting spot was an excellent location. With a mini golf course and a carousel, the park will be packed with visitors and tourist. Barry called his friends and told them where to be at two o'clock. He described what Afrika and Black were wearing then ended his conversation.

Around one o'clock, Afrika and Black was returning to the room to retrieve their product then placed it in the leather bookbag and left the room carrying their portable radio. They walked across the street and descended the speedline entrance. Hearing the train approaching, they picked up their pace. Buying a round trip ticket, they descended the stairs and sprinted to the train catching the door just as it was about to close. They found seats near the window and look over the Delaware River as it climbed the Ben Franklin Bridge. The first stop at 8th and Market. They walked down Market Street until they reached 6th Street then turned right and proceeded towards Arch Street. As usual, the streets were packed with people celebrating the end of school and the beginning of summer vacation. As they entered the park, parents with their children were running freely around.

"How in the hell did you find this place?" Black whisper staring at the abundance of white people in the city of brotherly love.

"I was doing my hobby when I met a young lady inside of Victoria Secret and she invited me to hang out. She brought me here."

"Well, I like this" he shared staring at several exits if necessary.

They found a nice cool spot on a bench under a tree then turned on the radio and W.D.A.S started playing the latest tunes. They were there approximately fifteen minutes when a predominate group of white guys and girls stared up the slight inclement at them. Not knowing what to do, a honey complexion young lady slowly approached them.

"Excuse me," she apologized staring in their eyes. "Is one of y'all Afrika?"

"I am" he replied smiling down into her grayish eyes. "How are you?"

"I'm fine" she replied returning his smile.

"Yes, you are my Queen" they complimented her together while taking in the contour of her body and causing her to slightly blush.

"How can I assist y'all?"

"Barry told us to meet y'all here" she replied waving her associates over.

"Hi, everybody" Afrika greeted them slightly smiling. They all spoke and had friendly smiles. "So, what are y'all looking for?"

"We need a total of eight halves and six ounces if you have it with you" she replied.

"We have to charge you an additional two hundred for the delivery."

"That's cool" they replied together smiling over at him.

"How about y'all come and have a seat on the grass with us" he informed them leading them further into the park and taking a seat on a grassy hill over-looking everything around them. As they sat down in a circle, Afrika brought out what they were requesting and instructed them to give their money to Black. As he made the count, several of them could not wait to get back to the dorms or apartment to test what they had just purchase. As a couple of the took a hit, they shook their heads vigorously at the purity.

"Wow!" declared a young lady rubbing her nose. "I want another one of these" she started counting out an additional ten Franklin's.

"Damn, Afrika" another white boy called out smiling. "This is some pure ass shit, man" he told him as he watched his nose lit up like Rudolph as his eyes were watery and turning reddish.

"I will only put out the best product" he told him watching his taking another snort and shaking his head vigorously.

"Well, you have" the honey complexion young lady cosigned. "By the way, my name is Daisy."

"Glad to officially meet you" Afrika said lightly shaking her hand. Her naturally curly auburn color hair made her extremely sexy to him.

"Can we get your number?" she asked slightly apprehensive.

"Sure," he replied extending a card to them individually. "I am only requesting that you spend a minimum of ten thousand dollars. If you are trying to hook up like we did today, I will not charge you that extra delivery fees if you do."

"We appreciate that" they chimed together smiling over at him.

"Well, ladies and gentlemen" he said suddenly getting to his feet then extending his hand down to assist Daisy to her feet closely followed by her friends. "I have genuinely enjoyed this interaction and introduction. Hopefully, we will establish a good relationship."

"I'm sure we will" the main guy Brandon assured him shaking his hand. "Nice meeting you, Afrika. You too, Black."

"Just hit me up when you are in need, later y'all" he told them as they disburse. In a short ten-minute meeting, they were returning to Camden with close to fifteen-thousand dollars. If they knew the drug game was this lucrative, they might have venture into the game a lot earlier. They hooked back up with their partners a little before three o'clock. With two sororities houses having parties the coming weekend, they justify buying their coke earlier on Thursday because they wanted to make sure they were covered, but since coming out of the gate, they have never been dry. They wanted the extra coke because they desired it and would be back Saturday night to spend more of their money. Their routine the entire summer was partying and snorting cocaine continuously.

Their junior year was almost a blur. Besides staying on their grind, they didn't really have a personal life. They would hook up with a couple of home girls and get their freak on, but other than that, they were about getting that money. They were now purchasing thirty keys to accommodate their new clients in Philly, but Thunder wasn't complaining. He was hugely impressed by their operation, but he wasn't telling them. None of them have gotten pinched by five-o or Office Friendly of the Rutgers University Police Department. They were over at his business house when Thunder gave them something to think about.

"Gentlemen, we had a very profitable two years, and I can't wait to see what transpires this year" he openly smiled at him. "I know y'all bank accounts are bursting at the seams because none of y'all have flaunted what you have acquired and for someone as young as y'all, I am extremely impressed, but it's time for y'all to get some wheels. Get some wheels, gentlemen."

They stared at one another then over at him and said, "Okay."

The next day they returned to their parents houses to hit their stash. Afrika would sneak into her home when she had an appointment or to go food shopping. When he walked in, his mother was elated to see him physically. Although he meet every one of her desires, she hadn't laid eyes on him in over a year and a half. He spoke to everyone as he went to his old bedroom. He locked the door and turned on the radio to conceal him removing the slab from inside the closet then counted out thirty-thousand dollars then adjusted him book. None of them could put their money in a bank especially without having a legitimate J.O.B. All they would need is some zealous employee snooping around and putting five-o on them. Na, placing their money in a bank wouldn't be smart, not yet. Once everything was in place, he turned off the radio and walked out holding a folder. He peeked at his mother but never broke his stride as he walked out the front door.

They hooked back up around eleven o'clock at 6th and York then went down town to jump on speedline or bus to go in their separate directions. They had hit the internet last night and knew exactually where they were headed. They will hook back up inside Camden High Park no later than two o'clock. Afrika was the first to arrive. He brought himself a fully loaded metallic gray Chrysler 300 with a Panasonic sunroof from over in Philly. Tek9 and Kimba was the next to arrive. Tek brought a metallic blue Cadillac CT5 while Kimba brought a white CT5. Murk pulled up five minutes later whipping a brown Acura MDX then Black driving a funky Audi A7. Bear stole the show arriving in a funky black Escalade Platinum Edition. As they congregated near the basketball court, they could feel the people staring over at them and wondering. What in the hell are they doing and where?

"A 300, Afrika" mentioned Black shaking his head at him.

"He is one cheap motherfucker" teased Tek snickering at him with the others.

"I am not cheap?" he corrected him.

"Afrika, you are cheap man" Bear tried cosigning while grinning.

"I am not cheap" he reiterated. "I'm just money conscious, brothers" he shared causing them to stare at one another then burst out laughing.

"No, man. You are cheap" they insisted, still laughing at him ignoring them.

Entering their senior year, they arrived at school in Bear's Escalade and Black's Audi A7. They pulled up on the students parking lot under watchful eyes of some of the students then climbed out and grabbed their leather bookbags. "What were they about?" was the subtle whispers that filled the halls. Granted, they have a very nonchalant disposition and motherfuckers didn't know how to determine it. The ladies that were constantly conversing with them could not shine any light into their personal life although some have spent time in their alleged apartments. No, they did not have a girlfriends because they were constantly on the go doing something. Although several had tried to get their clutches in the impeccably dressed young men, girlfriends were too demanding on their time, and they put it out there for all to hear especially those that had private aspirations. They did let it be known that they will be attending their senior prom since they didn't attend their junior prom, and this caused the young ladies to start jockeying for position.

Since their initial conversation three months ago, Afrika found himself conversing with Daisy almost every day. After concluding business one afternoon, she asked if he was in a hurry. He replied that he wasn't. She wanted to treat him to lunch and what type of man would refuse a free lunch being offered by an extremely beautiful and sexy young lady? From that initial lunch engagement, they started having lunch every Saturday in one of the restaurants in Center City. The conversations that he would initiate has caused her some thought-provoking confusions even with the answer being right in front of her face. She was program to accept certain things and alleviating from those embedded belief can be shattering to a person ideologies. Like she innocently mentioned being a Christian and he jokingly said he wouldn't hold it against her with that adorable impish smile he possess. When he asked her what was Mary's father and mother names, she had to admit she didn't know. Or why she never knew the touch of a man hand? He never told her, but she know the answer to both questions now. There were numerous of questions that she asked about religion and was dumbfounded by the things she read. A lot did not match what she was systematically taught. Did you know two of the four rivers that surrounded the Garden of Eden still exist today? The other two are subterrain now but can still be detected using modern technology.

She had observed several young women vying for his attention when they were out, but he acted like he didn't notice their subtle flirts. Him being very attentive eased a lot of thoughts that she had fabricated in her mind especially concerning her complexion. But none more than if he had a wondering eye and he did not. She had always admired an attentive man but reciting things that she might have said a month previously to solidify his opinion on something was not appreciated especially when he flashes that impish smile. Granted, she did make the basic inquiries like if he had a girlfriend, but he never inquired if she had left anybody back in Mississippi.

"When a woman ask you your age, she is extremely interested in you" Winston educated him.

And that is actually what occurred one night in the middle of a conversation while they were listening to the Quiet Storm on WDAS, he openly confessed to being seventeen for another two weeks. She adamantly refused to accept his answer and her laughter co-signed her opinion. His intellect and attire is not that of a seventeen-year-old. He display a maturity controlling his tongue that a lot of men much older could not or would not display considering she has a tendency of wearing a lot of provocative attire. With Afrika, he always complimented what she wore, but never said anything illicit towards her or had lust consumed his eyes with a hidden ulterior motive. He had to actually display his driver license to her three days later to confirm his age.

There were far too many reasons why she accepted his invitation to spend the weekend with him As she was climbing the Ben Franklin Bridge in her white Jaguar XJ, her mind was all over the place. Would she really have an enjoyable weekend or would it be cut short because of some of indiscretion on his part. It appeared that as soon as she crossed the bridge, the ride to his apartment complex was less than twenty minutes away. Pulling into his complex, she pulled next to his car then climbed out and grabbed her over-night bag then secured her car. She open the outer door to his building then ascended the stairs to the second level. Standing in front of 2D, she could hear "When Love Call" by Kem. She lightly tapped on the door then took a deep breath and slowly exhaled.

The door opens seconds later, and he stood there smiling down on her. "What's up Daisy?" he asked staring at her from head to toe and admiring how her hips flare out in her white cloth spandex pants and matching top.

"Hi, Afrika" she replied grinning up at him.

"Please, come on in" he invited stepping aside for her to enter and admiring how the thongs she was apparently wearing made her ass cheeks move like independent shocks.

"Oh, my goodness!" she declared admiring the décor he created. "This is beautiful, Afrika" she complimented admiring a poster size picture of him and his partners and started giggling.

"Thank you and the picture isn't that funny" he replied. "You can place your bag in the first bedroom. I will be out on the balcony" he informed her heading in that direction.

"Okay" she replied as she continued to take in the scenery. Once she placed her bag in the bedroom, she came out to inspect his apartment more closely as only a woman can. There weren't any pictures of a young lady just his partners over the years. There were no indication that a young lady stayed with him periodically or consistently. No extra toothbrush or lingerie that were purposely forgotten. The bathroom was clean with no scrum in the tub or stains around the water line in the toilet. She heard herself lightly giggling as she inspected the kitchen realizing that he was domesticated. Opening the screen door and stepping out on the balcony, she stared out at the forestry and small creek with a quaint smile. "Now, this is a lovely scenery" she said.

"Yes, it is" he replied in a tone that caused her to look over her shoulder at him admiring her ass. "Did you have any problem getting here?" he asked averting his eyes and extending the blunt he was smoking to her.

"No, thank you" she said refusing the blunt. "Once I crossed the bridge, the ride was smooth. So, can I make myself at home?"

"You better because I am not going to be your personal butler all weekend" he told her pulling from the blunt while grinning.

"I guess I need to get my own glass, huh?"

"Recommendable, if you are thirsty" he replied trying to contain his smile but failing.

She didn't say a word as she got to her feet then plucked him in his head as she went inside. She slightly paused hearing him snickering then continued to her bedroom before grabbing a glass from out of the cabinet. When she returned, she didn't have just the glass but with a small make-up compact. She took a seat and poured herself a glass of Parrot Bay before opening her compact. There was an abundance of cocaine inside. More than what she would need for a weekend or was it? As she snorted two lines with each nostrils, her eyes instantly became watery while her nose illuminated a reddish glow. She removed her stilettos then wiggle her toes before elevating them on the ottoman. As H-Town sang, "A Thin Line Between Love and Hate" in the background, their voices and laughter floated on the slight breeze for three hours.

As the sun gradually descended over the trees, he stared over at her. "Are you hungry?"

"Slightly, are you taking me out?"

"No" he replied. "I can hook up something light for us to eat."

"How did I know that you would say that?" she asked giggling. He refuse for her to pay for a meal that he could prepare himself and a hell of a lot cheaper. He didn't have a problem gripping her fingers and walking out of a restaurant if he felt their prices were too excessive.

"I can prepare something for us in a half hour" he said getting to his feet.

"I'm going to sit right here until the meal is finish and continue taking in this view."

"No, problem" he replied opening the screen. "I will call you when it's prepared" he told her while walking inside and closing the screen door.

As she sat there staring out into the forestry, she spotted several animals drinking from the creek. She took several more hits of coke then slowly exhaled. What is she going to do with Afrika? She was extremely impressed by him and the contents of his conversation, but his age still had her slamming on her brakes when she found herself lowering her guard. Yes, age is just a number, and his maturity confirms that especially since some of the guys she had dated were in their early and late twenties with no substance at all in their conversations. Is she going to keep him as just a friend or bite the forbidden fruit? If she continued to refuse to taste the nectar he had to offer, her three closet girlfriends said they would instantly especially if she step aside, but she could not for some strange reason. Why was she being selfish and dick blocking her girlfriends lustful desire for him? Her friends had told her that her reasoning was very immature. Her girlfriends laughing and teasing her made her realized just how dumb she was acting as a twenty-one-year-old, young lady. She was actually embarrassed by her apprehension. The scent of the meal invading her clogged nose is what interrupted her thoughts.

"It's ready, Daisy" he announced from the screen door.

She got to her feet leaving her stilettos on the balcony as she walked inside. Admiring the meal that he prepared, a quaint little smile creased her lips. Bake salmon with steam vegetables and a bake potato with sour cream on top.

"Mmmmm," she smiled tasting the salmon. "You do have some skills."

"Just a little" he replied, stuffing some vegetables into his mouth. "So, what do you want to do this evening?"

"Do you have any suggestions?" she asked, in a little flirtatious tone.

"Yes" he replied using the same seductive tone. "How about you allowing me to show you off tonight? Is that alright with you?"

"Sure" she smiled. "I don't mind being the envy of the young ladies tonight" she admitted lightly giggling. "Do you have some place in mind?"

"I would love to take you over to Philly to Smooths, but I don't want to travel that far. I know an excellent place in Madison called Shanghai Jazz."

"What time was you planning on leaving here?"

"Nine o'clock to catch the ten o'clock set."

"No, problem" she replied grinning. She had more than three hours to get ready.

Around eight o'clock, she went to take her shower while he sat in the front room listening to Jimmy Smith playing "The Sermon." When she came out wearing a towel and smiling down the hallway at him, he got to his feet to take his shower. They were completely dressed by eight-forty-five. He was wearing a light brown Armani suit while she wore a red one shoulder strap sequin slit mini gown by Norman Kamala. Her breast appeared so much larger and full. The only make-up she wore was eyeliner to accentuate her doe like eyes. She allowed her natural beauty to be displayed. Her shoulders were acme free and smooth.

"Damn, Daisy" he replied taking in the full contour of her body while trying to contain his impish smile. "You truly look elegant."

"Not too provocative for you?"

"Woman, please" he openly chuckled. "Nothing that you might wear would be too provocative for me" he shared displaying his impish smile.

"Time will tell" she replied giggling.

By nine-fifteen, they were cruising to Madison. As Luther Vandross sang, "If Only 4 One Night", he was enjoying his blunt while she was constantly powdering her nose. He was under the assumption that the two ounces that she brought that one was for someone else, but observing her, both were definitely for her personal use. Pulling up on the parking lot, they found a parking spot then climbed out of his vehicle. She stood on the sidewalk waiting for him as he walked around the car. He instinctively gripped her fingers as they walked towards the main entrance. He had surprised the hell out of her when he initially gripped her fingers. She found it so romantic. Her other dates never attempted to hold her fingers or hand. He explained that he witness too many people walking between couples as they walked, and he found that so disrespectful. A guy should never allow anyone to walk between him and his date. To eliminate that possibility and the possibility of him fucking some guy up, he would simply grip her fingers.

As they proceeded towards the end of the line, she caught the lustful stares from guys with their dates, but while they were lustfully staring at her with their eyes, their dates were devouring and disrobing Afrika with their eyes and flirtatious smiles. Walking into the quaint place, he walked towards the middle and noticed a vacant table in the slight shadows then claimed it and placed their orders. A six-piece band from Cleveland was providing the entertainment for the night. The lead person was a trombonist and he played like a young J.J Johnson or Slide Hampton. Daisy had never experienced a live jazz performance. Witnessing the music being created in front of her, she had a broad smile plastered on her face that wouldn't go away. For the next two hours, they enjoyed the music while continuing their conversation. As he would be stressing a point, she would be getting distracted because she was enjoying watching the women salivating over him and this caused as impish smile to come to her face. When he eventually inquired what was going on, she always responded nothing, but he knew her well enough to know when she was purposely lying. She like being mischievous too much.

A little after one o'clock, she was grabbing her clutch purse as she got to her feet with Afrika then smiling over at two tables specifically at the young ladies that had continuously tried to gain Afrika's attention before gripping his fingers and casually walked towards the main entrance. She would catch the eyes of several guys as she walked pass then stared up at Afrika then back at them smiling. Stepping outside, the early morning breeze had Afrika wrapping his suit jacket around her shoulders as they proceeded towards his car. Once inside the car again, she powdered her nose again while he lit a blunt. The half hour ride to his apartment took fifty minutes as he cruised in the second lane while listening to her sharing her life before arriving in Philly. Once they were back inside the apartment, they both took quick showers and changed into their sleep attire. He was sitting on the balcony listening to an assortment of jazz singers wearing his usual shorts with a wife beater when she came out in a red sports bra and a matching pair of micro shorts that was pressing firmly against her camel toe. She could definitely dress provocatively. They sat out there until three o'clock before walking inside. They exchanged a light kiss before retiring to their separate bedroom. She was awoken by the scent of breakfast. Tonight, he was going to reveal a peek at his personal life by introducing the rest of his partners and his mentor at his spot on the stripe called Winston's. For her, the weekend ended much too quickly. She had not enjoyed herself so much on a date ever because Afrika didn't have any ulterior motive except getting to know her better. Having continuous conversation on the phone is fine but witnessing a person facial expression can bring a more extensive conversation. So, when he said that he hoped that she will spend another weekend with him, she wanted to ask if she could spend every weekend and shout it out, but instead she said, only time will tell.

For three years, they have been flying under the radar. Rutgers University Police had been watching them closely initially. They sat three blocks off of campus and out of their jurisdiction. Yet, when they are approached and questioned, they were always respectful but were not giving up too much information except living in North. Five-o had gotten used to seeing the immaculately dressed young men playing chess or some unusual game name Twix. When they weren't playing their games, they would sit around in little clusters conversing with the students. Watching one of them in particular, the guy named Afrika always seem to have a small crowd around him. Walking among the students, he could be discussing the duality in the law especially when it's not being administered equally. Most had to admit witnessing something that had happen to a person of color by five-o that wasn't warranted especially their racist and derogatory language but not saying nothing about it. How do we mend our fences when you witness boundaries being crossed but remained silent. Malcolm advised them in his era to concentrate on changing the mind set of their peers and not try to join his movement. Although most was genuinely disappointed, Afrika would only give his opinions on social issues for a half hour then apologize for abruptly ending their conversation. He would either read for the next half hour or leave the scene completely. They were definitely an unusual group of high schoolers.

For the last two years, Bunny have been pressing up on Bear continuously after getting slain while Susan was trying to figure out the combination to get her claws into Afrika. She would be graduating next year, and her fantasy has not been fulfilled. Although all of her girlfriends have climbed into bed with one of his partners, he have remained very elusive. She wanted to experience what it would be like to make love to a black guy, also. She wanted to see if she would scream and moan for mercy like all of her girlfriends. She wanted to experience being over-whelmed by passion. She had to wonder was there something unattractive about herself? She waved the thought off as soon as she formulated it. Na, she was attractive according to the fellas attending her school including his partners. She have even heard some Black guys complimenting her body. Some said her body was like a Black woman's body and she adored the compliment. Yet, she could not figure out Afrika. She has watched him socializing with several white girls and causing them to openly blush from the things he was whispering to them in their ears. The look of adoration was engulfed in their eyes when they would end their conversation. She had always admired the way he and his partners would show their affection when in public even with them. She only would become jealous when Daisy would come over from Philly with her friends to join their exclusive parties. Although he was still very sociable and invited some guests to join them, he was so damn attentive to her needs and the things she would whisper to him. Although he was very respectable and flirtatious with his white female friends, she had never seen him dating one. She openly said one Saturday night in her frustrated, addictive, feeling rejected, state of mind if he was a racist. A loud hush came over the room by those sitting close enough to hear her outrageous statement and stared over at her in shock. Most were under the impression that they were having a tight relationship until that statement filtered pass her lips. Her girlfriends leaped deep in her ass over her unwarranted and unjustified statement. Although he never addressed her verbally, it was evident he took it offensively because of the distance it created between them. He would still greet her warmly, if it were too late to walk away, and take her money but that was the extent of their communication and interaction. As subtle as she tried to apologize, he was not being receptive.

Maybe it was because of her embarrassment or frustration that she decided to get with one of her black friends from school. Ronald have been sniffing after her since their sophomore year. He was the typical Negro by wearing khaki pants and penny loafers. With his high yellow complexion and corny ass joke that the fellas just didn't get, he was very shallow and perceived by his white friends as nonthreatening. She started inviting him to their exclusive parties a month after the incident. She would appear to be receptive to the things he was whispering as they snorted up their cocaine. Her laughter could be overheard over other people conversations and music. She would dance very provocative, as she learned from watching her black female students. Ronald didn't have the vaguest ideal to do with her dancing so provocatively and illicit. The fellas were snickering their assess off. What did she think Afrika would do by flaunting him in his face? Was he supposed to jump completely out of character over another person actions? Whatever reaction she was hoping to materialize never did. He remained very cordial to the young ladies and guys around him while showing no interest in what she thought she was doing. Her girlfriends tried to tell her to pump her brakes with Ronald or some other girl was going to snatch Afrika up. Instead of taking in what they were saying, she said "Fuck Afrika!"

Late one Saturday night, she sat staring at him from across the room as Ronald's kept himself entertained with some of his friends. She watched as Melissa grabbed Afrika tie and pull him closely to whisper something into his ear before kissing him lightly on the lips and making him smile as she walked away. More than usual, white girls were flocking to him, and she knew she had a hand in that unfortunately. He could be a Venus flytrap if he wanted to be, but he was a better man than that. Her accusation is what brought all this unwanted attention to him, and they were proving that she had misrepresented his character and the truth.

As she snorted another two lines of coke then leaned back, she knew any hopes of getting her fingers on him was lost especially after flaunting Ronald around him with her childish antics in front of his partners. She had asked herself several times, how could she make such a derogatory accusation towards Afrika? She felt so belittle by what she said, and her girlfriends still have not truly forgiven her. She remember when the fellas surprised them one Saturday night and took them over to Philly to experience South Street by public transportation. He was so attentive to her, and she felt like she was on top of the world. She had never portrayed the apple of someone's eyes, and this is how he made her feel while ignoring the snarls of the black women that they walked pass. They never allowed anybody to even contemplate saying anything disrespectful or slick towards them. Her statement brought back a conversation they shared later that night while they were walking back over the Ben Franklin Bridge, when they were at the half way point and taking a seat. "Am I a racist from the things I have experience and witness or what you bestow upon me?" She had bestowed upon him, and it severed their friendship. She could only shake her head at the thought. She did not want to think anymore. She tapped Ronald and started gathering up her belongings. As she said her goodbyes to those sitting around her, she eventually got to her feet. She stared over at Afrika catching his eyes briefly before putting her arm around Ronald's waist then headed towards the door. She took one last peek over her shoulder at him before walking out the door, but he was right back into his conversation with a young lady. She was not even an afterthought and it infuriated her. She decided at that very moment she was going surrender to her curiosity with Ronald since Afrika wasn't making himself available. The experience was not what she expected or desired. It was not anything like her girlfriends described and experience. There wasn't any long slow erotic journey through foreplay or intimate conversation. He did not make love to her with passion. He fucked her and that was not she wanted or expected. He was like fucking another white guy while intoxicated off of cocaine. She did not want animalistic lust but erotic passion.

For three weeks after that incident, she had gotten low from her girls, the scene and especially Ronald. Although he would come through with his predominant white friend and socialize, he was secretly searching for Susan. His calls have gone unanswered, and she was M.I.A from their private little watering hole. She was so piss with herself by her embarrassing action that she wish she could whip her own ass. She had settled and got precisely what she deserved. A useless ass fucking. Bunny tried to pull her back into the scene, but she was not ready to face her friends, Afrika's partners, or him. Weeks later, she happen to run into him over in Philly on South Street. She stood gawking at him talking to a young lady before they went in separate directions and a slight smile came to her face. Initially, she started to stay out of sight and continued where she was going, but she found herself gravitating towards him. He looked so sexy in his black Versace suit and handsome as hell in his small brim hat. Cutting across his line of sight, she caught his eyes and the softness in them caused her to slightly smile. She offer to buy him lunch and she was pleasantly surprised when he accepted.

"Afrika, you know I didn't mean what I said, right?" she asked as they sat at their table overlooking the skyline.

"Yeah, I know Susan" he replied smiling into her blue eyes.

"Coming to Rutgers from Texas, I have never socialized outside of my race. I was very skeptical of about Black men from the stories conjured-up as I was growing up. There will always be bad people in all races. I know that now. My false accusation of being a racist is a testimony that anybody can be considered a racist or bad person" she shared avoiding his eyes while slightly shaking her head. "I guess the color of my skin didn't carry any weight on that issue when pertaining to you around those that know you" she slightly grinned.

"No, it didn't but it caused a lot of young lady to invade my space."

"Yeah, I'm sorry about that" she replied grinning. She remember bumping into him and his partners inside the Cherry Hill Mall over a year ago. How they got on the conversation about being privilege she so not remember, but she does remember the revelation. He asked her to cosigned an accusation and watch how things evolve. He had gotten Bunny to tell security that she think that he stole her cell phone as his partners fanned out smiling. When they approached him, they almost instantly became aggressive. When he tried to politely make a statement against his accuser, they waved his comments off. They were trying to get him to come to the security office to conduct a search. He became slightly adamant about being illegally detained and search because of someone's accusation. When Susan interjected her false statement, they instantly grabbed for their handcuffs and tried to grappling him up as a crowd formed and his partners were laughing their assess off. He was constantly trying to explain himself to the four white security officers as they persisted in trying to place handcuffs on him as he kept pushing them off. When Black finally dialed her cell snickering by the escalators, the four security guards stopped their attack and stared over at her with the crowd as she searched frantically for her cell phone. Afrika was standing there shaking his head at them.

"Hey, baby!" she greeted like a school child smiling then stared around at the crowd that had accumulated then said, "What? Every Black man is not a thief" she commented flinging her hair then walking away switching her Chic jeans flat ass. She never apologized for disrupting the peaceful environment of the Mall or the boisterous accusation. Security stood there looking dumb as a motherfucker thinking they had just harassed an innocent black man off the word of an arrogant and ungrateful white bitch. As some of the by-stander shook their heads at them, others had a look of anger or slight snarls on their faces, but they were smart enough to keep their thoughts and comments to themselves. She never forgot that "life lesson" as Afrika called it, and they are subjected to this form of irony every day of their lives. "Why wouldn't you get with me?" she blurted out staring across the table at him.

"I was somewhat involved with Daisy" he somewhat lied. Although they have been secret lovers for over a year, she was engaged to some guy in Mississippi. They had come to a mutual agreement that they could date other people. Neither had explored the world around them. Since junior high, they were the others shadow. They city they lived in, Hattiesburg, was a relatively small close net community. Each had peeked on several friends while growing up but was unable to explore what might happen. With distance between them and the ability of exploring past interest freely, the long conversations they initially shared eventually got shorter. The enthusiasm that usually accompany their conversations were gradually diminishing. From talking every day to twice a week but neither were complaining.

She had concluded that no matter how she felt about Afrika they could never be anything permanent between them except what they were enjoying, one another company. He was too young for her to take home according to society and staying in Jersey with him wasn't happening for her. She missed being home. She accepted that city life was too fast and dangerous for her especially, to raise children. She would be on pins and needles every time one of their children would go out. But what frustrated her the most, he wasn't even out of high school got damn it, but when it comes to being intellectually stimulating and a beast between the sheets, she had found her dream man. Her personal Mr. Good Bar. Neither of her previous two older lovers she had since leaving Mississippi fulfilled what she was seeking. Accepting an invitation on her birthday from Afrika, she was still uncertain about him, but he has never pressed up on her sexually even when she was noticeably intoxicated. This is why he earned her trust and the clothes she wore around his apartment was a testimony to that trust. Braless and wearing some form of spandex shorts or cheeky boy panties while sitting out on the balcony as she sun bath. Yeah, she have become extremely trustworthy of him.

Laying awoke in her bedroom after celebrating her twenty-first birthday and hearing the soft instruments of jazz filtering through the air vent, she found herself crawling out of bed and methodically walking towards his room. With his door slightly ajar, she stared in at him sitting on the floor reading a book called "Twins" while the rice paper lamps illuminated the room just enough. A slight breeze carrying the scent of her body wash and perfume invaded his nostrils causing him to slightly raise his head and inhale deeply. He turned and stared into the shadow of his door unable to distinguish a silhouette until she gently pushed open the door revealing Victoria's latest exotic night attire secret. The yellow thong she wore grabbed his attention and caused his eyebrows to unconsciously arch but viewing her perky breast through her sheer top had him closing his book and staring up at her with that impish grin she admired so much. Although Daisy and her man back home had promise to confess if either stumble upon someone that truly tickled their fancy, neither were strong enough to confess. She could not confess simply because of his age but he couldn't confess because he was dating a white girl that they knew since junior high and knew she would be highly disappointed in him.

Allowing her sheer top to hit the floor and stepping out of her thongs, he got to his feet as she stared up into his eyes and kissed him lightly on the lips as she crawled up on the bed. Crawling between the sheets and staring at him stepping out of his stretch underwear, she quietly gasps staring at the length and thickness of his manhood. Although she told herself to leave her emotions on the other side of the bedroom door, she could not. The passion and ecstasy that she craved was found in Afrika's arm. He actually had her feel like a virgin again. He had induced multi orgasms and caused her to actually squirt for the first time. She did not know what the hell was happening when it occurred, and he thought it was funny as hell. All of her moans and groans had her pleading to him as he took her to sexual heights that she did not know exist. For the next year, he was like an aphrodisiac to her, very addictive and alluring. When she needed to taste his passionate kisses and feel his strong arms, he always made himself available to her.

"I thought y'all was seeing one another" Susan suddenly giggled. "But I saw you with so many girls conversing" she said grinning.

"I love talking to y'all" he simply replied.

For the next hour, they sat talking like old friends. By the time they left the restaurant and lightly kissed on the sidewalk, she was floating on cloud nine. Through everything that they discussed and laugh over, she was just elated to have her sexually alluring friend back.

Their senior year in high school had brought a lot of changes into their personal lives. With Barry and Brandon over in Philly graduating, Bunny and Susan wasn't far behind, they were introduced to new clients. Their money never slowed down through the transition, in fact, it increased. The night Bunny and her crew were throwing their last exclusive party was filled with exotic fun. How his partners convinced the ladies they were fucking to explore a menage trio is a mystery, but they had ventured to Atlantic City and acquired adjoining room to get their freak off. Susan finally figured out the combination to get Afrika between the sheets before she went back to Texas after reflecting on who mentor him. She proposition him ten thousand dollars and it work.

She remember the night that Winston told him to never fuck for free except home girls because they don't have anything to offer but an enjoyable evening. All others desiring their fantasies to be fulfilled needed to be charged and charged accordingly. Susan had the money, or her parents did. Around midnight, when everybody was high and starting to openly get a freaky, she gripped his fingers and escorted him out the suite. She had reserved a suite on an upper floor. Her knees buckled seeing his manhood. He took her on the slow deliberate sexual journey her girlfriends had experience. She remember crying like a baby at the dormant feelings he brought to the surface. With her perspiration running down her body, she begged to him constantly to stop, and he would follow her instructions until her body stop quivering all the while he was smiling down at her. She have never pleaded so much in her young life while making love or laughing at herself for the incoherent words she would utter. He had hit her G-spot while she was on her knees and had her leaping off his dick then staring back at him like a deer staring into the headlights of an approaching car. Apprehensively, she asked to try it again and he was glad to accommodate her wish. By the eight stroke, she was screaming again and leaping off his dick while tumbling off the bed. She sat on the floor staring up at him while rubbing her battered garden of love. They looked at one another then burst out laughing as he helped her back onto their playground.

With the rising of the morning sun caressing her body, she slowly open her eyes to find him staring into her blue eyes. As she shifted her weight, a pleasurable pain exploded between her thighs causing her to slightly groan then smiled. She confessed to being extremely attracted to him during their initial meetings and what they have shared last night will last a life time. She did confess that she will be trying to proposition him to come to Texas at least once a month before she gets married and get this money, she will be holding for him. He never responded but he knew he was going to go and get it. Who wouldn't want to make love to a beautiful, natural blonde with blue eyes? They laid talking for about an hour when he tried to make love to her again, but she wasn't having it. She was not going to be walking around like she had been horse riding a little too long. She did stop by 4th Street three days later to holla at him before she left to catch her flight at Philadelphia International. She gave him a small package then kissed him passionately before rubbing his face and climbed into her friend's car. His partners were shocked by the open display of affection by her. She blew him a kiss while wiggling her fingers as they pulled away from the curb. Watching the car turning up Cooper Street, he open his gift as his partners flocked around to see what it was.

"Damn!" they replied as Afrika just smiled.

She had brought him a diamond Cuban link wrist band with her cell number.

"Damn, man" Tek9 mentioned fingering it then passing to over to Kimba.

"That motherfucker has to cost at least twenty G's" Black informed them since he was into jewelry.

"So, that is what you get for keeping your dick in your pants, huh?" Bear asked smiling over at him.

"This and ten G's" he shared while laughing at their shock expressions engulfing their faces.

"You finally fucked her" Bear asked.

"She figured out my soft spot, man" he acknowledged smiling at him.

"Wait a minute! Wait a motherfucking minute!" insisted Bear trying to make sense of it. "Susan fine ass paid you ten G's to fuck her?"

"Yup" he replied taking his present from Black fingers.

"Winston warned us" Black said shaking his head. "I know Bonnie would have paid if I had played my hand differently. Damn" he said shaking his head at the smirk on Afrika's face.

Graduating from the High was a great accomplishment for them. Most guys coming from out their North never complete high school. Afrika was the only one heading to college. College was not and will not be a part of his partners plans, right now. He had several offers wanting him to attend their universities on partial academic scholarships. He even had an offer from Morehouse, but he decided to attend Rutgers to obtained his law degree. With a GPS of 4.0, he could not argue being called a bookworm ever again by his laughing partners. His speech as valedictorian consisted of the mistrust and deplorable experiments conducted on black people. Between 1932 and 1972, he made reference to the unethical Tuskegee Experiments by the United State Public Health Department. They wanted to see the effects of untreated syphilis in black military men. On a positive note, Tuskegee also had a fighter pilot training program and produced the legendary Red Tail Air Squadron. The highest and most successful all black fighter pilots, during World War II under the Command of Col. A.J. Bullard. America has also ignored her black inventors like Lewis Latimore who invented the light bulb in1881, but Thomas Edison got recognition, but look at the times. Garret Morgan initially invented the first traffic lights in 1923. He also invented the gas mask. Until America corrects the false things she advocates, young black youths won't know of their rich history and not just the history of black people forced enslavement.

"Teach! Teach!" his partners told him throughout his speech while boisterously laughing. When he gets on a roll, he reminded them of the passion that Malcolm X displays on the videos they had seen.

One week after graduating, he received a round trip ticket to Corpus Christi International Airport. He had to actually look up where Corpus Christi was located, and a coy smile came to his face realizing that it was Susan. She had reserved him a suite at the Holiday Inn Expressed and a vehicle to get him to his hotel. He drove to Philadelphia International Airport that following Friday morning and parked in the over-night garage. He told his partners that he had some personal business to attend to and they gave him that same wondering stare. "What are you getting ready to do?" As he checked in at the ticket desk, he would be departing from gate nine and the flight will take approximately three hours. With the announcement to start boarding, he was directed to the first-class seat and found his window seat. He pulled out the book "ATM and J-Lo" out that he had started then lean back and got into the story once the plane had level above the clouds. He was just snickering at a situation in the book when the announcement came over the intercom to place all trays in the upright position. After landing and retrieving his garment bag, he followed the other passenger's towards the main terminal. Spotting the car rental, he went inside and showed his identification then a black Karma GSe-5 pulled up outside. He stood on the sidewalk staring at it while shaking his head. This was the last thing he needed standing six feet five. He climbed inside the bullet with his garment bag then entered the address of the hotel into the navigational system. Leaving the terminal, he turned right onto RT.44 to RT.358 and connected to the I-37. In less than thirty minutes, he was pulling up on the hotel parking lot then peeled himself out with his garment bag. He have never seen so many ten-gallon hat wearing, cowboy boot styling people in one place in his young life as he casually walked through the lobby towards the receptionist desk. After displaying his I.D and signing a card, he was given an electronic key to room 810. Swiping the key, he pushed the door open and walked inside. He smiled at the massive size of the room with a sitting area. He placed his garment bag inside the closet then turned on the radio searching for a jazz station. He eventually found KCYY. He picked up his cell phone and called Susan.

"Hi, Afrika. Are you here yet?" she asked unable to contain her enthusiasm.

"Hi, yourself and yes, I am here" he replied.

"I will be there in forty minutes after I get you some weed."

"Alright" he replied as the line went dead.

Thirty minutes later there was a light knocking on the door. He pulled open the door and smiled down on Susan smiling face. She steps inside then instantly kissed him passionately after the door closed. She was unbuttoning his shirt as she walked him further into the room. Taking off his shirt and admiring his muscular body again caused an impish smile to come to her face as she eagerly stepped out of the sundress she was wearing and allowed it to hit the floor. Wearing a white thong set on her darken sunbath skin, she looked sexy as hell. Releasing her 38B from their restrictions, they perked right up and so did her nibbles as she stepped out of her thong while staring in his eyes smiling.

Although it has only been two months since they last made love, she felt like it was the very first time. She once again pleaded and cried over the ecstasy that he was able to induced. Making love to her future husband since being back, his peter felt just like that, a peter and not a dick. Afrika was moving and widening walls while digging deeper into her most sensitive and softest place on earth. Just two hours later, she surrender to his strength and stamina as she insisted that he stop, so she could slowly float back to earth. Since her fiancée lives in Kingsville, she felt safe getting a room in Corpus Christi. After snorting some more coke, she was ready for round two as she laid back smiling at him. After slaying her again and sharing a shower together, she had to get back home but not before giving him the ten G's and scheduling something for next month.

How was he to know that Susan was sharing her secret rendezvous with a black man to an exclusive set of friends after wonder why she was suddenly glowing? Their curiosity had him meeting them two months later. How was he to know that her girlfriends were admiring his physic and whispering in her ears if they could make love to him also? When she approached him over the phone about making love to her and her girlfriend, he initially thought she was joking and laughing at the suggestion, but when she mentioned the money he could make, he knew she was sincere. When he arrived the following week and walked into the suite, she was standing there, a natural red head named Peggy Sue, of course. With perky looking titties and a petite frame, she openly asked him to take off his clothes a half hour into their introduction causing Susan to burst out laughing as Peggy Sue was salivating. He got to his feet and got butterball naked then stared down at her sitting on the love seat. She gasp but got on her knees while unconsciously smacking her lips then smiled up at him before inserting it into her mouth. He saw another side of Susan that afternoon. A very naughty side as she or her girlfriend showed no inhibitions. The way they maneuver on him on the king size bed made it apparent that they have definitely done this before, but not with him. He demolished Peggy Sue in less than twenty-minutes while Susan was whispering illicit shit into her ears and giggling as she pleaded and begged for mercy, but none came then Susan willingly got slayed as Peggy Sue enjoyed the show. An hour later, Peggy Sue was ready to go again, and the same sexual journey occurred again except tears of rapture fell from her eyes. While they lay in bed, Peggy kept fondling his dick as they talked and got high. She would suddenly place it in her mouth and moan as she would suck it then shake it while smiling.

Their first rendezvous lead to an unexpected exotic summer for Afrika. He had started going to Texas twice a month to get that money from Susan and Peggy Sue, but as their friends saw the subtle but apparent changes in them, they wanted to know their secret, but they adamantly denied that they were changing. Their friend Betty Jane was the one that pointed out how their walk had changed, and it wasn't from riding a damn horse too much as they claimed. She had boxed them in a corner one night, and finally confessed to what they have been secretly doing. And yes, she was openly shocked to hear two of her best friends fucking a black guy, but she was also extremely intrigued also after hearing their stories. The introduction took place the very next weekend and Betty Jane remember asking Afrika to marry her just before reaching another climax.

After the word got out, Susan started pimping him out to all of her girlfriends that had been secretly desiring to make love to a black guy even at ten G's a pop. On numerous of occasions, Susan would have two or three of her girlfriends waiting to meet him and he would gladly slay every one of them. He was clocking in well over a hundred G's a month and knew he was in the wrong profession as a drug dealer. When he had to tell his partners what he was doing and how much he was making, they wanted to join his lucrative erotic party part-time. With pictures of them in her cell phone, she showed them off to their girlfriends and eagerly put them to work. Boy did they have a summer to remember and laugh about although they refused Susan invitation to attend her wedding. They can only imagine what she had set up for them at the bachelorette party if they had foolishly accepted her invitation. What a crazy and profitable ass summer Susan created for him and his partners.

Afrika and his partners often reflect on those earlier years and burst out laughing. They definitely had angles watching over their dumb ass even though they didn't believe in angles or the presence of God with all the misery around them as they should. The path that they took, or should it be said, Afrika took, was an unusual path but supported by his partners. You see, today is especially important for him and his partners. He was graduating from Rutgers University of Law. He was third in his class with a 3.85 grade point average. He devours the hypocrisy that existed in the law like a fat kid in a candy shop.

As he sat on his balcony over-looking the Delaware River, he thank God for his partners and Ramona G.

When he accepted Rutgers partial scholarship in May after he was certain of his decision, he paid the balance off. Walking the halls during June got him slowly acclimated to where everything was located since not many students were attending summer classes. He spent numerous of hours at the law library studying as clients were pleasantly surprised to hear that he was a first-year law student. Two of his four law professors took a liking to him or the ideologies in his head and was constantly requesting that he read his report out loud for the class. The professors would ask the students to debate on what they didn't agree with, and this caused their classes to be highly informative and revealed the bias thoughts of some students. It was those bias thoughts that he craved to debate so he could tear them a new asshole. By the time September arrived and the abundance of students arriving from summer vacation, he was firmly in place and how to maneuver around campus. He was taking fifteen credits his first year. When the summer semester had ended, he had acuminated six A's and two B's. He was now a half a year ahead of his graduating class by sitting his ass in class during the summer, but still filling his obligations to the students over in Philly.

Before starting his sophomore year, those crazy Q's were having a party. He entered their sorority house with his partners and the scent of marijuana consumed their nostrils. Greeting those that they knew, they venture further into the house exploring every room in the three-story fraternity house. Something was jumping off on every floor. Returning back down stairs, he was getting his freak off all night, dancing. He peeked on this bronze complexion young lady and asked her for a dance. From their initial conversation, they naturally click. She was born and raised in the suburb of Atlanta. She is prissy as he claims, and he is thuggish as she proclaims. Opposites truly attracts. When he would get low from his classes periodically, she would jump in her red Honda and cruise through his set. He had warned her hard head repeatedly about cruising through his set and unescorted because somebody was going to jack her high-yellow ass for her car. His word went in one ear and out the other because she said, "You will get it back." No truer statement could be said.

There were numerous of funny things about Ramona's disposition, and one specifically was that she couldn't cuss for shit especially coming from her perceived prestigious background. Can you image the smirk he would have on his face when she call herself chastising him by using intellectual laced profound word? "You are just incorrigible" and other synonyms to describe him having a "bad boy" persona. Her little chastisement usually work for about two or three weeks before the alluring sounds of the streets would start whispering to him and he would slowly, gradually get low on her again. She was subtly trying to keep his mind entertained, but he seem to be always plotting, as she claims. "His mind was always on his partners not plotting" he wanted to tell her. But, if it were not for her constant nagging over the years with Bear and Tek9 staying in his ears also, he might have answered the call to return to the alluring and addictive streets.

He remember the last phone call he received from Daisy after she had graduated from Temple University. She had asked him to come to her apartment one Thursday night after they closed up shop and that was very unusual or out of character for her. She usually only wanted to hookup on the weekends and at his apartment. When he parked inside the Broad Street garage and caught the elevator to the 10th Floor, he could hear Keith Sweat singing "Nobody" filtering through the door as he lightly tapped on it. Moments later, she opens the door wearing a broad smile and damn near nothing else. The red lace boy shorts were pressing firmly against her camel toe as her breast were restrained by her sheer bra. As she slowly walked towards the front room where two glasses of wine was waiting, he closed the door admiring her cheeks hanging out from those cheeky silk panties. He removed his suit jacket and folded it then placed it on the arm of the chair before taking a seat next to her on the couch.

"What's wrong, Daisy?" he asked seeing the stress in her eyes.

"Why do you have to be so damn young?" she asked lighting up a blunt and extending it to him.

"You are only four years older than I" he replied, grinning over at her before hitting the blunt.

"Four years might as well be ten by the way people think today. If you were four years older than me, nobody would utter a damn word" she shared slightly hardening her eyes. "I could very easily give you my heart, Afrika" she sighs, while staring over at him slightly smiling.

"I hate to burst your bubble, Daisy but the first time we made love, you gave me your heart" he informed her still smiling.

"Yeah, I guess you are right" she admitted returning his stare and smile. She did have strong feeling towards him even though she tried to keep them in check but every time they made love, it came running to the forefront of her lips, but she tried to suppressed the words. Her whispering words of admiration and love that she knew she should not have shared although they were truthful. She informed him that she was returning home in a couple days and wanted to feel his embrace before she left. That night was almost a total blur to her, as the erotic feelings he had induced slowly subsided, she do remember openly crying in his arms knowing that she could never legally or morally get with him again once she gets married and this broke her heart. She wasn't losing just a terrific and adorable friends, but a hell of a lover. She awoke to find the blanket tossed on the floor and the top sheet wrapped around her lower body. As she stared around, she noticed that he was gone. Peeking at the clock on the night stand, the clock had one o'clock. "Shit!" As she rolled on her back to reflect on the previous night, she had to confess that she was a freak or sexually explicit in the things she enjoyed when she was with him. She found herself giggling over something that he once told her. "You might not be a freak for me or the guy turning the corner, but somebody will bring it out of you." And he did, he kicked her doors of inhibitions off of its hinges and freeing her. She had wanted to embrace him and taste his kisses one final time before heading home, but she would not get the opportunity. She would have to be content with hearing his tranquil voice before she climbed on her plane. Although she tried to remain strong, tears flowed freely from her eyes as she told him goodbye. The way and tone that she said goodbye to him, he knew that she meant it.

It was during their sophomore year that his and Mona's friendship really started to blossoms. He was gently pulling her out of her cocoon. Spending time with him, she witnessed the love he received from the streets and wondered why? Was he once a famous basketball player because of its height or something else, but she did not have the vaguest idea what it could be. She never understood why he wouldn't drive her car and insisted that she drive his whip when they are together until she asked, why?

"I like looking at you especially when you have to concentrate" he replied nonchalantly while staring out to the people walking past and staring at the vehicle.

He still remembered the first time she invited herself over. Dee-Dee was from St. Louis had been peeking on him for a minute, but could not decide if he was a player or not? With her acme free, no make-up smooth chocolate complexion with medium lips, she stood five feet ten on a medium frame and wore her hair in a young Toni Braxton style. Make no mistake about it, they young lady was beautiful. She had watched him attending several parties around the city and watched his socializing even with the white students. One thing she knew intuitively about him, he like, no, love to dance and was constantly pulling women off the wall to dance. She watched him make the heavy weights feel beautiful like princesses as he request dances with them. Revealing this characteristic or disposition made him very appealing to a lot of young ladies including her. Besides staying impeccably dress, he was always polite and share a smile occasionally. She just so happen to be standing a line trying to get inside Winston's for an old school party with four of her girlfriends that extended half way up the block. He was walking past with his partners when he noticed her and paused to tap her on the shoulder and asked if she was being escorted for the night? When she responded that they were unescorted, he suddenly gripping her fingers and gently pulled her out of the line as his partners did the same for her friends. They spoke to several people as they waked past, but nobody cracked slick about the line being behind them or where they were going as they stood in front of four fashionably dressed silver back gorillas.

"Big Mike" they greeted, smiling up at him.

"What's up, North?"

All that night, they dedicated most of their conversation and dances to the ladies, but never refusing a friend's invitation to dance. They would excuse themselves then proceed to the dance floor gripping the young ladies fingers. She realized that he had a humor about himself that would escape those not paying attention as she constantly does. He was just getting better acquainted with Dee-Dee when Mona used her key and let herself in.

"Excuse the intrusion, sister" she apologized slightly smiling coming over and giving him a light kiss on the lips. "But I need to holla at you, Afrika."

"Who is she, Afrika?" she asked, responding to statement.

"I'm a friend" she replied answering her question. "I need to holla at you, Afrika. She can go or stay. I really do not give a damn" she informed her glaring over at her as she seductively walked towards the balcony.

"What?" she asked getting to her feet glaring over at Mona who paused and turned around. Her St. Louis disposition came to the forefront.

"I excused myself. What else do you want? Like I said, you can go or leave. I really don't give a damn" she reiterated returning her glare.

"Excuse me, Dee-Dee" he said getting to his feet trying to contain his grin at the expressions that had engulfed their faces.

"Is this how you roll?" she asked glaring over at Mona's harden eyes standing by the balcony screen door then stared up at him.

"If something was troubling you and you needed to talk to me, I would make myself available to you also Dee-Dee" he told her staring down into her brown eyes. "I hope that you don't go, but if you do, I could never hold it against your fine ass" he smiled causing her to slightly blush before turning and walking towards the balcony then stepping out. "Okay, what is this about?" he asked closing the screen then taking a seat next to her.

"Things have changed between me and my man" she stated firing up a blunt. "He said that it's me" she snarled hitting the blunt then passing it to him. "Of course, there will always be growth in people and their lives especially when they leave the confines of their cocoon, I hope, or you will be just existing and not living. I did not know how much about life I have not experienced or witnessed until I met you" she declared staring over at him then getting to her feet.

"Sometimes I wonder how you would have been without me" he stated staring up at her with the full moon illuminating behind her.

"More square and naïve than I am" she admitted smiling fully. "You definitely came into my life at the right time. I might have gotten involved with someone who would not have looked out for my best interest as you do" she smiled accepting the blunt from him.

"More than likely" he replied, watching Leo discussing her with his boys at a Q's party. Two of them have made their play and struck out. They were comparing notes to formulate a more conservative approached. They were famous for doing scandalous shit against unsuspecting young ladies. They were known for sneaking a date rape drug in their prey drinks and making a video of their antics. Well, Afrika interjected himself into their plans as Leo was in route to make his play. He ignored their cold stares. They did not want any trouble with him or his partners, especially Tek9 and Kimba crazy assess. "Okay, now tell me what this is really all about" he asked her while extending his hand to her then gripping her fingers and assist her back into her seat.

"Don't ask me questions that you know you are not ready to accept or respect" she blurted out hardening her eyes. "He called me about an hour ago inquiring who is occupying my time because we have not been talking as frequent as we use to, and I mentioned you. His next question of course was if we were lovers and I told him that we were not, but he is implying that I was lying to his punk ass, and I resent that."

"Come on, Mona" he stated revealing that impish smile that she secretly love seeing on his face. "A lot of people are curious about our friendship" he reminded her. "They see how you cuddle up to me when we are hanging out confusing them more than they already are."

"Yeah, I know" she replied giggling. "I love being devilishly mischievous."

"Look at you, baby" he spoke softly causing her stare deep into his eyes. "You are not just a beautiful young lady but sexy as a motherfucker especially when you are in your patient hipster jeans" he shared grinning over at her. "I personally would not have allowed you to leave town and go out into this world alone. Na, I would have worked something out."

"Could you go a year without sex?" she bluntly asked staring over at him.

"Me, personally" he replied slightly grinning. "I couldn't endure a month without the embrace of a woman" he confessed.

"Are you serious?" she asked genuinely surprised.

"Yes, Mona."

"Supposed you was in love?"

"Lust and desire have its own rules, young lady. I would want to know why I would have to go a year without making love if I am supposed to be in love someone?" he asked again, staring over at her. He had asked her on several occasions why she have not gone home and got tighten up or why he haven't made it his priority to come up and see her. She has never given him an explanation that was acceptable, or he would not keep repeating the same question to her. "If y'all agreed on seeing other people, lust and desire is part of that equation that should have been considered also. Promises made in good faith does not mean either is a liar. Who can predict, or who fault it would be if you or him, stumble upon someone intriguingly interesting?"

"Intriguingly interesting like you, huh?" she mentioned with a coy smile.

"Why have y'all decision became a problem now?" he asked ignoring her statement.

"I think he is looking for a way out instead of being honest" she shared her suspicion. "Like Toni Braxton said, "Be a man about it" she quoted then stared out at the Delaware River. "When I asked him who was occupying his time, he naturally said no one. Damn liar" she suddenly snarled. "When I mentioned to him that he was seen at several occasions with Liberty, he them tried to clean it up. Punk ass motherfucker" she snorted causing him to snicker. "They have been peeking on one another since our sophomore year at high school. If he wants her tricking white ass, he can have her."

"If that is true, baby. Why are you so upset?" he asked softly.

"He would not be honest with me as I am with him. He is actually accusing me of having a sexual relationship with you, Afrika."

"And what would be bad about that?" he asked returning her stare.

"Now is not the time for your bullshit" she replied causing him to burst out laughing. "He is only accusing me because he got something going on with Liberty."

"If you have put all the pieces together, you can accept what is going on because you y'all previous contract or move on, Mona. Only time usually heal wounds and broken hearts, but I have hugs for you whenever you desire them."

"You are so sweet" she sighs while smiling and waving off the blunt. "I have to go" she said suddenly getting to her feet then leading the way back inside holding his fingers. "Sister" she called to Dee-Dee. "I apologize for the intrusion" she slightly smile then kissed him again before opening the door and walking out.

"How many of your friends have a key?" she asked watching him coming around the couch then taking a seat.

"Not counting my partners, she is the only one."

"Y'all are that close?"

"Yup, that's my girl" he replied smiling over at her. "Are you ready to get your butt whip on this chessboard?"

"You have gotten a lot better, grasshopper, but six moves ahead is where I'm at" she replied pushing the queen's pawn then taking the blunt from between his fingers as Hiroshi Suzuki's trombone played "Cat" in the background.

In May with their finals completed, he drove Mona to the Philadelphia International Airport to catch her flight home for the summer. This was the first time she was returning home since she first left. As they entered the terminal clutching fingers with her eyes shielded by a pair of Gucci sunglasses and his hidden by a pair of retro sunglasses, both wear fashionably dress bringing attention to themselves. He was wearing a gray Versace suit while she was wearing a white silk Adrianna Papell pant suit. You would have thought that she wasn't going to see him again as emotional her departure was. He stayed staring at the jet until the wheels lifted off the ground and soar above the cloudy sky.

During the summer months after he got out of class, he and Black were concentrating on getting that money from over in Philly. Every day except Sunday they would arrive at one o'clock at their designated location on that shady hill then set up the chessboard and play with jazz was playing softly while they conducted their business. They were making more than a hundred thousand dollars a week from the colleges. From Drexel to temple over to LaSalle and up to Haverford, they had all those students seeking them out. They would slightly socialize until three o'clock when they start putting things away and descending the hill. On Sundays, they would enjoy one another's company or take care of some personal business like getting with their mothers to give them a few dollars.

In early July, he received a telephone call from Mona requesting that he come down to spend her birthday with her. Of course, she made reservations for him that following Friday morning. She told him to take the flight to DeKalb-Peachtree Airport instead of Hartsfield-Jackson because it was closer to where she live. She told him that she would be waiting when his flight landed, but he told her not to. He told her he would rent a car then call her to inform her which hotel he would be staying. She was not too keen on his idea but what could she really do? Afrika does things his own way and thinking she would occupy all his time wasn't happening. His plane landed at ten o'clock that morning. After acquiring his garment bag, he followed the others towards the main terminal then walked inside Hertz Rental to acquire the four-door black A7 he reserved. Since driving Black's, he had fell in love with the way they handle especially around the curves. He signed the necessary paper work then walked outside to the waiting vehicle and placed his garment bag across the backseat before climbing inside. After adjusting the seat and mirrors, he found jazz on 91.9 then enter the Waldorf Astoria address into the navigational system then follow the instructions to I-285 circle it reached Rt.400 heading north towards Peachtree Road. Pulling into the underground garage forty minutes later, he exit the car on the second level then proceeded towards the elevator and pressed L. When the door opens, he walked straight to the receptionist desk.

"Good morning, how can I assist you?" a mid-thirty black woman asked admiring his attire.

"Good morning, ma'am" he replied slightly smiling. "I made reservations under the name of Muhammad.

She started hitting a few keys on her computer then stared at him. "Afrika?" she asked staring up at him.

"Yes, ma'am."

"May I have some form of identification, please" she requested as he was already reaching for it.

"Here you are" he said extending his driver's license to her.

She took it then hit a few more keys before extending his license and an electronic key to him. "You will be in room 1424 and I hope you enjoy your stay."

"Thank you" he replied replacing his license then casually walked towards the elevator and climbed aboard. Pressing his floor, he stared at the arrow on the wall that indicated in which direction he had to go to his suite. He inserted his electronic key hearing the lock released then pushed the door open and walked inside. "Damn, is this what four hundred a night gets you" he openly smiled walking towards the bedroom. He put his clothes away in the walk-in closet and his under garments in the dresser draws then took his hygiene products and placed them on a face towel in the bathroom. He walked into the communal area and placed the radio back on 91.9 then took his toothbrush that contained his blunts and went out on the balcony to take a seat. He was laid back for hours admiring the skyline and scenery. It was almost three o'clock when his cell phone suddenly rang, he smiled at the number before answering then he told her where he was, and she said she was on her way. She arrived forty minutes later banging on his door.

"Why are you knocking like five-o?" he asked slightly snarling down on her while admiring her acid wash hipster jeans with a mid-level, pull over play bunny shirt.

"I knew you were out on the balcony" she replied kissing him lightly on the lips as she rubbed his face then gently squeezed him. She stared up into her best friend eyes. "Damn, did you get more handsome" she asked smiling up at him.

"I love the deep bronze glow you got from this southern heat" he replied ignoring her statement and watching the sway of her hips as she walked straight to the balcony. "Wow, what a beautiful scenery."

"Yes, it is" he commented staring at the pantie lines of her cheeky-short.

"Oh, I feel your eyes on me, sir" she said turning and smiling at the impish smile on his face. "I really missed you, Afrika."

"It hasn't even been two months yet, Mona" he replied extending his blunt to her.

"It appears much longer" she admitted returning his stare. "I saw you almost every day on campus when you weren't trying to bet low" she mentioned grinning. "How are your partners?"

"They are good. Have a seat" he invited.

"No, if I sit down, we might never leave this beautiful suite. I want to show you, my city."

"Are you going to take me out to a club later?"

"Definitely" she replied displaying her full smile. "I'm going to take you to a club named Blue Mist to get your jazz groove on" she informed him. "For right now, I need you to come with me" she insisted slightly whining.

"Can we at least finish this?" he asked holding up the blunt while staring up at her.

"Bring it" she replied heading back inside.

He extinguished the blunt then got to his feet and place it back inside the toothbrush holder. He closed the balcony and turned off the radio then grabbed his small brim hat and electronic key. "Lead the way" he said opening the door for her then closed it behind them.

"So, exactually when did you arrive in town" she asked as the elevator door open and they stepped inside.

"Around ten o'clock" he replied waiting for her natural reaction.

"What!?" she replied as the elevator door was closing as she peeked at him then punched him in the stomach causing him to burst out laughing. "You aren't funny Afrika. If I hadn't called you, what time would you have called me?"

"I don't know" he replied honestly while grinning down on into her grayish eyes.

"Knowing, your slick ass."

"I am not slick" he corrected her still grinning.

"Yeah, right" she slightly snarled. Your would have called me tomorrow. You would have found a jazz spot tonight and venture up into it alone" she read his hand to him causing him to openly grin. "Well, I got your black ass now" she replied as the elevator stop on the main floor then the door open. She clutched his arm as they walked out and casually walked through the lobby. Catching the eyes of several people as they walked pass, she found herself unconsciously giggling at them. "I can never get enough of the stares we receive together" she whisper up to him.

"As beautiful as you are, I would stare also" he replied opening the outer door for her to walk through.

"Every time you tell me that I believe you because you are so genuinely sincere" she smiled rubbing his face as she walked pass.

"You know I have nothing but mad love for you" he replied stepping out behind her.

"That I am certain of also" she replied over her shoulder smiling at him.

"By the way, when did you get that naval ring?"

"You like?" she asked with an impish grin catching his eyes on her ass again.

"You know it's sexy" he replied shaking his head at her smooth and golden silhouette.

"Here we are" she stated stopping in front of a missile.

"What the hell is that?" he asked watching her walking around as she unlocked the doors.

"It's Maybach Exelero" she replied smiling. "Climb in."

"Nope."

"Stop being a punk. Get in" she said shaking her head at him as she was climbing inside. He hesitated then eventually climbed inside. The V12 roared to life.

"Oh shit" he said fastening his seatbelt. "Do you have full body protection cushions for this beast?"

"What do you think, silly?" she asked pressing on the accelerator causing him to melt into the soft leather.

With Brownstone singing "If You Love Me" through the speakers, she leaps on I-285 and slightly opens her up causing an impish smile to come to her face as she concentrated on the road. They cruised though many sets around and inside of Atlanta. She introduced him to Ansley Park, the Botanical Gardens, which was beautiful, and other sights he would have never visited. It was almost eight o'clock when she finally returned him to his suite, she will be picking up at ten o'clock. The two hours appeared to zoom past. He was staring up at the star filled sky when he knocking came to his ears. Opening the door, he staggered backward clutching his heart like Fred Stanford admiring her attire.

"Damn, Ramona" he shared unable to contain his emotion. She was wearing a red one-piece stretched dress that complimented her muscular calves with a thin gold chain around her waist. The form fitting dress from Yves St. Laurent revealed every curve of her body. "Damn!"

"You said that" she replied slightly blushing while kissing him as she entered. "I see you are GQ down as usual" she smiled at the light gray Versace suit he was wearing. "Don't have me fucking up some bitch tonight" he warned him grinning. "The ride should take about thirty minutes."

"More than enough time to get our groove on" he replied shaking his toothbrush holder.

"Are you ready?"

"Just let me grab my hat" he replied closing the balcony door then walking into his bedroom. He returned seconds later adjusting his matching hat and grabbing his key. He followed her out the door then caught the elevator to the main lobby. Walking through clutching fingers, they quietly whisper among themselves. Walking towards the parking lot, he was looking for the missile she was driving previously, but she was driving something looking supersonic. "Now, what in the hell is that?" he asked staring at the beautiful metallic gray vehicle.

"It is a Zenvo ST1" she replied opening the door and starting to climb inside. "Are you coming?"

"I don't know" he replied still gazing at the beautiful vehicle. "What is the top speed?"

"Two-twenty."

"Two-twenty! Nope, I'm not getting in there" he replied shaking his head and slightly backing up.

"You are such a punk" she replied giggling at him. "If you love me, you will get in" she said with a coy smile.

"Now, that is hitting below the belt" he replied opening the door and climbing inside. He felt like he could stick his hand out the window and file his fingernails. The car appears that low. "Whose car is this if you don't me asking?"

"This was my graduation present from my parents."

"Your high school present?"

"Yes."

"Whose car was you driving earlier?"

"My mother's" she replied placing the car in gear and peeling rubber out of the parking lot while on-lookers stared in amazement.

Jumping up on I-285, she transfer over to I-75 and found what she was secretly seeking. Pulling up next to her was a white Ford Shelby with two white boys inside, they were inviting her to open her up, but Afrika was adamantly saying no, but she did of course. When she pressed on the accelerator, the beast leap like a carnivore on its prey as her giggles filled the interior. She left them wondering where in the hell did, she go that fast. She had disappeared just that quickly as she maneuver the car like an extension of herself through the last evening traffic. Although they traveled thirty miles outside of

Atlanta, she arrived at her destination twenty minutes later trying to contain her giggles but smiling from ear to ear.

They entered the Blue Mist Café around ten-thirty, and he gawked at the exquisite scene with dimmer lights at certain locations. As she escorted him pass booths and a lounging area, guys eyes were devouring the silhouette of her body and he couldn't blame them. Finding a table against the far-left wall, they placed their orders with the waitress. He suddenly pulled her chair closer to him and causing her to burst out laughing. He always seems to catch her off-guard whenever he did it and he does it all the time. Not having it done in several weeks, she was delighted to know some things about him will never change. He would whisper into her ears the crazy things that his partners were doing, and her laughter would erupt causing her to clamp her hand over her mouth while pushing him away. She had missed his stories tremendously. From the outside looking in, you would think they were young lovers and genuinely enjoyed the others company.

They had an up-and-coming protégé saxophone player named Q being mentor by Joshua Redman playing tonight. Although only sixteen years old, the young man had an old soul and felt the notes he was playing by the way he was rocking with his eyes close. During Q's set, they took in the scenery. Several tables were occupied by women, and they were all dress to impress. They would peek over at them catching Afrika's eyes and very subtle give him a smile or openly tip their glasses to him. She always admired the way he contained himself to the obvious attention that women gives him when they were out together. Granted, men were constantly openly flirting with her with their eyes when they were out also, but they knew they better not utter a word a single derogatory or illicit word while in his presence. Yeah, she heard their lust filled words and felt their eyes on her body when she went to the bathroom, but their words fell on deaf ears.

Between the jazz sets, the DJ played the latest R&B tunes while staying away from hip-hop completely. They would slow dance to Mint Condition's "Breaking My Heart" and ole school songs like the Intruders "I Wanna Know Your Name" and the Dells "Stay In MY Corner." He had her on the danced floor whispering in her ears causing her to giggle like a school girl or pushing him away laughing when he said something extremely illicit. He refused to dance to Wild Cherry's "Play That Funky Music White Boy" as she would get to her feet and request a danced from one of the many eager brothers. All night they laugh and caught up on things. They did not realize how much they have missed their interaction. It was almost three o'clock in the morning when they exited the club, the slight breeze felt refreshing to them as they walked back towards her vehicles clutching fingers. She gave him the wheel and laid back watching him enjoying himself. They arrived back at his hotel a little before four o'clock.

"Can I spend the night?" she asked softly staring over at him.

"When did you ever needed permission" he inquired as he pulled into the underground garage and using his electronic key to gain access.

They took the elevator to his floor then inserted his key and the lock released. As soon as she walked through the door, she removed her stilettoes and carried them towards the bedroom only pausing to place them by the love seat. She unwrapped the dress she was wearing and allowed it to drop to the floor revealing Victoria's lates secret. A plum color sheer bra and thong set. Her ass was so beautiful in the dim lights of the room. When the moon caressed her body as she climbed up on the bed and stared over at him getting undressed, how could he have forgotten how beautiful her body was? He turned on the stereo and Betty Carter with Ray Charles was singing "It's Cold Outside." When he crawled next to her, she grabbed his arm and wrap it around her. She inhaled deeply then slowly exhaled. In less than five minutes, her breathing slowed, and she could be heard softly snoring. He knew she would get up some time later and go to her bed, and she did.

The morning sun woke him up around nine o'clock. Mona was still sleep in the other room. Her snores could be heard filtering out the ajar door as he went to take his morning shower. He returned to his room twenty-minutes later and put on a pair of shorts with a wife beater. He grabbed his toothbrush holder and exit the room. He turned on the stereo and inserted a Sara Vaughn CD he had brought yesterday then went out on the balcony and took a seat. He stared out at I-285 as traffic slowly increased with the height of the sun.

It was almost noon when Mona appeared. "Why didn't you wake me?"

"For what?" he asked passing a blunt to her and she accepted taking a seat next to him then stared out at the city.

"I want to take you to my old house so I can change my clothes" she informed him.

"Who live there now?"

"Nobody" she replied giggling at his expression. "We still own the house. My parents brought a recent home a couple of years ago, but my mother kept the house she grew up in for one of us one day. I just got to stop there first."

"Okay, what time was you thinking about leaving here?" he asked with his feet up on an ottoman.

"As soon as you can get dress" she replied returning his stare.

"In other word, right now, huh?"

"You know me so well" she replied extending the blunt back to him.

"I can be ready in fifteen minutes" he said getting to his feet with the blunt and walking back inside with her hot on his heels. He grabbed a pair of black dress pants, a gray silk shirt with black and gray cufflinks and a black pair Ferragamo shoes. His small brim black hat completed his transformation. Mona was sitting on the love seat staring at his bedroom door when he appeared. A broad smile creased her lips. "Are you ready?" he asked grabbing his key then staring over at her. "What is that dumb expression about?"

"Nothing silly" she replied opening the door with him following her out then closing the door.

They took the elevator to the garage then climbed into her car. She started up the car and it roared to life as she place it in gear then pressed on the accelerator. The monster took off stopping just inches from the gate arm. She stared over at him smiling then said, "It doesn't matter how close I get as long as I don't touch" she giggled as the gate slowly raised then she pressed on the accelerator slightly fishtailing out. She took the ramp to I-85 for about twenty minutes before exiting at DeKalb. As they drove up Peachtree Road, Brookhaven Country Club was to his left as they pulled into a quiet single-family home community on Terrance Drive NE and East River

NE. They stayed there a half hour before heading to his parents new home. Pulling up in front of their home, there were several cars parked on the parking pad.

"Is this your parents' home?" he asked staring at a small castle. The white front and gray roof gave the house a beautiful curb appeal.

"My father is here" she stated ignoring his question while slightly hardening her eyes as they climbed out of the car. "Let's go around back" she suggested opening the privacy fence and stepping inside. "Damn!" she whispered staring at a group of adults sitting around a patio table.

"Hey, Ramona!" a woman greeted her. There was no doubt that she was her mother. They looked that similar.

"Hi, Mom" she greeted accepting a hug and kiss. "Father" she greeted flatly. "This is my friend Afrika."

"So, you are the young man that my daughter speaks so highly of" her mother shared shaking his hand while smiling.

"Hi, Mrs. and Mr. G" he greeted.

"I was wondering who was influencing my daughter's development" he mentioned staring him up and down with his fat ass stomach, but not offering to shake his hand. "Where are you from, young man?"

"Camden, New Jersey" he replied. "North Camden, specifically" he stressed returning his stare.

"Camden, huh?" he asked with an unusual stare.

"Yes, sir" he replied returning his stare. "Is there a problem?"

"I'll tell you later" he replied with a coy smile that did not go unnoticed by those sitting at the table.

"I will be right back, Afrika" Mona told him staring over at her father with malice in her eyes.

"Let me holla at you" Mrs. G informed her wrapping her arm around her waist while escorting her into the house.

"I'll keep him entertained!" her father shouted to her.

"His name is Afrika!" she shouted back at him with a cold stare.

Afrika moved away from him as soon as his eyes fell on Mona then took a seat near one of the young trees in their massive yard. He watched her father pull out his cell phone and spoke briefly before ending his conversation. He stared over at Afrika with that same coy grin on his face. About ten minutes later, three guys walked in. A high yellow guy went straight to Mr. G and shook his hand vigorously while smiling from ear to ear. When they glanced over at him, he got to his feet tipping his hat to them then walking out the back yard. He was sitting out front for ten minutes before Mona appeared from the back yard with her eyes looking to rip someone a new asshole.

"Let me drop you off and hook back up with you around ten o'clock, okay" she stated walking towards the car and climbing inside then starting the engine. He barely fasten his seatbelt when she pressed on the accelerator causing his body to instantly melt into the soft leather. All the way to his suite she remained quiet addressing her private thoughts. Pulling up in front of the hotel, she leaned in and kissed him lightly. "I will see you in a couple of hours."

"Alright" he said opening the door and climbing out. The door was barely closed before she peeled away An impish smile came to his face watching her leaning as she turned right, he could only imagine what she was about to set off at their home. He turned staring at the small spectators grinning them proceeded towards the main entrance. As he casually walked through the lobby, he pressed the elevator button and walked aboard then exited on his floor. Once inside his suite, he turned on some jazz then changed his clothes. He grabbed his book called "Retribution" and sat on the couch. Two hours later, sleep had unknowingly gripped. Opening is eyes hours later, the clock had seven-thirty. He swung his feet to the floor then stretched before getting up and walking towards the bathroom to take a shower. He was walking out fifteen minutes later with a towel wrapped around him. Standing the closet trying to decide which suit to where, he decided on his dark blue Armani with a light blue French collar silk shirt and a pair of brown wingtip Stacy Adams. He laid them out on the bed then put on his undergarments with a pair of shorts then walked out on the balcony with a glass of Parrot Bay coconut and took a seat before lighting up his blunt. Staring up at the stars, he had to admit he liked the quietness. No sounds of the hectic city. Checking his watch, it was ten o'clock. "She should be here in a half hour" he said to himself grinning. Anybody that knew her would naturally put an additional hour on her initial time. He have given her even more time when necessary because she was definitely worth it. He was almost dress when a light knocking to came to his ears. Opening the door, he actually gawked at her again.

"Close your mouth please" she said kissing him on the lips then lightly rubbing his face as she walked pass.

"Damn, Mona" he commented closing the door watching the sway of her waist and her phat little apple bottom ass. Dressed in a light blue Louis Vuitton shirt set that hit her mid-thigh. The black stockings she wore reminded him how attractive her legs were with her constantly wearing some form of pants. With her naturally shoulder length hair pinned up like a professional with a couple of strands pulled down on both sides of her face. The girl looked not just gorgeous but sexy as hell.

"Are you ready" she asked taking a seat and relighting his blunt.

"Give me five minutes" he replied heading back into the bedroom to finish his transformation. He reemerged five minutes later and wearing his gangster like hat. "Are you ready?" he asked staring over at her.

"Indeed" she replied smiling at his complete transformation. He always appeared GQ and she adored the stares they received while clutching fingers as they walked. Guys would say little slick things to her when she was out with other guys, but Afrika was not one of those guys. His eyes alone let a person know he is not to be fucked with and did not have a problem flashing his canines if persisted. Most guys would check themselves instantly or suddenly ignore them and keep it moving. She had witnessed him defending her honor twice and both times, she thought that he was going to commit a homicide. He was that brutal and unmerciful. Two characteristic that she thought were not a part of his demeanor or D.N.A. He explained later that he was making an example out of them for anyone standing in shadows contemplating the same dumb disrespect towards her. At both of those clubs, nobody has ever stepped out of the shadows since those incidents.

They arrived at Kate's on Piedmont Avenue NE around eleven o'clock. With him standing six-five and with her stilettoes making her stand six-one, they brought a lot of attention to themselves as they were clutching finger and getting in line.

Although she possesses a natural sexy walk, stilettos only accentuated it like she need more attention. They were in line for ten minutes before finally walking through the foyer. She gripped his fingers and directed him to a middle table, but he wasn't feeling being surrounded by a bunch of strangers.

"If you love me, you will do this for me" she whispers slightly smiling up at him.

"You are hitting below the waist" he replied allowing her to lead him.

He pulled her chair out and assisted her into her seat before taking his seat. After placing their orders, he pulled her close causing her to start giggling. They were there a half hour when the emcee came to the microphone.

"Okay, ladies and gentlemen" he stated dressed in a loud yellow zoot suit with matching gators. He was definitely representing the dirty south. "Let us get this night started, who will be first?"

As different people took to the stage, they would sing songs from the karaoke machine. Some actual sound really good while others had a little too much alcohol convincing them they could sing. When Ramona suddenly got to her feet and strolled towards the stage, she received the cat calls and whistles she desired. He had heard her singing a few times, but he didn't think she was bold enough to sing in front of strangers. He laid back with an impish smile on his face. When she gripped the mic, her impish smile came to her face and his male intuition started banging and loudly.

"Ladies" she called out smiling seductively at them. "Let me reveal to y'all just how much we are loved by my extremely close friend. Maybe our men are not putting in the quality time that he should, and we deserve, to keep our love on a solid foundation. Well, this is what you could be missing staying with an unappreciative and self-serving knucklehead ass man. Afrika, come tell these women of the love you have for us" she called out to him in the diminished light, but he was ignoring her as those sitting around him knew she was talking directly to him. "Afrika don't let me come and get you, sweetheart" she smiled staring in the slight shadow at him.

As those that didn't see where she came from was staring around, those that knew was staring directly at him and smiling at him. Reluctantly getting to his feet while slightly shaking his head, all eyes followed him to the stage as he climbed the stage. He came to stand next to her.

"Tell me how beautiful we are, sweetheart" she requested with an impish smile.

He stared at her then out at the silhouettes of the darken crowd then walked to the karaoke machine searching the menu. Finding what he desired, he pressed play and Kool, and the Gang's "Summer Madness" began to play. He walked over accepting the microphone from her hand then pulled her close to him. With the music playing in the background, he kissed her lightly on the lips then focus out on the crowd with an impish smile and walked towards the edged of the stage.

"What you see before you Queens, is a man in love...my love for you, extends further than the stars above. Like the rain quenching the thirst of a flower... I wish to bath in you, for hours and hours. I surrendered my love to you from the very start...because you are, the pendulum of my heart. I tried to deny myself of you, yeah, I tried that... but you are as alluring, like a Venus flytrap. I personally like staring into your eyes and admiring your full lips...all I want to know is, are they filled with bliss. Every day when I walk these streets, oh, I see you.... the only women that can change my gray skies to blue. Like Romeo and Juliet, a love that have endured the tests of time...I wish our love to ripen also, like the sweet taste of a wine. Like the moon caressing your body at night...I too will be holding you oh so tight. Becoming intoxicated by the scent of your perfume...as your moans and groans filled our bedroom. My love for you should not breed doubts or maybe's...because y'all are the only ones, I want to call, baby. Take this kiss and place it on your most sensitive spot...or let me do it, until you plea and beg me to stop" he requested in an exceptionally low and alluring voice. "So, before this evening ends and you tell me goodnight...consider how romantic it could be, if you allow yourself to get caught by the morning light" he slightly grinned staring over at Mona then extending the mic to her.

"Ladies, should I get caught by the morning light?" she asked revealing her impish smile.

"Hell, yeah!" they screamed out at her causing her to giggle to mix with their laughter.

He couldn't contain his laughter as he gripped her fingers and escorted her off the stage.

"You blew their minds" she whispers staring in the eyes of some of the women as they proceeded back to their table.

"Does he have any brothers at home?" a chocolate complexion woman asked staring in his eyes.

"Sorry, sister" she smiled over at her table. "God wouldn't know what to do if there were another one of him" she replied giggling with them.

It was almost four o'clock in the morning when they finally left the club, they had met some genuinely nice individual that evening. All of them wanted to know where he was from with his accent. Finding out that he was attending law school in Jersey and that was where they met, the women all sighed at their romantic journey. Neither shared with them that they were just close friends. They did not want to blow their fantasy. They allowed them to have their perceptions. Arriving at the hotel, they drove into the underground garage then took the elevator to his floor. Mona was definitely slightly intoxicated from enjoying herself tremendously. Opening the door, he allowed her to enter first then closed the door. He assisted her to her bedroom. She flopped down on the bed staring up at him with a very seductive smile.

"Come help me out of my clothes, baby."

"Nope, not this time" he replied causing her to burst out laughing.

"Stop being a punk all the time with me. Nobody is going to mess with your punk ass."

"Nope" he replied backing out of the room.

"I just want you to hold me tonight, Afrika" she stated trying to look serious but unable to contain her giggles at the expression that had engulfed his face as he closed the door behind himself. "Stop being a punk!" he could still hear her and her giggles as he entered his bedroom.

He took a quick shower then put on some shorts and a wife beater. Peeking inside her bedroom, she never completed taking off her clothes. He walked inside contemplating the task that laid before him. He admired her nibbles through the sheer yellow bra and her public hair protruding through the matching thong. All he could do was smile at her beauty as he took her clothes off. She whisper something incoherent then giggled before passing back out. He pulled the sheet over her then extinguished the light then quietly closed the door.

When she finally woke up around two o'clock in the afternoon, she was slightly confused as she stared around then a smile engulfed her face as she thought about the previous night. She has always been able to get him to jump out of character and do what she desired especially reciting his poetry. She was constantly giggling at the young ladies expressions that had join them last night. When she finally peeked at her watch, she could believe it was after two o'clock. She swung her feet to the floor then grabbed her blouse then strolled through the suite searching for him. She found a note of the balcony door informing her that he has taken an earlier flight home to avoid the sadness that would have engulfed her beautiful and alluring eyes. All she could do was sigh and shake her head smiling. He was right. She would have cried like a little girl. She took the blunt from the note then opened the balcony door and stepped out. She stared over the city then noticing a small box. She opened it and stared at the bracelet she saw two days previously that caught her attention. "You are something else, Mr. Muhammad" she said to herself smiling as she placed it on her wrist. She did not have to leave until six p.m. She sat back with her feet on an ottoman then lighting up the blunt. She sat there reflecting on the past two beautiful days then the first day came back to her thoughts and she found herself slightly snarling.

"So, what happen when you went back home?" he asked as they were leaving the MLK Memorial on Auburn Avenue NE.

"My mom was waiting in the driveway for me when I return. She knew I was about to get my shit off" she admitted slightly hardening her eyes "She took me aside to cool me down or I would have gone at my father raw. When we finally went back into the yard, my father had enough common sense not to mentioned or ask where you have gone. With their friends sitting at the patio table, I still air it out. "You must think it is okay for a guy to cheat on your daughter? I requested my best friend to come celebrate my birthday with me and you are going to shun him without even knowing anything about the substance of the man. He is the reason for my transformation. A transformation that a man like you can't appreciate and damn sure don't approve because I am not that fragile little girl that left here four years ago with her heart broken. I wanted my Daddy to side with me and not the person that broke your daughter's heart. When you did that, you was no longer daddy to me but simply father, with no of the attributes associated with being a daddy like my love and affection. You abandon me for his high yellow ass" she snarled over at Theo. "So, stop asking for my motherfucking forgiveness because you will never get it" she apologized for her profanity as she snarled over at him then at Theo again with his two friends. "I emerged from my cocoon a much stronger and confident woman. I personally don't care who likes it. I'm not asking you to, but here I stand and never regressing back to that shallow girl I once was."

She privately wished that she could convince him to join her in Atlanta after graduating. The only thing that could keep him in Camden is his partners. If she pleaded her case to them, they would cut him loose, but the final decision would still be his.

During his internship, he had to pick two law firms to learn under for six months each before they could take the bar exam. Rutgers had their annual open house for different law firms to make their introductions and possible, future pitch. Afrika's introductions to most of the firms was not being very receptive or warm towards him. The tones of their words revealed that even though the right words were filtering pass their lips, their whole demeanor and body language was saying something completely different. Absent was all the zest that would influence him to consider the firm, but he made a notation on the paper after acquiring their signature to show he had been interviewed, then he would move to the next firm. Every student had to have a minimum of ten signatures, and he obtained the minimum. Hines Brother would be his primary and Barnes and Barnes would be his secondary. His favorite professor, Professor Dickerson flipped his choices. At first, he thought that he was joking, but then he realized that Professor Dickerson was always teaching. He knew he would choose the Hines Brothers not because of the substance that they could provide but because of the color of their skin. So, he flipped his choices.

Entering Barnes and Barnes, he was met with a slight resentment but that was expected. As long as no one disrespected him or say anything racially derogatory, things would be peaceful. If not, he would plea temporary insanity after beating the shit out of their racist asses. He also had some gangster bitches on stand-by for the woman that was cosigning the bullshit. His immediate supervisor was a guy named Rodger. He placed a recent assault case in his hand and told him to dissect the charges and evidence. His first draft covered every possible angle including the back door that prosecutors like creeping through. Daniel Jackson, the lawyer that he had prepared the brief for was extremely impressed with hiss investigative technic. He and two other lawyers were constantly requesting for him specifically from Mr. Rodgers. He acquired some lessons under Barnes and Barnes exceptional and reliable professional lessons under Barnes and Barnes. They taught him not to just defend for his client but counter what the prosecutor might conceived. All the briefs that he wrote under their tutorage cover everything like the branches of a tree. He actually sat as third chair in a criminal case during his span there. He was very professional with a unique eye for pointing out discrepancies on several charge papers eventually getting their clients reduced charges or getting an acquittal. When he arrived at the Hines Brother six months later, Robert was blown away by his brief writing techniques and professionalism. Professor Dickerson once again gave him another "life lesson" to take with him as he continued his journey. "Learn your lessons the right way then alleviate later if you chose to but lean your lessons, Afrika." He had learned his lessons well.

Hours before their graduation ceremony, he was sitting on his balcony listening to bassist Ron Carter while enjoying the warmth of sun on his deep mocha complexion body and face. A sudden breeze caused the curtain to move indicating that someone had just entered his apartment. Turning and staring inside, he spotted Mona's honey complexion heading his way. She had on a pair of white acid wash hipster jeans revealing her diamond naval ring on slightly develop abs while carrying her stilettoes in her hand. A mid-range white silk blouse revealed the red bra she was wearing. The woman is bad with two D's.

"Hey, stranger" she smiled down on him then giving him a light kiss and taking the blunt from between his fingers before taking a seat next to him. "What's up with you?"

"Nothing much" he replied, taking his feet off the baboon table while putting on his wife beater. "When did you get here?"

"A couple of hours ago" she replied. "I am going to miss you so much" she sighs after hitting the blunt a couple of times.

"I'm just a phone call away, young lady" he replied avoiding the sadness that was creeping into her grayish eyes.

"Atlanta isn't right around the corner, Afrika."

"No, it is not" he agreed returning her stare. "It's just a flight away."

"I don't want to lose what we have acquired over the years" she stressed. "You are the first guy that I can honestly say is my best friend" she smiled over at him then extending his blunt back to him.

"We have built an extremely solid foundation for our friendship, Mona. There is nothing on God's earth that can ever destroy that, and I mean nothing" he stressed slightly hardening his eyes.

"Yeah, you have shown me that" she admitted smiling. "The times you have caught me disrespecting myself by dancing a little too provocative or just a little too intoxicated, you never flipped your script on me. You would stay cool and remained the loving person that you are" she shared smiling at him. "You would only shake your head at me with that impish smile I say I don't like but actually adore, and simply tell me it's time to go home. You are actually my knight in shining armor protecting me from myself" she admitted giggling. "How could I not fall in love with you?"

"Aaahhhh" he replied causing her to harden her eyes at his sarcasm. "I truly love you too, Mona" he said staring in her eyes trying to assure her again but still wearing his smile. "I'm a friend, Mona."

"Stop saying that, Afrika!" she insisted hardening her eyes then slowly lowering them. "You are more than just a friend, baby. Those nights I came stumbling through your door, tore up from the floor up, you have never taken advantage of the situation or used your position with me to take advantage. I would awaken the next morning slightly disorientated, but my clothes were never touched and so was I. At one time, I thought you didn't find me attractive" she shared staring in his eyes then slightly blushing.

"Yeah, right" he smirked waving off her comment. "You know damn well you are not just attractive, but sexy as hell. So, you can drop that nonsense. I will never forget the first time you came over stumbling through my door giggling like a school girl. All I could do was shake my head and assist you to your bedroom. When you asked me to assist you out of your clothes, I eagerly accepted the invitation. I damn sure was not prepared for the unveiling of Victoria's latest secret under those hipster jeans that you like to wear in the summer. Bronze color lace boy shorts revealing your close shaven garden of love and your bra revealing your nibbles pressing firmly against their restraint. The image have been permanently engraved into my memory bank and when I close my eyes when I'm thinking about you, I can't escape the memory" he shared with that impish smile that caused her to blush. "I told myself, I will never do that again. Never!" he stressed staring at her smiling face. "So, don't ever think I'm not attractive to you, Honey Buns" he shared lightly snickering.

"I heard what you are saying, but I still had my reservations, Afrika."

"And you came to this conclusion, how?"

"You never tried pressing up on me for one thing. Sure, when we are out socializing, you have always been extremely attentive but…"

"But what?"

"Why didn't you play your hand? To be portrayed as the apple in someone's eyes is desired by all women. My girlfriends don't understand our relationship and sometimes, I honestly don't understand it. You know we are feeling one another. So, what is up?" she asked staring in his eyes. "I have never kissed you passionately and that is a shame."

"First of all, young lady. You shouldn't want to kiss me passionately, that can confuse our relationships" he said gripping her fingers and pulling her to her feet then pulling her into his arms. He kissed her so passionately that all of their hidden passion and desires overwhelmed them as he pressed his body firmly against hers. When a deep low moan escaped her throat, she had to gently push him away as she seem to savor the taste of their kiss with her eyes closed.

"Damn that felt so erotic" she confessed slowly opening her eyes. "So, why haven't you step up?"

"Listen" he insisted as they reclaimed their seat. "I knew this conversation would come and bit me on the ass. Although my explanation will be truthful and I know my explanation won't satisfy you, but you know it will be the truth."

"What will be the truth?" she asked a little apprehensive.

"Do you remember the first time I met your parents?"

"Yeah, I invited you down to celebrate my birthday during our sophomore year."

"Correct, your parents were very receptive to me, despite your father" he replied slightly smiling. "Your father asked me where I was from, do you remember that?"

"Yes."

"Well, he must have gotten a private investigator to get the 4-1-1 on where I was from, not on me because there isn't anything out there on me. When you went to show your mother your dorm room, he decided to have a frank conversation with me. Through all the bullshit he was uttering, I understood that he was allegedly grooming you to marry some guy named Theodore."

"Theo!? What is in the hell is that name doing coming out of your mouth?" she asked openly snarling at him.

"Well, you know I didn't place it there" he replied with slight smirk. "Apparently, your father has lofty expectations for you and your future, which doesn't include somebody coming from the third most violent city in America. His fat ass actually had me feeling a little embarrassed that I didn't qualify to date his daughter" he admitted, slightly shaking his head.

"I am so embarrassed" she replied slightly lowering her head. "So, he has plans for me, huh?"

"Apparently and without your knowledge" he lightly chuckled seeing how piss she was.

"Is that why you asked me if I had anyone at home?"

"Yes" he admitted. "And when you didn't mentioned Theodore, I was wondering why?"

"I didn't tell you about him because he is no longer a factor in my personal life" she replied. "He seen I wasn't the same meek and naïve little girl that left there to go to school. Both of my parents expressed how I have changed. My mother adores my new confidence and strength but my father, he is scared as hell of me, and he needs to be unless he wants to get his bitch ass feelings hurt, again" she stressed hardening her eyes. "So, I honestly don't give a damn what he thinks or anybody else think about my transformation. I love you for helping me transform."

"My pleasure, but don't think it was easy keeping my emotions in check because it wasn't easy, Mona. It was not easy at all."

"Can I ask you something?"

"When have you needed permission?"

"No, seriously Afrika. Now is not the time to be joking" she insisted hardening her eyes. "During our internship, Barnes and Barnes were very interested in you and so was a lot of other prominent law firms, but you turned them all down, why?"

"I couldn't accept it Mona even with their lucrative offers because I have to pay restitution to my community" he shared in a tone that forced her to stare at him unusually and thinking about the subtle message he was giving her.

"What do you mean?"

"Think about it Mona" he insisted returning her stare.

Mona has this habit of biting her lower lip as an unusual expression would engulf her face as she would concentrate. This gleam would gradually come to her face as she figured out his subliminal message.

"I have always had my assumptions about you ever since you introduced me to your partners a couple of years ago" she admitted, grabbing the blunt from between his fingers and pulling from it. "Although it wasn't obvious what they were about even with the fashionable way that they dressed, I just couldn't understand how y'all became such close friends. As I watched you closely and observed your tendencies, there are the unconscious things that you naturally did when we are out. You always face the door at an angle and kept your eyes on the rear exit, and that was when it finally click. You was or are a part of their entourage until you started school. I don't even expect you to confirm that because I know you won't. You would place that question on your wifey to know only shelf" she snickered at him. "And don't get me started on the love and respect y'all receive when we are on the streets. Once a group of guys started getting fresh with me, until two of them recognized me as someone that was always with you, and they ceased their comments plus apologized repeatedly" she shared smiling at him. "Some of the people you know are straight up gangsters and pimps once you invited me inside Winston's. I couldn't believe the part of your hand you revealed to me. I still get astounded sometimes. I knew there was more to you than what the eyes see."

"Just a little bit, Mona" he replied indicating how much with his fingers. "If hooking up with you wouldn't bring you no drama especially from that father of yours, I would snatch you right up."

"Then do so, my father will eventually accept you once he gets to know you" she replied.

"I'm sure that his fat ass would, but I demand respect coming out the gate not after you think you know me. Your father don't see where I'm headed. He sees only where I came from. Since he couldn't respect me as a man but snob at my social and financial environment, I don't ever want him to know me" he shared slightly hardening his eyes.

"But."

"There is no buts, Mona. Your father has aspiration of Theodore waiting on you."

"You aren't funny" she snarled at him extending the blunt back to him.

"No, I am not but Theodore name is" he replied snickering just escaping a punch from her.

"Nothing is etched in stone with me" she informed him. Just like the seasons change, I have also. I don't see Theo being able to handle the changes in me. All I am concerning myself with is you. I need you to stay connected to me or I will come cruising through your set" she warned him.

"Your, crazy butt probably would" he replied smiling at her. "Atlanta isn't that far away, girl. You will see me."

"Do you promise?"

"I promise" he replied using that word very rarely.

"I'm going to hold you to that" she replied lightly giggling.

"Woman, look at the time. We have two hours before show time" he said getting to his feet and stretching his six feet five frame. "Are you going to wait on me or what?"

"I have been waiting on you" she replied seductively then openly laughed at his expression.

He waved off her comment as he proceeded down the hallway to take a quick shower. He emerged forty minutes later dressed in a pin-stripe gray Versace suit with his small brim hat. She nodded her approval while grinning.

He had slaved his ass off trying to be the valedictorian of his graduating class, but Roman won the honor followed closely by Suzi Wong and then him. A couple of years ago Mona's subject would have been on some bullshit like world peace or expectations of America, but this wasn't a couple of years ago. She has evolved since then and removed her blinders. He didn't know what her subject would be about, but he was certain that it would be interesting. Her subject was on the death penalty and the unfair practice by America's judicial system of administering it more frequently to people of color. The statistics she quoted substantiated her thesis.

"Preach! Peach!" his partners would shout fanning her fire and laughing their assess off. Can you imagine how red in the face those white people sitting in the audience were and the look of embarrassment on her father's face as though she was embarrassing him specifically. Her mother stared up at her in awe and smiling from ear to ear.

Several law firms and the city finance department contributed for its annual internship program being held at the Philadelphia Convention Center in the 1300 block of Arch Street. It was at this function that he became acquainted with the Hines's Brother, Robert in particular. He watched the many aspiring lawyers selling themselves like a top-notch whore for consideration in one of several prestigious law firms. He watched the many interviewers closely as they talked to perspective employees especially when a potential prospect was a person of color. There was no sincere enthusiasm in their greetings or a friendly disposition that was bestowed on the other prospects. He had to get a certain amount of signature and he would obtain them, but he wouldn't give them his manuscript. All he wanted was their signature so he could keep it moving.

"Excuse me."

"Yes, sir" he replied, pausing, and staring into his blood shot eyes.

"I'm Robert Hines of the Hines Brother."

"Glad to make your acquaintance" he replied shaking his hand.

"I've been observing you since you walked in. From what I have seen, you really don't care if a law firm hire you are not."

"That's not true, I'm just not going to act like a Negro to be considered for my internship" he informed him. "I will let them hear the book knowledge that they place so much value in, but I have so much more to offer."

"Like what?"

"Let's just say, I know people that knows people that is always looking for a good lawyer" he replied never averting his eyes.

"I believe you" he grinned at him. "Here is my card, I hope you consider doing part of your internship with my firm."

Since it was mandatory by his favorite professor, Professor Dickerson, to do our internship at two separate law firms, he choose the Hine's firm as his primary and Barnes and Barnes as his secondary, but Professor Dickerson flipped his choices. He was always giving "life lessons" if a person was receptive and he was. He didn't take it personally when he flipped his choice. He did it because he knew how afro-centric he was and knew he would make the Hines Brother as his primary. "Learn your lessons, Afrika" he had told him. So, he worked for Barnes and Barnes for the first six months of his internship. The experience and knowledge he obtained was exceptional. He even worked a trial as third chair and pointed out discrepancies that had escape the lawyer. He was overly impressed with Barnes and Barnes. He shared this with Professor Dickerson. When he walked into the Hines Brother dab environment, Robert was extremely impressed with his brief writing skills covering everything, especially his back door.

At the end of their internship, they had to go back to those he had gotten a signature for the final meeting before taking the state exams to be a certified lawyer. As he was retracing his previous path, those interviewers that displayed a nonchalant or snobbish disposition were left with their hands in the air as they tried to shake his hand after he reminded them of their previous disposition. They had heard about him through the revue he received from Barnes and Barnes. Although they tried to make amends for their previous actions, he reminded them that you have only one chance to impress a person and he wasn't impressed with their alleged professionalism.

On June the 21st, he walked into the Hines office at 31st and Charles Street in Pennsauken with his B.A and law degree.

"May I help you?"

"Yes, ma'am. I have an appointment with Robert Hines."

"What is your name?"

"Afrika Muhammad."

"You are the new lawyer?"

"Yes, and why are you looking at me like that?" he asked smiling over at her.

"Because you look like you should still be in high school" she replied returning his stare while smiling.

"Thank you, I think" he replied still grinning.

"Just a minute Afrika" she said grabbing the phone and talking into it briefly then returning the phone to its cradle. "Robert will see you now. Go right in. His office is on the left-hand side."

"Thank you" he replied following her instruction. He nodded to the three lawyers he had as he walked pass then lightly tapped on his door.

"Come in."

He pushed open the door and the scent of alcohol instantly invaded his nostril. Robert was sitting inside with his younger brother James. "Good morning, gentlemen" he greeted them.

"Morning Afrika" Robert greeted his shaking his hand. "This is my brother James."

"Nice meeting you" he said shaking his hand. "I got things to handle. I'll talk to you later, Rob" he said checking Afrika out from head to toe as he walked pass and out the door.

"Listen, I seen your performance at Barnes and Barnes, and so have so many other law firms. I know their offer will be substantially higher than what I can offer, but if you come work for me and my brother, I promise to make it up to you. If my hunch is correct about you, this office is about to make a drastic change and I will reward you with an associate partnership after four years. Will you accept my promissory note?" inquired Robert trying to read his eyes, but they were blank of expression or indication that he will accept his offer.

He accepted the contract with the promissory note attached. That weekend, he got with his partners to celebrate his good fortune. They hit the clubs Friday night in Camden and left his cards at all the locations. They travel over to Philly Saturday night to hit the clubs around City Center. Sunday, he tried resting but his partners were snatching him out and kept him out until seven o'clock that night. Monday morning, things started jumping and I mean jumping quickly. Pimps, gangsters, drug dealers and many more that dwell in the darkness was calling and making inquiries about if Afrika worked there. Once it was established that he did work for the Hines Brothers, they made appointments. All the small firms near them should have folded or closed their door permanently.

After the first year, the Hines had to hire five more lawyers and four full time interns or money would be escaping them and that wasn't about to happen. With him able to show how he make his money, Afrika went out an brought himself a three-thousand square feet, four bedrooms with two-and-a-half-bathroom Colonial off of foreclosure for a little over five-hundred-thousand dollars. The house was a leisurely forty-minute drive from the suburb of Moorestown. The house originally was going for seven-hundred and fifty thousands, but with no interest from potential buyers over the years, the owner had to lower the price or watch the house continue to deteriorate. The realtor that hooked him up was the mother of an ex-client. Once he signed on the dotted line and obtained the keys, he contacted South Jersey Painting and Remodeling in Maple Shades. With all the specifications he wanted, the total came to one-hundred and fifty thousand dollars. With his massive backyard, he got an inground swimming pool with a tarp to cover it during the winter months and a large gazebo that could sit fifteen people comfortably. Ramona had brought him a portable hammock that he seem to constantly be on while reading and listening to his jazz. He did all of his lawn work including keeping the edges manicured. With the addition of a balcony from his master suite, he was the only one in his community that had one and brought substantial value to the house.

He was barely twenty-four and didn't have a worry in the world. He gradually got into a routine for his nosy ass neighbors. You could virtually set your clock to his movement, and he was certain that some of their wives did, seeing window blinds subtly moving. Monday thru Friday, he was out of the front door by eight o'clock and back home by five o'clock. He would change into his workout gear and hit his heavy bag after doing his exercise for ninety minutes then take his shower and eat a healthy dinner before peeking at the idiot box to catch up on the sports news. He was usually in his bed by ten o'clock and fast asleep by eleven-thirty then start the routine all over again. The weekends were a crap shoot especially if his partners could get their hands on him.

Everybody should have a hobby to release a person stress whether its bird watching or playing or attending some sport event. Some prefer going to museums or attend symphonies to listen to Bach, Beethoven, or Mozart's concerto#21 although his hobby had an ulterior motive. Most Saturday's after he left the law library, he would venture over to Philly to prospect, if you will. He would venture into the numerous women clothing, shoes, and lingerie stores in Center City especially on South Street and Chestnut Street prospecting. During these little adventures of his, he have become very conscious and knowledgeable about women fashions. He would comment on a piece of clothing that a young lady might be contemplating, and he would voice his opinion. Like, in lingerie stores, he would whisper what color would look even sexier on them while in clothing stores, he would suggest what color would complement their complexions or style that would accentuate her shape. Women would be suspicious of him and rightfully so. Men are known to be dogs. Up until he suggest them trying on something from Donna Morgan or Suzi Chin while slightly hippy women had their hips accentuated by a dress from Adrianna Papell.

"Go and try it on, please" he would suggest returning their stares then allowed them to see him taking a seat and crossing his legs while smiling at them. When they emerged, they would walk like a model admiring what he had suggested. Their broad smiles would give him the liberty to suggest then trying on something from Saks or Veronica Beard. Usually, his suggestions were right on point. They would slightly lower their apprehension and conduct a friendly conversation. He never referred to complimented their anatomy during these small talks. Some would offer their telephone numbers to stay connected. They always seem to call him when they were ready to up-grade their wardrobes. Several had actually taken him up to New York to do their shopping. His ploy didn't always work mainly because some women are just not friendly, but he have become very acquainted with a lot of women in Philly.

He was walking back towards his car on 8th and Market parking lot when a poster staple to a telephone pole caught his attention advertising a mystery boat ride with ole school music, dancing, and an open bar tonight at six o'clock. Checking his watch, it was five-forty-five. Being very spontaneous, he jump into his car then race down to Penn's Landing. Calling his partners to pull their coats wouldn't do any good, they wouldn't be able to get here in a reasonable time. Swinging into the parking area, he found a parking space then grabbed his toothbrush holder and noticed he had five blunts inside. Placing it in his breast pocket, he climbed out the car and notice a people approaching the ship. He notice several people buying tickets at the gangplank and a broad smile came to his face. He slow his pace then brought a forty dollars ticket and boarded the three-tier ship. On the lower deck was the main party, a bar extended along one wall with six bartenders and several waitresses. He order himself a glass of Moscato at the bar then took in the sights while having a casual conversation with two guys. His head was constantly on a swivel admiring the various fashions that some of the women were wearing. Even when he was dancing with a sexy woman, he still couldn't ignore the beautiful black women that surrounded him. Some were in packs of three and four. A smorgasbord, I must confess of women for a single man. After partying and conversing for three hours, he eventually had to surrender to the heat and walk out on the deck. The first two tiers were occupied by lovers and couples. So, he continued to climb to the third tier. There were only three couples on the deck. He found a semi-isolated spot with the wind against his back then fired up one of the blunts. He was half way through when the wind suddenly shifted. A few seconds later, an incredibly attractive young lady suddenly appeared following the scent straight to him. She slightly hesitated grinning then proceeded towards him. She stood about five feet nine with locs that extended down to her shoulder blades. A deep smooth mocha complexion contributed by the summer. Removing a funky pair of retro sunglasses from Juicy Couture, she had eyes like Dawn of En Vogue. Full lips and an hour glass figure, seeing her in a pair of hipster jeans reminded him of Mona. With the slight glitter of her naval ring from the moon's light, she held his full attention. He didn't know if she worked out or not, but the naval ring was attached to slightly muscular abs. The bracelet she wore on her right wrist was from Mark Loren. The woman was a walking fashion show.

"Excuse me" she apologized slightly smiling down at him. "May I hit that."

"I'm no cheap trick, sweetheart" he replied hitting the blunt while staring up at her and containing his smirk.

"I didn't think that you were" she slightly smiled studying his attire. "I'm referring to the blunt that is between your fingers."

"What are you willing to sacrifice?" he asked suddenly gagging from the blunt.

"What are you requesting?" she ventured staring into his mysterious eyes.

"Your name" he replied.

"That's not too expensive" she replied smiling fully and he thought that the sun had suddenly risen. "My name is Aziza (precious)."

Getting to his feet and seemingly towering over her, he gripped her hand. "I'm Afrika with a K."

"Nice to meet you Afrika with a K" she smiled watching him pulling out a toothbrush holder then opening it and extending a blunt to her.

"Nice spot" she confessed accepting the blunt from him.

"Are you married?" he bluntly asked admiring her eyes.

"If I was, would you hold it against me for being here with you?"

"No, being married doesn't mean you couldn't be friendly or socialize, but it would eliminate a lot of my conversation" he admitted smiling down on her as he took his seat.

"Supposed I didn't want you to limit your conversation" she inquired seductively with a coy smile.

"As disappointed as I would be later, I would have to decline your offer. I'm not the type of man you are seeking" he replied honestly returning her stare.

"That's good to know" she replied before she burst out laughing then gradually gain controlled. "No, I'm not married" she finally answer and taking a seat before lighting the blunt. As she pulled from her chest, he thought she had lost her got damn mind. He thought he was the only fool that did that. As the smoke filled her lungs, she suddenly gagging uncontrollably. He extended his handkerchief to her to catch the snot that was trying to escape her nose. As hard as he tried to contain his laughter, he was unable. It took her about a minute for her to recuperate. "Damn this stuff is good" she stated revealing how reddish her eyes has become. "Where did you get this?"

"Over in Camden."

"Camden? Is that where you live?"

"That's where I grew up" he shared.

"I'm originally from East Orange" she shared smiling over at him.

"A home girl" he replied grinning.

"So, are you married Afrika with a K?" she asked hitting the blunt a little too hard and started gagging and coughing again.

"Na, too young to consider marriage" he replied smiling at her trying to catch her breath. "And no, I don't have any baby momma drama either" he included.

"A man with no true responsibilities, huh?"

"Oh, I have responsibilities, but a woman with a child of mine isn't one" he slightly smiled over at her.

"I don't know if I like that little smirk on your lips or not" she replied studying him closely.

"It grows on people" he replied still grinning. "Are you enjoying your evening?"

"I must admit it has picked up" she replied staring in his eyes while respecting the blunt as she hit it again. "I started to back away when I stumble upon you after following the scent."

"I'm glad that you didn't. So, what is your profession?"

"What makes you think that I am a professional?"

"I could start with the St. Laurent blouse you're wearing or the Mark Loren you are wearing" he replied admiring it on her wrist.

"Damn boy, I'm impressed" she admitted giggling. "Are you in the fashion field?"

"Na" he replied slightly raising his head into the slight breeze. "I love the scent of Chloe when it mixes well with a woman's biochemistry, and it mixes well with yours" he shared.

"A man that freely gives compliments too" she smiled shaking her head trying to contain her blushing. "Do you have a girlfriend?"

"Na, y'all are too expensive for me" he replied nonchalantly causing her to giggling again while staring over at him.

"No, we aren't" she counter shaking her head. "So, you don't have a girlfriend?

"Na, not the way that you mean it. I do have female friends like I know you have male friends."

"Oh, you think I do."

"I know you do" he replied admiring her silhouette. "Don't you?"

"Of course, I do" she admitted grinning.

"So, what is it that you do?"

"I'm a corporate lawyer on Broad Street" she shared. "What about you?"

"You are a corporate lawyer. Well, I'm impressed" he complimented. "I'm a trash man."

"Don't even try it" she burst out laughing for several seconds. "You are so funny when you lie. Trash men don't wear Armani or that Rolex that you are trying to subtly hide" she continued still giggling while staring in his eyes. "What do you do Afrika?"

"I'm a defense lawyer for the Hines Brothers."

"I've heard of them. They are in Pennsauken, right?"

"Yeah."

"They have suddenly blown up in the last eighteen months. Most law firms thought that they would have folded by now. Their alcoholism and shady dealings had gotten a lot of people incarcerated. I don't know what turned them around."

"They seem to have obtained a new lease on life. I hope that they value it" he replied slightly hardening his eyes.

By the time she was half way through the blunt, they were talking like old friends. Their laughter and the scent of their blunts floated on the air. Three couples eventually joined their private party. They brought out more blunts and a canister filled with Moscato. The intrusion brought out their true demeanors and love for life. The fellas found themselves eventually defending themselves from the women opinionating ideologies that men are dogs. Afrika informed them why they felt that way and put into evidence to substantiate. With so many brothers being locked down, addictive to drugs or alcohol, standing on the corners not being productive and homosexuals to name just five category of men, the ratio of men to women are extremely high, especially in the black communities. Some women understands the shortage of productive men while others never consider it at all. Each woman has a decision that she has to make personally. Some women don't mind sharing their man with another woman instead of being alone. It is a hell of a lot better than thinking that your mate is being monogamist when he isn't. Thus, we are classified as a dog because he wasn't being truthful. His opinion had the women looking at it in a whole new perspective. Time seem to have slipped pass them even after their intrusion had left almost two hours.

"I have got to go Afrika" she suddenly announced getting to her feet causing him to get up and stare over at her.

"Did I say something wrong" he asked softly.

"No" she smiled up at him. "My escort has been on the second level twice looking for me" she sighs.

"Is he an escort or a date?"

"You are playing lawyer on me. Now that is cute" she replied giggling. "He's just an escort but I really have to go. I really appreciate the love you showed, the conversation and laughs."

"I hope to run into you again" he replied sincerely.

"If it is going to happen, it will" she replied mysteriously as she turned and headed towards the stairs.

He stood there admiring the seductive sway of her hips as she walked. She was just about to descend the stairs when she turned and stared back at him. His eyes were still disrobing her. She smiled shaking her head blushing then descended the stairs. Just as she melted into the crowd, he realized that he didn't get the name of the law firm she worked on Broad

Street. He remained on the upper deck an additional half hour before rejoining the party. His presence was missed by the women who openly confessed it. He dance, laugh, and joked with so many people that night. He was holding in his arms a honey complexion young lady whispering the most erotic things into his ears as The Moments sang "To U With Love" but his eyes were fixed on Aziza eyes while she was in the arms of her escort. Although he wanted to infringe on her to obtain the information he needed, he decided to stay in his lane. The mystery ride was to Valley Forge then turned and came back. They were docking a little after midnight. From his position on the second level, he watched the people descending the gangplank when his eyes rested on Aziza. The high yellow guy escorting her had a walk like Gomer Pyle. He had to smile to himself. Just as he was about to leave his position, Aziza suddenly looked up in his direction and waved while openly smiling. Her escort stared up to see who she was waving to. He waved back to her while ignoring the cold stare from the guy. "Yup, I'm the guy that held her attention for over two hours" he said to himself then tipping his hat to the guy and smiling.

Monday morning came quicker than he had hope. As he was cruising down Rt.130, he fired up a white boy (joint) and pushed the CD he brought from the DJ on the cruise ship then Cameo's "Why Have I Lost You?" filled the interior. His mind reflected back to the conversations he had with Aziza and found himself lightly laughing. "So, men aren't really dogs, the productive one are in high demands, huh?" she asked when they were alone, and she had to admit that some women does go after another's woman's man. So, the conviction is in the man to be monogamist and not how you perceive us to be. If we are dogs as perceived, why would anybody throw meat at us? He knew he was shaking her foundations with his ideologies, but she could never say he didn't have solid evidence to substantiate his beliefs.

He was pulling up on the Hines parking lot a little before nine o'clock then climbed out of the car and proceeded towards the main entrance. He walked out of the elevator and retrieved his messages from Tweety. He spoke to the staff as he walked pass while winking at Shakira. She has been working for the Hines almost fifteen years. Something went down in a case leading to a mistrial and Robert carried it like she lost the damn case. Whatever his dumb as motive, but he never assigned her another high-profile case. How do you keep a thoroughbred like her locked down? The fresh face lawyers look towards her for guidance and that say a lot about her knowledge of the law.

When he enter his office, he instantly realized that his shit, was out of place starting with his chair. Turning on the stereo, Duke Ellington filter through his speakers instead of Billie Holiday as it should. As he sat there wondering which Hines was violating his space, his office door suddenly swung open, and Robert came bursting inside holding a folder in his hand.

"Drop everything that you are doing and get right on this" he stated dropping the folder on his desk.

"And good morning to you" he stated staring in his bloodshot eyes.

"This case…"

"Good morning!" he raised his voice while hardening his eyes. "What's up with you and your brother? I know your mother taught you common curtesy. This barging into someone's space isn't cool and I'm tired of constantly reliving it."

"Morning" he replied flatly. "That case is yours."

"Give it to someone else. I have an important case to prepare for."

"Fuck that case!" he heard himself say with the scent of alcohol accompanying his words.

"Pardon me!" he replied staring at him like he was crazy.

"I need you on that!" he pointed.

"Why do you constantly throw profanity out of your mouth at me? In the two years that I have been here, I have never disrespected you, but this has become a routine for me and it's making it a very unhealthy environment for me. Give that to someone else because I don't bail out on my clients."

"They aren't your clients! They are mine!" he corrected him while returning his stare and snarling.

"You know what, you are absolutely right. Until I have my own firm, they are your clients" he conceded suddenly smiling at up at him. "Give your client to someone else."

Realizing what words had just filter pass his lips there was no way he could retract them. His alcoholism had his lips slipping again. So, he took a different approach. "Listen Afrika" he requested as his tone was completely different than when he first walked in. "That client father is in my office right now. He is an extraordinary high-profile individual."

"If that is true, tell him to hire himself a high-profile lawyer" he suggested leaning back in his chair.

"He has" he mentioned. "He hired you."

"I appreciate the compliment, but the answer is still no" he replied being defiant and knowing how it pisses him off.

He stood there motionless and staring over at him. One thing that nobody can do is get Afrika to do something that he won't do. What threat can he throw at the most honor lawyer in his firm. "Okay, how about briefing the statement of facts?"

He stared into his bloodshot eyes then reached for the folder and opens the fold. He stared at the charges and his eyes instantly became harden. "Sorry, but I don't fuck with "short eyes" Robert" he informed him tossing the folder back on his desk.

"Short eyes?" he repeated looking confused. "What is short eyes?"

"Individuals messing with under age children" he snorted. "I refuse to defend the actions of a morally degenerate rapist. Those that put their hands on a woman have better have a damn good excuse also or they are on their own with me also" he shared his conviction and snarling.

"You will represent whores, murderers and drug dealers but not someone accused of rape."

"I understood becoming a lawyer I would have to compromise my integrity but that doesn't have anything to do with my morals" he informed him staring coldly into his eyes. "Who is this guy father?"

"Butch Williams" he replied watching to see if he recognized the name, but he had his nonchalant disposition as usual. "Do you recognize the name?"

"Yeah, I have heard the name" he acknowledged. Butch Williams is better known as The Terminator in the criminal world. There are rumors that he stretched out well over fifty people getting his business established and maintained. To converse with him, you would never think that he was the most notorious and unforgiving motherfucker walking the streets of Camden. Although well into his sixties, he physically still look as strong as a bull. Controlling the drug game in Camden and surrounding counties for over thirty years, he's one man not to be fucked with.

"Will you at least come to my office and explain your position to him?" he wasn't asking but pleading.

"I don't have a problem with that" he assured him getting to his feet. "Lead the way" he instructed following him out of the office and heading towards his. Shakira had a smirk on her face as he walked pass. As they enter his office, two fashionably dressed gorillas stared at him coldly. Sitting in a chair wearing a gray pin-stripe Versace and smoking a Havana cigar was Butch Williams. As he move to his left, he admired the diamond pinky ring he was wearing. He slowly looked him down to up into his eyes.

"So, you are Afrika?" he mentioned getting to his feet to shake his hand.

"Yes, sir" he replied. "Glad to make your acquaintance, Mr. Williams" he said shaking his hand then taking a seat across from him.

"I've heard some impressive things concerning you, young man" he assured him. He had done his homework and got a profile of what he was about or once was, nobody know for sure except his partners and nobody was crazy enough to inquire. "You are from out of North, correct?"

"Yes, sir."

"Young man, the streets has a lot of love for you and not just the people that you have defended. Even those so-called haters have admirable things to share."

"Thank you, sir but what is tis about?"

"Preserving my youngest son freedom" he replied seriously as his eyes took on a menacing stare.

"That case that Mr. Hines showed me is pertaining to your son?"

"Yes, it is" he replied. "Word on the streets is that you are the person I should contact. So, I'm reaching out to you."

"That may be Mr. Williams but I won't touch that case."

"And why not?" he replied blowing a smoke ring before focusing in on his eyes while slightly snarling.

"Sir, there are certain charges that I won't defend or be associated with, and short eyes is my number one. I know you can respect that but being a parent, you're not trying to hear what I am saying" he slightly smiled at him. During his reign of terror, Butch Williams has never allowed a bullet to harmed a child or woman while putting in work. "I will alter my integrity but not my morals. I will represent gangsters, pimps, whores, drug dealers and murderers, but short eyes, that profoundly disturbs me. I truly so understand your dilemma sir."

"You know I feel what you are saying and normally, I would go with the flow but on this, I must be a parent and hypocrite. You can understand that, right? He's my baby, Afrika" he stressed, revealing a weakness in his armor.

"Yes, sir."

"Do you know the heat my son is gonna encounter with a skin charge?"

"Yes, sir. I can imagine" he assured him returning his stare.

"Afrika, there are numerous of people that is locked up that knows what my son is facing. Niggers and cowards will seek him out then turn him out because they are too afraid to face me" he shared his thoughts revealing a father's concern as fear engulfed his eyes.

"Do you blame them?" he asked surprising him but causing a slight grin to crease his lips.

"No, not really" he confessed. "I did have a very unusual journey. There are lot of dormant enemies lingering in the shadows for an opportunity to touch me, directly or indirectly. I really need your assistance, young man" he stressed again.

"What are you will to sacrifice for him?"

"Everything except my life" he replied.

"Can the victim parents be persuaded?"

"You mean brought?"

"No, sir that would be illegal. I said persuade?"

"I don't know" he replied grabbing for the string of hope.

"If they are willing to come to a financial agreement, would you honor it?"

"Of course, I will" he unintentionally raised his voice.

"What is your son name?"

"Jamaal (he is pretty), why?"

"I heard something about this, but I didn't know it was your son. Have you spoken to him about this?" he informed him.

"Extensively" he replied. "He assured me that he didn't rape that girl."

"Supposed I was to tell you that he isn't guilty of rape as the charging documents states, but he is guilty of seducing an underage girl."

"I would advise you to be certain of your claim and where you obtained your information" he told him never averting his eyes.

"I got my information from the streets" he informed him. "People have been whispering for months and now I understand why? The accused is your son."

Butch turned in his chair and stared at his two bodyguards for confirmation or denial to what was being said, but all he got from them was an evasive stare. He had instilled so much fear that even his bodyguards didn't want to be the bearer of unwelcome news. He couldn't fault them for being apprehensive because his past dictated such apprehension. He reached into his suit breast pocket and pulled out his cellphone. He pressed a preset number then got to his feet and walked to the window then stared out waiting for a response.

"Hey, Pop's. What's up?"

"Is your brother home?"

"Which one?"

"Jamaal."

"Yes, sir. He's chilling in the family room watching Sports Center. Why, what's up?"

"Romello, I just had a very intriguing and interesting conversation over here at the lawyer's office with Afrika."

"Afrika? He's one solid brother, Pop's. What's up?"

"He said that Jamaal isn't guilty of rape but fucking with a minor. Is this being said about a son of mine in the streets?" he asked, but no response came back. "Hello?"

"I'm here Pop's."

"So, the rumors are true, huh?"

"Yes, sir" he replied solemnly.

"It is" he replied astounded. "What do you know?"

"Pop's, the girl that this mess is over is the sister of a brother that I went to junior high with. Dino is as cool as the other side of the pillow Pop and a straight up soldier when he has to be. He requested Jamaal to stop driving his little sister around and getting her intoxicated because she is only fifteen.

Jamaal actually told him to back off, but Dino wasn't having that just like I wouldn't have it if the script was flip. Dino tried repeatedly to come to a peaceful conclusion, but the more he humble himself, the more Jamaal tried to whore him. Jamaal don't know Dino as I do. On this particular night, Jamaal was so lucky. Dino was getting ready to reveal his whole card until someone impeded him and pulled his coat that Jamaal was my youngest brother. If that person hadn't pulled his coat, he was going to stretch Jamaal out and pay restitution to your wrath afterward. Jamaal is using your name and reputation in the streets to disrespect people, Pop's and people are getting fed up with his antic. I even got with him, but to a certain point because he is going to do what he wants and I'm not getting my butt chew out from you for trying to protect his dumb butt. If somebody doesn't check him, he can easily be a contributor to the murdered statistic."

"Why didn't you tell me, Mello?"

"Come on Pop, every time I tried to talk to you about Jamaal, you shut me down. Ever since Mom pass a way, you kept a pacifier in his mouth. Me and Doc worked our butts off cutting grass and doing chores around the community to acquire our first used cars when we were sixteen, but you go out and buy him a brand new 750 Beemer. You was so elated to see his expression, but you never too notice your two previous sons. We were piss, Pop's. He doesn't even try to please you as we do, but you constantly keep rewarding him and for what? Doc has been on the honor roll numerous times and you don't even praise him, but I do. Sometimes Pop's, I can't even stand my own baby brother. I know it is wrong but so is you and him.

"Does Doc feel the same?"

"Na, Pop's, worse. He is the middle child like you are."

"Indeed, I do" he replied slightly shaking his head. "Where did I go wrong?"

"You have been catering and protecting him since Mom pass away. Whenever me and Doc tried to harden him up, he would go running to you crying and you would bring down the wrath of God upon us. Enough finally became enough. So, we started treating him like he treated us, a stranger. When we saw him on the street, we would act like we didn't know him and casually walk away. I'm sorry to mentioned this Pop's but when you was on vacation for three years, he started toughing up because you wasn't around. He realize that if he intends to hang and survive in the streets, he had better learn how? When he came to us to learn how to defend himself, we didn't turn our backs on him. He is still our baby brother. In a year time, he was back in good grace with us. We started introducing him to our friends and hanging out together like "good fellas" then, you came home. Your enthusiasm wasn't directed at me or Doc, but we somewhat expected it. How could you allow Mitchell to be a second thought? She expected to receive the love that a daughter is supposed to receive from her Daddy especially since she resembles Mom, but she watch you give it all to Jamaal. You crushed her heart Pop's, but you was too over joyed to see her pain because you wanted to see your baby."

"Damn" he replied softly.

"In less than three months Pop's, once you was home, he allowed you to place that damn pacifier back into his mouth and he eagerly suckled from it then regressed back to his old selfish and spoiled self. When we stared at him one day, he had this little smirk on his face that let us know, he was back in the saddle again and dare us to touch him. So, we left daddy's little boy alone, permanently."

"I never peeked on what I was doing" he replied in a low tone and filled with pain to know what he had been unconsciously doing for years. He had promised his first and only love that he would take care of their babies, but he haven't except for Jamaal. He didn't know if he, being naïve, enraged him knowing that his son had been playing him for years. No motherfucker walking the streets of Camden would dare try to play him and especially lie to him without paying the ultimate sacrifice, but his son had broken both infractions. "Son, I'm going to make it up to you, your brother and sister. I honestly didn't realize what I was doing."

"Yeah, we know Pop's."

"Why didn't y'all just force me to sit down and listen to y'all?"

"We rationalized that sooner or later the truth will be revealed to you, and it has."

"I want to talk to Jamaal. Put him on."

"Yes, sir" he replied laying the phone down then calling to his brother. "Pop's want to holla at you."

Footsteps could be heard approaching then the receiver being picked up. "What's up ole man?"

"Why did you lie to me?" he blurted out while seeing his eyes hardening in the reflection from the window pane.

"Lie about what, Pop's?"

"Are you telling me that you have been pulling the wool over my eyes so long that you don't know which lie I am referring to?" he asked as his anger slowly mounted.

"What was I supposed to have lied about Pop?" he asked unknowingly revealing his apprehension in his voice. He had told so many lies over the years that he didn't know what specific lie he was pertaining.

"This motherfucking situation you got yourself in got damn it!" he exploded. "Do you know some guy name Dino?"

"Vaguely" he lied.

"Who is he?"

"The brother of Denise."

"Did you and him have a discussion concerning his sister?"

"Yes, sir."

"How many times?"

"I don't remember Pop's" he continued to lie. He couldn't tell him that they had talked on six or seven times.

"So, you have knowledge of this guy and not vaguely as you claim."

"I guess Pop's."

"When he requested that you leave his sister alone, did you threaten him?"

"Not really, Pop's."

"Either you did, or you didn't. Which is it?"

"I did" he finally confessed.

"Why?"

"I don't have a good explanation, Pop. Me and Denise was just shooting the breeze together."

"Just shooting the breeze, huh?" he lightly chuckled. "If you request some guy to leave your sister alone, but he kept acting like a knucklehead, what would you do?"

"I would grab a baseball bat and shut him down" he replied low but with conviction in his voice.

"You don't know it but that is actually what Dino was about to do to you, shut you down. The only reason why you are still breathing, and we aren't crying at your funeral is because someone pulled his coat that you was Mello's knuckleheaded little brother. You caught a blessing from death and your dumb ass didn't even know it. Who in the hell do you think you are to be piggy backing on another person's reputation, especially mine's. Listen, after I'm through over her at the lawyer's office trying to clean up your shit, I will be heading home and straight to you. Don't leave the house. Do you understand me?"

"Yes, sir."

"Put your brother back on."

"Okay, Pop's" he replied placing the receiver on the table and walking away.

"Yeah Pop's."

"If he try to leave before I get home, you have my permission to put your foot up his ass like some nigger on the street. Do I make myself clear?"

"Absolutely" he replied with an impish smile that didn't go unnoticed by Jamaal.

"I will be leaving here soon, watch him."

"Like a guard dog" he replied grinning at Jamaal diverting his eyes.

He continued to stare out the window after ending his conversation until his anger slightly subsided then turned around and face the group of men. "Afrika, will you do something for me?"

"If possible, sir."

"Would you mediate an out of court settlement with the child's parents? I'm not asking you to represent him but to mediate for him and me. Whatever you think is fair?"

"Since the restitution is at my discretion, I'll do it. I will get over there sometime this afternoon and get back with you with their decision. I will do this free of charge unless the Hines want their consultation fee?"

"No, no. No charge at all" he replied wearing a phony smile.

"In that case, do your best son and I won't forget it either" he said shaking his hand again then turning. As he was about to walk through the door, he paused and turn around then address the Hines brothers. "Robert, I know you won't do right by this young man and that is a shame. He is going to come back and bite you square on the ass if you don't change your scandalous ways. Watch and see" he warned him then staring over at James slightly shaking his head before walking through the door as one of his bodyguards closed the door glaring in at Robert and James.

Afrika stared over at Robert and James then realized that what Butch was saying was already happening. They don't appreciate what he has done for their firm. They will never do right by him even especially when it benefits them financially. So, he needed to start formulating a plan within the next two years that didn't include the Hines Brothers Law Firm.

He kept his morning appointments and around eleven-thirty he was heading for the Parkside section of the city. The sun was just burning through the clouds as children was already running up and down the street. As he turned off of Baird Boulevard, the Crusaders "Lilies of the Nile" filter out the open sunroof. He studied the descending numbers until he came upon 1224. He found a parking spot and climbed out. As he was approaching the house, he noticed two adults sitting on the porch relaxing. The woman was reading the morning paper while the man was nursing a bottle of Thunderbird. He stood at the gate staring up at them.

"Excuse me, ma'am and sir" he called getting their attention. "Are y'all the parents of Denise Covington?"

"Yes, we are" the man responded looking pitiful. "What do you want?"

"To help you" he replied.

"Help us, how?" he asked taking a big swig from his bottle then smacking his lips. "Who are you?" he asked with slurring words.

"My name is Afrika and I'm a lawyer affiliated with the Hines Brothers law firm."

"You aren't with the prosecutor's office?"

"No, sir."

"So, why should we talk to you?"

"You really don't have to sir, but listening doesn't hurt anyone" he replied.

"Negro…"

"Shut your mouth Harold before you say something even dumber. What do you wish to discuss with us, young man?"

"Ma'am, if you give me twenty minutes of your time, I will utilize it very productively. May I come up?"

"Sure, come on up and take a seat" she offered.

He pushed opens the gate then proceeded towards the porch. He shook their hands then requested to go inside the house for some privacy. Their neighbors were trying to ear hustle like a motherfucker.

"Harold, move out of the way so the gentleman can get pass" she ordered as she lifted her frail frame and got to her feet. She was in her early fifties. "Move damn it!"

Harold cradled his bottle and moved out of the way. She was definitely the back bone of the family as she open the front door and led the way inside. When he walked inside, the place look like it had been rammed shacked. The entire down stairs was in disarray. Empty wine bottles were placed in a specific corner as though they had some value. The air was thick with the scent of extinguished cigarette butts and alcohol. The scent of stale urine was also detected. Dirty clothes was thrown around. Dirty dishes found a home where they were left and provided the roaches with a smorgasbord daily. The chair she offer to him was soil with stain and funky looking. He sat on the edge of the chair being mindful not to over react to the squadron of roaches peeking out at him from between the cushion.

Just as he was about to make his presentation, a deep bronze complexion young girl descended the stairs in a pair of "fuck me" shorts. As hard as he tried to contain his eyes, he was unable. Wearing a light blue stretch strapless top, her 36 C breast would spill out if she ran or bend over. Her nibbles were spike and winking at him. The skimpy jeans or "fuck me" shorts she was wearing left nothing to the imagination as her ass cheeks over-flowed out. Her camel toe was openly evident as she stood on the landing staring down at him with a coy smile. She purposely turned to tie her sneakers allowing the jeans to creep further between her phat little ass like a thong then peeked between her thighs at him. Her pussy lips revealed themselves while the hair of her garden over-lap. Slightly bow-leg with a natural provocative walk, the guy was a definitely and eye catcher. If she persist on the path that she was venturing, somebody just might pimp her out. She was already a Bonafede freak and that is undeniable.

"Mom, I'm going to the park" she announced disrobing Afrika with her eyes and not hiding her lust. "Who is this?" she inquired unwrapping a lollipop and inserting it into her mouth.

"Afrika, this is my daughter Denise" Mrs. Covington informed him.

"Glad to meet you Denise" he replied staring into her light brown eyes.

"Is Afrika your real name?" she asked coming closer and the scent of the cheap perfume she bath in consumed his nostrils.

"Yes, it is."

"Who named you?"

"My father" he replied watching her allowing her full lips to protrude out as she pulled the lollipop out.

"I like your name. Is you married?"

"Denise!" interjected Mrs. Covington. "Don't ask so many personal questions."

"I just like what I see Momma" she replied licking her lollipop in a seductive way while staring in Afrika's eyes smiling.

"Young lady, you need to check yourself. He is too old for you."

"Age is just a number, right Afrika?" she asked with a coy grin.

"Not when you are pertaining to the law, Denise" he informed her ignoring her smirk. She had heard that statement so much that now she was using it to seduce men.

"Denise, if you are going to the park then go but have your butt home by six o'clock for dinner. You hear me girl?"

"Yes, Momma" she replied putting a little more twitch in her switch. "I hope to see you around Afrika" she openly flirted with that impish smile she possessed.

"Maybe but enjoy your day, Denise" he wished her.

"Oh, I will, and I want you to enjoy your day also" she replied winking at him then giggled as she walked out the front door.

The way she openly flirted in front of her parents; he see how this mess all unfolded. The young lady was a Bonafede freak with a slight retardation if you listen closely. If she weren't more careful out in those streets, something more traumatic could easily manifest itself.

"Mrs. Covington, how old is Denise?"

"She turned sixteen two weeks ago" she informed him.

"Sixteen" he replied with a slight smile and shaking his head. There is no way in the world a person would think that she was sixteen. She could easily pass for eighteen and if she is telling people that, they wouldn't denounce it even after she opens her mouth revealing her immaturity. Most adult men would welcome someone as sexually vibrant and naïve as her into their beds. Fuck the consequences. "As I was saying outside, Mrs. Covington, I'm in a position to change your living condition."

"How are you able to do that, Afrika?"

"I am not representing this young man in court. I am here on behalf of his father. He asked me to see if y'all came to a financial agreement."

"Are you trying to offer me, us a bribe?"

"No, ma'am" he stated adamantly. "Bribery is against the law. I am here for you. Mrs. Covington, if this goes to trial, this young man father will hire an investigator and his only job will be to follow and record Denise every movement. Catching her in the attire she wore out of here today and her promiscuous disposition, she would be giving them the evidence that they would need to win their case. A jury just might believe that she told this young man that she was eighteen as he is claiming" he stated staring in her eyes. "I'm not here to discourage you from going to court, but I must make you aware of how his father will play his hand. What do you honestly get with either results? A conviction gets you satisfaction while a not guilty verdict gets you nothing but frustration. I can offer you satisfaction without the frustration."

"You can?" she asked returning his stare. "What is he offering?"

"What is a fair settlement for you?" he asked flipping the question back at her.

"Oh, I don't know" she admitted looking over at her husband for assistance, but he was studying how much wine he had left. "How about ten-thousand-dollars?" she asked apprehensively.

"Ten G's, Mrs. Covington" he repeated returning her stare. "I'm personally not comfortable with that number."

"How about five thousand?"

"Mrs. Covington, when I said I'm in a position to change your living condition I meant it. I also said that I am here for you not him. How would I be looking out for you if I allow you to accept either of your offers?" he asked staring over at her. "Although Denise appears to have adjusted to her ordeal, I'm still appalled by the accusation. I wouldn't allow you to accept anything under two-hundred-thousand dollars."

"What!?" she asked staring over at him then at her husband who also heard the offer. "You can get that for us?"

"At least but I do have one stipulation."

"Stipulation?" he said not liking the word. "What stipulation?"

"Allow me to hook up with a friend of mine to purchase you a home outside of the city and a small car for you to get around in. You will have money left over to purchase modern furniture also. Is that too much to ask?"

"No, Afrika" she suddenly smiled, and he saw just how beautiful she actually was.

"Mrs. Covington, I would never purposely be disrespectful, but Denise needs to be put in check. Although immature in her mind, her physical attributes is far beyond her intellect to understand that some men doesn't care about her age. There are a lot of devious and scandalous individuals out in the streets. It would honestly break mt heart if something were to ever happen to her."

"I know I need to put her in check, and I promise I will. She might not like the changes I'm about to institute especially her style of dress if I get this new home."

"Not if, Mrs. Covington" he corrected her causing her to smile again.

"How old are you Afrika?"

"Creeping up on twenty-four" he replied grinning.

"Do you have any children?"

"No, ma'am. I'm still searching for my queen."

"You will be an excellent parent because your heart is in the right place. Most lawyers would have exploited my ignorance and kept the balance themselves. I deeply appreciate your honesty and integrity. Thank you so very much."

"It's really been my pleasure, Mrs. Covington" he stated getting to his feet and casually plucking off three roaches. I will have the balance of your money in your hand within a week or two after I purchase this house. If you have any questions, give me a call" he told her extending one of his cards to her.

"I will" she replied getting to her feet then demanding a hug and a kiss on the cheek.

He walked out the house feeling good about his offer. If more were needed to fulfill his promise, he will get it. Granted, he comprised his morals slightly but at a cost to Butch Williams and he will live with that. As he descended the porch steps, he ignored her signifying neighbors. He walked back down the street and climbed into his vehicle then hooked a U-turn retracing his previous route. As he jump on Admiral Wilson Boulevard, he fired up a blunt. He initially started to head back to the office, but his impulsiveness had him hooking another U-turn and heading towards Philly. He wanted to see what his hobby could manifest. He called Aisha (life) while climbing the Ben Franklin Bridge and told her the size house he needed. She assured him that there were plenty of homes available outside of the city limits.

Two weeks later at nine o'clock in the morning on Saturday, he was pulling up in front of Mrs. Covington's house. They were all congregated on the porch enjoying the brisk morning temperature. He was introduced to Dino then requested that they come with him. They all piled into his vehicle then proceeded to the Pennsauken side of town to a single home with four bedrooms and two bathrooms with a finish basement. Stepping out of the car, they all walked towards the house smiling then climbed the steps to the stone front porch. He extended the keys to her. She stared at them then up at him and her radiant smile came to her face. Accepting them, she unlocked the door and walked inside. Thick light laminated floors extended throughout the entire house. He had brought contemporary furniture including stainless steel appliances from Dent and Scratch at ridiculous prices. As she marvel at the first floor then climbed to the second floor, Dino tapped his shoulder.

"Afrika" he stated watching his parents and sisters turning the corner. "I want to thank you for what you have done for us. I have seen you and your partners around. Now I understand why there is a lot of love for you on the streets. Thanks, brother."

"My, pleasure" he assured him grinning as they hugged. "Besides, I couldn't have you stretching out my client's knucklehead son" he shared returning his stare and smiling as his parents started descending the stairs. The look he gave Afrika caused him to lightly chuckle.

"Afrika, this house is beautiful" she smiled gripping his hand.

"I'm glad you like it" he replied smiling down on her.

"Like it! Baby, I love this!" she stated looking around and smiling.

"I'm glad you love it" he replied pulling out the deed then extending it to her. "Rent is a thing of your past, Mrs. Covington. I needed more money than what I initially quoted to you, but Mr. Williams was glad to accommodate you" he smiled at her again reaching inside his breast pocket and pulled out an envelope then extending it to her. "There is fifty thousand dollars in there. I'm insisting that you take care of yourself before taking care of the family first as mother's usually do. Will you be selfish just this once?"

"Yeah, Afrika" she replied giving him a tight hug then smiling up into his eyes trying to contain her tears of joy but failing.

"Thank you" he replied still smiling down on her. "If you are going to go shopping, you need something to get around in."

"Oh, I can get me something now" she replied smiling.

"I didn't say I didn't get you a car, Mom. I brought you that white Camby outside because I didn't know what color you would prefer" he said extending another set of keys to her. "I hate to run off, but I have some other business to attend. If you ever need my services or just information, you have my number" he told her opening his arms to her and she eagerly accepted his hug. "Family, it's been a pleasure. Later, Dino" he said grinning.

"Later, Afrika" he replied tapping his knuckles as they followed him out the door. They stood on the porch watching him climbing back into his car and pulling away from the curb while the Last Poet's "When The Revolution Comes." They stood there watching him until he turned the corner. They looked at one another then embraced. "He is one solid brother."

"He was a blessing" his mother commented methodically walking towards her new car smiling. "And young lady, you are about to get a rude awakening" her mother slightly snarled at her from over her shoulder causing her to slightly repel.

Wednesday morning while heading to work, he received a surprise call from Tweety informing him that Mr. Williams was requesting his presence at his home for breakfast in Voorhees, an extremely high echelon community. Pulling over on a parking lot, he entered the address that Tweety text him into his navigational system. He jump on Rt.73 then followed the instructions. He wasn't inviting him to his home but to his mansion. Pressing the button on his electric gate, he stared into the camera then the gate slowly opens, and he drove through. Driving up to his massive home, he instantly fell in love with the scenery and tranquility the slight forestry provided. He would love to be able to afford something like this. Climbing out of his car, he admired the three new cars with temporary tags still on them. A white BMW M2 coupe, a black Corvette, and a metallic gray Jaguar. He assumed Butch brought them for the three children he had unconsciously been neglecting. Before he reached the door, Butch Williams was wearing a broad smile.

"Afrika" he greeted shaking his hand. "Good morning, young man" he wished him revealing his jubilation."

"Good morning, Mr. Williams. How are things?"

"Things couldn't be better. The prosecutor office contacting me informing me that all charges have been dismissed for lack of evidence" he shared pulling him inside. "Have you had breakfast?"

"I had a couple pieces of fruit."

"Na, which won't do. You need more nourishment than fruits" he advised him leading the way through the vestibule. The house open up to reveal marble floors throughout the first floor. The tallest fireplace he have ever seen at seven feet has a portrait of him with his family. The woman was gorgeous with her cat eyes and natural impish smile. There were other pictures of his children but no more of him or his associates. A man with his status tries to keep his identity of his children to a limit. As he entered the dining area, his children were sitting around. His breakfast was actually a smorgasbord. If you desired it, more than likely it was being served.

"Family, this is Afrika" he introduced him. "She's my first born, Michelle. He's my oldest son Romello, Doc, and he's Jamaal" he mentioned with a hint of discuss in his voice that he wasn't trying to hide.

"Family" he greeted placing his hand over his heart while slightly nodding his head then accepting the seat that Butch pointed at. "I must say this, or I would be kicking myself later, but Michelle" he called getting her full attention. "You are as beautiful as your mother and I'm ready to put my foot up anybody butt that say otherwise" he expressed slightly hardening his eyes to show his conviction.

"Damn, thank you Afrika" she replied blushing and unable to return his stare.

"She isn't all that" mentioned Mello snickering with Doc.

"Tell me you don't see the glow that surrounds her?" he told him slightly grinning.

"She has a slight glow, but you don't need sunglasses" he confessed but still teasing her.

"Just like your eyes adjust to darkness, your eyes have grown accustomed to her immolating glow."

"You need to chill Mello" suggested Doc smiling over at him. "His tongue is too slick when defending a woman."

"Truth is easy to confess" he replied still grinning at them.

"Afrika, you can complement me all you want" Michelle replied then sticking her tongue out at them.

"Afrika, I truly appreciate what you did for this family and especially me."

"I'm just glad that I could work things out for you."

"From what I gathered through the grapevine, they were willing to accept ten G's. Why did you charge me so much?"

"You gave me an open check, Mr. Williams" he reminded him slightly grinning. "Despite Denise very promiscuous disposition, a jury would see just how incompetent she actually was" he shared peeking over at Jamaal who caught his eyes.

"Just because Mrs. Covington was gullible, I would never take advantage of her or her situation."

"What did we tell you!" Mello suddenly interjected and laughing with Doc. "You owe me and Doc a hundred dollars!" he shared laughing as he and Doc tapped knuckles as Michelle was giggling.

"Sshhhh" he insisted grinning.

"Their living condition warranted a change and since you are able to provide it for them, I couldn't resist being devilish" he shared smiling over at him. "Besides, what lesson would Jamaal have learned if ten G's made his problem go away. Na, he needed to understand the severity of his actions and the extremely vulnerable position he placed you in unknowingly" he mentioned slightly hardening his eyes at Jamaal. "Now, I'm giving you the peace of mind you requested and without murdering him" he included with a faint smile causing Michelle to start giggling and his brothers to try and contain their snickers.

"You make some good arguments" he admitted peeking over at Jamaal who diverted his eyes.

"You should be extremely thankful that you aren't white. I would have demanded your nightmares also" he said smiling.

"Oh, I am very thankful" he burst out laughing with his children especially when Michelle spit out the orange juice she was just starting to drink. He like this young man. Very outspoken and honest. You have to admire and respect that even if you didn't like it. He paid is own way through college just like his two sons insisted and he never forgot his roots or his partners. Hearing that he still hang out with his partners is a testimony to their love for one another and five-o didn't know what to make of their relationship. They had been peeking on them over the years, but nothing have ever materialized. He knew that five-o was photographing him with them while politicians were baffle especially when you have five-o whispering in their ears. When they were asked to substantiate their suspicions, they couldn't. What truly shocked him was hearing that Afrika was very prolific with not just his hands but with his German made Glock .40 and have stretched out numerous of people trying to step into his lane. Tek9 and Kimba wasn't no joke but Afrika, he was a completely different kind of predator.

Afrika didn't know how much he missed sitting down for breakfast with family members. His partners used to come over every Sunday morning until they reached Kingpin status and wouldn't stand too close to him even though he made his presence known at all of the big functions. Interacting with Butch family brought back fond memories and hilarious conversations. As the maid sat in the kitchen reading a book, his children started cleaning the table and placing the dirty dishes in the dish washer while two others were placing think back in their position. Once everything was completed, Michelle and Jamaal went upstairs while Doc and Mello headed towards the basement.

"Mello."

"Yes, sir."

"Get that for me in my room."

"Yes, sir" he replied diverting his direction as Doc proceeded down into the basement.

Entering his office, he walked behind a cherry oak desk then offer him a seat. He open his cigar box pulling out a Havana cigar then licking it before lighting it with his gold cigarette lighter. After blowing a couple of smoke rings, he asked. "How long are you going to stay dedicated to the Hines?"

"I wish I knew, Mr. Williams. I still have a little over two years on my contract."

"You do know it was you and your street connections that revitalized their piss poor company, right?"

"Yes, sir. I would like to think I had an influence."

"Young man, you did. You was a life preserver for them. Let me pull your coat to those scandalous, lying, self-serving, alcoholic motherfuckers" he suddenly snarled at him. "A smart man would already be locking you in as a partner, but they won't until their backs are against a wall then you still can't trust them. I don't know why they are keeping my girl Shakira in the starting blocks. The woman is a beast."

"I will admit that things are on shaky grounds with the Hines, especially James."

"Put your fool up his bitch ass" he suggested as a light knocking to came the door then Mello walked in and extended an envelope to him. "Thanks, son" he said watching him walking back out. "This is for you" he said extending it to him.

"That's not necessary, Mr. Williams."

"Take it or I'll have one of my men hand deliver it to Robert" he threaten with a smirk on his face.

"Na, I'll take that" he replied smiling and placing it inside his breast pocket then suddenly getting to his feet. "I enjoyed the breakfast and conversation."

"My pleasure" he replied walking around the desk then escorting him back through the house to the front door. "Enjoy your day, Afrika."

"I will" he replied shaking is hand then climbing back into his car. Thirty yards from the gate, he broke the red beam with his car and the electronic gate slowly opens. Pulling out the gate, he drove towards Rt.73 then pulled over before climbing the ramp. Opening the envelope, there was twenty thousand nontaxable dollars. A broad smile came to his face as he pulled back into traffic. It was almost eleven o'clock when he pulled up on the Hines parking lot, exiting his car, he spotted Robert looking down on him from his office window. He exited the elevator and winked at Tweety as he proceeded towards his office. As usual, it didn't take him long to realize that someone had been in violating his space again. His chair was out of position, again. He had a hunch who was the guilty person, but he needed more than just a hunch. He needed proof before he could unleash his wrath. He had barely taken his seat before Robert came barging in.

"I heard you had an appointment with Butch Williams this morning."

"It wasn't an appointment it was an invitation" he corrected him.

"An invitation to what?"

"Breakfast" he replied.

"Breakfast?" he repeated.

"Yes, breakfast. Is there a reason for this intrusion?"

"I was wondering did Butch give you anything for assisting him?"

"We didn't discuss anything that had to do with this law firm especially money wise, but if you think he owes you something, I can give him a call" he said reaching for the phone.

"No, that isn't necessary" he stammered then headed towards the door.

"Hey, Robert" he called getting his attention. "Do you use my office when I'm gone?"

"For what?" he replied staring at him puzzle. "I have my own damn office."

"I was just wondering" he replied watching him walking out the office. His assumption was correct. It was James violating him. Before he knew it, he was getting to his feet and walking out his office. Shakira had seen this disposition of him a couple of times and a broad smile came to her face. As he knocked on James door, he didn't wait for an invitation to come in. James was sitting behind his desk with the shades pulled and sipping on a glass of brandy.

"Yeah, what do you want?" he asked revealing his dislike for him.

"Why do you constantly invade my office space and use my shit without permission?"

"Aren't nobody taking shit from you" he stated still snarling over at him.

"Oh, I know nobody will take anything from me" he assured him. "I asking you to stay out of my office and leave my belongings alone. Do I make myself clear?"

"First and foremost," he stated refilling his glass. "This is my office and I do dame well where I please. Unless you have something important to discuss, you need to get to work" he ordered taking a sip from his glass while glaring up at him.

"Alright, boss" he slightly smiled while staring in his eyes. "I'll get to work" he told him, but he didn't fully understand his subtle message.

The rest of the week went relatively quick. He would shoot James a cold stare every time they were in each other's presence. Robert picked up on the animosity between them during their weekly meeting, but he remained in his lane hoping that they would work it out. Afrika was leaving for the day when he received a very pleasant surprise. Leaning against her lip stick red Benz was Aziza. Wearing a powder blue Adrianna Papell full length dress with a matching blue six-inch stilettos from Michael Kors and a funky pair of retro sunglasses from Juicy Couture to shield her eyes, the young lady looked very sexy and professional while clutching her purse. Spotting him approaching, she suddenly flashed her radiant smile.

"Hey, stranger" she called getting up from her car. "How have you been?"

"Ms. Aziza, thanks for finally seeking me out" he openly confessed while smiling. "I was truly smitten by our first meeting."

"Was?" she replied removing her sunglasses and placing one of her hands on her hip. "You're still not smitten after a month?" she teased.

"Well, actually yeah" he smiled staring into her brown eyes. "So, what is the reason for this unsuspecting visit?"

"Your monogram handkerchief" she replied reaching inside her purse and pulling it out. "And yes, I washed it" she shared extending it to him.

"Thank you."

"Do you have any plans for this evening?"

"I'm sorry to say that I do" he replied seeing a slight surprise come to her eyes.

"Can you cancel?" she couldn't believe she heard herself asking. She had decided to explore him further by taking him out to dinner and if their conversation flowed like it did on the boat ride, she wanted to go out dancing.

"If it were anybody but one of my young partners, I would. He turned twenty-one, today" he slightly smiled.

"Na, you can't cancel that" she agreed reaching in her purse and pulling out her business card then extending it to him. "How about hitting me up tomorrow?"

"Oh, I can definitely do that" he assured her placing it in his breast pocket.

"Do that and you don't have to be shy."

"Shy?" he burst out laughing like he heard the funniest joke. He still haven't figured out why women think he is shy, but he always found it hilarious. Was this the persona he was naturally displaying to lure his prey like a Venus flytrap?

"Oh, excuse me" she replied grinning up at him. "Hit me up Mr. Afrika with a K" she said walking around her car and climbing inside. She stared out of her sunroof at him.

"Yes, ma'am" he replied as she started up the vehicle and Brown Stone's "If You Love Me" filtering out causing him to suddenly think about Mona. She placed her vehicle in gear then accelerated away. He stood there grinning like a little boy as she turned off the parking lot then proceeded towards his car. He got home later than usual. Breaking his routine was nice and needed. He had decided to run over to Philly to pick up his new tailor Armani and Louis Vuitton suits then get his fade tighten up instead of Saturday. It was a little after seven o'clock when he finally pulled up on his horse shoe parking pad, Freaky Freda damn near ran to the bay window after hearing his car pulling up. She position herself to display what she was wearing this evening. She was wearing a long sheer white gown revealing her red thong and bra set. All he could do was smile and throw her a kiss as he walked into his home. If her husband knew he was admiring the latest Victoria's Secret he was paying for before him, he would truly be upset, maybe. He has been spotted by his partners hanging around Rutgers since his house warming party.

He climbed the stairs to his bedroom and strip down to take a shower. Twenty minutes later, he was exiting and putting on his under garments with a pair of shorts. He put on some Louis Armstrong on the CD player then sat out on his screen in balcony to smoke his blunt as usual. He knew his neighbors were jealous how he had transformed the once dilapidated house into the best and most expensive in their neighborhood. As the lights came on in his neighbor houses, the stars lit up the night sky as a thought about Aziza made him smile. Glancing at his watch, he leaped to his feet seeing it was almost ten o'clock. He grabbed his three-button dark blue Versace suit with a white French collar. Grabbing his diamond Rolex and his little gangster hat, as Mona called them, he descended the stairs and grabbed his car keys then set the house alarm before climbing into his car. His watch had ten-thirty as he cruises down Rt.130. He was buzzing from the blunts and glass of Parrot Bay as he entered Camden. Cruising up Broadway, the streets were pack with individuals on their own private journeys. Prostitutes were staring inside cars as they drove pass seeking their next trick while others were seeking their drug of choice. Turning onto Kaighn Avenue, pimp cars dominated the area with their elaborate colors and styles. Winston's is like a gentlemen club but without the strippers. His clientele consisted of pimps with a couple of their whores, gangsters, players, high level drug distributors and a few adventurous minded individuals. Professional athletes from Philly, New York and Baltimore visit the place regularly without being harassed. Five-o didn't stand a chance of penetrating his door without a search warrant because an arrest warrant wasn't getting you through the door. They would have to wait for the person to leave and that could be for days if the person were that connected.

Afrika was patiently waiting on the corner when he spotted his partners turning off of S. 8th Street. Finding parking spots, they all were wearing broad smiles while teasing the birthday boy Amir (populous). Bear had taken him under his wings about eight years ago and turned the aspiring stick-up boy around. He was the first boy in his family to graduate high school without a criminal record especially being the youngest boy. He was supposed to follow in the footsteps of his three older brothers and be incarcerated by the time he was eighteen until Bear snatched him up and told him that anybody can put a gun in a person face but that doesn't make them tough because you are now a ward of the state. All of your responsibilities are gone including those that made you a father. Being tough is getting through the traps that America had set for you, if you want to impress someone, impress America that you made it through her traps. He will be graduating college next year because they all contributed to his tutorage, tuition, and future. Tapping knuckles, they approached the line that was extending around the corner. As they walked pass the waiting patronages, they tipped their hats to the people and couples that they knew. Approaching the three well-dressed silver back gorillas with stern faces, their faces suddenly lit up spotting them.

"Kackalacks in the house!" boasted Big Mike smiling. "What's up fellas?"

"What's up Big Mike?" they chimed together allowing his two younger brothers Freight Train and Punisher to search them.

"How is the family?" inquired Afrika allowing them to inspect his hat.

"Those boys are pure knuckleheads" he shared.

"You weep what you sow" they chimed together then burst out laughing at his expression.

"So, they say" he sighs while shaking his head as they proceeded inside.

"Hold up little man" insisted Punisher staring down on Amir.

"Yo, fellas!" he called out causing them to pause and turn around then staring at him.

"Kackalacks, do y'all know him?" inquired Freight Train staring at them.

They stared at one another then Bear asked, "Have you ever seen us with a high motherfucker before?"

"Na" he replied.

"I never saw him before in my life."

"Fellas!" called Amir as his body was suddenly elevated off the ground. "Fellas! Come on y'all!" he insisted.

"Bear, do y'all know this guy or what?"

"You know we don't fuck with light skin niggers" he snorted staring coldly at Amir.

"It's time to go partner."

"Bear!" he pleaded. "Is this how y'all are going to play me!?"

"Big Mike, he's the birthday boy" Bear finally told him causing the fellas to burst out laughing at Amir adjusting his suit jacket and looking furious.

"Not funny" he told them pouting and causing them to snicker again as he brushed his way pass them and causing them to laugh even harder. They were escorted to their reserve booth and place their orders. As they laid back enjoying the scene, Winton's protégé and partner Kali introduced another group he stumble upon up in New York. They seem to extend new musician a platform but not rap. Tonight's group was called Brothers Keepers from out of Harlem. Their lyrics were like Gil-Scot Heron and Public Enemy with their band playing smooth jazz. They were spitting out some knowledge to those that were listening and not flirting with the young ladies, but by two o'clock, Amir's patience had worn thin.

"So, where is my birthday present?" he asked staring around the table, but everybody was ignoring him. "Bear!" he slightly shouted.

"You are going to have to wait on it" he replied nonchalantly never averting his eyes from the group.

"Wait on it!"

"Yeah, wait on it."

"Why?"

"Because I said so" he replied taking his eyes off the band and placing them on him before returning them to the band as light snickers could be heard coming from the fellas.

"Afrika!" he called staring at his smiling face.

"My name isn't Bennett, so don't put me in it."

"Fellas" he called staring at them ignoring him.

"Patience grasshopper" Bear requested never averting his eyes from the band as light chuckles invaded Amir ears again.

"Patience!" he snorted at him. "That's all I have been displaying these past two and a half years, patience. I couldn't do anything to make money on the streets. The threat you made, and your partners cosigned had me like the plagued to the street hustlers" he expressed his frustrations while staring at Bear seemingly ignoring him. "If you wasn't so got damn big, I would fuck you up?" he threaten staring over at him.

"And why you are imagining fucking me up, what do you think my partners will be doing?" he asked revealing his smirk but never averting his eyes from the band.

Amir stared at the group of young men snickering. Although he has known them for eight years, he very subtly became very aware of them by the time he was sixteen and what they were capable of doing by the time he was eighteen. They are the most laid-back brothers in the game and the most notorious when necessary, so don't make the necessary, necessary. Although Tek9 and Kimba can be vicious, Afrika is unmerciful with his fighting skills and grabbing a gun as a form of retaliation would be detrimental to your health especially with witnesses having to testify, he was just defending himself. Bear might be out front, but Afrika is the heart that keeps their click pumping. He still didn't know why Bear extended his hand to him and he have thought often about it over the years, but he grabbed it like it was a life preserver because of the misguided dark path he was venturing on. He was just approaching the fork in the road when Bear became his life preserver. Without Bear and his partners, his life would have been dramatically different. He didn't believe in angles, but these six guys were actually that, angles that just so happen to carry guns. "You can be such a pain in my ass" he stated staring over at Bear.

"I wouldn't have to be if you just do the right things" Bear replied keeping his eyes fixed.

"I do the right things" he countered.

"Oh, what about last month?" he asked peeking over at him before staring back at the stage, but the fellas ears perked up and small smiles creased their lips as some revelation was about to be revealed.

"I haven't done that in months, but you carried it like I do it regularly."

"Don't skip class and you don't have to worry about me pressing up on your high yellow ass" Bear advised him. "How is that cute little thing I caught you with anyhow?" he asked smiling but never diverting his eyes.

"Traumatized after seeing your big ass" he slightly snarled at him causing to the fellas to snicker at an incident that had escape them.

"Oh, it wasn't that traumatic" he waved him off laughing. "You need to stay on your side of the tracks anyway. What was you going to do with her prissy little ass anyway?"

"You have finitely got to give us the 411, Amir" insisted Afrika, grinning.

As he stared around the table at them individually, they were trying to contain their smirks but failing before speaking. "Last month, I finally got this beautiful intellectual young lady named Honey to finally bite my hype to come over to the crib. I have been shooting my not impressed game at her for months, not weeks while wearing a bib to catch my salivation.

She had gotten extremely comfortable with me. I was chilling at the library organizing a report that was due the following week when she approached me wondering why I haven't pressed up on her. She actually had the audacity to ask me if I was still a virgin" he shared staring at them perplexed and causing Black and Kimba to spit out their drinks as they burst out laughing. Once he had reached his mid teen years, he had obviously been influenced by those with the responsibility of educating him. He has always been described by them as an undercover whore created in the image of a male. "When she asked me to prove it, I damn near fell out of my chair. Brothers, she actually wanted me to prove to her that I wasn't a virgin. Is that not a sheep being led to the slaughter" he said looking over at them with an insane expression causing them to burst out laughing again. "Brothers" he called in a lowering voice and getting their attention. "This young lady is fine as hell."

"I can cosign that" admitted Bear still keeping his eyes fixed on the band.

Amir shot him a cold stare before continuing as the fellas lowered the snickers. "She asked me to take her to my apartment, but I told her that I had a ten o'clock class and we could hook up afterward. She actually started giggling like I was procrastinating or scare. Me" he stressed returning their stares but not the laughter they were containing. "Before I knew it, I allowed my ego and lower head to control my foolish decision then said let's go, but here's the punch line. She placed her damn car in the shop earlier that morning to get her breaks fixed. How unfortunate for me."

"Yes, it was" replied Bear as chuckles could be heard again.

"I suggested hooking up the next day and her laughter filled my ears again" he shared still snarling over at Bear. "As soon as we left campus, I had my head on a swivel looking out for Bear's big black ass. I went to the main speedline terminal down town in hopes of catching a cab, but as usual, none was around when you desperately needed one and I needed one desperately. It takes two buses to get to my damn crib, two damn buses. A leisure drive of twenty minutes in a car take ninety fucking minutes on those damn buses" he complained hardening his eyes. "We were three blocks from my crib when I spotted Bear's Suburban turning on Westfield Avenue. I damn near shoved her into the store then peeked out. I quietly prayed that he didn't see me, but when he hooked that U-turn, I knew I was done. D.U.N" he spelled it out causing them to burst out laughing again. "Of course, I came out of the store, the way he came speeding back up the street then slamming on brakes, he scared the living shit out of her. She stood slightly behind me gripping my arms staring at the driver's door opening. When he pulled his six feet seven gorilla ass out of his SUV, she coward behind me while gripping my coat tightly. As she stared at his hostile and aggressive expression on his face, she dug her fingernails into my back.

"Amir" she called out softly.

"Everything will be okay, Honey" he replied never averting his eyes from the hidden smirk Bear had on his face.

"Are you lost" he asked making his voice deeper than usual as Honey rested her head against my back.

"Na, I'm not lost."

"Where are you supposed to be?" he asked making a lust filled stare at her.

"You know my schedule" he replied returning his stare.

"Indeed, I do, and you aren't supposed to be on this side of time until one-thirty. You need to get to where you belong."

"Looking over to him for empathy would be senseless" he shared causing them to snicker again. "I'm on my way now."

"Your class will probably be over by the time you get there."

"Probably."

"Well, we can't have that. Jump in" he said starting to walk back to his Suburban.

"No, thanks. We will catch a cab or the bus."

"You are under the impression that I am requesting. Well, I am not" he growled as Honey was quietly pleading that he didn't accept the massive man request. "Climb in."

Honey was totally confused by their conversation. He never hesitated as his sudden movement caused Honey to lose her balance. He gripped her fingers and directed her towards the back door then tried to climb in beside her, but Bear wasn't having that. He informed him that the front seat is reserved for him and waited for him to close the back passenger's door. As he stared in Honey eyes, all I saw was confusion and fear as he closed the door then climbed into the front seat. Her quietly asked herself why would he willingly accept a ride by an apparent menacing and threatening person? As he pulled away from the curb, he turned up the radio slightly then leaned in to have a private conversation. There were numerous expressions exchanged. Both appeared to be adamant about they were expressing but the big guy had the final words and Amir humble himself.

"A couple of days later, Honey finally caught up with me in the library and confided that she thought I had stumbled onto the wrong side of town and that the shit was about to hit the fan. Her biggest concern wasn't about my safety, but not knowing how to get the fuck out of where she was at. Three blocks from River Road and she's lost" he shared slightly shaking his head.

"Did your whorish ass ever get back with her?" Tek9 asked trying to contain his snicker.

"Yeah, she still thought I was scared and procrastinating because I had tests on the days she wanted to hook up. So, she brought her prissy ass over one Saturday afternoon and got slayed. The girl started looking for me with a flashlight during the day time, brothers. Now she wants me to meet her mother like that is ever going to happen" he shared causing them to burst out laughing again.

"So, what are you whining about?" Bear asked.

"I'm not whining but you don't have to drop the hammer on me. Okay, I fucked up during my freshman year and abused your trust, but I apologized for that. You asked me to keep my academics up and I have with Afrika scrutinizing every report I intend to put in" he peeked over at him slightly smiling. "In all the conversations that we had before I started college, you never mention the smorgasbord of vibrant and adventurous young ladies. You know how women like my high yellow ass and saying no, to a sexual invitation is not in my vocabulary. I have just completed my junior year because Afrika is paying for my summer classes. I will be a senior this year. A full year ahead of my graduating class and will pass the bar exam on my first attempt under Afrika tutelage. If I had a set of wheels, I wouldn't have these petty ass problems. I can't work to purchase my own set wheels and y'all damn sure aren't going to let me whip y'all pimp."

"As long as you know it" they chimed together then burst out laughing at him pouting.

"Are you finish complaining" inquired Bear.

"I'm not complaining. I'm just stating the facts."

"Are you finish stating your facts because I'm trying to listen to this brother lyrics?"

"One day, I'm going to go insane and whip your big ass" he threaten again.

"Yeah, yeah, yeah. I'll pluck your feathers Big Bird" he called him causing the fellas to burst out laughing again.

"I'm tired of your complexion jokes also" he mention revealing his slight intoxication.

"Or what" he asked taking his eyes off the stage and placing them on him. "Or what?" he reiterated still staring at him.

He had learned what that subtle stare meant. He had challenged it just once to know to never challenge it again. So, he said, "Nothing" then leaned back in his chair.

"Yeah, I thought so" he replied causing the fellas to start snickering again especially at seeing Amir pouting again.

For the next hour, they teased one another over the dumb shit they had done. Although some close female friends tried to infiltrate their tight circle, they had to shut them down, but Amir found one seemingly interesting. Almost three o'clock, Bear's cell phone suddenly rang. He had a quick conversation then looked around the table and nodded his head. They down their drinks and got to their feet then headed towards the front door before Amir noticed them leaving. He looked around confused then excused himself from the young lady he had in his fishnet. He had to catch and release this night. He down his drink then rush to catch up with them. They were standing on the sidewalk enjoying the early morning breeze when he finally arrived. He noticed how quiet they were and learned to take the same disposition. People escaping the heat or desired feeling of the slight breeze or were just socializing, stared at them. They all knew who they were and where they were from. Two minutes elapsed when two Honda Accords turned the corner of S. 8th Street and double park on Kaighn Avenue with the flashers on. Both drivers got out of their vehicles then approached them smiling.

"What's up fells and looking GQ as usual?"

"What's up Roberto?" they chimed together tapping knuckles as his partner laid back watching the interaction.

"Are you the birthday boy?" he asked staring directly at Amir.

"I'm no boy but it is my birthday" he replied, slightly hardening eyes.

"Happy Birthday, brother" he wished him slightly smiling then tossing him a set of keys. "Later fellas" he said turning and walking back to the red Honda then climbing in on the passenger side and pulling away.

Amir stared at the key then the white Honda with tinted window and fully loaded with a navigational system and all. "Don't fuck with me fellas."

"Happy Birthday, knucklehead" they wished him smiling at him.

"No, no!" he shouted walking over to inspect his car through the open sunroof. By standers stood around admiring his birthday present. He turned with his head and walked into Bear's opening arms. "Thanks, big brother" he slightly smiled up at him unable to contain his tears.

"Our pleasure" he replied cupping his head.

"Much love, brothers" he said walking over and hugging them individually.

"We don't want to catch you or hear about you zooming around the city like some damn juvenile or we will take those keys from you" he warned him.

"You won't big brother. I won't abuse y'all trust" he told him with conviction in his voice and eyes. "Can I whip her?"

"You don't have to ask permission to drive your won whip, damn" he told him snickering.

He tapped their knuckles wearing a broad smile then pimp walk towards the car and climbed inside. He adjusted his seat and mirrors then turned the radio to WDAS and rocked his head to "Summer Time" by the Fresh Prince and Jazzy Jeff. "Tell all the mothers to hide their daughters because there is a new player in the game!" he shouted through the sunroof while laughing and pulling away. They didn't hear or see him for a month. When he came stumbling through Bear's front door as they fellas were entertaining, he looked like a stray dog that had been marking new territories. He looked that worn out but wearing a broad smile.

Saturday afternoon, Afrika cell phone rang, and he stared at an unfamiliar number. "Hello?"

"I can tell by your tone that you didn't lock my number in. I don't know who I should feel about that."

"Hey, Aziza" he greeted lightly snickering.

"What are you doing?"

"Laying back listening to jazz and reading. What are you doing besides signifying."

"Can I see you?"

"Sure, when?"

"Now" she replied. "Unless you have something to do, again" she included.

"Na, nothing that I can't put on the back burner" he assured her.

"So, if you don't mind text me your address."

"Sure, where are you now?"

"I'm about to leave Moorestown Mall."

"Okay, I'll send it to you now" he replied ending their conversation then sending the text. He figure it would take her thirty minutes to reach him by Rt. 295 and thirty-five minutes if she took Rt. 38. He laid back continuing to read and listening to his jazz. About thirty minutes later, he spotted her car coming up the street then pulling up on his property as he walked inside his bedroom then descended the stairs. He was just opening the front door as she was casually strolling towards his house admiring the exterior. Wearing a pair of stretch white jeans that accentuated her thighs and hips, a coy smile crept across his lips.

"What a beautiful home" she complimented. "Is this your parents' home?"

"Na, it's mine" he informed her opening the door wider for her to enter. "Come on in" he invited" leading the way.

"Wow!" she declared as she walked through admiring the décor and African artifacts.

"Do you want to sit outside or chill inside?"

"I rather we sit inside of you don't mind" she replied admiring a poster size picture of him with five other dusty looking kids when they were about twelve. "Look at you" she giggled.

"Yeah, funny hu?" he asked grinning. "Would you like something to drink?"

"Surprise me" she told him continuing towards the family room. She stopped at every picture to admire them including the ones with young ladies. She was staring at a picture of him and his partners looking all GQ. There were something in their eyes that she couldn't understand, but they all possessed it.

"Here you are" he said extending a glass to her with ice.

She took a small sip then stared over at him. "Mmmmm, this really taste good Afrika. What is it?"

"Parrot Bay coconut" he replied taking a seat.

"How long have you been living here?" she asked taking another sip.

"A little over four years" he replied.

"You live here all alone?"

"I'm never alone especially at home, but I do live alone" he assured her smiling.

"And you don't have a girlfriend?"

"No, y'all are too expensive and time consuming."

"You said that the first night that we meant" she suddenly giggled. "I'm beginning to think that you mean it."

"Oh, I do mean it" he reiterated extending a blunt to her.

She accepted it then walked into the kitchen to grab some napkins then returning. "I know the young ladies are memorized when they come over."

"Na, I haven't invited any over" he shared surprising her as she fired up the blunt.

"Are you serious?" she asked doubting him with a coy smile.

"I have no reason to ever lie to you, Z. Besides my house warming party for a selected group of friends. I haven't invited any woman over as a date or anything else. This is my place of tranquility and I'm going to keep it like that" he told her adamantly.

"Well, I must have made a good impression to be invited over" she smiled hitting the blunt then started gagging while clutching her napkins.

They sat and talked for hours getting better acquainted. Before they realized it, he was turning on the lights to illuminate the room and their faces. Although she didn't intend on staying as long as she did, she was contemplating asking him if he wanted to go to a club so she could get her freak off, but she found sitting in his house very relaxing and informative. Around eight-thirty a group of people suddenly invaded their serene environment and private party. She was initially startled that someone would just barge into his home, but he never reacted. As the group made their way into the family room, she recognized the guys from the pictures except they were with dates. They were more handsome than the pictures portrayed.

"Why are y'all over here?" he asked getting to his feet tapping their knuckles while kissing the ladies on the cheek.

"Because you don't mind cleaning up after us" replied Black causing them to start snickering.

Removing their stilettos and placing them out of the way, the ladies moved around the house like it was a usual occurrence while he talked to his partners. After invading the refrigerator of its vegetables, fruits, wheat crackers, mixed nuts, they returned with a serving tray and placed it on the coffee table before them. Philadelphia Cream Cheese or an onion dip, the choice is yours. They grabbed several large slender glasses, refilled the ice bucket, and uncorked two bottles of red wine with a bottle of Moscato. Afrika gripped Aziza's finger and directed her to one of the two love seats. As they commandeer the couch and other love seat, they also pulled up four ottoman's. After the introductions were done, they got down and party. The dancing she desired were fulfilled. Laughter filled the night as she melted into Afrika's arms dancing to Etta James "At Last." By the end of the night, she felt like she found somebody that was truly intellectually stimulating and funny as a motherfucker. It was almost four o'clock in the morning when they started cleaning up then making their way home. She grabbed her stilettos and was heading towards the front door when he requested another dance. He searched his alphabetical CD finding what he desired then placed it in the CD player. Melanie Fiona's "It Kills Me" began to play. He pulled her close and allowed their hands to lightly roam over each other's body. As the final notes were about to strike, she peeled herself from his arm then searched the CD rack finding the song she desired. Angie Stones "No More Rain" filter through the speakers as she crawled into his waiting open arms smiling. As the last note struck, she stared up into his eyes then kissed him lightly on the lips.

"I really enjoyed myself and the intrusion" she mentioned giggling then grabbing her stilettos and walking towards the front door with him clutching her fingers. Opening the front door, she slipped her feet into her stilettos then step outside. He open her door for her to climbed inside then assisted her into her seat before closing the door. "Call me."

"Maybe" he replied as she slightly harden her eyes before flashing her radiant smile. She pressed on the accelerator and pulled off turning left off his property.

Out of impulse or frustration over the Hines brothers deviousness, he found himself purchasing a round trip ticket to Atlanta. Although he talked to Ramona at least three or four times a month, nothing replaces a face-to-face conversation especially with her. He could hear the loneliness in her voice and her need to reconnect with him. So, he found himself packing a weekend bag then giving his partners the 411 as where he was headed. They offered to rent a car for him, and he knew they had something devious planned. He drove to Philadelphia International Airport and parked in the overnight parking garage then grabbed his carry-on bag. He enters the terminal and proceeds to the reserved ticket counter to obtained his first-class tickets. As he made his way to gate 12, he could feel people staring at him like he might be a pimp, an undercover gangster, or some professional sports person. He has never got comfortable with people gawking at him even if he did stand six feet five. He knew if he had down played his attire, instead of dressing GQ, they would have look at him as just another traveler. He watched under the cover of his Gucci sunglasses as several young ladies being accompanied would peek at him and subtly smile or flirt as they walked pass.

Climbing aboard the Delta 747, he found his window seat then open the book "The Destruction of the Black Civilization" he has been dissecting for the previous week. As the turbines thrusted the plane skyward, he watched the massive buildings and structures gradually dissipated as they climbed above the clouds to view clear blue skies for miles then level off. As he meditated on the things being advocated in the book, he heard the announcement to place all trays in the upright position and fasten your seatbelt. He had to check his watch. His watch had eleven-thirty, but their arrival time was supposed to be noon. They must have had a strong tail wind. As the wheels touched down, an unconscious coy smile crept across his lips. Gathering his garment bag, he joined the others departing the place and casually walked towards the main terminal then spotting Hertz Rental. He walked through the door and approach the receptionist that was smiling.

"May I assist you, sir" she asked smiling up at him as he removed his sunglasses.

"Yes, ma'am" he replied admiring her smooth mocha complexion. "My name is Afrika Muhammad and I believe I have a vehicle reserved for me."

"Let me see" she said hitting a couple keys on her computer. "Yes, you have reserved a Corvette Stingray Z06" she seen to recite then looked up at him with a usual expression. "The Z06" she reiterated.

"I don't know what that is, but my partners have a warp sense of humor" he shared smiling at her.

"I can definitely use friends with a sense of humor like your" she expressed arching her eyebrows as she lifter the receiver and spoke into it briefly. "May I have some form of I.D." she requested accepting his driver's license. "You are from New Jersey, huh?"

"Born and raised."

"Are you here for business or pleasure?" she inquired extending his driver's license back to him.

"Neither I'm visiting a friend" he replied replacing his driver's license back in his breast pocket.

"I hope you see some of the history our fair city has to offer."

"I have some destinations that I'm going to visit."

"There you are, Mr. Muhammad" she nodded towards the front door.

He turned and stared out the front door and shook his head. "Just what I needed, a damn rocket to ride inside" he shared while listening to her giggling. "Enjoy your day, Monica" he wished her staring at her name tag then grabbing his garment gab then heading out the door. He laid his garment bag on the miniature back seat then climbed inside adjusting the seat and mirrors. He searched the stations for a jazz station and came upon WCLK 91.9 then enter two addresses into the navigational system. As the first directions came upon the screen, he slightly stepped on the accelerator, and she leap forward like a predator. Taking the ramp to I-85, the bullet took off. He drove North getting the feel of the high-performance beast. The slightest turn on the steering wheel and she instantly responded. "Oh, yeah" he suddenly smiled. "I like this." Turning off the interstate, he spotted the Hilton Gardens. Turning into the parking lot, eyes followed the powerful and expensive car. Walking towards the front door, he ignored the stares he was receiving as he entered the main lobby and approached the receptionist desk. He signed in and received his electronic key then proceeded towards the elevator and getting off on the 10th Floor. He swipe his card at 1020 then pushed the door open and step inside taking in the scenery. He walked into the bedroom and placed his garment bag in the walk-in closet then went into the living space and turned the radio to 91.9. As jazz filled the quietness, he walked over to the balcony door and step out. He could see Atlanta in the distance. He suddenly turned and went back inside then grabbed his key then walked out the door. Minutes later, he was back on I-85 heading to the nearest hood. As he drove up Central Avenue, he drove through the River Park area off Norman Berry Drive when he spotted some guys sitting in a small park on a bench smoking a blunt then pulled over. Peeling himself out, their eyes went to him then to the car.

"Damn, she is one funky looking car" a light skin guy complimented.

"Thanks, brother. I'm looking to buy some weed. Can you help me or direct me?"

"What are you looking for?"

"I'm here for the weekend. I'm looking for at least an ounce."

"Two hundred" he replied, exchanging stares.

"Make it happen" he told him never averting his eyes.

"Go get that Skippy" he instructed as a dark skin guy instinctively started skipping his first few steps. He went to a bush then stared around before reaching inside and eventually coming out with an ounce then handing it to the light skin guy.

"Here you are" Afrika said extending two Franklins to him and receiving his weed.

"So, what is the top speed?" the light skin asked.

"Two-twenty but I'm not messing with her" he replied grinning then turning and retraced his steps back to the vehicle. He hooked a U-turn then went to the liquor store he spotted previously to buy some blunts and see if they sell Parrot Bay before going back to his room. It was almost two o'clock when he returned to his room and got comfortable on the balcony. Witnessing the sun descending, he anxiously stared at his watch. "Damn, where did the time go" he said getting to his feet while gathering his stuff and went inside to take a quick shower. It was a little after five o'clock when he climbed into the vehicle, he was cruising with the evening traffic up on I-85 smoking a blunt and enjoying the jazz. Taking the Stone Road exit, he drove up the one-way street admiring the single-family homes that lined the street. Spotting the address, he was seeking, there were several cars parked on her parking pad. Climbing out, he heard music coming from the back yard and proceeded in that direction. The bronze color leisure set he wore allowed the slight breeze to filter through keeping him cool. As he stood by the gate staring in, he spotted Mona entertaining several young ladies near her inground swimming pool. Stepping through the gate, he casually walked towards the group carrying his present. It was a light skin young lady that spotted him and kept her eyes fixed on him.

"Who in the fuck is that fine motherfucker? Damn!" she whispers causing her girlfriends and Mona to turn around.

"Afrika!" shouted Mona leaping to her feet and dashing towards him then leaped into his arms. "Hi, baby!" she greeted kissing him lightly on the lips. "What are you doing here?"

"If my timing is wrong, I can come back later" he replied allowing her feet to touch the ground.

"Funny" she replied nudging him with her hip then gripping his fingers and swinging their hands like a little child. "This is ladies is Afrika" she introduces him wearing a broad smile.

"So, you really do exist" the light skin girl said smiling. "I'm Donna."

"I'm T.T." a mocha complexion girl introduced herself. "Will you marry me?" she asked returning his stare while smiling.

"Don't get your weave twisted" warned Mona slightly hardening her eyes causing them to burst out laughing.

"Don't go there. You know this is my real shit" she corrected her grinning.

"The other two more conservative ladies are Ebony and Tamira."

"Glad to make y'all acquaintance" he said admiring their individual beauty. "This is for you" he said extending the package to her.

"What is it?" she asked accepting it and started tarring off the paper cover then stared at it intensely. A tear almost instantly started to swell in her eyes as she showed the picture to her girlfriends.

"Damn, Mona!" stated T.T. "Girl you look sexy as hell."

"Look at y'all" snickered Ebony. "Y'all look like lovers instead of just good friends."

"Where was y'all at?" inquired Donna smiling at the picture.

"We were attending a costume party during our sophomore year" she shared admiring the picture. They always complimented one another in every picture they took together.

"Y'all really look good together, Mona" admitted Tamira smiling at the picture then over at them.

"So, how long are you staying?" inquired Mona unable to contain her enthusiasm.

"I'll probably bounce Monday."

"Monday?" she repeated staring up at him smiling. "I have you for three days" she started giggling.

"Only if you can stand it, young lady" he replied grinning.

"Oh, I can stand it after dealing with your ass for four years" she assured him. "Where are you staying?"

"At the Hilton Gardens."

"Na, I got plenty of room here. We are getting your stuff."

"No, we aren't" he corrected her and bursting her bubble. "We can probably get it tomorrow, maybe. I paid for my solitude especially tonight" he smiled at smile.

"Okay, what do you want to do tonight?" she asked still tickled that he was here.

"It's Friday, what do you think I want to do being escorted by some beautiful young ladies?"

"Show us off" she replied smiling.

"Let's take him to Club Ellery's" suggested T.T.

"Na, how about Back Stage?" countered Ebony.

"We will do Ellery tonight and Back Stage tomorrow night" suggested Mona. "Ladies, it's six-thirty. You have three hours to get back here" she informed them. "Don't sit there gawking at him. Move ladies" she said causing them to react while smiling over at him. They gather up their belongings and scurried out the back yard giggling. "It is so good seeing you, Afrika" she said gripping his fingers and leading into the family room then taking a seat as she placed the picture on the coffee table. For the next hour and a half, they sat talking and laughing before she excused herself.

Around nine o'clock, her girlfriends returned looking like models. Hair in place while the exotic scent from their perfumes invaded his nostrils, they were like an aphrodisiac. They were extremely alluring and sexy as hell. When Mona descended the stairs, she was wearing a white form fitting knit dress from Louis Vuitton. If there were any imperfections on her body, the dress would have revealed them, but she didn't possess any. Her breast were still just as perky and full while her ass had a little wiggle than he used to remember. He knew the thong that she was wearing allowed for such movement.

"Na, I am not wearing this" he informed them staring at them individually. "I am not escorting five beautiful women in this."

"You look fine, Afrika" they insisted.

"Nope, not happening ladies" he told them adamantly returning their stares and causing Mona to burst out laughing.

"But you look fine, Afrika really" insisted T.T smiling affectionately at him.

"Nope, not going to happen sweetheart" he told her staring into her doe like eyes.

"Ladies, you will lose this battle" interjected Mona snickering. "Yawl can go ahead, and I'll ride with him. We will catch up with y'all later."

"Okay, but he really do look fine" Ebony insisted.

"Not really ladies especially when he goes out" she replied with a coy smile as they filed outside. "Are you driving that?"

"My partners ideal of course" he replied.

"How are they?"

"Just fine" he assured her opening the door then assisting her inside. He climbed inside then retraced his route back to the hotel. Eyes followed them all the way to the elevator. "Make yourself at home" he said turning on the radio then walking into the bedroom. He reemerged ten minutes later wearing a light brown pin stripe Armani suit with a silk tie matching the pen-stripes and a soft bottom pair of brown Salvatore Ferragamo shoes with his patient small brim hat.

"Now you look like the little gangster I know" she teased as he collected his key and exit the room after her. She admired their reflections in the stainless-steel door. Strolling through the lobby clutching fingers, a devilish smile came to her face.

"I missed the stares we receive when we are together" she admitted whispering up to him. Stepping back outside, "Can I drive?"

"Here you go" he replied tossing the keys to her.

"Oh, yeah!" she gleam climbing inside. Starting up the engine and hearing the roar, she stared over at him with an impish smile he have never seen before.

"Oh, shit" he said staring into her unusual eyes.

"You might want to fastening your seatbelt" she mentioned pressing on the accelerator and causing the tail to swerve as her giggles filled his ears. Mona loved speed and all of her fantasies were being answered as she zoom up I-85 to I-285 doing damn near a hundred and ten miles per hour. The look of thrill was plastered on her face and blew away any var that dare to challenged her. With her giggles and eyes, the size of a fifty-cent piece, she was in erotic heaven as she descended the ramp doing seventy onto Campbell Road SW. She made the tires screams as she slammed on breaks while giggling then looking over at him sighing. "I'm in love" she shared giggling. Finding a parking garage up the street from the club, she pulled inside and found a parking spot on the second level then exit the car and proceeded towards the elevator. Exiting at street level, they clutched fingers then crossed the street. It was barely eleven o'clock and the line extended down the street, they climbed in line, and he was glad he changed his attire. He could have gotten away with what he had on previously, but suits did dominate the scene. Jeans and Tims couldn't even make it pass security. Paying the entry fee, they walked inside and her took in the scene as she searched for her girlfriends.

"They are over there" she pointed leading the way while gripping his fingers. He exchanged glances with several groups of women sitting at different tables as she led him.

"Damn, Afrika" Ebony stated grabbing everyone's attention while checking him out from head to toe. "You are GQ like a motherfucker" she complimented admiring his tailor suit. "Is that a Johnny Dang you're wearing?"

"Do you planning on sticking me up?"

"She is into jewelry" Donna informed him. "And so am I" she shared peeking at his Cartier Santos watch.

"Come and dance with me" invited Mona gripping his fingers. "Two Parrot Bay, ladies" she told them before leading him to the dance floor as Luther Vandross "If Only 4 One Night" filter through the speakers. "I almost forgot how safe and secure I've always felt in your arms" she mentioned resting her head against his chest and inhaling the scent of his cologne. "I missed you tremendously, Afrika."

"I miss you too, Mona. When I hear certain songs or see a woman wearing a pair of hipster jeans, you come rushing to the forefront of my mind" he confessed staring down into her eyes. "I woke up yesterday with the urge to see your beautiful face and hear that ridiculous funny laugh that you possess" he lightly chuckled. "So, here I am."

"That is so sweet to know" she replied admiring his mysterious eyes. "I would hate to think you weren't thinking about me like I am constantly thinking about you."

"You will always have a permanent spot in my heart. No matter who is in my life or yours" he stressed returning her stare.

"You will always have my heart also" she reiterated again. She could never hide the love she been storing in her heart for him. Her eyes always gave her away by saying what her lips wouldn't dare confess. He could have taken advantage of her on numerous occasions by simply using her affections for him against her, but he never did. Although her life has changed tremendously since meeting him, he had remained a permanent fixture in her heart and in her life. She was elated to show her father the two write ups they had on him in the Black Lawyers Paper praising his professionalism and the high demand for his firm in a tri state area. When the song ended, she smiled up at him then escorted him back to the table when he heard their private song. He led her back to the dance floor as Backstreet's "Before I Let Go" started to play. Staring at them and the exotic way that they dance, you would never believe they were just extremely good friend and not lovers. No way.

The remainder of the night he got to know her girlfriends. Listening to them dropping dimes on one another about the crazy incidents they have shared, kept him laughing. Mona told stories on how she would cruise through Camden alone and how he would have a hissy fit causing them to burst out laughing. He would counter with how she got jack for her car one afternoon while in Camden then come crying to him with a snotty nose mixing with her tears. Nasty, he said causing them to burst out laughing. They snitch on one another all night causing tears to creep into their eyes. Guys would try to interject themselves into their little circle by requesting dances, but they were right back at the table after a couple of dances. Trying to pull them to conduct a private conversation wasn't happening tonight. Afrika was in town, and he kept them all fully entertained. It was almost three o'clock when they finally said their goodbyes on the sidewalk, he hugged them individually before hugging Mona and lightly kissing her on the lips.

"I'll see you later today, right?"

"Yeah" he assured her slightly smiling.

The next morning around noon he was checking out. He placed his garment bag on the back seat then headed over to Mona's house. Pulling up in front of her house, there were two cars parked on her parking pad. He grabbed his garment bag then approached the front door. Before he could ring the doorbell, the front door swung open by Donna wearing a pair of acid wash jeans and a white silk blouse with black and white Jordans.

"Hey, Afrika" she greeted wearing a very sexy smile.

"What's up Donna?" he asked stepping inside then kissing her on the cheek.

"Put your clothes in the back bedroom!" shouted Mona from the family room.

"I'll see you when you get back" she said turning to join her friends.

Her admired her walk before climbing the stairs and proceeding towards the back bedroom. He placed his clothes away then came back down the stairs. Mona was sitting on an ottoman in her patient hipster jeans revealing her birthstone naval ring with a mid-section black T-shirt with a picture of Angela Davis on the front.

"Good afternoon" she greeted extending blunt to him.

"What's up baby?" he replied kissing her lightly on the lips before accepting the blunt then taking a seat between Donna and T.T. "How are you doing, T?" he asked kissing her on the cheek.

"I'm okay" she replied returning his stare. She tried to hide her attraction for him, but it was useless. From the moment he said hello and asked him to marry her, she has been smitten by him. Watching a small transformation in his style of dress last night, only heighten her attraction for him. Him requesting a dance with her on Mint Condition's "What Kind of Man Would I be?" had her floating away feeling his embrace and the intoxicating scent of his cologne. She could barely remember the full content of their conversation, but she did catch his subliminal message, he gave to her through the words of Stokey. What kind of man would he be if he acted on his impulse? What kind of woman would she be if you did the same? How sweet and considerate he was to reveal his attraction for her also but won't bite the forbidden fruit at the expense of a mutual friend's feelings and love. She remember the alluring tones he would use occasionally while complimenting her bedroom eyes and how inviting her full lips appeared. All she could do was blush like a school girl and hold him a little tighter. Yeah, she was definitely attracted to him, and she confessed it to her girlfriends last night except to Mona.

She could see how they all were attracted to him as hard as they tried to hide it especially Tamira shy self. She found it all very charming and cute. She had told them so much about him since being home that they thought he was a figment of my imagination or a mirage until he suddenly appeared like a genie and flashed that adorable impish smile at them. "So, what are we going to do today?" Mona inquired while pulling from the blunt.

"Go to the Atlanta Zoo first then hit a coupe spots I have in mind."

"The zoo" repeated Mona snickering. "I haven't been to the zoo since junior high."

"Good, maybe you will enjoy yourself" he said lighting his blunt.

"With you, I know I will" she giggled.

"So, Afrika" called T.T getting his attention. "How come you're not married yet?"

"I'm much too young to consider marriage, T.T" he confessed grinning. "There is a lot of life I have yet to experience, and I couldn't experience them freely if I have to consider somebody's else feelings."

"Like a wife or girlfriend?" mentioned Donna.

"Especially a wife or girlfriend" he replied. "I see beautiful black women surrounding me every day and the way y'all reappeared last night to hang out actually blew my mind especially the red wrap you wore Ebony. You have some beautiful legs" he said causing her to slightly blush. "T.T, I can only imagine the bliss in your lips. Donna, I like when you let your hair down and yourself. Nobody is going to bite you unless you want them to" he shared causing them to giggle. "I could complement each one of y'all on what I found so attractive, but I won't, y'all heads are big enough" he said shocking them before they started snickering and giggling while nudging him in his ribs. "But really, are your lips like bliss T.T?"

"Afrika leave my girls alone" Mona said lightly giggling at T. T's stun expression and the look of admiration on the rest of their faces.

"I was just asking a question, Mona" he told her in a soft alluring tone with his impish grin on his face.

"No, you weren't" she corrected him while slightly shaking her head. "I didn't know how much I miss that about you" she lightly giggled again. "Do you see what I meant about him ladies? He is as beautiful and alluring like a Venus flytrap. Before y'all knew it, he had all four of y'all ensnarled" she giggled as they stared over at him ignoring Mona's word while smoking his blunt. "Oh, don't get it twisted ladies" she said slightly hardening her eyes and getting their attention. "He meant every word that he whispers to you especially while in his arms dancing. Oh, he is wondering about your lips T.T and how you would perform in bed Ebony, but he also know, he better not act upon those impulses, or I will fuck him up while he sleeps. He is too good with his hands ladies to get him while he's awake" she shared grinning. "Look at him" she requested as they stared at his nonchalant disposition then he suddenly burst out laughing.

"Oh, he is so wicked" Donna said shaking her head at him.

"Oh, he could be but then he wouldn't be my first and only true male friend" she shared smiling over at him.

"Do you have any children Afrika?" inquired T.T.

"I'm always ready to go through the formalities, T.T" he replied causing them to burst out laughing at T. T's expression.

"Didn't I tell you to stop?" Mona said.

"Okay, okay. No, T.T I do not have any children. I adopted a motto from y'all."

"What motto?" Tamira asked.

"No glove, no love" Mona shared causing them to stare at him then burst out laughing.

"You know you are naturally sexy, right?" Ebony shared her opinion.

"I think y'all are sexy especially when you hold me in your arms."

"Watch him, Ebony" warned T.T peeking over at her grinning.

"Imagine going through this every day in college" Mona said watching Ebony surrendering to his alluring charm. "I couldn't have handled the attention he gets if I didn't come to understand him and eventually trust him. He is an exceedingly rare find, ladies" she shared sticking her tongue out at him grinning.

"I will cosign that" replied Tamara coming from the kitchen and staring over at him.

"How come we never hooked up?" Mona asked the question that was secretly plaguing their mind.

"Theodore" he answered then tried to contain his snicker.

"You know Theo?" Donna asked surprise by his answer.

"Na, but I have seen and heard of him" he replied grinning.

"You need to get that grin off your face" she told him slightly hardening her eyes while taking the blunt from between his fingers.

"How is Theodore anyway?"

"Just fine Afrika."

"If all the small talk is over, can we start this day?" he asked getting to his feet.

"Are you driving?" Mona asked with a devilish grin.

"Nope" he replied bursting her bubble. "We can jump in whoever is driving that Yukon. Come on, ladies" he said heading towards the front door.

"Damn, he's just going to step off like that" mention T.T admiring his disposition while gathering her belongings.

"I see you are gathering your shit" replied Donna giggling over her shoulder while catching up with Tamira.

They all climbed into T.T Yukon. Mona and Afrika took the third-row seat.

"I know I said it last night, but I love throwing that article in my fathers' face. He tried enticing me with a car of my choice but I'm not accepting anything from his hypocrite ass. He can keep his damn peace offering. Plus, Theo been sniffing around for the past couple of months, but he is very apprehensive and rightfully so. I will cuss his square ass off. I have changed from the school girl crush I once possess for him. He has a high mountain to climb if he plan on reaching me" she shared her conviction while hardening her eyes. "My father still has hopes of us mending our differences."

"There is nothing wrong with maintaining hope" he casually said.

"True" she replied gripping his fingers. "I've maintained my hopes" she shared with a faint smile.

"What hopes?" he asked already knowing the answer, but would she openly confess it.

"You moving down here to be with me, Afrika" she confessed in the ears of Ebony and Donna. "Who would be better for me, than you? And who would be better for you, than me? You and I have been in love with one another for years or am I reading this wrong?"

"No, you are not reading this or me wrong" he admitted returning her stare.

"Leave the harsh streets of Camden and live here, in this house, with me Afrika" she slightly pleaded.

"I still have restitutions I still have to administer, Mona. You know this sweetheart. Although I have accomplished a lot, there is so much more I have to complete before my journey is over. I wish I could pick up and leave for your love, but I can't yet, darling. I truly can't and it breaks my heart" he confessed returning her stare.

"From where your roots are embedded to where you are, you have accomplished so much baby over the years. All I want to be is your reward for the things you have done at the end of your day" she said softly.

"I don't know a of a more alluring contract than one with you, but I can't baby, not yet."

"I know" she admitted while surrendering to the battle she tried to fight on numerous of times over the years within herself except this time, she open her heart to him and vocalized her words but got the response she thought she would receive.

As they entered Southeast Atlanta, they were cruising down Cherokee Avenue then turned-on Georgia Avenue for the entrance of the zoo. They walked around enjoying the scenery like school kids. They brought cotton candy while the ladies threw their peanuts at the elephants as Afrika ate his. They walked around for three hours before getting pimp for some overpriced mementos. While still on the Southeast, they drove down Hillard Street to explore the MLK Natatorium. Reliving their grandparents peaceful demonstrations during the fifties and sixties in black and white pictures then witnessing them being brutally attacked by police, and backed up by the national guards, to keep in place a segregated America, brought frowns to their otherwise smiling personalities and Afrika incorporating his two cents only further their discuss. It was almost six o'clock when they were finally drop off back at the house. They agreed to a ten o'clock patch up time to go to Back Stage. Ramona and Afrika went to their respected bedrooms to get a power nap in.

The alarm clock sounded at nine o'clock that night. As they rolled out of their beds to take their showers, music could be heard coming from their individual rooms. It was forty-five minutes later that Afrika emerged from his bedroom and descended the stairs, he was chilling in the family room smoking a blunt and sipping on a glass of Monet while listening to Duke Ellington with Sara Vaugh doing vocal when Mona appeared.

"Damn" was all he could say methodically getting to his feet. His eyes said everything that his lips didn't or wouldn't say. She found herself blushing at the lust that had crept into his eyes. Wearing a brown two-piece brown skirt from Versace that revealed her muscular thighs and calves with a tan camisole and matching red bottom stilettos, the woman looked gorgeous. "Damn" he reiterated lightly kissing her on the lips.

"You clean up pretty well also" she smiled adjusting his tie then taking the blunt from between his fingers. The gray pin-stripe Louis Vuitton was tailor to his muscular body with a dark gray shirt matching the pinstripes. "You look handsome as usual" she stated taking seat next to where he was sitting on the couch. She had brought him a bottle of John Varvatos cologne during their junior year. She loved the intoxicating way his body chemistry mixed with it. She had brought Theo a bottle for his birthday and several male friends as gifts, but it didn't do anything for her. On Afrika, it was erotically intoxicating and stimulating. The aroma was hypnotizing and enticing her to willingly do something naughty like getting butterball naked.

Her girls rolled through around ten-thirty being fashionably late as only a woman can be. As he stared over at them smiling, the competition was tight, but Ebony slightly edged out T.T. The off the shoulder white stretched dress revealed every contour of her body especially her phat little ass and he did wonder how she would handle in the curves.

It was a little after eleven o'clock when they enter Back Stage, they found themselves a table on the far-left wall and got comfortable. As the night heated up, Afrika could himself in T.T arms dancing to 702 "Stello." Their bodies thrust and grind against one another erotically until they had to pause and laugh at themselves as they walked off the dance floor in one another arms. Mona could only shake her head at how her girlfriends became smitten by his natural charm and positive spirit after just two days. She enjoyed watching their interactions especially prissy acting Donna. She surrender to his charm and openly admitted to them that she could easily fall in love with someone like Afrika, but could she deal with all the attention that receive. Her self-esteem would be tested constantly. They had to respect her honesty, but that wouldn't prevent them from stepping up. Having him their fingers and whispering illicit words in their ears would be more than enough to appease their self-esteem and they haven't even considered how he would perform in bed they admitted laughing.

Back Stage was one of a few clubs that closes at two o'clock in the morning. Afrika and Mona had slip away to the outside deck to enjoy the breeze and for some privacy when the lights started flashing indicating it was time to get the fuck out. Descending the stairs, they found the ladies conversing with a couple of guys and exchanging cell numbers then headed out the club with the others. Arriving back at Mona's house, the ladies continued home with the promise of catching up with them tomorrow. It was three o'clock when they finish taking their shower and crawling between the sheets. Afrika always left a dim light on as the sound of jazz filled the room. Just as sleep was about to grip him, he heard faint footsteps approaching then his bedroom door quietly open further. Mona stood by the door staring in at him. He lean up engulfing her body with his eyes. She was wearing a pair of white cheeky panties and nothing else.

"Are you sure you want to venture down this path?"

"No but I know we love each other and that would sustain our friendship no matter what unfold between us" she replied unfolding her arms and revealing her full perky breast and slightly hardening nibbles.

He pulled the cover back inviting her to join him as she step through the door slightly smiling. Crawling inside next to him, her spoon her while allowing his hand to lightly caress her body while the warmth of his breath accompany his kisses on her neck and shoulders. She turned and faced him staring deep into his eyes. Their passionate kiss revealed their lust and desire for one another. As he engulfed one of her breast into his mouth, he suckled and gently bit her spike nibbles sending electricity throughout her body. As he kissed the contour of her body, she could feel his fingers gripping the rim of her panties and slightly elevated her hips for him. As he continued on his southward journey, her breathing became more spasmodic. Feeling his lips and tongue protruding through her light garden of love, she gasp out and gripped his head firmly. When he suck on her clitoris, her body elevated off the bed.

"No, Afrika" she whispers. "No, baby" she pleaded feeling an orgasm approaching quickly. "Afrika, Afrika. Stop baby, please" she pleaded as she suddenly gripped his head firmer and started rotating her hips to the erotic pleasure he was inducing with his tongue. "Yeah, baby, yeah. That's it. Yeah, baby, yeah!" she scream out as her climax made her body quiver as she became light headed. "Wait" she insisted panting as he made his journey north pausing slight to suck on her nibbles then she flipped the script. She reached for his dick then released it thinking it was an anaconda. The length wasn't the only thing that brough apprehension to her eyes, but the thickness was well. She struggled to give him head, but she did her damn best, as her saliva ran over her hand and down his shaft. As he laid her back, she could feel the head of his dick at her entrance and took a deep breath before slowly exhaling. Forcing himself inside, you would have thought that she was a virgin as tight she felt around his manhood. With each slight thrust, she allowed more of him to enter as another orgasm forced her thighs further open for him. She found herself catching multi orgasms as their perspiration tried to cool their lustful passion. She remembered hearing herself crying, moaning, groaning, and pleading for mercy, only to tell him not to stop, from the euphoric feeling of bliss he was inducing. She doesn't remember becoming unconscious. Was it from catching another orgasm or being overwhelmed by him. Only the late morning sun creeping through the window eventually stir he awoke. As she slowly open her eyes, she stared up into his brown eyes and smiled. The sudden movement of her leg reminded her of the pleasurable pain filled night she just experience. She reached over and engulfed his face in her hand then kissed him passionately.

"I love you Afrika" she informed him softly.

"I'm in love with you, too Mona. I honestly am. I'm not naïve enough not to realize that Theo will be putting his best foot forward in hopes of reclaiming your trust and love, but I don't blame him" he shared slightly hardening his eyes. "I'm mad as hell that I can't accept the love you are offering. If anything changes in my life the next year or two, I will definitely be placing my resume in your hand with the other admirers" he told her slightly smiling.

"You don't have to submit a damn thing, just come."

"Supposed you are seeing someone, Mona."

"They will be receiving their walking papers" she replied grinning. "I wouldn't dwell on what I was losing Afrika because I know what I will be gaining a hell of a lot more" she told him with conviction in her eyes and voice.

"Yes, you would" he cosigned then kissing her again. Before he knew it, his hands were exploring her body again and was enticing her to experience the scenario of last night and she was very receptive. It was almost one o'clock when they finally untwined their bodies and took a shower together, they were down stairs in the family room talking when her girls arrived around three o'clock with dates. They sat around talking, dancing, laughing, and getting their heads bad listening to the latest songs through Dr. Dre's "Beats" speakers. It was almost eleven o'clock when they finally said their goodbyes. Afrika kissed Mona girlfriends. He promise he wouldn't stay away so long and that he will convince his partners to come with him the next time. Mona shared his bed that final night to feel his embrace. She was still able to tighten her thighs days later and feel the remnant of their exotic night then a devilish smile would come to her face. Her girls had caught her numerous of times with that same unusual smile and started presuming that she finally got with Afrika, but she wouldn't deny or confirm their suspicion. You never kiss and tell. Neither she nor any woman could handle him straight out the gate unless they were a season professional escort. A woman would need time to get acclimated to what he was slinging. He was a real-life Mandingo. She had caught herself unconsciously giggling several times causing her girls to peek at her suspiciously, again. She had the nerve to call him nasty when she was allowing him to get his freak off while enjoying it immensely. "Damn, I'm nasty" she admitted at her desk reminiscing on the sexual acts she committed and initiated. Saying goodbye at her front door wasn't as hard as she thought it would be. He promise that he would be back, and he never break a promise because he doesn't make them often.

In the weeks after the brutal murder of Munchie, a well-respected and honorable brother in the game, up in Collington. Certain distributors, like Bear's crew, shut down their business for a week as a show of respect. The streets became psychotic as the need for heroin and crack had the addicts screaming out for mercy. The relief they were seeking as their bows broke, the craving increased, the aches and pains from withdrawal symptoms wasn't coming. Most took to the speedline over to Philly to answer their addictions demand. Fuck that they were venturing into some dangerous neighborhoods To ease their craving, they would walk through the door of hell if necessary than give their money to some bullshit dealer watering down his product for a bigger return. Although rumors ran rampant throughout the streets, there was no definitive evidence to associate to anybody and thank goodness. The Terminator was searching for answers also and that wasn't something that a conscious motherfucker wanted or needed in their life. People started speculating that the people responsible for the hit was from out of town, but if that is true, who put them on Munchie and why?

Every small-time dealer or little click were vying for his vacant territory. Squads from several sides of the city thought that they could cut themselves a small piece of real estate on the outer crust. If you are in the game, you should never underestimate your opponent, or you could be walking straight into a hornets nest. It didn't take too many bodies being stretched out from different crews from around the city to understand that just because you are from the county doesn't mean you're not a soldier. Remember, they were affiliated with Munchie, and he only kept soldiers in his crew. Anybody that truly knew Munchie would laugh at the notion that he kept soft motherfuckers around him.

With five-o being on certain people payroll, if was confirmed that the hit consisted of five individuals according to the five different caliber shells recovered from the crime scene and ballistic confirming it. Two came from two separate street sweeper and a Mack 10. A lot of fire power for him and his partner Bones. So, when different crews came at them, they repelled every attempt at a takeover and insisted that they keep bringing it. With the body count steadily rising grass root communities advocates took their concerns to their city council representatives and the chief of police with the mayor's office being their next move.

Police Commissioner Naomi Brown was conducting a special meeting with the commanders in her precinct. Known for being fair while instituting the law, her men knew she was a woman to be trusted and would have their backs, but she was incorruptible. "So, what can we do about this steadily escalating violence, gentlemen?"

"We need to initiate that special drug enforcement squad we discussed last month, ma'am."

"I agree but who can we get to run it?" she asked staring around the table at her majors.

"I have been doing a survey of perspective candidates, but one kept grabbing my attention. He's a ten-year veteran. He has been on the undercover drug force the past five years. Detective First Class Shaun Mulligan has a good reputation around the city for getting things done, ma'am."

"What problems does he bring to the table?" she inquired returning his stare.

"Accusations of heavy hands but none have been substantiated, ma'am."

"You mean he have never been brought up on charges" she countered returning his stare.

He stared back at her with his hands folded in front of him then said, "Ma'am, if your house is being over-run by mice, you can simply get a cat and your problem is gone. You wouldn't throw a sheep amongst wolves; you throw another wolf. A wolf with specific markings that all the other wolves recognize and respect even if they find the wolf repulsing. A wolf that will get the other wolves in line or out of their territory. If you want a head banger to take control of these streets, he's the man for the job ma'am or you can throw another sheep out there."

Naomi leaned back in her chair as a faint smile came to her lips. "I want to have a meeting with Mulligan tomorrow morning at ten o'clock."

"Yes, ma'am" he replied slightly smiling at her coy smile.

The next morning around ten o'clock Mulligan was strolling through the halls heading towards the Commissioner Office. He wore one of his three suits that he possess. The thought of hitting it with an iron must have never enter his thought process. His thoughts since last night were consumed with why Commissioner Naomi Brown wanted to see him. Has a complaint finally reached her desk? Shit, he hope not because he wouldn't know what complaint he would have to address. His own Captain couldn't surrender any information because the order came from their Major. One thing he despised was walking blindly into any situation. Pushing open the outer door, her secretary stared up at him.

"Sargent Mulligan?"

"Yes, ma'am" he replied.

"They are waiting on you" she announced pressing the buzzer for him to enter the next door. Who in the hell is they? As he approached the door, he took a deep breath and slowly exhaled before adjusting his suit jacket then lightly tapped on the door.

"Come in!"

Opening the door, his major was presence and so was the City Council President.

"Have a seat Sargent" Naomi invited him as he took the vacant seat between the two gentlemen as Naomi took in his attire from behind her desk. "You are here this morning because some of my Majors feel like you are the man, I need for the situation plaguing our streets. Do you recognize the gentleman to your right?"

"Yes, ma'am" he replied staring at him then laced his eyes back on her.

"He has concerns with what I am about to initiate because of the complaints that have been filed against you in the past from several community leaders, but as I stated to him, you have never been formally charged with any offense. Now with that out of the way. I want you to head up a special undercover drug enforcement squad. I need you to decease this senseless violence that's occurring around the city. Create a squad six but your Major has final approval of your selections. Do I make myself clear, Sargent?"

"Yes, ma'am."

"And Sargent" she said staring over at him closely.

"Yes, ma'am."

"Watch what you do out there because people will be watching, understand?" she asked slightly hardening her eyes.

"Yes, ma'am."

"Then go do what you do, I expect my first report on my desk by next month. If there is nothing else, you can leave."

"Yes, ma'am" he said getting to his feet then walking out her office. Walking through the outer door, a broad smile suddenly came to his face as he felt like he was floating. "There is a God" he chuckled pulling out his cell phone and pressing a preset number then waited.

"Hey, what are you doing? Meet me behind Our Lady of Lords Hospital" he said ending his conversation.

A half hour later he was cruising up Haddon Avenue into the Parkside section of the city and cross Kaighn Avenue. He spotted White Boy and Red Neck parked on Donkey's parking lot then they pulled out following him to their destination. Pulling up behind the hospital, Dog was joking around with Smooth. They bail out of their vehicles and greeted one another.

"What's up Mulley?" Dog asked shaking his hand vigorously.

"How you been Dog?" he asked returning his smile. "What's up fellas?"

"Same old bullshit" replied White Boy grinning.

"Guess who had a meeting with Commissioner Brown this morning?" he asked wearing a smirk.

"What did you do now?" inquired Dog snickering.

"Nothing" he replied laughing with him. "You will never guess who is the head of an exclusive drug enforcement squad?"

"Who got bless?" asked Smooth staring over at him.

"I did" he burst out laughing.

"Bullshit!" denounced Red Neck.

"Na, I am serious" he replied controlling his snicker. "I'm supposed to get a squad of six. Are y'all down?"

"Are you serious?" inquired Smooth unable to contained his enthusiasm.

"Hell yeah" replied Dog. "When do we start?"

"I will have my captain contact y'all supervisors later today."

"You mean me, and you are back in the saddle again?" Dog aske surprised by the revelation.

"Shit, you are my nigger, Dog. I called you first" he assured him smiling. "The only hick-up is our sixth person. Captain have given us this guy named Morales. He's been qualified for a position on a drug squad except there were no position for him. Now that I'm leading this, I'm forced to take him. Does anybody know him?" he asked staring around the small circle.

"Yeah, I know the guy Mulley" Smooth replied. "He will fall in place."

"If not, I will assist in his transfer" Mulley told them.

"So, we start tomorrow?" Dog asked staring in his greenish eyes.

"Report to your regular precincts but you will receive transfer paper sometime tomorrow morning" he told them grinning.

Sure enough, by eleven o'clock the next morning, they all had their transfer papers in their hands and packing up their belongings. When the Commissioner initiate something, there is no procrastinating. Motherfuckers meet her demands. As they were boxing up their belongings at their respective precincts, Mulley had taken possession of a small building near Cooper River Park as their private headquarter. The building was spotless with cameras located at the front door and two on the back parking lot. As they started filing in around noon, they all claim their desks. Smooth quickly took control of the radio and tuned it to WRTI 90.1, a jazz station. No hip-hop, R&B, country and definitely no hillbilly music. Morales was the last one to arrive. All eyes feel on him.

"Morales, I'm Mulligan or Mulley: he introduced himself. "If you become uncomfortable with the things that you witness, request a transfer and I'll obtain it for you. Do you understand me?"

"Yeah" he replied staring into his eyes of his coworkers glaring over at him.

"No, I need you to understand me" he insisted coming closer and staring down on him. "I know and trust these guys, but I don't know you. I've been in the trenches with them, and they know that I have their backs. So, if you witness anything that makes you uncomfortable, you need to inform me and get out the squad. Do I now make myself clear, officer?"

"I understand" he replied staring up into his eyes.

"Since Smooth is cosigning for you, he will be your partner."

"Alright, Mulley" he replied staring over at the smiling face of Smooth then took a desk near him. He had seen Smooth around in the last two years since transferring into the district. He's very laid back but deeply knowledgeable about the streets. He has been trying to patch into An undercover squad for the past three years but didn't have the experience and nobody was willing to give him a chance to obtain the experience they persistently cried that he needed although he qualified for the position. He didn't want to believe it was racially motivated until he was slap in the face with it. A white officer with the scent of baby food still on his breath was given the opportunity that wasn't granted to him, and it did have a profound effect on him especially how he looks at his supervisors. He had heard of Mulligan from his cousin and the tactics that he uses to extract information. Yet, when his captain approached him about an opening in a fresh new squad being run by Mulligan, he still leaped at the opportunity. He never thought about the gradual transformation that would occur in him or the amount of illegal money that would flow into his hands.

Two weeks later, they were formally announced at a nine o'clock news conference. Commissioner Brown stood firm as she made her prediction that the violence associated with the drug game will diminish within three months as she stared over at Mulley and his newly formed squad while making the prediction. After answering questions from the reporters, she had a brief conversation with Mulley and his men then released them upon the city. Driving in three sets of wheels, they went out to administer their form of justice upon the communities.

The first place they hit was at 9th and Atlantic Avenue. There have been three shootings in the previous two weeks at that location. Somebody wanted the money associated with the corner and they were willing to sacrifice their soldiers, not themselves, to get it. Well, Mulley was going to shut the corner down. They swoop down on the crowd so fast that nobody had a chance to run especially with two Mossberg shotguns and several 40 caliber Glocks pointing at them. They found out how Dog obtained his nickname. The man was so uncanny and with the senses of a dog to smelling out their stashes in the most unlikely places as though one of the guys in the squad had told him. Their first swoop surrender four guns, an abundance of crack and heroin and over ten thousand dollars. They were making serious hits around the city. They would double back a few days later and arrest the next wanna be drug dealers.

During every hit they made they were recovering illegal weapons, and some was connected to a previous unsolved homicide making the individual who's fingerprints on it as the prime suspect especially if he doesn't snitch as to where or who he got the weapon. The choice is yours. Take the fall for someone who willingly placed a dirty gun in your hands with hopes that you remain quiet as most dummies do or you can consider self-preservation like the guy that placed that gun in your hands. What are you going to do? As they said, the choice is yours. The month alone they brought down four prominent drug corners that were easily making twenty G's a day selling their products. Convincing corner boys to flip on their sergeant in arms was an important tactic for what they were planning. Known felons being caught with a fire arm was an automatic five years when associated with the drug game, but some chose to get their sergeant in arms pop for their perceived freedom. In one swoop at a stash house from a reliable snitch, they confiscated three street swipers, eight fire arms of different caliber, approximately eight keys of dope, over a hundred thousand dollars plus several mid-level distributors. Commissioner proudly allowed the newspaper reporters to take pictures of the accomplishment of her Special Drug Force and blast it on the morning paper for all to see especially the drug dealers.

As their names started filtering through the grapevine, corner boys convinced their lieutenants to invest in Donks (little corner boys to alert them when five-o was in the area). Kids as young as eight where being recruited as lookouts and would earn fifty dollars a day. Most would hooky from school to get that money in hopes that their parents didn't find out. With fifty dollars, most could feed themselves during the week or go to the second-hand store to buy more jeans and button-down shirts to improve their appearance. Most Donks were the product of a drug induced dysfunctional home. Some parents have actually asked their child for money so they could obtain a blast instead of disciplining them as a parent should. Those dealers that didn't invest in Donks found out the hard way that it was cheaper to invest in Donks, than constantly hearing that another crew got snatched up and having to pay bail them out. Even when they tried to cover their back doors using Donks, Smooth would walk up on an unsuspecting Donk then snatch him off his bike or off the steps he was sitting on then handcuff him to a pole or through somebody metal rail. Fuck if it was illegal to treat a child like that. Mulley's advice to the irate parents was simple. "Teach your child not to be affiliated with the drug game."

Main distributors realized that higher security was necessary to protect their merchandise from Mulley and his squad. Higher security meant more than fifty dollars a day. Infiltrating Mulley's tight circle wasn't happening and will get you touch suggesting it to any of them. So, they subtly put on the grapevine wanting information concerning which cops would put the color green over the color blue. All five-o could really be is a high price corner boy with communication ability to the main communication station. They might, I repeat, might be able to warn their private employers only seconds before a hit or a minute if they were lucky. When it came to Mulley, he doesn't always use the communication center.

Using the few snitches, they have acuminated, they had just crashed their first substantial stash house. They acquired a hundred bricks of suspected cocaine, cutting solution, scales, packaging material, a small quality of marijuana, two assault weapons and three hand guns. Staring at the bundles of money, Mulley nodded to Dog, and he grabbed six stacks, and five keys then placed them in a small black gym bag. He walked out the back door and placed it in their vehicle then rejoined them in the front room to finish searching and identifying those that they caught inside. Smooth caught the eyes of one of the three young ladies that were inside. As the men were being escorted out to the paddy wagon by uniform officers, the honey complexion young lady was offering a proposition to Smooth. She would get her girls to party with them if they didn't receive distribution charges. This was how their erotic adventures began. Once the fellas were taking away, Smooth took their ID's and wrote down their information then cut them loose with the understanding that they will be contacting them in a couple of days. They allowed them to leave by the back door. After completing their reports with Mulley finalizing them, they summited everything they recovered into evidence room. Mulley and his men hooked up on the upper deck of a parking garage in Collingwood to distribute the money. Each stack contained twenty-thousand dollars. Hearing how much drugs and money were collected during their preliminary, two of the accused peeked at one another. Bum rushing certain corners, they could catch them sleeping and easily take ten G's off the main man. It wasn't a lot of money but hitting three corners a day, the nontaxable money wasn't bad.

With the increase of illegal money, problem will arise. Like Biggie said, more money more problems. How are they supposed to hide the illegal money they were stealing? Placing it in a bank in New Jersey wasn't happening, but maybe, one of the surrounding states like crossing the bridge to Philly or up to New York; going down south to Chocolate City (D.C) was also an option. Until a decision is finally made, they will keep stashing their money where they were hiding it. With Smooth's suggestion, they obtained two apartments outside of Camden near Westview for their little private rendezvous with the young ladies that got caught up. From their initial hook up with the vibrant legal teenage and early twenties young ladies, they were instantly addicted. Admiring them surrendering to their every desire was like a dream come true. Prancing around in bras and panties or nothing at all by the more adventurous ones, they were in heaven. Granted, they would kick them a few hundred dollars for their services, but they didn't care, the money wasn't really theirs. The videoing got started by Butter's freaky ass. She wanted to revisit their sexapades while getting high and Red Neck was quick to be the producer.

Since their inauguration two years ago, they have out shined every drug enforcement squad in the city including the Feds. Numerous of hot spots around the city have been eliminated as several grass root organizations congratulated Commissioner Brown for the job her special drug force was doing. Violence associate with the drug game have diminished over percent throughout the city. Two years ago, there were three-hundred and twenty murders associated with the drug game. Last year, there were one hundred and forty associated directed with the drug game. With their high rate of arrest and convictions, they received several prestigious awards and accommodations for their exemplary work. The Commissioner and Mayor's office took their success to justify their ballooning over-time.

With success comes accusations of police brutality, extortion from drug dealers and racketeering, but with no evidence, they continued their routines and antics. They eventually earned their nickname from the streets. They were called the Nextel Boys because everybody in the game was secretly wondering who was going to tell next? Mulley was known for catching a small fish with fear in his eyes of incarceration and dangling freedom in front of him for a gun. While reducing the number of illegal guns on the street, he was privately building his private little world. He would give them a half hour to return with a gun and most dummies do without knowing the history of the weapon.

Usually on Friday and Saturday nights, they would be contacted by mid-week by one of their regulars or they would contact a specific girl. Grinding to the latest R&B and hip-hop tunes, the E-pills and marijuana they provided to the girls had them on some exotic island. Cries and pleas coming from the young ladies during sex acts only heighten the men lusts. Rumors of their parties eventually hit the grapevine as other eager young ladies vied for their attention especially the money they were offering. While lying in Mulley's arms one night, Domino suggested who they should hit next and on which night. She provided him with the location and whole layout. What she neglected to tell him is that she had a personal vendetta against the guy because he fucked a girl that he knew she didn't like and boasted about it. When she had approached him about it, he shut her straight down in front of her friends like she was some cheap trick even if she was tricking. Her embarrassment was like a wound that wouldn't heal and only fester until she could get her revenge. Nothing can be compared to a woman's scorn, nothing.

With the money they were extorting and the territory that they controlled with the drugs that they stole, threats of retaliation was common. Although they were five-o, they weren't Teflon Dons. So, they hired the best security that money could buy. Blackout is a very feared and extremely vicious homicidal individual. There were rumors that he stretched out over thirty people to get Diamond's business firmly rooted until he caught a three-year vacation inside Rahway State Prison. He refused to accept an early parole because he didn't want to have time held over his head if he did fuck up again or have to report to some snobbish ass parole officer. Returning to the streets and seeking to put his unique skills back to work, he was shocked when Mulley and Dog approached him about an employment opportunity. How could he refuse such a lucrative proposition? Getting paid by five-o to do what he was bred to do, kill a motherfucker without remorse, was hilarious to him. Who could ask for a better employer and protection policy. Only a fool would not accept such a lucrative proposition and Mulley put his straight to work.

When he first step to Yogi, he asked him if he understood when Muley told him to shut it down or get in line with the other dealers; he said he understood but said, "Fuck Mulley!" So, he tried to have a civil conversation with the young man because he was only twenty-three, but you know how some twenty something act. They actually believe the dumb shit that they say, and Blackout always allowed a person to express themselves then asked the original question; are you going to get in line or shut it down? Yogi's laughter informed him that this young man was misjudging him and that was okay. He just turn and casually walk back up the street. He returned the next evening around eight o'clock for his definitive answer and while he was laughing, Blackout blew his brains out the back of his cranium with is beloved 44 Magnum while his crew stared on in horror then he casually walked back up the street in the shadows. Word got out quickly as to who was running security for Mulley and small-time dealers got lower while those that couldn't had to negotiate or close up shop. The third option was getting a visit from Blackout.

Mulley's men didn't have a problem breaking people's Constitutional Rights, black people specifically, but Morales were starting to struggle with his morals. He actually joined the force to make a difference not to become implicated as a co-defendant in a criminal case. He constantly fought with his consciousness and shared some of his concerns with his wife, but not the stolen money he had stashed and definitely not the provocative parties he had attended while telling her he would be on another stakeout. He wasn't that stupid. The illegal drugs that they confiscated off of drug dealers were forced in the hands of drug dealers on the opposite side of town to sell except the marijuana, perks, and E-pills. Accepting the stolen money didn't actually bother him, but being a drug distributor, this was his problem and what is he supposed to do, resign the position, or say, snitch? Snitches are despised on the streets, and many have gotten taken out for breaking that street code, but on the force, it can be just as dangerous and lethal. Who could he trust to have his back in violent situation like a gun battle. He would hate to be classified as a victim of a friendly fire scenario.

"Listen up, gentlemen" ordered Mulley at roll call. "The information I have obtained on these fresh players are solid. Dog and I drove pass, and something is definitely jumping off. They are supposed to be from out of South Camden and they are trying to establish a corner near Collingswood. They are getting off the speedline at Ferry Avenue then walking over. The setup is like this. At the end of the one-way alley, two young ladies are there as lookouts. They have to be taken down first before we can move. Smooth, come from the east and do your thing. Red Neck, you and White Boy will be approaching from the south. We will be coming straight at them. Does everybody have their assignments?"

"Yeah" they replied in unison and hardening their eyes slightly.

"Let's get paid and gentlemen, please be careful."

Smooth and Morales turned on Van Hook Street cruising at twenty miles per hour in a white restored Escalade blasting Jay Z's "I Got Ninety-Nine Problems." With the New York tags standing out like a black man attending a KKK rally, the Forge series Sleeper chrome rims has a value easily thirty G's. What appears to be Johnny Dang glittering around their necks had several young ladies waving them over, but they kept their flow. As they approached their destination, they spotted their targets. Smooth slowed down even more as a light skin girl stare at him and slight smiled. He stop down the street then started backing up and they did what he had hoped. They left their position.

"Excuse me, young ladies" Smooth apologized smiling to reveal his diamond studded fronts. "Me and my partner was wondering where two strangers can go to have some fun?" he asked placing his elbow on the door and revealing his diamond studded Rolex.

"What kind of fun are you talking about?" a thick chocolate girl asked walking further from her post while salivating at the glitter.

"Not to be disrespectful but we were hoping for some adult like fun. If y'all are busy right now, we can hook up later. Everything will be on me and my partner, Chico."

"All that is expected but what are y'all going to put in our pockets?" the light skin girl asked, not just wanting a high and a wet ass for her time.

"May we get out to introduce ourselves properly" Smooth requested still smiling at the light skin girl. "I'm sure we can come to some kind of mutual agreement."

"Sure" they replied together nudging one another while giggling.

They climbed out wearing shirt cargo pants with a black New York Yankee jersey and a black fitted hat with a pair of Dolce Gabbana sneaker. Just as they were in arms-length, they flipped out their badges and gaffle them to the ground despite their cries of police brutality.

"Eyes under control" Morales informed the squad as they hooked them together to a metal pole.

"What kind of fucking shit is this!?" snarled the light skin girl.

"Shut the fuck up!" insisted Smooth. "Y'all can still get out of this shit if y'all are willing to cooperate."

"Cooperate how? We aren't snitching on anyone."

"I would never put you in such a predicament. You are too damn cute" he told her smiling. "I'm talking about that party we were discussing."

"Do we still get paid?" she asked returning his stare but not his smile. "If not, you can take our asses to jail."

"Baby, we got you" he winked at her before entering the mouth of the alley.

Creeping through the alley, the music from the portable radio drown out their slight sounds. "Freeze motherfucker! Don't move!" ordered Mulley catching them totally by surprise. "Everybody get on your knees and clamp your fingers behind your head! Now, motherfuckers!" he ordered as his men pointed two shot guns and their Glocks at the group.

The six teenagers froze in their tracks staring at the barrels of the weapons pointing at them especially the two Mossberg shotguns being held by the two white boys and the badges as they followed the instructions. Once they were secure in tie-up plastic cuffs and patted down for weapons. White Boy took well over thirty-thousand dollars off of one guy. They also retrieved two nine millimeters and a Glock, fully loaded, near where they were sitting.

"I wonder who fingerprints are on these?" Mulley asked smiling while placing them in paper bags not plastic bags to assure the prints don't condense, fade or smear. "So, where is the stash?" he asked staring in their eyes individually. "What nobody got nothing to say. I just heard y'all quoting T-Pain's "Whatcha Gonna Do?" he asked still wearing his smirk. "Dog, go find it" he said staring at the group smiling.

Only twice in two years was he unable to locate a stash. Only twice. No matter where you hide it, Dog will sniff it out. As he slowly left the group and venture, he trailed their footsteps to a small opening between the two vacant houses. You can hear him kicking things then the storm drain suddenly collapsed. Dog re-emerged smiling and carrying a plastic bag containing twenty bundles of crack cocaine. Twenty vials were in each bundle. Two of the bundles contained a brownish substance believed to be heroin.

"Well now" Mulley smiled accepting the bag and looking inside. "Nice" he smiled then looked over at the group of teenagers. "The drugs are one thing but finding these weapons with a possible body attached is something else and guarantee us a conviction unless" he paused slightly hardening his eyes. "Unless we can work out some kind of deal" he mentioned studying their eyes.

"I don't know Mulley" Dog stated getting their attention. "I don't they are wise enough to know when they are catching a blessing."

"Look here, gentlemen" stated Mulley getting their attention again. "Who is going to be the mouth piece because

I don't like repeating myself?" he asked waiting for a response, but none came his way. "You are right, they are dumb as hell. Call for the wagon and charge them all."

"What are you offering?" a dark muscular guy asked snarling up at them.

"Freedom" Mulley replied walking over and standing in front of him. "Can we talk?"

"Talk" he replied still snarling.

"I was hoping to talk to you in private."

"Na, that, is not going to happen" he replied still snarling up at him. "My partners have to hear what you are offering."

"Okay, here's the deal. Either you work for me or y'all go to jail. No partial agreements to grind for me. All or nothing at all."

"You want us to grind for you?" he asked surprise and shock.

"That's right, work for me" he reiterated returning his stare. "You can work this spot with no interference from my brothers in blue. You will receive thirty percent of the profits. Do that sound fair?" he asked trying to contain his smirk.

"Hell no!" he replied adamantly as he flashed his canines. "How long do we have to slave for you?"

"Six short months and your slavery chains come off" he replied slightly grinning.

"Six fucking months? Damn!"

"That's my offer and it's non-negotiable. What is your answer?" he asked lighting up a cigarette and inhaling deeply from it then exhaling. "Well?" he asked hardening is eyes more at the guy.

The mouth piece stared into his partners eyes and saw the fear of incarceration in them. They never truly consider incarceration until reality smack them in their faces. They wanted the high and perceived status of selling drugs especially the money, but when it comes to paying restitution then the bitch surface in them. If you can't do the time, don't do the crime. He have been jailing since he was fifteen but none of them have ever been detained at "baby booking" as juveniles. Their eyes were pleading with him to accept the offer and not decline. "We will grind" he said swallowing the bitter pill.

"I thought so considering most of your partners are pissing in their pants" he shared looking at two guys specifically and grinning. "Be here tomorrow at noon and we will lay out our plan. Gentlemen, you don't want to try and get low on me because we got niggers everywhere and we will cross paths again. So, to eliminate any repercussions on your part, please show up. Cut those tie ups off and get their identification" he told them watching the look of discuss creep across Morales face and it didn't go unnoticed by any of the members in the squad.

As it was on most nights especially after a good sting, Morales would go home to his wife while the others would go to one of the two apartment's. The two young ladies that Smooth had pinch earlier in the day would be coming over around nine o'clock with a couple of her girlfriends. With the money being right, they expected a night filled with erotic passion with young ladies that wasn't afraid to reveal their voyeurism. Every known drug they have confiscated was kept at the apartment. From X's to cocaine and marijuana, they had it all for the adventurous young ladies to consume. Between the mass consumption of drugs and alcohol, most nights were a blur. Reliving their experiences via Red Neck's video, the following weekend, they would laugh their asses off at their antics while complimenting some of the exotic positions some of the girls were attempting. The atmosphere was like a scene straight out of Caligula.

"Listen up" Mulley told them after partying and the girls had left. "I particularly don't like what I have been seeing in Morales eyes."

"He's alright, Mulley" Smooth replied pulling from a blunt.

"Na, Smooth. That rice and bean eating motherfucker isn't alright" countered Red Neck slightly hardening his eyes at him.

"Why because he doesn't hang out with us as much anymore?" he asked returning his stare. "He is a married man."

"Na, that's not it" interjected White Boy Mike. "That motherfucker has been snarling at us strange for months now. I personally think he needs to transfer out."

"I'm cosigning that" Red Neck said returning his stare.

"Well, I'm not cosigning that bullshit" he replied staring over at both men. "I'm the one that is spending time with him in that SUV and I'm telling y'all, he's alright."

"You are standing too close to the tree, Smooth" Mulley said catching his eyes. "There is something jumping off in his eyes. If it doesn't disappear soon, he will have to transfer out."

"But where can he go, Mulley? There is no openings anywhere."

"That is not our problem" he told him looking over the rim of his eyeglasses. "I refuse to allow him to become a problem for us. Either he gets back on board, or he need to transfer out. The decision is his, Smooth."

Tuesday started out as usual as Afrika made his way to the office and just as he pulled on the parking lot, his intuition warned him that something was about to jump off. He have had this same unsettling feeling for the past couple of weeks without nothing materializing, but he wasn't just going to ignore his intuition, only a fool would. Pulling into his parking spot, he stared up at the shades in his office slightly settled. He instantly started snarling as he climbed out his car and approached the building. When he exit the elevator, Tweety informed him that the Hines were waiting for him in his office. He barely acknowledged Shakira as his strides took a purpose causing some of the staff members to snicker or giggle. Entering his office, James had his feet up on his desk and listening to his jazz collection. The look he gave him would have made a conscious person aware of their actions, but not this arrogant stupid alcoholic motherfucker.

"Can you take your damn feet off my desk!?" he asked shooting him a glare as he slammed the door shut. "I didn't give you permission to touch my shit?"

"I was just listening to your damn music" he replied taking his feet off the desk and getting to his feet.

"Buy your own. You are making a hell of a lot more than I am."

"Afrika!" interjected Robert. "We need to talk."

"About what!?" he asked still glaring at James moving in the opposite direct he was taking to get to his seat.

"About progress" he told him smiling as he took his seat then lean back. "We are about to purchase this new building next week."

"Good for you" he replied nonchalantly while clamping his fingers. As he stared over at James, he wanted to grip him by this throat and squeeze the last bit of life out of his alcoholic ass.

"James and I want to give you a nice corner office overlooking the skyline with a private secretary. A nice reward for what you have done for this company over the past two years."

"Apparently, what I contributed wasn't shit considering the promissory note and your brother constantly invading my space" he told him staring coldly at James. "What is really troubling to me is your actions. You witness his disrespect but don't say a damn word. You could have easily had him take his feet down."

"Nigger, you need to chill."

"Nigger?" he repeated getting to his feet. "Who in the fuck do you think you are calling a nigger? You fucking Negro."

"Boy, if you don't!"

"What? Boy?" he said coming from around the desk, but Robert impeded him with as much strength he could muster.

"Stop it! Stop!" Robert insisted staring at both men. He had told his brother on numerous occasions about fucking with Afrika personal belongings, but did he listen? Why didn't he tell him to get the fuck out of chair when he spotted him coming? If they were going to put their plan into effect, they needed Afrika aboard. Without him resigning his contract next year, their plan would falter and the money they would lose could have them back on life support or shut down completely and they didn't want that. They would lose all the materialistic things they have acquired by fulfilling the settlement including their homes. "Listen Afrika" he requested trying to ease the tension. "Patience will pay off in the end. Trust me."

"Trust isn't given, you must earn it. Don't you know that?" he asked staring in his bloodshot eyes. "Is my incentive supposed to be a larger office with a secretary?"

"What do you want?"

"The partnership you promise when I initially signed with you."

"Partnership!?" snapped James moving closer to the door. "Nigger, you must be crazy" he chuckled. "The only way you will become a partner is when I retire and that's not happening any time soon. So, make other plans" he smiled over at him.

"Be glad that you are standing over there by that door calling me a nigger again. You alcoholic bitch!" Afrika called him with venom in his eyes. "Perhaps I just might take your advice James, make other plans."

"Whatever nigger" he snicker waving him off as he walked out the office.

"Afrika, I am going to increase your pay by fifteen-thousand dollars, and I will get my brother on board about your partnership capacity also. I promise."

"Think about the things that you told me, Robert. Don't have me considering self-preservation" he warned him staring in his eyes.

"Don't make any irrational decision, okay?"

"I'm never irrational" he smiled at him grabbing his folders. "I'm taking the rest of the week off" he informed him easing past then heading out the door and walking towards the elevator. He have had enough of this bullshit, but what is he going to do? Joining another firm like Barnes and Barnes wasn't desirable even with their lucrative offer. If the path you are traveling isn't producing fruits, pioneer another path.

Mulley had several dealers that were starting to smell themselves and coming up short much too frequently. He need to send a message and make a statement that would run through the grapevine, and he did. He leased Blackout upon the city. He would walk in the shadows searching for his intended targets. Once found, he would casually walk pass like a regular Joe then pull out his 44 Magnum and blow their motherfucking brain out then continued casually up the street. Only once did a guy's partner fire back at him, he was very deliberate as bullets zipped pass and blow the guy away. He was extremely prolific with his baby. Most motherfuckers on the streets don't know shit about sight alignment. As he stretched motherfuckers out, those that thought they were soldiers leap their asses back in line. When the mention of the violence reached their supervisor, Mulley would shut him down but kept the fuse lit. he was getting five G's a week just being on standby and ten G's for every mid-level distributor he had to touch. He made thirty G's last week alone. When he had to approach other dealers after sending his message, they were all very receptive to the things he was telling them for Mulley. Those that tried to buck his system was rewarded with an additional three months of slavery.

Afrika had called Mona late one night informing her that he was coming down and with his partners. She was ecstatic and would put her girls on point. They got with their clients and informed them that they would be leaving the city for the weekend especially those over in Philly. Just as suspected, Thursday they had three times the volume than usual. They rationalized that they rather have an abundance than not enough. Afrika and Black made well over a hundred and fifty-thousand dollars that afternoon over in Philly. They were also forced to keep their business open until two o'clock because of the demands and one of the fraternities were having a party.

When they tally up the money at the end of the night, they were astounded by the money they have acquired. Tek9 was the one to suggest taking every other weekend off and forcing them to load up again. The ploy actually worked and freed up their weekends to take quick trips to the various Caribbean Islands.

Friday morning, they were cruising down 95S heading to Philadelphia International in Bear's Escalade and parking inside the over-night garage then climbed out with their garment bags. Entering the terminal looking like a squad of gangsters, they received their first-class tickets then proceeded to the boarding gate. Being directed to their seats, Afrika pulled out his book as the fellas flirted with every young lady that stared a little too long. Their flight to Atlanta ended too quickly for them.

Exiting the plane with their garment bags around noon at the DeKalb-Peachtree Airport, seeing seven black men professional dressed and with their eyes hidden by sunglasses, people naturally wondered who they could be. Their attire left no doubt that they weren't from Atlanta or the swag that they all possess. They enter the Hertz Rental to acquire the two Suburban that they requested. After placing their garment bags inside, they climbed inside then headed up Bobby Brown Pkwy to the Radisson Suites at Hardin Avenue and Lee Street. After checking in and receiving their electronic keys, they took the elevator to their rooms. Afrika and Bear went to the location he first obtained his weed. The same group was still holding down the spot. They spoke warmly to one another as Skippy retrieved the three ounces he requested. He stop at the liquor store to buy thirty packs of Cloud 9 and ten bottles of Moscato before returning to their suite. He called Mona when he got back and they agreed to meet at Ellery's around ten o'clock, but he warned her, they probably wouldn't arrive until close to eleven o'clock or a little later.

When they enter the club a little after midnight, every eyes were on them including security. All GQ down but their attire gave the impression that they were more than what meets the eyes. They stood scanning the place like a group of hit men before Afrika finally located them and pointed out the ladies to his partners. He located Mona and T.T on the dance floor getting their groove on while Ebony, Donna, Tamir and Monica was carrying a conversation with three guys that wasn't getting them anywhere. After the song ended, both ladies slowly made their way back to their booth. Just before sitting down, Mona glance at the door spotting a group of guys entering and disappointment came to her face as she took her seat. Taking a sip from her drink, her eyes focus in on the shadows and the silhouettes of several men. As they started moving in the shadows towards their direction, a broad smile came to her face as she methodically got to her feet ignoring the questions of her girlfriends and the guys vying for their attention. As they turned to see what had grabbed her full attention, they spotted seven young men heading in their direction looking very intimidating especially the six feet seven bear, although very handsome and facial beard well-manicured.

"Hey, knuckleheads" she greeted flashing her radiant smile then hugging Afrika and kissing him lightly on the lips. She walked into the open arms of all of them and kiss them on the cheek individually.

"Damn, Mo! You got finer girl" complimented Bear.

"Finer? What kind of word is that?" she teased giggling. "I have always been fine" she corrected him while smiling up at him smiling. "Ladies, these are the bad influences of Afrika like he needs one. This teddy bear here" she said hugging him again. "Is Bear, that's Tek9. Kimba, Black and Murk" she introduced them. "This young man here must be Amir. The young man that they have been mentoring. Please say a pray for him ladies" she giggled then shaking his hand.

"Ladies" they replied while tipping their hats.

"Hi, fellas" they chimed together.

"Fellas, these beautiful young ladies is Donna, T.T, Tamira, Ebony and Monica" she introduced them.

"Y'all can get low gentlemen" Tek9 told the three guys staring in their eyes individually and they left without saying a word.

"Damn!" T.T said giggling with Donna and Ebony as the three guys obeyed his command like little children.

"Pull a chair up" invited Mona smiling at them. She didn't know how much she missed them and their disposition until now. They used to have her in tears the way they shut down so-called tough guys like the three walking away with their tails between their legs. She was just thankful that they didn't flash their canines at them and just left. Security couldn't have arrived fast enough to preserve the fur on their asses.

Instead of pulling up chairs, they pulled up tables to the displeasure of security but none of them approached them as Mona burst out laughing at their antics. For the remainder of the evening, they got better acquainted as certain ones clique like Donna and Tek9 and Monica and Kimba. Mona and Afrika found themselves up on the balcony having a private moment and conversing. She admitted to dating Theo again to the pleasure of her father, but not giving him the monogamist relationship he desperately craved and desired. No, she wasn't fucking every Tom, Dick, or Harry. She has more respect for herself than that, but she was leaving her options opens. His journey to acquire her trust again wouldn't be an easy task. He could keep the flowers and words of endearment. She didn't desire either. Time will only heal what was ailing her and not his promises or some damn flowers.

While the fellas took in the city with her girls, he and Mona took quality time for themselves. They made extremely passionate love. He have witness and caress some beautiful women bodies, but none could compare to Mona, not even Aziza and she had a banging ass body. They laid in one another arms whispering and laughing for hours. Their embrace that morning felt different as each knew that things in their private lives were about to change, especially Mona's. Neither spoke of the love that they obviously had for each other, but they knew subconsciously life has its own plans and journeys for everyone. They could not predict the next time that they would see one another or fell the embrace of the other. The weekend ended much too quickly for them. Tek9 and Kimba were very reluctant to leave, but they had responsibilities at home that demanded their attention. As they whisper to Donna and Monica, you could see both young ladies had been smitten by them and they were also smitten. Catching the fellas sneaking out of town together every other weekend, they could only shake their heads at them. Climbing on the plane, he never conceded not seeing her for a year, or he might have shared what was hiding in his heart to express. The conversation he had with his partners earlier that morning surprised the hell out of them, but they understood his reasoning. They had watched them over the years and how they interacted. Although he never stepped up, they have been in love with each other since their sophomore year. So, him contemplating on leaving Jersey to build a life with her in Atlanta; they gave their blessing but what about Aziza? Have an unspoken decision been made concerning their, on and off, slow revolving relationship?

Aziza wishing to go out for dinner was the best invitation he had all week. In the past year, they have become much closer, but neither has ever mentioned anything about a commitment during their conversations. Hearing stress in her voice as they tried to decided where to eat was unusual. She had shined a small light on the situation that was transpiring at her job, but she never elaborated fully, and it must be coming to a head. He was sitting outside smoking a blunt when she pulled up on his horse shoe parking pad around eight o'clock. He waked over opening the passenger's door and climbed inside then closed the door before accepting a kiss from her. He fasten his seatbelt then lean back. They decided to go over to Philly at Kisha's in Center City for dinner. She was heavy in thought as they climbed the Ben Franklin Bridge. Twenty minutes later, they were escorted to a table over-looking the skyline. While the candle slowly burned, they were relatively quiet until have way through their meal.

"How long have we been dating again, sweetheart?" she suddenly asked with a serious expression on her face.

"Including our two departures?"

"Yes, darling" she answer solemnly.

"Coming up on fourteen months in July, why?"

"There are several things that I love about you and make you so damn attractive, but your brutal honesty can be devastating. When you told me, you are man enough to answer any questions I desire but be prepared as a woman to accept your answers, you had me pumping on my breaks. You said a woman is extremely inquisitive and to watch out because she might see something that she wish that she didn't. Listen, I'll get back to that conversation because that is not why I invited you to dinner" she sighs and took a deep breath then slowly exhaling. "Do you remember that promotion I was pass over last year?"

"Of course."

"Well, two more positions have open up. Me and this Caucasian sister got the promotions."

"I want to say congratulations, but your eyes are telling me not to, what's the hook?"

"One promotion is here, and the other is in Atlanta. Which one do you think my racist ass boss Mr. Dickweed has me in place to accept?"

"Atlanta" he replied slightly grinning at the fury coming to her eyes.

"I mentioned that I taught the white bitch the ropes and my seniority to him, but he actually shrugged it off like it didn't mean a thing. He said it was my decision to accept or decline. I wanted to leap across that desk and slap that motherfucking smirk off his face. There is no way I'm going to maintain a long-distance relationship with you. They never work because like you said, it makes the heart wonder. What am I going to do, baby? I can't ask you to give up what you are building to come with me."

"Sure, you can, and I would come" he told her causing her to smile. "From where I'm sitting, you and I have the same problem."

"And what's that, sweetheart?"

"Our respected bosses doesn't appreciate what we bring to the table. Queen, I've watched you bring some very prestigious clients to your firm with your beautiful smile and genuine personality. I've witness how you interacted with them, and they genuinely adore you. You are a particularly important lawyer to the firms and losing those accounts depends on you. If you refuse the promotion and stays, like he hopes, the accounts remain firmly in place even if you go to Atlanta" he informed her. "If you resign, his bosses will want to know why especially if they have a conversation with you first" he said slightly smiling at her. "As for myself, the Hines are trying to pull wool over my eyes. I had a heated conversation with James, and he allowed that alcoholic tongue slip some information that he shouldn't have let slip. They don't have any intentions on making me a partner" he shared slightly hardening his eyes.

"A partner!" she smiled over at him.

"They are trying to deceive me, again Z" he slightly grinned at their antics. "They are throwing pipe dreams at me, baby. I know I gave them a new lease on life with my street connections, but I can also be their grim reaper also" he slightly snarled. "I don't like where my head is heading."

"What's in your head, sweetheart?"

"Deviousness" he admitted staring coldly into her eyes. "They have been boasting about this new building they purchased and the corner office with a secretary for me, like I need a damn secretary" he snorted. "I've known about this move for weeks. I got the 411 from Tweety. You never reveal your hands to me if they aren't clean and theirs are filthy. When scandalous thoughts materialize in my thought process, the person initiating them should watch out and I referring specifically to the Hines."

"I wish I could shake things off as easily as you do" she admitted slightly shaking her head.

"I'm not going to allow anybody to break my peace, especially the Hines. I'm going to sign on with their pipe dreams verbally, but when it's time to resign my contract with them, they will get the biggest surprise I can muster" he slightly grinned again. "As they have taught me, deception is the core essence of a liar. With my connections on the streets and my bank account, I can initiate my aspirations."

"What is that?" she asked taking a sip from her glass of wine. He have never shared his aspirations with her.

"Owning my own law firm" he announced.

"What?" she stated starring over at him. "Baby, that, is going to take a lot more money than what's in your bank account."

"Do you know what's in my account?"

"Of course, not but what you are contemplating will take a couple of hundred thousand dollars and maybe using your home as collateral but that will be for a small office."

"I know baby" he grinned at her. "You are very important to my plans after listening to you over the past year."

"Me?"

"Yeah, you. You should have never educated me about business law and the money that's out there. I want you to run the business section of what I want to do."

"Me?"

"Is that the only word you know?" he asked smiling at her. "Yes, you Aziza. I have a strong financial support group behind me if I need it. All I need to know is if you are down?"

"If you are leading, yeah but I have a few things I need to air out first. I'm going to make my supervisor aware of the prejudicial tendencies being practice when it comes to promotions. I have some very business conscious friends that are also being held back from promotions also and would love a change of environment once we get things off the ground."

"Try not to worry and drop all of your apprehensions. I got this and you" he told her with that impish smile that she haven't determined if she likes it or not. One thing for sure, he had an ace in the whole that he wasn't ready to share with her yet, but rest assure, he have done his homework thoroughly.

Two weeks later, they were packing their things and having their property transferred to a quaint building near East Orange. The Hines were certain that their clients would travel a little further to have them represent them and they were right. Several highways connected to their new location including a bus route for those that don't drive. Sitting in their massive office over-looking their accomplishment, the Hines felt like they were on top of the world. Their fall will be that must greater if they didn't change their scandalous ways.

In May, Afrika received a surprise invitation informing him of the marriage of Ramona Garrett to Theodore Roosevelt in July. He stared at the invitation shock. He didn't know how he should feel about her reunion. Joy damn sure wasn't one of the emotions. He wasn't losing just an extremely good friend, but also, one hell of an excellent lover. The question that kept plaguing his mind was why? Why him after all she had shared with him about Theo? Just as soon as he formulated the question, he knew the answer. Because of him, she had waited all these years and kept a flicker of hope alive that he would commit to her and surrender to the love he possesses for her, but he wouldn't or couldn't. If he requested that she come live with him in Jersey, she was positive that she would and there lies the threat. Being associated to the drug game, he couldn't, no wouldn't put her in such an unnecessary style of life. Someone might get a scandalous idea to touch her and that wouldn't be healthy for the person entire roots. None of his partners have a main lady because of that exact reason. Who wants to lose their loved one to a game they weren't associated with simply because you can't dictate who your heart will love?

He remember lying on the couch listening to Peggy Lee singing "Black Coffee" his junior year when the front door suddenly opens. A smile came to his face. She had told him that she would never use the key he had given to her last year, but she finally did. She uncharacteristically dropped her crossbody bag on the floor then climbed upon him as she rested her head against his chest then wrapped her arms around him. The scent of her biochemistry mixing with the perfume she was wearing had his heart fluttering like a little boy and beating slightly faster as he inhaled deeply. Feeling her breast against him only heighten what was affecting him. Her fingers slightly rubbing his abs had him slightly restricting them. Only when he felt her tears dropping did his exotic journey cease and he froze. He slightly adjusted himself and held her gently as she eventually went to sleep. Hours later when she open her eyes, he was still holding her but reading. She smiled up at him then lightly kissed him for the first time before peeling herself from his arms and grabbing her bag. She shook her head at him then gave him that mysterious smile that has always caused a certain expression to engulf his face. He didn't have the vaguest idea what the expression was signifying, and she wasn't sharing shit, but she would always start giggling before walking out the door.

Not the one to play the single scene, she regressed back to what she was familiar and once comfortable with even if it wasn't entertaining. Theo was forced to decide either accept the drastic changes in her personality or step the fuck off. He apparently got aboard or would have lost her for life. Her father was so delighted for him while mother showed and told her disappointment to her husband. She knew her daughter held a flame in her heart for Afrika. They have gotten so close since returning home like a mother and daughter relationship should be. She had fallen in love with Afrika, just like her daughter did, from the numerous of hilarious stories she shared. He was definitely a rare find like Mona had attested and found herself openly admitting it to him when she interrupted their phone conversation. She did subtly try to coerce him to move to Atlanta when he passed the bar exam where a well-paying job would be waiting for him on his arrival. He was openly flatter but had to decline. She remember the night Mona suddenly came to their house with cloudy eyes and pulled her aside. She confessed to being so in love with Afrika that it hurts pleasantly but she was going to accept Theo's marriage proposal. How was she supposed to say congratulations when she wasn't marrying the man that she actually love but a substitute. One day, she must tell her about Kali (energy).

Afrika was still contemplating if he was going to ask Aziza to escort him or leave her to her private life. He haven't heard from her in two days but that wasn't unusual anymore. When his partners announced that they were flying solo, the decision was made for him. On Saturday morning, they were climbing on their ten o'clock flight at Philadelphia International for Dekalb Peachtree Airport in Georgia. They arrived at their destination at eleven-thirty and went straight to the Hertz rental to retrieve the two Lincoln Aviator's they had reserved. Arriving at the Atlanta Marriott Suites Midtown on 14th Street and entering carrying their garment bags, all eyes feel on them. Seven professionally dress young black men with their eyes hidden by sunglasses. As Bear and Afrika signed everybody in and retrieve their electronic keys, the fellas was scanning the place for prospects as usual. Minutes later, they came back dispensing keys then taking the elevator to the fifteenth floor and walked to their suites. Bear and Amir was sharing on as was Tek9 and Kimba. Black and Afrika had separate room because they knew he needed his space. They knew how he felt about Mona and the dilemma that he was now facing. After placing their clothes away, they made their calls.

"Where are you?" Mona asked smiling from ear to ear with music and cackling women in the background.

"At the Midtown Marriott" he replied. "Congratulations" he said solemnly.

"I can tell you don't mean it, but I won't hold it against you."

"I appreciate it" he replied slightly smiling. "So, where is this bachelorette party being given?"

"Where ever you are at?" she replied softly with an impish grin.

"You know where I am."

"I'll be there by nine o'clock. Looking at Donna prissy butt and Monica, I can tell they are talking to Tek9 and Kimba. I'll see you in a couple of hours" she said ending their conversation.

Around nine o'clock, the ladies arrived and wearing broad smiles as they hugged one another. With everything that they need for an enjoyable evening, they sat around the living room and out on the balcony socializing and dancing. It was around midnight when Mona clutched his fingers and walked out the suite. They enter a suite on the seventh floor that she had reserved. There was white, red, and pink rose pedals leading from the front door to the bedroom. White representing their friendship, red for the love and pink for the passion they held for one another. As they walked on the rose pedals, she instantly started disrobing with Afrika following her lead. The bed was completely consumed with pedals. They made intense and passionate love until three o'clock in the morning. Tears flowed freely from her eyes as he took her on her final erotic journey with him. Lying in one another's arms, neither knew what to say.

"So, who is she?" she asked staring up at him while lying on his chest.

"Her name is Aziza."

"Do you love her?"

"I thought I did once" he admitted softly. "If I was truly in love with her, I wouldn't be here with you Mona and enjoying myself immensely without any remorse" he confessed never averting his eyes from hers.

"No, you wouldn't be here with me" she admitted smiling up at the seriousness in his eyes. "I don't know what's going on up in that sister's head and don't care why she haven't won your love either" she shared grinning. "Do you still love me?"

"Make no mistake about what I am going to say, Mona. I will aways be in love with you, especially internally and it breaks my heart that you aren't marrying me. With the things going on in my private life, and you getting hurt because of it, I would go insane with rage and my partners will willingly follow me. I won't place any of y'all in danger. I won't baby especially you" he finally told her, and the weight of the world seem to be lifted.

"You know how naïve I can be even when shit is right in front of my face?" she asked grinning.

"Yeah" he replied lightly snickering.

"Well, not this time. I suspected everything that you just said. The first time I saw you defending my honor wasn't very pleasant for the person, but I saw your conviction, you are willing to not just protect me but defend my honor. Who couldn't fall in love with a knight like you?" she asked grinning.

"Theo, Mona?"

"I know, I know" she sighs rubbing his face. "He look so pitiful, Afrika."

"Like you did?"

"Yeah, but look at the woman you assisted in creating from those burning ashes like a rising Phoenix and I will always love you for that. I'm not marrying Theo because I'm in love with him. He knows I am not. I'm in love with you and if you told me not to marry him, I wouldn't" she confessed not denying the love she still possesses for him.

"You know I won't do that, but I do know a special part of my life is coming to an end" he shared staring into her grayish sorrow filled eyes. "Only time will ease the pain I am feeling. I honestly don't know if I will ever get over you."

"You better not" she smiled up at him. She always knew what his lips wouldn't confess until now. All she could do was lock his love away and hold tight to the memories they have created together over the years.

Her wedding took place at two o'clock sharp. As friends and loved ones of the groom and bride took their respective sides of the isle, Afrika was noticeably absent from the festivities. As much as he wanted to witness her in her gown, he couldn't witness her marrying Theo. The person that actually broke her heart. The person that when she needed her Daddy for assurance and that everything will be okay, his bitch ass instead sided with the foe. How can any man respect a man, especially a father, that choses foe over family? When the minister asked, if there was anyone that opposes to this union, he might have stood up advocating why she shouldn't marry a punk ass motherfucker like him. Her father would probably have caught a heart attack as her mother was screaming out "Halleluiah!" standing behind Mona's smiling face. The parents of the groom would be wondering what in the hell is transpiring and who in the fuck is this stranger that had the girl that their son was about to marry so got damn elated? His partners would have been laughing for weeks after witnessing such a spectacle. The thought made him suddenly chuckle. Na, he didn't need to create a comedy with his antics because it wouldn't have been no drama. They would have shut them down. All of that might be a fantasy of his but nothing brought a broader smile to his face than when Bear called him whispering, she is refusing to allow her father to escort her down the aisle and openly asked where you was to escort her or she will talk alone, but not with him. Now that was hilarious. As Afrika sat there watching the sun gradually descending over Silver Lake, he took a deep breath then got to his feet.

When he attended the reception, he kept his distance although they exchanged stares often. Her parents also watched them and knew their daughter had not married with her heart, like her mother, but out of convenience and familiarity. She had watched the six well-dressed young men that had accompany Afrika keeping their distance from him also while peeking at Theo with sightly harden eyes then flashing their genuine warm smile at her. How do prissy ass Donna know that gentleman as well as she does openly clutch his fingers and giggling? The same could be said about Monica. They are apparently smitten by them. They reserved all songs for them and them only. Observing how the small group interacting, have they ever gone to Camden? Na, they must have meet down here but when? Arriving yesterday wouldn't produce what she was seeing. She found herself methodically getting to her feet with her glass of brandy and walking in Afrika's direction. She exchanged a brief stare with her daughter as she continued on her unknown journey and intrude on his private thoughts. She needed to have a private conversation with him that she hopes he wouldn't avoid.

Seeing her approaching, Afrika got to his feet. "How are you, Mrs. G?"

"How are you being the better question, Afrika?" she counter ignoring his question.

"I thought I could witness my best friend getting married, but I wasn't strong enough" he admitted grinning down on her. "Have a seat, please" he offer as she accepted his invitation. "Your daughter and I have been in love with one another since our sophomore year, but I knew she needed a friend not a new lover to heal her wounded heart and I became that for her. My perceive status doesn't dictate a person self-worth or morals. "Your husband" he suddenly snarled staring over at him.

"When I heard what he said to you, I was appalled" she admitted hardening her eyes. "I'm the bread winner in this monarch not his broke ass" she shared slowly softening her eyes. "I adore what your interaction with Mona have produced" she smiled revealing where Mona had obtained her impish smile. "She is so confident and strong."

"And she is hard headed as heck" he included grinning.

"Who Mona?" she asked surprised.

"Yes, ma'am Mona" he replied suddenly smiling. "You are going to need a stiffer drink" he warned her as they stared over at Mona staring at them very peculiar then they burst out laughing at her. He actually revealed his hand to her and don't know why he did, but he did. He confessed to doing things in the streets that he must pay restitution and wouldn't put Mona in harm's way as he does. That is the only reason why he never ask her for her hand for marriage. Everything that he has been accomplishing was a direct reflection from Mona's nagging butt. He shared little stories with her that Mona would never share with her causing tears to fall from her eyes from laughing so hard and insisting that he wait a minute before continuing. Her light touches only heighten and revealed her respect for him. When she got to her feet with him and open her arms to him, Mona watched their interacting and smiled. He had won another woman over.

Her father was also watching their interaction and was shocked to see her giving him a hug after their conversation.

Watching her genuinely laughing and touching him, his jealousy had the audacity to raise its head. She really appreciated him for the transformation he was responsible for in their daughter. He have repeatedly tried to apologize to her, but she wouldn't be receptive and rightfully so. He did abandon his own daughter in her time of need. She refusing him the privilege of escorting her down the aisle was her conviction and feelings towards him. Yes, he did scrutinize Afrika without getting to know him. How was he to know that they guy wasn't playing her for the money that she will inherit upon her mother's demise? He was coming from out of ravage torn Camden and the report he obtained from the private investigator warranted his skepticism. How was he to know that young man would know his own law firm and come highly recommended in the northeast according to the Black Lawyers Association at the age of twenty-five? The picture of them in her bedroom revealed their friendship by the smile that consumed her face and in her eyes. She was so happy standing near him, but now, he kept his distance like she was the plague. She will now have to find some form of happiness with Theo and not him. When he wouldn't accept his weak ass apology, he knew he would never get the chance to truly interact with him and see why even his wife adored him. Everything that Theo will acquire will be coming from his parents, but he couldn't say the same for Afrika.

They went to change their clothes around eight o'clock after taking their pictures. When they returned, she went looking for him. She methodically walked around looking for him everywhere. She found Donna and Monica in Tek9 and Kimba arms. Bear and Amir was flirting with some friend of Theo. Black was discussing something with T.T that caused her to burst out laughing then engulfing his face with her hands still giggling. She searched everywhere but Afrika was M.I.A.

"He subtly left over an hour ago to catch an earlier flight home, baby" her mother walked up behind her whispering causing her to turn around.

"What?"

"He left Mona" she repeated staring at the sadness creeping into her eyes. "I really like that young man."

"So does I, Mom" she replied staring into her eyes while trying to contain her tears but failing. "He's the man of my dreams" she signs as her mother held her tightly.

"I must tell you about Kali" she heard herself say.

"Who?" she asked gently pushing her out of her arms and staring at the impish smile on her face.

"The man I should have married instead of out of convince" she replied peeking over at her husband then back into her eyes. "By the way, you aren't as innocent as you portray either, young lady."

"What are you talking about, Mom?"

"Cruising his set and getting your car jack. Did you actually asked him to help you get out of your clothes and on numerous occasions?" she mentioned causing Mona to burst out laughing.

"He told you all that?" she asked trying to contain her giggles, but her mother's expression was priceless.

"From your snotty nose about your car to your constant nagging like a wife" she told her while giggling. "He only told me what he knew I could handle" she shared smiling.

"That's why I love him so much, Mom. He never took advantage of my vulnerability or my undeniable attraction to him, but I'm still going to punch him in the mouth for snitching on me" she said slightly hardening her eyes and causing her mother to burst out laughing again. "I'm going to miss him dearly."

"He's never too far away sweetheart. Never" she said cupping her face in her hands and kissing her on the cheek then walking away.

His flight home was a complete blur. He could vaguely remember boarding the plane less alone walking through the terminal. The two young ladies that were trying to strike up a conversation must have thought he had some form of mental condition for ignoring them. Exiting the plane, retrieving his garment bag, and exiting the terminal was also a blank to him. He do remember climbing into the cab but not being driven home or methodically walking towards his house ignoring Freda's attempts at getting his attention. He took a couple of days off from work surprising everybody. He didn't realize that he was in a state of depression until days later when he stared into the mirror. The individual staring back at him looked beaten down from the inside out. A FedEx driver delivered a package that needed his signature a week later and he took it into the family room then open it. He stared at the present. It was a picture of them at Café 290 on the night she got him to recite a poem. There was a look of love undeniably in their eyes that caused him to suddenly laugh for the first time since returning home and his depression was suddenly gone. Someone in the club had taken the picture and shared it with her when they ran into her. He blew the picture up to a poster size then placed it on the basement wall, next to his partners, in front of the couch so he could always see it.

When he saw his partners days later, they were glad that he finally snapped out of his state of depression and was smiling again. They around in his family room sharing intimate thoughts especially concerning their futures. Tek9 and Kima damn near had their bags back to move to Atlanta. Bear shared how Amir had been whispering to him about getting out the game. They all had more than enough money to sustain them comfortably. Trade school was also mentioned. Through everything that they discussed, no mention of when they would institute their exit plan. Afrika knew it would be his responsibility to tell them that it was time to come home.

Aziza made a surprise visit one Saturday afternoon. He was down in the basement listening to Louis Armstrong singing "Hello Dolly" live then he heard the doorbell. He got to his feet and ascended the stairs then casually walked through the house and opens the door.

"Hey, what's up?" he asked kissing her lightly then closing the door.

"Nothing much" she replied following him through the house. She was surprised to see him continuing through the house and heading towards the basement then descending the stairs. She had been down there only once in the past year. He would spend the time there occasionally especially when he was in heavy thought and didn't have a problem telling you that he needed time alone. He wasn't asking you to leave his home but definitely wanted you out of his space. She remember waiting almost three hours while he was working something out for his partners. With the lights extremely low and jazz playing, she took a seat next to him. He had a glass of Parrot Bay in front of him and several blunts spread out on the coffee table with a book called, "The Product of My Environment" that he was reading. She peeked up and noticed a massive picture of him with another woman. She found herself getting to her feet and walking over to inspect the picture closely. The look that was engulfed on their faces caused her to turn and stare at him before asking. "Who is she, Afrika?" she asked in a low soft voice while walking over and seeking his eyes in the dim light then taking a seat next to him.

"Her name is Ramona" he asked extending a glass to her which she accepted.

"A friend?" she asked apprehensively.

"Since our sophomore year at Rutgers" he shared. "When you first step off from me, she was the one that help me keep it together."

"Was y'all lovers?" she intrusively asked while staring in his eyes.

"Yes."

"Where is she? Does she live near Camden?"

"Na, she lives in Atlanta. She got married six weeks ago" he shared.

"Was you there?"

"Of course, she's my girl" he replied grinning.

"Did you love her?"

"Did? No, still do" he replied honesty returning her stare.

"If you still do, why aren't you with her?"

"Different sides of the tracks" he offered as an explanation.

"No, I need more than a quaint answer" she insisted.

"Moving to Atlanta wasn't an option, I'm making restitution here" he reminded her. "If I told her to join me in Jersey, she would have without any hesitation, but she knows of my obligations" he shared. "Anything else?"

"No" she replied softly. "Y'all do look very much in love."

"People said the same thing about you and me but did that keep you by my side?" he reminded her.

"No" she replied lowering her eyes. "But that didn't mean I didn't love you."

"What did it mean, Z? Self-preservation or selfishness?" he asked slightly hardening his eyes while hoping for some clarity.

"I don't know Afrika, but it didn't mean that I didn't love you" she replied but not returning his stare as she lit a blunt and pulled from it before extending it to him. How can she tell him that it was for self-preservation that made her walk away from him and the love he was openly displaying. She had heard of this Mona character from ear hustling around his partners and their part-time girlfriends. They all spoke highly of her and her humorous disposition. She never expected her to be so motherfucking attractive. If they had hooked up, she would have lost him for sure. Now all she could do is stare into the eyes of the woman that he loved and be thankful for this third chance to get it right.

Two months later, Afrika was being accompanied by Aziza for an appointment. Butch Williams was surprised to receive a call from him, and his curiosity only heighten when he requested having lunch. Most people that sat across from him were making illegal transactions and he knew this lunch engagement wouldn't consist of anything illegal, or would it? As he and Aziza enter the exquisite restaurant in Cherry Hill, they removed their sunglasses then scanned the area. Butch Williams was sitting towards the far-right corner over-looking the pond. He motioned to the hostess to allow them to pass. His two bodyguards got to their feel and scrutinizing the two strangers approaching until Butch waved them off as they reclaimed their seats.

"Brother Afrika" he greeted getting to his feet with a broad smile and shaking his hand.

"How have you been, Mr. Williams?" he asked returning his smile. "This is my lady Aziza."

"Glad to make your acquaintance" he replied shaking her hand lightly then motioning them to take a seat. "Are you the same Aziza Jackson that works at Michael's over in Philly on Broad Street?"

"Why, yes I am" she replied surprise that he have heard of her.

"I hope those foolish white boys know your worth."

"I assure you that they don't" she replied slightly hardening her eyes causing him to lightly chuckle.

"I used to see you and Afrika around a lot. So, I made an inquiry about you. I hope that doesn't offend you."

"No, it doesn't Mr. Williams but you could have gotten your information straight from the horses' mouth."

"Oh, I like her Afrika" he suddenly burst out laughing.

"Yeah, I'm starting to like her also" he shared avoiding her elbow.

"I know you are not here to freeload a free lunch: he mentioned grinning. "So, what is it son?"

"You told me a couple of years ago that if I ever needed you to reach out to you. Well, I'm reaching out" he replied returning his stare.

"What is it that I can do for you?"

"I heard through the grapevine that you have several buildings that you are trying to relinquish" he shared.

"So, you are finally ready to step off from the Hines, huh?" he asked ignoring his question.

"Yes, sir" he admitted. "There apparently isn't any future for me there."

"I rationalized that about two years ago" he said grinning. "I ran into them at a social event about six months ago. With the alcohol loosening their alcoholic tongues, they boasted about the seven million dollar building that had just purchased. I thought it was rather high for that location" he voiced his opinion. "If you aren't hungry, I have something that I want to show you."

"I'm not hungry baby" replied Aziza. "I'm very curious about that smile on his face" she admitted staring across the table at him.

"Time will reveal" he replied suddenly getting to his feet. "Can she ride with me Afrika?"

"I don't need his permission" she informed him while smiling over at Afrika then gripping Butch arm. She was a good five inches taller than him.

"She's that independent woman that has most guys running from her, Mr. Williams" he replied following them out the restaurant with his bodyguards close by.

They climbed into his Big Boy Benz and proceeded towards Marlton Pike while he followed them. When they pulled up on a parking lot and climbed out, Afrika instantly like the building curb appeal and the location was ridiculous. A one bus ride from down town Camden will take a person thirty to forty minutes to reach the location and a fifteen-minute ride on the speedline with a ten-minute walk to the building. Entering the main entrance clutching fingers, they took the elevator to the second floor then exited. The place wasn't large but humongous. Bathrooms were located by the elevators for clients with two additional sets further back that could be utilized by staff members only. There were eight offices encased in glass with an open floor plan just waiting for some definition. Down the only hallway was two huge offices also encased but in a smoke glass with opposite views of the skyline. Private bathrooms were in both offices with a secretary desk and all the amenities our front of the offices.

"Well, what do you think?" he asked staring at the couple.

"Impressive to say the lease" admitted Afrika.

"I have a hook up for everything a new budding company would need. From desks to phones to file cabinets to comfortable chairs for your staff. I have it all. From fax machines to copiers, electric typewriters, and computers, I have it all for you at a discount price" he mentioned still grinning.

"With everything included and because it is you, give me five million dollars."

"We will take it!" interjected Aziza before the final syllable had escaped his mouth.

"Damn, Z" Afrika said staring over at her. "With you salivating like some damn rabid dog, you left no room for negotiations" he said slightly shaking his head at her.

"I'm sorry sweetheart but no time for bullshitting" she replied kissing him lightly on the lips then smiled up at him. "We will take it, Mr. Williams."

"No hesitation huh young lady?"

"I know a good deal when I hear one" she replied. "How much do we have to put down?"

"Nothing" he replied.

"Nothing!?" she replied smiling over at him then at Afrika's stern expression and her jubilation slowly dissipated as she stared at the two men exchanging stares.

"Na, I can't accept that Mr. Williams" he informed him. "As long as I have a note on this building, the longer I am a slave for you. Five million., huh?" he repeated not like the possession he was suddenly in, but this was his dream. Fuck it. "I can have it in your hands by tomorrow" he informed him causing him to slightly react and so did Aziza. "Do you want it in a cashier check or in cash?"

"Cashier" he replied.

"I can be at your office by ten o'clock tomorrow."

"I will have my lawyer gather all the necessary papers for your signature later today. If you give me a couple days of advancement, I can everything in place and to your specification, okay?"

"Yes, sir" he replied while shaking his hand and smiling.

As they proceeded back to the elevator, Aziza gripped their arms like a little girl in a doll store. Butch was definitely smitten by her charm and warm disposition. Once they said their goodbyes, he assisted Aziza into her seat then proceeded towards maple shades for their late lunch. Jumping on Rt. 38, she fired up the blunt she was smoking previously then stared over at him seemingly concentrating on the road.

"I can't believe your good fortune. That building is in a prime sweetheart and worth easily three times as much in today's market.

"I didn't know" he replied casually cruising with the late afternoon traffic.

As they road in silence, she was in heavy thought. She would peek at him occasionally and a faint smile would crease her lips then dissipate. She took a deep breath then slowly exhaled. "Honey" she called softly grabbing his attention from the jazz he was listening enjoying and catching his eyes.

"Yeah, what's up love?" he asked taking a quick peek at her then focusing back on the road.

"Do you know what me and Mr. Williams were discussing traveling to the building?"

"How beautiful you are?" he replied accepting the blunt from her.

"Na, our break ups" she replied causing him to peek over at her again. "When I asked how did he know about them? He told me that people stop seeing us together. They knew that something personally had to occurred, but nothing came on the grapevine about our break ups. The circle that you travel in is too tight and people had enough common sense not to inquire through one of your partners. He made me see that at one time we were inseparable" she slightly smiled. "It didn't take me long to understand that you are the man for me, despite your faults."

"No one walking this earth is, Z" he stated peeking over at her as he extended her blunt back to her.

"I can't dispute that" she admitted accepting the blunt then leaning back and staring out the window. There were factors in their separations. Factors that didn't have anything to do with them personally but with her inquisitiveness. There were a lot of things that she needed to know concerning him although he was brutally open and honest, but he was also extremely secretive. He had warned her several times to be careful of the questions that she asked because he was man enough to answer them and let the cards fall as they will.

She was absolutely positive that he was monogamist although women were constantly vying for his attention, but he always made her feel and know her position in his heart. Yet, her inquisitiveness one night had her asking a very inappropriate question concerning his finances. If she had studied his eyes more closely instead of his smile, she would have retracted the question.

"Are you sure you want to know like it is important?" he asked, and she said yes. He didn't know how she was going to react to the information that he was about to share, but he knew he had to confide in her eventually and let her make her own decision concerning them. So, he confessed to being a drug distributor while obtaining his degree and still does sometimes when needed. The look of surprise that engulfed her face was expected, but he was admittedly shocked when she took a step backward. At no time during their interactions in the streets or at the exclusive functions that they attended, did business interfere with them or the love that was gradually building between them. There was no doubt that she found him extremely charming and witty with his ability to recite what was shared weeks before. He could do it word for word if necessary. He was that attentive when he wants to be. Sexy as a motherfucker but also so grounded, you have to laugh at him sometimes not understanding how handsome he is. Not quick to share a smile around strangers, but when he does, he could illuminate the entire area. No, he didn't want a ride and die bitch although he found their dedication very admirable. He couldn't stand losing the woman he love to the streets that he sometimes call home. Na, he desired the woman he loves to be home safe and raising their children. With all the information he had shared with her, she still found herself stepping off. His eyes pleaded for his lips, but she ignored them. She kissed him lightly on the lips then walked away. After witnessing him weeks later socializing with different women and watching them becoming lost by his charm, she knew she had better come to a definitive answer concerning him or keep doing what she was doing, absolutely wasting her time on different dates. The guys weren't seeking anything permanently but subtly trying to convince her to share her bed or their beds. She found herself showing up at his home unannounced one night. How was she to know from that blissful night that she would lose him again weeks later from another selfish act except this time for over a year.

"So, what are your next moves? How are you going to get five million by tomorrow morning?" she asked not seeing any indication in his private life that he could get his hands on that much money overnight. Granted, he did possess a high credit score, some awfully expensive tailor suits and very few jewelries. The only collateral he actually have is that gorgeous home he owns but its valued at a million-one now. "How baby?"

"I have the money already, Z" he replied nonchalantly while peeking at her.

"What?" she heard herself say. "You have the money already?"

"You know what I used to do full time and I'm not about being flashy about what I have" he informed her. "Plus, I have people that owes me on the streets, and they need to pay up if they ever want me to represent them again" he said slightly hardening his eyes as he pressed on the accelerator.

She was openly stun that he had the money. Where? How? The latter she knew but the initial question remained elusive. Why does he still drive that Chrysler 300 when he could afford almost any car he desired. She had to stop and reflect for a minute. He was always ready to impress her with his culinary skills when she offer to take him out to dinner. He would rather sit in the park enjoying the scenery than sit in a movie theater. He rather attend the free museums or art galleries admiring its artifacts than spend his money in any place that display an exclusion disposition by their service, but willing to take your money. His partners were always calling him cheap, but he would counter that he was just money conscious. He evolved from poverty-stricken Camden, and nothing is given away especially their money. Perhaps she needs to check herself. She spends her money much too freely especially since she didn't have any real responsibilities like a child. All she has is a car note and rent. Why haven't she brought her own home as he suggested then stressed three years ago? With what she paying in rent, she damn sure could afford a mortgage.

In the weeks since his meeting with Butch Williams, Afrika had stayed extremely focused and busy. His personal life, his hobby and extreme workouts all took a back seat while he brought forth his aspiration. His partners, Aziza and his few tight friends had to adjust to him suddenly being selfish with his time. He made himself unavailable even to attend three events dedicated to him that he usually would attend. He was burning the candle at both ends and it didn't go unnoticed by the staff or the Hines brothers either. He was always there before they arrived and was still on his grind long after they had gone home for the night. They just didn't know what to make out of his extreme dedication. His success rate was a staggering ninety percent and that doesn't include getting his clients an excellent plea agreement when necessary to avoid a trial. Circumstantial evidence didn't stand a ghost of a chance with him as the prosecutor's office have found out over the years. Dissecting and scrutinizing every alleged piece of evidence against his clients have bred doubt in the minds of some jurors. He had a natural flow with his deliverance like he had rehearsed a script and the alluring tones, as some female prosecutor classified it, captivated some women jurors. His mind was too much like a criminal's at times. He can be very devious and set a trap to stress a point. Although on the opposite sides of the penal, he had established an exceptionally good relationship with several prosecutors during the lawyers conference and social events.

Between setting up his secret law firm and closing out cases, he was placing large checks in Robert's hands while he spent every free minute preparing for his eventual departure. On Friday, he dropped envelopes on specific desks as he was leaving around two o'clock. The first time he have left early in weeks. As he waited for the elevator, he drop an invitation at Tweety desk also before casually walking on the elevator. He descended to the first floor then step outside and took a deep breath before walking to his car and climbing inside. Starting up the car, J.J. Johnson's "J Is For Jazz" filled the interior as he pulled away.

"Robert is you busy?" inquired James sticking his head in his office.

"Na, I was just sitting here thinking" he admitted taking another sip from his glass of bourbon.

"Thinking about what?" he asked coming further in then closing the door.

"Afrika" he replied staring over at him.

"So, have I" he admitted walking over to the mini bar and pouring himself a shot of Jonny Walker Red. "I think Afrika got something brewing up in his motherfucking head" he stated taking a seat in front of his desk.

"Do you really blame him?" he asked returning his stare.

"What do you mean?" he asked taking a sig from his drink.

"I'm trying to play with words, and he catches me every time. I have told you repeatedly about fucking with his shit, but my words are going in one ear and out the other" he reminded him slightly snarling. "You see these?" he asked holding several checks in his hand. "I am holding eighty-thousand dollars. How am I able to this? Afrika" he stated. "What is it with you and him anyway?"

"I don't like his arrogant ass" he stated coldly while slightly slurring his words.

"Arrogant?" he suddenly burst out laughing. "The man is extremely humble" he corrected him. "I stressed to you how important it is that he feel secure here or the motherfuckers we jump in bed with will be checking us out especially if he doesn't renew his contract."

"He isn't going anywhere. Throw his bitch ass some more crumbs" he suggested downing his drink then refilling the glass.

"He's not going to continue to be satisfied with those crumbs we have been throwing to him the past two years. We need to secure him with a partnership."

"Partnership!? Fuck that! Hell no!" he stated adamantly. "I'm not giving that motherfucker shit especially a partnership!"

"We need him, James."

"No, we don't. Look at where we came from and where we are. We don't need him, Rob" he insisted staring at him through glossy eyes. "Motherfuckers have heard about us now and they will keep coming" he insisted confidently.

"Put that damn glass down!" he told him watching him gulping down his drink. "Did you hear me!?" he asked slightly hardening his eyes as he followed his instructions. "Where we came from was a law firm barely breathing and on life support until Afrika walked through our motherfucking door then pump life back into us. Don't get that shit twisted in your dumb ass head. He single handed resurrected our scandalous asses. He's making some kind of restitution is the only reason why he chose us over the more prestigious law firms. I personally don't care what indiscretion he's making restitution for because who have done more fucked up shit over the years than us? Who?" he asked glaring over at him. "What he have achieved for you, and I is a remarkable. These" she said shaking the checks. "These are his work and connections not ours. Connections that you and I could never have acquired from the streets. What do you think these connections will do if he leaves? Do you really think they will stay with us?" he asked with a sudden chuckle. "Did you know other law firms are already vying for his attention? Did you?" he asked returning his stare. "Well?"

"No" he replied solemnly.

"Well, they are stupid. They know the contract with us is up in a couple of weeks and are putting themselves in a good compromising position with him especially Barnes and Barnes."

"Barnes and Barnes are still sniffing after him after all this time?" he asked totally surprised.

"Where have you been the past three years dummy? Have you or I ever been mentioned in the Black Lawyers Magazine?" he asked slightly shaking his head at him. "He's been mentioned five times and Barnes was the first to congratulate him, but you and I didn't. He's been invited to several prestigious parties by politicians and why do you think they are inviting him?" he inquired with a smirk. "Since he walked through that door, we have never profited like we have never profited in our best years and what have we done? We regressed to the same old scandalous motherfuckers we have always been except now; we don't have to make back alleys deals with the prosecutor's office for their little trinkets. I finally realized why you don't like him also. Because you and I don't possess an ounce of descent moral character or integrity like he does. We won't give him what he deserved because we are self-center and definitely psychotic, or self-destructive. The only way of surviving this shit we are in for the next ten years is to give him the partnership he deserves."

"No!" he replied snarling at the ideal.

"Supposed he goes out on his own?"

"How?" he asked returning his stare. "How is he going to finance any kind of staff? He couldn't even afford a small office anywhere. If he really had money, do you really think he would still be driving that old ass Chrysler 300? The car is at least six years old" he mentioned snickering and causing Robert, to lightly chuckled.

"Okay" he agreed trying to contain his smile. "Maybe he can't afford a new car or an office but there are other options out there he could consider and none in our favor."

"Options? What options?" he snickered again. "Working for another law firm will still have him as a slave."

"Those that are dwelling in the shadows is an option" he informed him watching the smile dissipate from his face. "Where do you think the majority of our clients are coming from? Don't forget about the relationship he has built with Butch Williams over the years. If he decides to take a chance on himself, he just might obtain the money from Butch to obtain a small office somewhere and another lawyer. Do you want that to happen? Well, do you?"

"No" he replied honestly.

"Then you need to get your head around him becoming a partner."

"I don't want to" he replied pouting while getting to his feet and grabbing his glass. He stared down at his older brother then killed his drink and placing the glass on his desk. "We have more than enough time before that decision has to be made. Until then, keep getting those checks from his punk ass" he smiled starting to head to the door.

"Hey" he called to him getting his attention and causing him to turn around. "Two things before you leave."

"Yeah, what are they?"

"Get that motherfucking glass off my desk and put it where it belongs" he stated staring up at him coldly then leaning back in his chair with his glass. "Secondly, if you keep disrespecting Africa's private property after I told you repeatedly, he's going to kick a mud hole in your drunken punk ass, and I'll be damn if I'm going to put myself in harm's way for your stupid shit. The man has some guns under his attire, and they don't have a safety either. Now get the fuck out of my office" he told him placing the glass in the sink then headed towards the door.

When he stared into Robert's eyes before closing the door, he didn't like what he was seeing. He was getting tired of his dumb shit, but he still wasn't feeling Afrika becoming a partner. He and Robert had brought themselves brand new vehicles the first year, but what have Afrika brought to show he was profiting? He haven't brought a got damn thing. He doesn't have anything to show for his work except those motherfucking crumbs at the corner of his lips. He found himself having a private laugh. He has always admired the Infinity's SUV but refused to pay the high price to keep her filled. Now he has one and his little toy for the young ladies, a Dodge Charger. To appease his wife, he brought her the Lincoln Continental that she likes so much and all of them are paid in full. Afrika isn't going anywhere with that yoke around his neck and he damn sure wasn't going to venture out on his own. He will continue bringing money through the door and be happy with the crumbs that they throw at him.

Days later, Robert was sitting at his desk long after everyone had gone home for the night. James never looks at the full spectrum of a picture or situation, but he does now. He learned over the years watching Afrika and the subtle traps he set for the prosecutors. He has won several controversial cases by covering his back door, something that he had never considered. What was going on at his back door? With all the money that Afrika is bringing in, why haven't he brought himself a new car or something to show that he was prospering? He suddenly got to his feet while finishing his drink and placed the glass in the sink. He opened his file cabinet and got Afrika's address from his initial application. He never noticed that he was living in Maple Shades. He thought that he was living in the city somewhere. He grabbed his battered briefcase and walk out his office extinguishing the lights as he went towards the elevators. Exiting the elevator, he locked the exterior door then walked to his car and climbed inside. Starting up the engine, James Brown's "Make It Funky" filtered out the speakers. He entered the address into the navigational system then lit a cigarette and pulled from it deeply allowing the nicotine to relax him. He placed the car in gear then gently pulled off the parking lot heading towards Rt. 130. As he drove, he realized that he haven't been in this area in years. Following the instructions and taking in the scenery, he admired the large single-family homes as the distance to his destination gradually lessen. As he drove down Maple Street, he couldn't believe the size of the houses. He had to damn near slam on his breaks when he realized he damn near drove up to his destination and parked then extinguished the headlights and sat low. He's been living here all the time. His house had things that distinguish it from the other houses like the screen-in balcony from the master bedroom. His home was gorgeous, but it is supposed to be the type of home that the owner of a law firm should own not one of its employees. Was he buying this place, or did he own it? You don't rent in this community. What was he having at his place tonight? Sitting in the shadows that a tree provided, he watched several expensive vehicles finding places to park. The professionally dressed people were stepping out of expensive cars and methodically walking towards the music coming from the back yard. He was stunned to see Frank from the prosecutor's off with his wife, Margaret walking with Naomi. When he spotted Butch getting out of his black Bentley Flying Spur with a date and not having his bodyguards watching his back, he must feel extremely comfortable with the people attending the function. As he started up the engine and pulled away from the curb, he took a final peek at the house. Half way down the block, he spotted Tweety getting out of Shakira's Audi A7 laughing. They were included in the festivities but him or his brother wasn't invited and that wasn't a good sign.

Monday morning, Robert exited the elevator and went straight to James office after exchanging a brief glance at Shakira. He pushed opens his door to catch him pouring himself a stiff drink.

"You want one?" he asked lifting his glass.

"Yeah" he replied loosening his tie as he went to take a seat in front of his desk.

"I went to our watering hole Friday night looking for you, but you weren't around" he mentioned walking around the desk and extending his glass to him. "Where were you?" he asked reclaiming his seat.

"Impulse had me checking my back door" he replied taking a sip from the Johnny Walker Red.

"What?" he asked taking a sip but staring at him perplexed.

"Something that I learned from watching Afrika" he replied slightly grinning while crossing his legs.

"Him again" he stated twisting his face. "Can we at least get the week started before discussing his motherfucking ass" he asked taking another sip while exchanging stares.

"Do you know where Afrika lives?"

"Na, and I don't care" he replied nonchalantly then said. "He's probably in some mouse and roach infested apartment somewhere in or near the city" he replied snickering.

"Well, he has a gorgeous home near Maple Shades" he shared watching the smile leave his face.

"How do you know it's his?"

"Because he was living in it from the first day he walked through our door" he informed him. "Plus, he was having a party there Friday night."

"What party?"

"The one you and I wasn't invited" he replied exchanging his stare. "But Butch Williams was there and so was Frank and Naomi."

"Judge Naomi? Frank from the prosecutor's office?"

"Yeah, including Shakira and Tweety."

"I didn't know he had a relationship with Frank and Naomi."

"Nor did I" he confessed. "Afrika drives the car he does because he chooses to drive it and don't give a damn about keeping up with the Jones. The bonuses he obtained from clients could have easily brought him a new car. He's not out to flashing his status to the world like most people. While we were boasting and spending out money freely, he was banking his. All weekend I was throwing up. I couldn't keep shit down after that revelation Friday night. If what I witness is going to be the basis for his new clients if he doesn't resign with us, we are fucked."

"Give him the partnership" he blurted out almost in a panic.

"Oh, now you want to act like you got some got damn sense. Why couldn't you have it last year?" he asked glaring over at him. "I told you that ship left port a long time ago" he reminded him.

"Give him an additional thirty thousand also" he offered up.

"What got you aboard all of a sudden?" he asked with a little smirk on his face. "You are thinking about your little elaborate lifestyle you had this weekend, huh?" he found himself giggling. "It is too late to make peace with him, he's not built like that. You can't shit on him and expect him to have any form of forgiveness. Like he constantly says, he is not a Christian" he repeated grinning then downing his drink and getting to his feet.

"You have to talk to him Robert" he insisted watching him walking to the sink then towards the door.

"I had him James, but did I do right by him?" he asked opening the door then stepping out. As he walked past Shakira's desk, he very subtly nodded to her causing her to look at him peculiar. He haven't knowledge her in years.

Late Wednesday afternoon, Afrika was returning from court and walked into his office. He turned on his music hearing Bessie Smith voice filtering through Bose speakers singing "Back Water Blues." He dropped his briefcase next to his desk then took his seat. He had to contemplate on what the prosecutor was offering as a plea bargain. Ten years with all suspended but five. The five years that they would be holding over his client's head was his concern. Could he remain law abiding even knowing the consequences of any indiscretions? There star witness is a young lady that his client lays down with sexually frequently. It is during these sexual encounters with these promiscuous and illicit young ladies that some men for some strange or dumb ass reason, discuss their personal lives and what they do in the streets. When ten G reward is offer for information and then S.W.A.T come kicking in your door, do you fault her for you running your mouth and patching her in on a conspiracy charge after the facts? Are your conversation so nonintellectual that all you can do is boast. Well. All he could do was place the offer on the table and hear what his client has to say. If he follows his suggestion, he will tell him to snatch that five up and keep his damn mouth close the next time he's laying down with any woman about what's going on in the streets. A subtle knocking at the door broke his concentration.

"Come in."

"Can we talk?" Robert asked sticking his head in.

"Sure" he replied closing the folder. "Have a seat in one of your chairs" he told sarcastically.

"Listen, Afrika" he began closing the door. "I will be the first to admit that you deserve the partnership in some capacity and it's yours" he told him returning his stare.

"In some compacity, huh" his words didn't slip pass him causing him to slightly smile.

"I'm throwing in an additional thirty thousand dollars increase also."

"Why couldn't you have done this initially, Robert?" he asked staring into his bloodshot eyes. "Why did we have to be where we are today? I was only expecting from you what you initially told me during our initial interview and nothing else, but you started using the word in some compacity."

"I know Afrika."

"If I don't leave up out of here, I'm going to put my foot up your disrespectful brother ass."

"I had a long talk with him, and he will respect your personal stuff. We can work this out. Trust me."

"How am I supposed to trust you again, Robert? Would you trust you, again" he asked flipping the question and smiling at his expression. "Yeah, I thought so. Nothing you are offering can convince me to get back in our corner. A person gets one chance to fuck me, and you have used your chance. Now if you don't mind, I have to figure out a way to convince my client, my bad, your client to accept this offer. So, if you don't mind, I need some privacy" he told him staring into his eyes. That was the nicest way for him to tell him to get the fuck out.

"Afrika" he called while getting to his feet.

"Save your words Robert. You are talking to a deaf person" he informed him returning his stare as he suddenly turned and walked out the office.

He walked back to James office where he was waiting to hear the results of their proposition.

"Well, what did he say?" he asked hoping that the offer would entice him.

"He threw the offer back at me" he replied flopping down in his chair. "He is not forgiving me for not keeping my promise."

"Why don't you let me try?"

"You!" he suddenly burst out laughing then slowly became serious. "All you would do is piss him the fuck off then get fucked up if you try talking back at him slick especially disrespectfully as you usually do. No, you need to continue keeping your distance from him and staying in your lane. I told him if things doesn't work out for him wherever he goes that the door is always open to him. He actually told me to slam it shut. He has no intentions of ever coming back our way again unless something drastically changes his mind."

"What are we going to do Rob?" he asked as apprehension and uncertainty consumed his eyes. "What are we going to do?"

"Watch our spending and wait to see what happens with him" he replied. "If he goes to Barnes and Barnes, we are fucked" he said getting to his feet and drained his glass. "Shit is about to get tight James. You need to cut back on those young tricks you like so much. I'll holla at you later" he said walking to the door and slightly opening it. "Penny pinch" he advised him slightly hardening his eyes walking out and closing the door.

One Saturday morning around eleven o'clock, Afrika's quiet neighborhood was forced to awaken earlier than normal as expensive strange vehicles invaded their community once again. Once again, they were surprised by the professionals stepping out of them especially the one white woman genuinely surprised them since the majority was black on this morning. Peeking out their windows at his home or at each other, they were wondering what he was having now? The party he had last month lasted two days like he was celebrating a special event. He has never invited any of them to his elaborate parties except for Freda and rightfully so. They did openly display a racist disposition towards him when he first brought the house five years ago. How he had remodeled it and allowed his neighbors to walk through only heighten some of their jealousy. The new appraisal knocked their shoes off. They never considered him being a lawyer at such a youthful age or would be reading about him in the Courier Post newspaper winning high-profile cases over the years. His parties always consisted of a diverse group of people although the majority were black. How they wish they could put some life into their static lives, but their initial act warranted the hand they held. Admiring his functions from a distance.

Everybody had arrived including those from Aziza's office. They followed the jazz music to the back yard where a light snack was prepared consisting of a fruit salad. He and Aziza purposely stayed in the kitchen watching the two two-groups introducing themselves and interacting.

"See baby, real recognize real" Aziza smiled using his words then kiss him on the lips then they went to join the group. They were clutching fingers as they walked out the family room.

"Ladies and gentlemen, I, no, we" he corrected himself smiling over at Aziza. "We would like to thank y'all for breaking your Saturday routine to accept this meeting. What we all have in common is unappreciative bosses and lack of growth. Although I am young, I have the connections to continue to prosper. I have brought a laws firm from the dead and its growing steadily, but not me or my position."

"I can cosign that" mention Shakira lifting her glass of orange juice to him.

"Well, I brought a building two months ago and its fully furnished and ready to go. All I need is y'all but with an understanding. I don't foresee anything keeping us from prospering. Nothing" he reiterated. "I am able to pay you what you are making now and don't worry" he smiled over at them. "I have y'all backs. Y'all will benefit as we prosper and not just me and Aziza. This is not a dictatorship company I'm trying to establish, but one comprise of family members. We will vote on genuine issue, but the final decision is mine's. I also will be doing the hiring on my side of the law firm while Aziza will be doing the same on the business side. All personal references will be highly considered. I know y'all have to go home and discuss things with your loved ones, but rest assure, our doors will always be open to you no matter if apprehension have you pumping your brakes" he told them smiling.

"We hope y'all chill for a minute" Aziza said grabbing the white girl's hand then walking away with a black coworker.

"Afrika" called Shakira. "I don't need to discuss anything with my husband. I'm in. I have witnessed what you did first hand. It will be priceless when the Hines finds out you're stepping off and taking me" she mentioned unable or unwilling to hide her pleasure.

"Thanks Shakira."

"When are you putting in your resignation?" inquired Jamaal.

"I'm supposed to be renewing my contract with them on Friday. They actually tried to get me to sign early" he lightly chuckled. "Instead, I will be placing my resignation paper in their hands and opening my firm the following week after my contract is officially over."

"I can't wait to see James face" admitted Tweety snickering. "As much as his fat ass spends on those young tricks, he won't be getting them anymore" she burst out laughing.

"I hope you keep that same smile once I tell you what me and Aziza have plan for you" he shared with a coy smile.

"Y'all have something for me. What?" she inquired enthusiastically while smiling.

"You will be attending school to acquire that final two years you need for your B.A. If you are going to be our private secretary, you have to possess the proper credentials."

"I can't Afrika" she stated as fear gripped her eyes as she slightly repel. "I can't afford it or have the time."

"We have it all worked out if you decide to join us. You will still be getting your full pay with a pleasant increase, but you will be in class by noon and out by four o'clock. We will hire a tempt for the hours you are gone" he informed her waving off her comment. "We have a seat already reserved for you at Drexel starting in September right over the bridge. Well?"

"Are you serious?" she asked leaping into his arms and squeezing him tightly as she kiss him on the cheek. "I can't wait to submit my letter of resignation" she giggled.

"I'm going to have a ring side seat with popcorn when this shit unfolds" mention Shakira snickering.

"Oh, I will be close" admitted Jamaal smiling.

"Excuse me, Afrika" a light skin guy apologized. "My name is Gregory. I'm a coworker of Aziza and her confidant" he told him shaking his hand. "Since you have been back in her life, I love the change I see in her. She is extremely impressed by you and that's a rarity coming from her. I don't know what tomorrow will bring but if she willing to back you, I am too."

"I appreciate the love" he replied giving him a light hug. "Besides, who couldn't use your hidden talent?"

"Hidden talent?" he repeated cutting his eyes over at Aziza.

"You can get a lot of information from a woman after making love to her" he replied smiling.

"Apparently, so" he replied looking at her with slightly harden eyes and causing her to giggle then raised her hand surrendering.

Gripping the white girl hand, she introduced her to Afrika. "I need everybody to take a ride with me and Afrika. Keep up if you can" she told them wearing an impish smile her coworkers have come to understand and admire. He left Freda to watch his house as his guests walked out the back yard then climbed into their respective vehicles. As Aziza weaved through the traffic, they eventually pulled up on a specious parking lot and everybody climbed out of their cars.

"The building is beautiful, and this is an excellent location, Afrika" commented Shakira seeing signs to the three highways.

Aziza gripped his fingers as they approached the building with everybody following closely. He unlocked the door by the electronic keypad then took the elevator to the second floor. The first thing that caught your attention wasn't the receptionist desk or the layout of the waiting area with several love seats, but the neon sign.

"Justice 4 All" quoted Aziza.

"Is that our name?" inquired Tweety grinning.

"Apparently so" she replied smiling.

Afrika hit a button behind the receptionist desk and jazz filled the interior causing everybody to stare up at the ceiling at the enclosed Infinity speakers.

"Right this way y'all" invited Aziza leading the way through a smoke glass and door enclosure into the body of the office.

"Wow, this is nice Aziza" complimented Gregory smiling at the hookup. "Y'all planned this out?"

"This all Afrika" she admitted beaming with joy. "Any of those offices are free" she mentioned watching them walking inside a few and inspecting the area. They all possessed an excellent oak desk with a leather reclining chair. The size allowed for a love seat and coffee table to discuss their client's cases in a more relaxed environment. With two copy machines that double as a fax machine, the area for additional lawyers and interns was also defined. He did do his homework, and everything was evolving as he said it would. By the time they left that afternoon, everybody was on board. Nobody expected his office building to be so appealing or ready to go, but it was.

Monday afternoon after he won a controversy murder case filled with deceptions and hidden evidence, he enter the new Hines building feeling good. This will be the final month of working for Robert and James Hines. When he exited the elevator, a small smirk came to Tweety face while Shakira openly flashed her devilish smile and getting some popcorn. He assumed her devilish smile was because of the envelop he was carrying in his hand. He tried to suppress his smile, but he wasn't able. He knocked on Robert's door then enter before being invited.

"Yeah, what can I do for you?" he asked in a flat tone. "We will have our meeting later or early next week" he said starting to return to what he was doing.

"Not necessary" he replied catching his eyes then laid the envelop on his desk. He turned ignoring his stare and walked out of his office. He could feel Shakira and Jamaal's eyes on him as he went to his office and took his seat. He press the remote to the stereo system and "My Little Brown Rock" by Duke Ellington and John Coltrane began to play. He laid back staring at the door and waiting with an impish smile. Two minutes later, Robert came barging in with a look of panic or disbelief in his eyes and carrying his resignation letter.

"What is this?" he asked holding his resignation letter.

"It's good to know that thing s around here stays consistent" he shared staring up at him grinning.

"What are you talking about Afrika?" he asked staring at him perplex but a response didn't come then slightly shook his head to get back on point. "What's this that you are handing me?"

"What part of my resignation you don't understand?" he asked returning his stare.

"You are resigning on me?"

"Just like the vodka you like so much, Absolutely" he replied never averting his eyes as he lean back in his chair.

"Why? I thought we worked things out, Afrika."

"You thought wrong, Robert. You should never assume anything especially when dealing with the law" he stated leaning forward. "I gave you ample enough time to do right by me, but it's not in you or your bitch ass brother's character. I shouldn't have doubted what Mr. Williams said in front of you, that you won't do right by me, but I did. I foolishly gave you the benefit of doubt" he shared slightly snarling at him. "I am the reason for the resuscitation of this firm, but you couldn't even acknowledge it by making me a full partner. You should have never said in some compacity. I would have gotten me to sign papers a full year before my contract expires to show my appreciation, but that isn't a part of your demeanor or disposition. Did you and your brother genuinely believe that I would stay satisfied with y'all crumbs?" he asked lightly snickering. "Wake up Robert. Your ride is over, so you might as well get off."

"Afrika don't do this, man" he unconsciously pleaded, not for his talent but for the money he was bringing into the firm. All he heard was his goose with the golden eggs talking about leaving. "Listen man, I'll make you a junior partner and will write up the papers right now. I will also increase your pay by that additional thirty G's as I said" he included. "What do you say?" he asked throwing him a life preserver and he threw it back at him.

"Na, I can do bad all by myself and not get fucked in the process" he said suddenly getting to his feet and grabbing his hat. "You are still trying to be deceptive with your words, like junior partner, and you will lose that battle every time with me, slick" he lightly snicker again. "Have a fucked-up evening, Robert" he said casually walking pass him smelling the scent of alcohol on him as he walked out his office leaving him with his thoughts.

The few that knew what had just transpired stared at him with little smirks on their faces as he had a look of determination in his eyes. He never looked or acknowledge them as he headed towards the elevators. Robert exited his office just as the elevator's door closed and walked methodically back to his office with his head noticeably lower. The wind seems to have been taken out of his sails. He opens his office door and walk over to his desk then flopped down into his chair. He reached into his middle draw and pulled out the contract he had prepared for Afrika's signature without any mention of a partnership. He violently shredded it and threw it at his office door. "FUCK!" he screamed out.

"Whoa!" a voice suddenly said causing him to raise his head. "Where in the hell is that bitch ass Afrika running off to?" James asked coming further I to the room and taking a seat. "How did he take getting that partnership?" he asked snickering.

"He's resigning."

"Yeah, right" he chuckled. "He's not going anywhere?"

"He's resigning motherfucker! Do you hear me now!?" he asked staring over at him coldly. "That's the fucking contract I was hoping for him to sign on the damn floor" he informed him as he peeked at it then back at him.

"Why?"

"Why? Are you serious?" he asked slightly shaking his head at him. "When we didn't make him a partner before his contract year, he knew he was being played and flipped the script on us. While we were boasting in the papers about our company, he never seek out the lime light, but it still tried to seek him out. I should have kept my promise to him. We are some dumb motherfuckers for trying to play him."

"Fuck him!" James stated adamantly.

"Fuck him?" he said getting to his feet and glaring over at him. "Nigger, do you understand what the fuck we got ourselves into and the people we barrow from? We have about two weeks to a month to convince him to reconsider his resignation or our asses is headed towards the grinder. We need the money he brings in or start liquidating our accesses quickly" he told him reclaiming his seat. "If I were you, I would hold tight to that fifty G's I gave you last Friday. Shit is about to get seriously tight. Now, get the fuck out of my office" he ordered him still staring at him coldly as he got to his feet.

"Robert, press up on him harder. He will listen to you" he insisted standing by the door.

"That ship has long been gone. What part of that statement you don't understand?" he asked solemnly. "We just didn't know it because of all the luxuries we have been indulging in the past three years. Self-center motherfuckers like us is always the last to recognize it until it hits us in the face" he told him leaning back in his chair as James opens the door and walked out.

Sitting in his office hours later and nursing a glass of bourbon, James was still trying to swallow what had just transpired. He can't leave. What will they do? The money he received last Friday is damn near gone. Splurging in Atlantic City with one of his secret young freaks. He showed her the time of her young life. Although she thought that she could play him, he was going to spend what he wanted, not what he wanted him to spend. Sure, buying her a couple pairs of jeans, some shirts and blouses with some cheap shoes wasn't shit. He was going to test ride her corvette every night after making his play for her. With the promise of getting a thousand dollars, she eagerly accepted his weekend rendezvous. She was just one of three girls that he fucks with that was barely over twenty-one. How do they return to their previous lifestyle when they got accustomed to a whole new one? What will happen to them when they start losing clients and unable to make payroll or worse, payments to their lenders? The thought brought a look of dread to his face.

On Saturday morning around ten o'clock, he got the janitor to open the door to the Hines building for him and his partners. They went to his office grabbing all the things that he had box up and transferring everything to his new office. They were there a good hour chilling before finally leaving. All that weekend while they party, they put it out on the grapevine about his move and where his office was located. They pass out his business card everywhere they party especially at Winston's. For the first week since resigning, he put the finishing touches on everything. Content with the final results, he stood staring out his window glaring at the scenery.

When Shakira and Jamaal offer their letters of resignation two weeks after he had resigned, Robert was blindsided especially by Shakira. He thought that she would be a permanent fixture with his firm. Where were she and Jamaal going? Did they too have something setup? Where in the hell was Tweety suddenly going now? Motherfuckers were abandoning ship already and they weren't even taking in water yet. Was this the beginning of things that was about to materialized. If so, this could turn into a nightmare quickly. All he could do from his office was watch them packing up their stuff and saying goodbye to those that they have become acquainted with over the past four years. Neither said anything to him or his brother as they left. They never even look in his direction. He poured himself another stiff drink then stared out his office window slightly shaking his head.

A month later, Justice 4 All was up and running. The Courier Post had found out that Afrika had branched out on his own and damn near gave him free advertisement. He had to hire three additional lawyers almost instantly especially with clients rescinding their wish to be represented by the Hines law firm once they were affirming that Afrika was no longer working or associated with them. Rumor had it that Robert had to lay off four of his lawyers and all of his interns except one. Just imagine, last year he was flying high among the clouds and telling the world to kiss their asses. Now reality was slowly creeping up on him and his punk ass alcoholic brother.

In the meanwhile, Mulley and his boys were making their weekly collections when Dog spotted a cranberry color Caddie sitting on chrome twenty-two's rims with slightly smoke windows pulling away from the curb from the opposite corner.

"Mulley don't that look like the Caddie we have been looking for?" asked Dog never taking his eyes off the vehicle.

"Well, I'll be damn" he replied watching the car going up the street. "I will get back at you Turk concerning this short and you can bet on that" he snarled at him. For right now, I have some business to contend with. Let's roll Dog" he instructed.

Mulley and his boys jumped back into their vehicles and pursued the Caddie. They closed the distance then followed it for a couple of blocks in hopes that he make a driving violation including freewheeling through a stop sign, but none was committed.

"Fuck this shit!" shouted Mulley speeding up then suddenly cutting in front of the vehicle forcing the driver to slam on brakes. They bail out of their car and surrounded the vehicle with their guns drawn. Mulley tapped on the driver's window with the butt of his Glock. The driver slightly opened the door and was suddenly snatched from the vehicle and the two passenger also got the same treatment.

"Can I help you, sir?" the driver asked openly nervous.

"License and registration" Mulley replied ignoring his question.

"Sure, officer. What did I do?" he asked retrieving his license and registration then extending it to him. "Excuse me, but you didn't answer my question?" he reminded him.

"Shut your mouth" demanded Mulley.

"What, I can't ask a question?"

"Not unless you want to go to jail" he replied returning his stare.

"On what charge?"

"Driving while black" he replied snarling over at him.

"Now, that was an unnecessary racist comment. What is your name officer?"

"Shut the fuck up" he replied.

"Na, you shut the fuck up."

"You have a smart-ass mouth, nigger. Don't let it get you in trouble" he warned him. So, I'm advising you to shut the fuck up."

"First of all, who are you calling a nigger!? And secondly, you shut the fuck up" he reiterated.

"Yo, Ice. Is everything okay?"

"Just the daily police harassment."

"Check the car" ordered Mulley.

"Whoa! You are illegally searching my car and you better not be planting any drugs either" he warned them as Dog and Red Neck commenced the illegal search.

"What are you implying, young man. You don't trust the city finest?" Mulley asked with a smirk on his face.

"You have got to be kidding me" the driver replied snickering. "Y'all are worse than the criminals."

Dog returned empty handed. "Search it again" Mulley ordered them. "Where are you headed?"

"To mind my business" he replied returning his stare.

"Watch your mouth you little bastard."

"My Mom and Pop was married when they had me. Can you say the same thing about your frigid trailer park mother?" he asked wearing a slight smile.

Mulley suddenly slap the taste out of his mouth and drawing blood.

"What's up with your hands, officer?" Ice asked revealing his animosity then spitting out a mouth full of blood and reaching for his cell phone.

"Put that cell away until after we finish doing our investigation" ordered Mulley.

"Investigation? What damn investigation? I didn't do anything wrong nor did my friends. I'm calling my father."

"Put it away."

"Man, whack what you are saying. I'm calling my father" he reiterated.

That was the extent of his conversation. All he knew he was looking up at him from the pavement. Yeah, his jaw was hurting but he didn't know why?

"You have anything else to say smart ass?"

His partners and witnesses had become irate after witnessing Ice being sucker punch by Mulley. Those that had witness the unprovoked attack became unmanageable so back up was eventually called. Upon searching the car again, Dog came up with a twenty-dollar bag of weed under the driver's seat. Ice adamantly denied any knowledge of drugs and so did his partner, and this escalated the situation even more. By the time extra officers arrived and with the paddy wagon, Ice friend assured him that he would be collecting witnesses names and telephone numbers who observed the racially motivated incident and prejudicial practice and illegal procedure.

The next morning around nine o'clock Mulley was instructed by his shift commander to report to the Commissioner's office. Naomi had come through the ranks to obtain her position. No back alley deals or secret rendezvous to obtain her rank. No one could spread dirt on her because her integrity was unquestionable. Mulley didn't have the vaguest idea why she wanted to see him. He damn sure didn't think yesterday's incident would have reached her desk that soon. So, he was confident lightly tapping on her door.

"Come in" her voice rang out.

He pushed the door open then step inside. "Good morning, ma'am. I got word that you wanted to see me."

"Yes, I do Detective. Have a seat and explain to me about the arrest yesterday of Malcolm Diggs?" she informed him leaning back in her chair.

"Malcolm Diggs? Oh, you mean that smart mouth kid?"

"If you say that he is" she replied never averting her eyes.

"We were conducting street interviews from a previous shooting when one of my men spotted him smoking a blunt" he lied. "Once we stop the car, the distinct smell of marijuana was prevalent. We ask everyone in the vehicle to exit when Diggs started being disrespectful. I asked permission to search his car and he gave it. Upon searching the vehicle, a small amount of marijuana was located then they were read their Miranda rights and place them under arrest."

"Did you omit anything, Detective?"

"No, ma'am" he continued with his lie.

"Did anyone run the car's tags?"

"I'm sure one of my men did" he persisted with his lie.

"Are you sure somebody did or are you just speculating?"

"I'm almost positive that one of my offers did."

"Well, I doubt that seriously Detective. If they had, they would have known that the vehicle is register to Samuel Diggs. Do you know who he is?"

"Yes, ma'am" he replied shocked by the revelation. "The City Council president."

"Exactually, the one and only" she assured him staring in his greenish eyes. "Now, I have known Malcolm since he was born and that is twenty-two years. That is how long I have known the Diggs. He and my two sons attends the same mentoring program at our church for the past five years. I would be surprised if he and his two cousins urine come back dirty. You can take it to the bank that his father will take them all for a urinalysis. I hope this doesn't come back and bite you in the butt, Detective. As far as the alleged police brutality charges, we will deal with that at a more appropriate time. I hope you crossed your T's and dotted your I's."

"My squad report will reflect everything that transpired, ma'am" he told her.

"I hope so Detective" she grinned looking over into his lying ass eyes. "I'm finish, you can return to duty."

"Yes, ma'am" he replied getting to his feet and walking towards the door then quietly closing it. "Shit!" he quietly said as he proceeded down the hallway.

Justice 4 All was gradually growing. In their second year of existence, they were mentioned in the Black Lawyer's Magazine as an up-and-coming firm that needs to be watch. With their clientele growing especially Aziza's department, her former boss reached out to her and needed an explanation for her sudden departure. When she explained everything that had transpired with Mr. Dickweed, they were furious and tried to persuade her to rejoin their firm, but that option was off the table, now. She have eight business lawyers under her supervision and abandoning her position, and man, was not going to happen. When they spoke to Dickweed about her sudden departure, he initially tried to lie but they stop him in the middle of his lie and informed him that they had talked to her and the fabricated lie you are trying to weave makes you even more guilty. They gave him an option. He could resign his position or take a pay cut in pay plus a demotion. The choice was his. He chose to remain instead of having any new potential employee calling them for a reference and having his whole card revealed.

Wednesday morning, Mr., and Mrs. Samuel Diggs strolled into the office holding hands. They requested to speak to Afrika, and he told Tweety to escort them back to his office.

"Good morning, Mr., and Mrs. Diggs" he greeted them getting to his feet and shaking their hands. "Please, have a seat. How can I assist you?"

"Have you heard about the incident concerning our son, Malcolm?"

"Yes, sir. The streets are buzzing about the news" he assured him while returning his stare.

"Well, that is why we are here. We are seeking legal representation. Will you take out case?"

"I personally can't, Mr. Diggs because I have a murder case that I am finalizing, but I do have the right person for you" he replied slightly smiling while picking up his phone and pressing a preset number. "Hey, what are you doing? Good, come get with me" he said placing the receiver back into its cradle. Seconds later, there was a light tapping at his door then it swung open. A petite fashion-conscious woman walked in. "Mr. and Mrs. Diggs, I would like to introduce you to Shakira Muhammad."

"Ma'am, sir" he acknowledged them slightly nodding her head.

"She will represent you in the criminal case and the civil case, if you desire to seek restitution" he informed them.

"Are you sure, Afrika?" Mrs. Diggs inquired revealing her apprehension.

"Oh, he's sure, Mrs. Diggs. I won't let y'all down" she tried to assure her returning her stare.

"Okay" she conceded, slightly smiling into her eyes.

"If you will follow me" she said as they got to their feet.

"By the way, starting Monday you will be responsible for all drug cases."

"What? Really?" she asked smiling from ear to ear.

"Yes, really."

"Can I have a private secretary?" she inquired grinning.

"Sure, as long as you are paying for one with the additional ten thousands you will be making" he informed her causing her to start giggling.

"Yeah, I thought you would say something like that" she admitted smiling. "Mr. and Mrs. Diggs, please follow me to my office." She was flying high and walking on Cloud 9 as she walked towards her office. From day one when he walked through the Hines door, he naturally click with her. She initially thought he was flirting with an older and married woman but came to appreciate his love for the black woman. She had to admit he was handsome as hell, but his faith in other people is what made him so attractive to her.

When the Inner Harbor finally open, tourist flock to it not understanding the violence and danger they were subjecting their families to. Car jackers and stick-up crews were waiting to catch a tourist sleeping or making a dumb decision like walking around the streets near the Inner Harbor. Venturing just two blocks away from the Harbor in al direction will reveal what the tourist guild neglected to mention.

Murk and Black was off from the block. So, they decided to go down to the Harbor and chill. Opportunities are always presence if your timing was right. They had been observing this group of guys walking back and forth then peeking at them for over a half hour. It was obvious that they were searching for something or somebody or have something on their minds.

"Should we assist them?" inquired Murk slightly smiling at a red hair guy staring at them.

"There is nothing wrong with extending a hand of friendship" Black replied grinning at the group.

Murk raised his hand to get the group attention then pointed directly at the red hair guy to join him. Nervously, he slowly approached them.

"Brother" the terminology surprised him. "You have been walking nonchalantly past us for a half hour. Is there anything I can do for you?"

"I don't mean to be disrespectful but I, we, are here in Camden for the next two weeks and we need a hook up."

"What are you looking for, Archie?"

"Some pot and cocaine" he replied subtly.

"How much weed and coke are you looking for?"

"An ounce of each" he replied. "I can provide that for you, but it will take twenty minutes to get here, Archie."

"My name isn't Archie it's Steve" he informed him.

"Not anymore, your street name is Archie now" Murk informed him grinning. "Here, take this tester" he said extending a twenty-dollar bag to him."

"Tester?"

"Yeah, to see what I am selling. It is free" he informed him as he took it. He told him that by the time he gets back he would have that for him but that he's not under no obligations.

"Okay" he suddenly smiled walking back to his friends then leaving the scene.

Once they left, they contracted Bear to have about five ounces and five halves ready for him. If Turtle were around, grab an ounce of weed from him and they would hook up at the entrance on S.4th Street. On their way back, they spotted Archie and his boys waiting on them under a tree. They requested three ounces of coke along with the weed they requested. Archie requested that they exchange numbers so that he could contract him, and Murk eagerly provided it for him. Archie eventually started introducing them to all of his coke sniffing friends. They were suddenly getting paid at the Harbor. Things were rolling like a donut until one day, they spotted a potential situation. Guys from Blood's crew started showing up and sniffing around. Spotting them posted up caused their curiosity to perk up. What was North doing at the Harbor? They laid back and pinch a tent. It didn't take them exceedingly long to observe what they were doing.

"You know they are peeking at us" mentioned Black.

"Yeah, I know" replied Murk.

"Trouble will be coming our way" he mentioned catching his eyes.

"Yeah, eventually" he cosigned touching his Glock in his hip.

As time pass, Blood's crew started showing up more frequently. The fact that they were coming didn't bother them, but the noise they were bringing did. Boom boxes played out in the eighties, so why bring one to the Harbor? Perhaps if they kept it playing low, especially around touring white folks, the intimidation factor wouldn't exist, but hearing lyrics from N.W.A saying "Fuck The Police" didn't settle too well with their ears. Seeing them dress like thugs, drinking forties and openly smoking blunts, tourist became a little leery and five-o is going to want to know why, eventually?

Things came to a head one day with Murk. He has had enough as they approached the group of five. "Brothers" he addressed them as they stared up at them. "I'm not trying to interrupt y'all thing, but y'all are making too much noise. The lyrics are making the white people jumpy. How about lowering the music some."

"Fuck those crackers" a medium complexion muscular guy stated laughing. "They can take their asses back out to the burbs."

"I hear you brother, but they are the ones buying my product. From the noise y'all are making, my customers are nervous that five-o might be peeking on us, and they don't want to get caught up."

"You can meet their lily-white asses someplace else" he suggested staring in Murk's eyes.

"You know that is not going to happen, partner" he assured him still keeping his cool. "With the things that y'all are doing, you are putting a spotlight on the area."

"Man, we aren't bothering anybody. So, why are you over here harassing us?" he asked slightly snarling.

Murk and Black ignored his question as they held a private conversation with their eyes. The Glocks on their waist wanted to spit fire but all they did was humble themselves and close up shop then started out the Harbor. They heard them laughing at them and Black had to grab Murk's arm because he wanted to shut them down permanently.

"I hope you know what you are doing J.B." commented a light skin guy.

"Man, chill" he insisted watching the two guys casually walking away. He knew he was wrong and being disrespectful for taking the disposition that he, but he was just following orders from Blood. He said that they wouldn't do anything, and he was right, but he wasn't fooling himself, he knew they would be returning. He spotted the Glock's on their hip and prayed that they didn't reach for them, or they would have been fucked. Hours later, the group was back down on S.4th Street blowing blunts and drinking from forties boasting about what had occurred hours later. When O.G Bumpy informed them of who they were describing and talking shit about, they almost piss their pants. All the joking and laughing definitely ceased. When one of the guys held the other back, they had caught a blessing. They definitely need to apologize and hope that they didn't demand any form of restitution like kicking them up their asses. If Blood had told them who they were, they would have refused his order especially fucking with a crew from out of North.

"I'm glad you decided to chill" Black said as they climbed into his A7.

"I wanted to shut his bitch ass down" he snorted. "I know you saw the bitch up in his eyes. He is definitely following orders."

"No doubt about that" he cosigned. "Slick must think he has a stronger hand. I told Bear that he should checked him. He is one devious motherfucker."

"No disputing that. This bullshit drama he's trying to produce is going to turn straight into a nightmare on his dumb ass. We need to pull Bear's coat to what's happening?" Black said lighting a blunt.

"Might as well" he agreed. "Let's see how he use diplomacy on this shit" he said snickering. Bear had an uncanny ability to see the truth through people's eyes. When a certain person was accused of stealing a stash, Bear was called and stared in the person's eyes then surrendered his opinion. His insight has never been wrong and spared several people their lives. If Slick doesn't flip his script, something traumatic will eventually occur. Who in the hell brings ladies to dance and grind on when you are supposed to be grinding? The answer is idiots.

The criminal trial against Mulligan finally began in late May. If it were just another young black man making the complaint of police brutality, the issue would have been sweep away, but this wasn't just another young black man complaining. He is the son of the City Council President and couldn't get sweep away. As far as the trial is concerned, news reporters as usual hype up the whole case. In one breath they were praising Mulligan and the Nextel Boys for their numerous accommodations in the performance of their duties, but with their next breath, mentioning the many complaints against them stemming from making arrests. This complaint isn't coming from someone with a known criminal background, not this time.

Shakira was wearing a gray two-piece gray pant suit, which complimented her grayish locs, from Gucci that was tailored to the contour of her body. As she sat at the defense table, she stared back at Afrika and smile. She was ready.

"All rise!" shouted the bailiff. "Presiding over case 993246 is the Honorable Maxine Brown."

"Be seated" she instructed taking her seat. "Good morning, ladies and gentlemen of the jury."

"Good morning" they replied together.

"Is the defense ready?"

Getting to her feet, she said, "I am, your Honor. Shakira Muhammad of Justice 4 All."

"Representative for the accused" she said staring over at him.

"James Swartz of the Police Legal Team is ready also, your Honor" he replied barely getting out of his seat.

"Very well, let's get started. Mrs. Muhammad, you may make your opening statement."

"Thank you, your Honor" she replied moving from behind the table and walking towards the juror box. "Ladies and gentlemen, I am going to talk to you straight forward. We are here today because Detective Mulligan didn't follow protocol and a simple traffic stop escalated out of control as the tendency usually is when dealing with a person of color. I will produce several witnesses including a retired nurse and son who were leaving Bible study class when they stumbled upon the abuse. There are several indiscretions between what actually happen and the story that Detective Mulligan alleged. As the trial progresses, his representative will try to discredit them, but he won't. He will boast about his squad accommodations, but this isn't about their or his accommodations, it's about him breaking the law that he was hired to enforced. Just because he wears a badge and carry a guy doesn't make him above the law, does it?" she asked catching a few of their eyes before turning and reclaiming her seat.

"Mr. Swartz. Are you ready?"

"Yes, your Honor" he replied getting to his feet and approaching the jury box also. "Good morning, ladies, and gentlemen. Mrs. Muhammad does possess a soothing voice but don't be fool by it. On the day in question, my client was doing exactually what he is paid to do by the citizens of Camden, control the drug scene. The incident that occur on April the fifteenth was the results of that gentleman being in a known drug area then mischievously pulled away from a known drug dealer when he spotted my client in his unmarked SUV. His action is what initiated a street interview and the mannerism of his passengers to do a more intensive interview. This is when the alleged brutality occurred. Once the facts are displayed, you will enter a not guilty verdict and allowed this highly decorated Officer to return to keeping our streets safe. Thank you" he said returning to his table and taking a seat.

"Mrs. Muhammad, you may call your first witness."

Getting to her feet, "Thank you, your Honor. I would like to call Vivian Pullman to the witness stand" she said staring into the gallery. The jurors and spectators watched the elderly woman approaching the witness stand clutching her bible as she climbed the steps and took a seat. Shakira had made the right move to call her first and to give the jurors a perspective of what she witnessed. As she related her story, the juror were very attentive to what she was saying. Mulligans lawyer was also captivated by the clarity she displayed in remembering what had transpired. He knew he couldn't shake her but maybe, he could poke holes in her testimony, and she would correct him every time he tried to misrepresent what she said. She wasn't biting his hype, and neither was Shakira but most importantly, the jury didn't either.

On the second day of the trial, Mulligan decided to take the stand in his own defense against his lawyer's advice and this brought an impish smile to Shakira's face. She was about to shine light where it was once dark.

"How come what your official report say is so different from what other witnesses had testified?"

"I don't know" he simply replied.

"Oh, come on Detective Mulligan" she insisted with a coy smile. "You have to have an opinion. I mean, how can every witness dispute your account?"

"They see only what they choose to see" he proclaimed.

"So, they choose to see three African Americans males being gaffle to the ground by the police. Is this what you want this court to believe?"

"I'm saying that it isn't always as it appeared."

"Like this case, huh?" she asked with a smirk on her face.

"Exactually" he snorted while exchanging stares.

"Okay, let's try this" she said raffling through her papers. "Why did you stop the car that my client was driving?"

"He was observed smoking what appears to be a blunt" he lied never averting his eyes from hers.

"Did you ever recover the blunt?"

"No" he replied.

"Did you ever lose sight of the vehicle?"

"No."

"Did anybody throw anything out the window?"

"No."

"Then why wasn't this alleged blunt never found?"

"Perhaps it was swallowed" he gave as an explanation.

"Perhaps, huh?" she asked with a coy smile.

"Yeah, perhaps" he stated looking at her with slightly hardening eyes.

"Supposed I was to place into evidence the toxicology report from the three individuals that was inside the vehicle" she stated pausing for him to stare at the piece of paper she was holding in her hand. "Suppose the results reveal that their system was absent of all drugs. What would you say?"

"I would say that anybody can beat a uranology if they buy the right product or have someone that they know that doesn't mess with drugs to give them their clean urine" he replied confidently.

"True and I thought that would be your response, so I requested a hair follicle test to be administered. Have you ever heard of anyone tainting, coercing, or beating that result?"

Mulley paused but had to admit the obvious. "No, I haven't."

"I want to submit into evidence the test" she said allowing his lawyer to view it first then extending it to Mulligan. "Will you read the highlight area for the court."

He read the results then stared at her before speaking. "Negative for all forms of drug."

"So, how did you determine that my client was allegedly smoking a blunt?"

"A pungent smell coming from the driver's window as I was approaching" he continued with his lie.

"What?" she said staring at Malcolm then back at Mulley. "The window was down?"

"Somewhat?"

"Somewhat? What do you mean?"

"The window was slightly down" he persisted.

"Could you see my client's face?"

"Yes."

"And he was smoking?"

"The smoke was coming from his window" he replied.

"So, you actually don't know if he was smoking, right?"

"If you want to play with words, you can do so. I know what I witness" he insisted returning her stare.

She showed a piece of paper that Jamaal extended to her to his lawyer to view then extended it to Mulligan. "What that you are holding in your hand?"

"A work order" he replied.

"A work order for what?"

"The electrical system" he replied.

"What time was the appointment?"

"Three o'clock."

"And what time was my client harassed then arrested?"

"At two-forty-five" he replied.

"Where is the shop located?"

"At 3rd and Benson."

"So, apparently, he was going to put the vehicle in the shop when he was two blocks from his destination when he stumbled upon you and your men. What is the work order for specifically?"

"The driver's window" his voice was almost inaudible.

"Pardon me, will you repeat that?"

"The driver window" he repeated with contempt in his voice.

"How did his cell phone get broken?"

"He wanted to make a call, but I informed him that he could make one after the interview was completed" he lied.

"That doesn't explain how it got broken, Officer."

"He insisted on trying to make the call when I reached for it and the phone hit the ground."

"By simply reaching for it, the cell phone broke, huh?" she said not expecting a response. "Officer Mulligan, how did things escalate so quickly?"

"One of my officers found a small quality of marijuana and from this discovery, the gentleman became belligerent."

"How many times was the vehicle search?"

"Three time" he replied.

"Three times and where was the marijuana found?"

"Behind the driver's seat under the floor mat."

"Wait a minute" she suddenly smiled shaking her head at him. "A highly decorated and accommodation squad took three searches to find the marijuana under the back floor mat."

"Yes, it did" he stated flatly while ignoring her faint smile.

"Why didn't y'all follow protocol before stopping the vehicle?"

"We did" he insisted.

"You did" she openly smiled at him. "Who called in the tag number? Now be careful, I might be holding the duty call log for that night" she warned him. "So, what is your answer?"

"Because of the evidence collected and the subsequent commotion, we might have neglected to call in the tags."

"When the registration was placed in your hand, you didn't recognize the name?"

"Not initially."

"You wasn't on you're a game, huh?" she smiled at him.

"Apparently not" he agreed.

"No further questions, your Honor" she said peeking at the jurors as she took her seat.

"Mr. Swartz, you may proceed."

"No questions at this time, your Honor" he replied.

"You are excused Officer Mulligan" Judge Brown informed him.

As Mulligan left the witness stand, it was evident that he wasn't just a liar but a defeated man also. The smile he gave to his men and associates was lifeless.

"Ladies and gentlemen, with the lateness of the day this court is adjourned until nine o'clock tomorrow morning."

"All rise!" shouted the bailiff as Judge Brown got to her feet and went towards her chamber.

Around eight-thirty, the next morning, Shakira had a message on her answering machine requesting an audience. Mr. Swartz had called her the previous evening. When she returned his call, he wanted to discuss a plea bargain. She informed him that she would have to get with her boss and the client's parents before she could give him an answer. When she took it to Afrika, he threw it back into her lap. Mr. and Mrs. Diggs also threw it back into her lap saying they have confidence in her decision. She assured them that accepting the plea bargain doesn't diminish their civil case. She decided to wait until she got to the court house to share her decision. She wanted Mulligan to sweat. When she gave them her decision, Mulligan was overcome with joy, but it was short lived. She placed in his hand a pending order for restitution in civil court. He nonchalantly shrugged it off because he gained his freedom and most importantly kept his badge at a modest one point three million dollars. Why should he care about the settlement, he wasn't paying it. As it was known, all fees by Justice 4 All was picked up by the state not his clients in civil matters.

Bear was sitting on his balcony smoking a blunt when his cell rang. Peeking at the number, a smile came to his face. "What's up man?"

"What's up with you?"

"Just chilling Afrika."

"Where is that shadow of yours?"

"His young ass just left here to go pick up a young lady" he mentioned chuckling.

"That boy is put of school next month; I know you are proud."

"You know it, but he'll never hear it from me" he suddenly laugh again. "So, what's the call about?"

"Tomorrow" he replied casually.

"Tomorrow?" he repeated. "What happening tomorrow?"

"My flight" he replied grinning.

"Has it been two weeks already?"

"Yeah man. You are working too much."

"Apparently, what time is your flight?"

"Nine o'clock."

"I'll be there by seven thirty. The traffic going toward Philadelphia International Airport shouldn't be that heavy that time of the morning."

"I appreciate it. What's on your agenda?"

"I'm going to try and have a civil conversation with Blood's dumb ass tonight" he informed him.

"Good luck with that" he lightly snicker. "I'll see you tomorrow, partner."

"For sure" he replied ending their conversation. He was so proud of Afrika and what he have accomplished since leaving their clique full time. Owning his own law firm at the age of twenty-five and having his name mentioned in the prestigious Black Lawyer Magazine several times over the years since coming on the scene. Who would have thought that a guy coming from out of North Camden would have accomplished so much? He had stayed grounded and never forgot where his roots emulated.

As far as Blood was concern, he could only hope that he don't start talking slick. The thing known about Tek9 and Kimba was they weren't the ones to display a lot of patience or having long conversations. He would hate seeing Tek9 smacking Blood in his mouth with the butt of his baby. Since they were young, there existed something between them that neither spoke on. The hatred that Tek9 had for him was never hidden. He displayed his animosity every time they were in the same social environment, or area code, Blood would eventually gather up his shit and his entourage then leave under the menacing eyes of Tek9.

Afrika was the only one that peeked on what transpired between them, but he never shared it with their other partners, and he respected him even more for that. If he weren't so damn attentive, he wouldn't have peeked it either. They were fifteen while Blood was twenty-three when he rubbed Tek9 the wrong way. He was still grinding for Mack 10, but he was making and banking his money for the big move. Blood used to think it was funny teasing them lightly about how dusty they look until that look would come into Tek9 eyes. He saw the danger in his young eyes while the others seem to ignore it. Blood would cease his jokes and move with his little entourage. Tek used to see this girl name Shy around the set. They were very friendly with one another, but their age difference, not what was in the heart, kept them in their respective lanes. She was eighteen years old with carnation milk still on her breath. She was a unique find in the hood. She was the type of young lady you would take home and introduce to your mother with a broad smile. Her smooth chestnut complexion covered a petite frame standing about five feet seven. Natural long eyelashes surrounded small doe like eyes with shoulder length hair even women smiled and complimented her natural beauty. Her laughter could make your heart flutter. Her intellect was acquired from the many books she read except one. "The Lessons and Experiences of Life" that cannot be duplicated, manufacture or learned in any books especially while the hood is your classroom. When Blood first spotted her, he was undeniably captivated by her.

Knowing that she smoke weed, which is how he introduced himself to her, he was holding a blunt and an impish smile that she didn't comprehend. Here is where the trouble started. Tek got out of his lane and pulled her up one day trying to pull her coat to Blood, but she was insisting that they were just friends. He told her with a friend like him, she would do better obtaining cancer. You have a better chance of surviving than interacting with him, but his words fell on deaf ears. How was she to know that his special blunts was laced with cocaine? A year later he had her sniffing coke laced with heroin. Within eighteen months, he had her strung out and doing things that a respectable young lady would never do. It broke his heart when he was cruising the stripe two years later and spotted her then pulled over to have a conversation with her. When she approached him from the passenger's window, she was fucked up off her new first love a speedball and trying to proposition him. She never recognized him. He excused himself never revealing his identity to her. From that night, Blood was on his secret hit list and a smart person would never want to be on that list.

The only reason why Blood is still breathing is because of his cousin Unique. She pulled him up and gave him a reality check. Nobody forced her to take those drugs and long before she became an addict, she knew something was changing simply by her craving, but didn't give a damn about seeking help or even acknowledging that she was becoming an addict. When she started snorting, is that Blood's fault? Sure, you can't blame him for her turning tricks, do you? All the reasonable things that she offered in his defense, she neglected to include that nothing is grown or produced without a seed. Blood was the seed that initiated the whole torrid scenario.

Cruising through the south side, the three vehicles maneuver through the afternoon traffic. The south side had predominately home owners while ninety percent of the people living in North rented. Traveling up S 4th Street and crossing Berkley Street, they had just entered into the heart of Blood's territory. Reaching Walnut Street, they turned left then found parking spots on Maceo's parking lot. If somebody wanted to reach out and touch him, he made it quite simple for them. Climbing out of their vehicles, they had a small smirk on their faces staring at his squad as they approached them. Most was noticeably nervous having North this far from home.

"North's in the house!" Blood announced for all to hear as the five well-dressed men approached. Blood was wearing a red Gucci suit with match gators and a red derby while leaning on his red Big Boy Benz. "What's up fellas?"

"What's up Blood?" Bear replied shaking his hand while his partners took their usual position standing slightly behind one another as they glared over at his crew. "How have you been?"

"I've been fine" he replied feeling the grip of Bear's paw. "And how have y'all gentlemen been?" he asked smiling.

"Gentlemen?" repeated Bear then burst out laughing. "You know damn well none of them are gentlemen" he corrected him still smiling.

"Yeah, upon reflecting" he said staring over at them. "There isn't nothing gentle about them" he admitted staring at their stern expression especially Tek9. "Where is Afrika?"

"Minding his motherfucking business" replied Tek9 snarling over at him.

"Do you know why I called this meeting?" Bear inquired bringing his eyes from Tek9.

"Yeah, it has something to do with the Harbor, right?"

"Yeah, they are making too much noise" he stated staring directly at Slick. "Five-o is starting to creep and snoop around. My partners are not trying to get caught up in their dumb and immature shit. What I am suggesting is this. We will continue to work the North side while your boys can work the south side and make all the damn noise they want."

"How about y'all working the south side and we work the north side?" he countered.

"Na, this is not an option" he informed returning his stare. "Murk and Black stumble upon the gold mind accidentally on the north side before your boys came snooping around and pitching a tent. Take the south side."

"Na, I'm still not feeling that south side shit" he replied making his objections known.

"Okay, how about this?" interjected Tek9 grabbing everyone's attention. "How about us giving you the north side then send a crew from 3rd Street to step to you every motherfucking day until you surrendered the whole harbor to us? How does that sound to you?" he asked staring at him coldly and with a smirk.

"Or we can take it our damn selves" Black informed them staring directly at Slick.

"I haven't gotten my hands dirty in a minute" Kimba shared snarling over at Blood's crew and flashing his canines.

"Brothers, I got this" Bear insisted never averting his eyes from Blood. "There is more than enough money to go around and together we can keep any other crew from crashing our little party or we can do as my partners are suggesting and put all the money straight into our bank accounts" he informed him with a faint smile. "If your crew continue bringing that loud as boom box and some of the nastiest looking bitches on the south side, my partners are going to react eventually. Who brings such distractions when they are supposed to be grinding? Bitches? You really need to consider what I'm suggestion."

Blood shot Slick and his Sargent in arms a cold stare. He will address this bullshit later but never in front of company. What kind of foolishness are they doing down at the Harbor.

"Blood!" called Bear snatching him out of his daydream.

"Huh?" he replied staring up at him. "Yeah, I got this. I will have one of my lieutenants checking on them regularly."

"No problem as long as they stay on the south side."

"Dig, man. I said I got this" he stated irritated that Bear made it clear to be on the south side.

"You need to check your mouth" Tek9 urged him while glaring over at him.

"What the fuck are you looking at him like that for? You heard him" cosigned Kimba glaring just as menacing.

To throw salt in the wound, Bear warned him. "Get your squad in check or we will checkmate them" he openly threaten him and his crew.

"Damn, Bear. You don't have to threaten me and my men" he stated returning his stare. "Oh, yeah" he slightly smiled. "Y'all don't make threats. Y'all makes promises."

"As long as you know it" they replied in Unisom still staring over at him and his crew.

"I'll have a meeting with my people this evening."

"You do that" he told him suddenly turning as his partners brought up the rear. Climbing back into their vehicles, they pulled off the parking lot retracing their route towards North.

Tek9 was noticeably quiet as they drove down Broadway staring out at the people. "You know he is plotting something" he finally said. "I think they want the whole harbor."

"That will never happen, and they call whoever they want to assist them" Bear slightly growled taking a quick peek at him. "I told him I will release Viet Nam on them as I stated if they try their weak ass hand" he told him still snarling.

"You do know that you are talking more like Afrika each year" he lightly chuckled. "I personally like it" he chuckled again then lean back. When Afrika became his right-hand man when they were seventeen, they couldn't be fucked with on the streets. He would listen to a person explanation then take restitution out of their asses. Squeezing that trigger was second nature to him if you threaten him or his crew. He might be the sergeant in arms, but Afrika is the scale of justice that determine your fate.

On the south side of Precinct 9, a car pulls up into the shadows slowly with its headlights off and turns the engine off. The two occupants sat motionless while staring at the building. Neither utters a word. Only the rising and descending of their chests were the indicators that they weren't mannequins. Both stares out into the darkness like they were waiting on somebody or something. They observed the night shift departing for the evening and still remained motionless until they thin out. Only then, did one of the figures move.

"Maria, I'll be back in twenty minutes" he stated softly still staring into the darkness.

"What's up Poppi?" she asked staring at his intense stare.

"Nothing" he replied opening the door and illuminating the interior. "Just sit here and wait on me, okay?"

"Yeah Poppi" she replied as he closed the door and darkness filled the interior. Something was up and there was no denying it. She felt it to the core of her bones. A couple of nights ago she caught him having a conversation with somebody in the bathroom. She couldn't make out who he was talking to or what they were discussing but she unmistakably heard her husband ask, "Do you think he could help me?" These words weigh heavy on her mind and on her heart. Realizing that he was talking to his gang banging cousin, Santiago later by checking the phone log didn't help the matter and conspiring anything with him was totally out of character. As she watched her husband, she could only hope that whatever was going on would end quickly so they could return their humdrum life.

Morales stood in the shadows peeking up and down

the street. Periodically, he would peek at his watch. In five minutes, he would know if he had a future or not. He took a deep breath before stepping out of the shadows and making his presence known. As he briskly walked across the street and step up on the curb, he was in the land of no return. He could only hope that the inside person would turn the camera before he reached the back gate. Peeking at his watch then around the corner, the camera was just starting to rotate.

"Yes" he expressed picking up his pace. He pressed the elevator button and waited. He could only hope that no one would be exiting. He had monitored the area for two weeks and had the routine down to an art. As the elevator door opens, no one was inside. He stepped inside staying close to the door and under the elevator camera. Once the door closes, he place a sticky paper over the lens then pressed the desire floor. As the elevator slowly descended, a nervous coy smile creased his lips. "After tonight" he whispers to himself. "I will sever all ties with Mulligan and the notorious Nextel Boys." What he witness and participated in could easily be described as disgraceful to those honoring the badge. Watching them smoking marijuana and sniffing cocaine with the young ladies they caught with their hands in the cookie jar, the fear of incarceration had the young girls humbling themselves to their sexual demands. Yes, he had smoke some weed because he had to. Being hit by friendly fire was always a possibility and even more possible if offers didn't trust you. Why would they video themselves doing the things they did was foolish and dumb? It only revealed much too late, how much above the law they have flown because of their accommodations and awards.

When one of the girls took it and got low on them, they didn't know which girl took it or when? Now, he was unanimously voted to break the law this time.

Yeah, he understood the risk he was taking but the rewards, freedom and his career was worth the risk. When he confided into his cousin what he was getting ready to attempt, he was glad he didn't hit him with "That's why we don't fuck with five-o." He needed him to be that same little boy he was when they stole candy from stores, and he was. It was his cousin, which gave him the strength to finally do what Mulligan and his crew suggested especially since Mulley had someone controlling the cameras.

As the elevator reached its destination and the door slowly opens, the officer in the evidence cage lifted his head then watching him approaching. He got to his feet while unhooking his keys then unlocked the cage. He placed the keys on the counter.

"I'm going to the bathroom for five-minutes. As far as I am concern, I haven't seen you tonight. Do you understand?"

"Yeah" he simply replied, exchanging stares with the late fifty officer as he walked pass.

"By the way, tell Mulley we are even."

Morales never responded just nodded his head. As he turned the corner, Morales leap into action. He had less than ten minutes to retrieve the tape, place the keys back on the counter and get back to the elevator before the cameras rotate to their natural position. He rushed to the area where audio and video evidence was store. Moving frantically, he spotted the special marking that White Boy place on the video and stuffed it in his jacket. Rushing back to the front, he was exiting the evidence cage as the elevator was descending. DING! He took a quick seat as the elevator's door swung open.

"Hey" the old white office greeted him. "Where is Draughty?"

"I don't know" he replied finishing like he was tying his shoes.

"He knew I was coming. So where in the hell is he?" he growled revealing his impatience.

"I'll go check the crapper for you" he suggested realizing that his window of opportunity was gradually closing. Just as he was half way up the hall, Draughty was turning the corner. He palm the key into his hand never breaking his stride as he continue towards the elevator. Pressing the button, he was glad that the elevator was still there. Stepping on, he check his watch again. "Shit!" He had one minute and there was no way he could reach the gate in time. Removing the sticky paper and stepping out, the cameras haven't started rotating and he gave thanks to God. Briskly jogging back to the gate, the camera started rotating back into position. He just turned the corner when the camera picked up his silhouette of his shadow.

Maria sat nervously staring in the direction that he had disappeared. The longer he took the more nervous she became until she spotted him briskly walking back across the street. A broad smile engulfed her face as she exhaled. Climbing back inside the car, they exchanged warm smiles.

"Where to now, Poppi?" she asked placing the car in gear.

"Take me to Santiago house" he replied as she pulled away from the curb.

She didn't object or say anything derogatory about him and he appreciated it. He had more than enough shit on his mind and didn't need her nagging at this time. He might have jump out of character and cuss her the fuck off. She was maneuvering the car through the late-night traffic like a professional wheel person. Occasionally, she would peek over at him and study the expression of determination on his face and in his eyes. She could tell he was hiding something inside his jacket. Whatever have been bothering him for the past year must have come to a head and he was ready to deal with it.

Twenty minutes later, they were pulling up in front of Santiago's house. He leaped from the car before Maria could ask if she was going to accompany him. He dash up the steps and pushed the doorbell. Moments later, the porch light came on illuminating the entire area and he stepped inside. Less than three-minutes later, he reemerged and absent was the slight bulge inside is jacket. As he climbed back inside, he took a deep breath and slowly exhaled.

"Let's go home, Mommy" he said leaning back then staring out the window with an impish little grin.

He tried to contact Mulley, but he wasn't answering his phone as expected. He was partying with the fellas and some new tricks they pulled during the week. So, he took advantage of him turning off his cellphone to call him seven times in one hour and never receiving a call back. Monday morning, he arrived with Smooth at their usual time.

"What in the fuck did you want Saturday night?" Mulley asked staring up at him.

"I was trying to inform you that the damn evidence is missing" he told him watching his reaction.

"What?"

"It's gone Mulley" he reiterated returning his stare. "I tore the fucking place apart in the five minutes that I had to search. With the markings that White Boy placed on it, locating it would have been easy but it's not there" he stressed.

"Where in the fuck is it?" he asked looking perplex by the revelation. "Who in the hell have it?" he asked not expecting an answer as he stared in his men eyes. The question plagued his mind. What was somebody going to do with it? Surely, none of his associates would use the evidence to extort them, or will they? Whichever, somebody still has it.

Although Afrika and Aziza displayed their affection daily, they haven't taken a vacation in three years. He was constantly on his grind getting Justice 4 All deeply rooted and he has. The Black Lawyers Association had requested an interview with Afrika, and he surprised everybody accepting, especially Aziza. He is extremely private. He gave them a small peek at his initial financial and upbringing on the North side of Camden. Afterward, Afrika and Aziza decided to take time for themselves. Nothing says I love you to a woman like seven days and six blissful nights vacation on a balmy exotic island in Barbados at the Hilton Barbados Resort. He placed Shakira as head of the criminal department while Susan was heading the business law side. They landed at Grantley Adams International about three o'clock. The light weight attire they wore was very appropriate for the Caribbean breeze. After passing custom, they climbed on a bus that would transport them to the resort. Peeking through the thick bushes, he spotted the shacks of some of the inhabitants. He rationalized that the resort money doesn't extend to them, but to the pockets of representatives of its citizens. He might be the product of the hood, but they are living in the slums. No way could you compare the two. No way. In 2023, we don't have out houses except in remote or isolated places in the rural south.

The resort jumped out at you with its vibrant Caribbean colors. Just one of several reflections of the cultural. As they climbed off the bus, islanders were checking them out closely as they entered the main lobby. Once they signed in and accepted their electronic keys, they took the elevator to the nineth floor to their room. They walked inside and place their garment bag near the bed with their suitcases. They walked out on the balcony staring at the multi color blue water of the Caribbean Sea. Putting away their clothes, he told her he would be back then walked out the room and took the elevator back to the main lobby. Exiting the lobby, he walked towards the beach and spotted what he was searching for. A couple of islander brothers were smoking a phat ass blunt on a wall.

"Brothers" he addressed coming to stand in front of them. "Where can a brother buy some of that?" he asked staring at him hand.

"You just arrived?" one asked ignoring his question.

"Yes, I did."

"Where did you come from?"

"The last Babylon" he replied staring into his reddish color eyes.

"America, huh?" he lightly chuckled. "How long are you stay?"

"Brother, I'm here to buy some weed not to be interrogated. Can you assist me, or do I have to continue my journey?" he asked returning his stare.

"Americans" he smiled over at his posse.

"I'm no American" he corrected him slightly hardening his eyes. "I only live in America. Can we do business or not?"

"What are you spending?"

Initially, he was going to spend a hundred dollars, but heard himself say, "Fifty dollars."

He nodded to one of his boys and he dip off. He returned seconds later extending a brown bag to him. He took it and peek inside. He peeked around to make sure he wasn't being set up with the abundance of weed inside. He gave the guy his money then returned to the resort but went to the commissary to pick up a few things before returning to his suite. Walking through the door, a deep chocolate young lady was standing behind the counter admiring him while smiling. He nodded and returned her smile but kept it moving. Finding the Tops paper and incenses, he stumble upon a small corn cob pipe with an Islander smoking a blunt wrap around it and a box of tissues to catch the snot escaping their noses after hitting that pipe. He took the items to the counter and placed them on top.

"Looks like a party" she inquired smiling. Her smile brought a sex appeal to her eyes.

"A private one" he shared returning her smile.

"You just arrived?"

"About fifteen minutes ago."

"You don't waste no time in handling your business" she grinned at his merchandise. "Are you going to party tonight?"

"Definitely but not on the resort" he shared.

"Wow!" she declared. "Most tourist stay close to the resort to spend their money while business on the island is struggling to survive" she said peeking around to make sure that no one had heard her. "Very few black Americans come and experience true Caribbean music and dance" she boasted with a faint smile. "We have a dance here called the Grind. Can you do it?" she asked with an impish smile.

"The Grind?" he asked unable to contain his impish smile. "I think I could learn that relatively easy. Do you have a club a could visit?"

"Sweet Thang" she mentioned instantly smiling broadly. "You can't witness anything truer to the culture styles of danced than at Sweet Thang. Brothas and sistas be grinding all night. Security is really tight also. Door open at ten and closes at four o'clock. I'm there every Friday, Saturday, and some Sundays."

"What is your name?"

"I'm Brenda" she replied extending her hand.

"I'm Afrika" he replied shaking her hand lightly.

"That's no American name" she tease him.

"I'm no American. I wouldn't know how it would feel to be an American" he counter slightly grinning.

"It is funny you would say something like that" she replied slightly hardening her eyes. "If I ever see you at Sweet Thang, I have someone I would love for you to meet."

"Who, your boyfriend?" he joked.

"Na, maybe the person you are having the private party with" she countered giggling.

"Good come back" he admitted snickering. "I really enjoyed the conversation and information. but I really have to go. I have somebody waiting on me."

"I'm sure she'll be wait as long as it takes you to return" she subtly flirted revealing her attraction towards him.

"Well, I'm not going to test those waters sweetheart" he replied gathering his items. "By the way, how far is this club from the resort?"

"About five miles from here" she replied. "You can rent a moped to get around and it's a lot cheaper than catching a cab."

"I'll consider that."

"Well, enjoy your day Afrika. That customer have been very patient. I might give him a little trinket for his patience" she said turning to take care of him. Her Caribbean muscular ass wiggled like it was alive. When he took his eyes off her ass, their eyes connected, and she openly blushed from the lust she saw in his eyes. All they could do was share a laugh as he walked out slightly shaking his head.

When he returned to the suite, Aziza had found a Caribbean station and stared out at the Caribbean Sea on the balcony. She had put on something more comfortable. She wore a yellow thin shoulder strap wife beater and a pair of black micro shorts. She would never wear them out in public but in the confines of her own space was something completely different. With the sun glowing off her complexion, she looked so sexy. As the beats of the music touched her, she was wiggling, rotating, and gyrating her hips. She must have felt his eyes caressing her body and burning a hole between her thighs as she slowly turned around smiling.

"How long have you been admiring the view?" she asked smiling.

"Oh, long enough to smile."

"Did you find what you was looking for?"

"Indeed, and more" he replied reaching inside the bag and pulling out everything then laying it on the table.

"Oh, shit!" she giggled. "A corn cob. It's been years."

"Good, while you are laughing and cry tears as I blow my brains out. I will be enjoying the same scenario when the script is flip" he assured her.

With the breeze constantly blowing, they had to go inside and sit at the table. The amount and quality of the weed he received was mind blowing. He top off the corn cob pipe and lit it. All he remember was the air surrounding him ceasing to exist as Aziza's laughter filled his ears. How ever he must have been looking had to be hilarious to her as tears fell from her eyes from uncontrollably laughing. When the script was flipped, she actually had to run to balcony in search of air, but none was provided. Tears fell from his eyes as she struggled to gain control. After one hit, they didn't fuck with that corn cob any more that night. They sat out on the balcony sipping on some coconut island wine while smoking "white boys" (joints). He informed her of meeting Brenda and the club Sweet Thang. She initially wasn't feeling leaving the resort or riding a damn moped, but eventually warmed up to the it considering she knew he would have gone by himself, and she wasn't going to allow any woman, especially a Caribbean woman, to seduce her man when all she had to do was simply escort him.

Around ten-thirty, they stepped off the elevator into what appeared to be mass hysteria. People were scurrying around like roaches when the lights come on. They were trying to decide which resort club to attend while others appeared too intoxicated to go anywhere. As they casually walked through the confusion clutching fingers, some eyes were following them closely. Aziza was wearing a white silk pant set by Adrianna Papell. She fasten just three buttons to reveal her diamond naval ring on slightly develop abs. With a pair of tan sandals that revealed her toe ring, she allowed her shoulder length locs to flow freely. He always like her to walk slightly ahead of him so he could enjoy the movement of her ass that thongs produces.

They arrived at the club a little after eleven o'clock. Now, he have seen some provocative dressing women in his years, but what he experience that night was straight out of an erotic dream. Most of the women appeared that they had pour themselves into their little sister's attire. Ass cheeks were hanging out of micro blue jeans that had been purposely cut or micro skirts were the norm. Victoria revealed all of her secrets in those short skirts. His eyes were staring at girls bodies like a little boy staring through a candy store window. He paid the entry fee then walked through a set of double doors. The scent of blunts and incenses invaded their nostrils. Being outsiders, they stood out like a Klan member attending a black rally. Damn near everybody was smoking on blunts or holding a bottle of Red Stripe beer. As he gripped her fingers, he directed her towards the bar. They found two stools and got comfortable.

"Brothas, Sista" a light skin brother greeted them wearing a genuine smile. "Welcome, what are you drinking?"

"How about one of your island's special?" he replied returning his stare.

"I got what you want" he smiled impishly turning to prepare their drinks. He returned holding two high glasses of a milky substance filled to the rim. "Now drink those slowly or you won't remember the night" he offered as a warning as he turned to leave them with their drink. Coconut and rum could be detected as they took a small sip then smiled. A sweet tasting nuclear bomb.

As he scope the club, he realized that people were people no matter where you live. American ballers and Caribbean ballers emulated one another like the distance cousins that they are. New York fitted baseball caps were being worn and other professional America teams emblems. Status will always be determined by your attire, and they didn't have a problem displaying their wealth in the gold and diamond they proudly wore. A silly way to place a spotlight on them considering the majority of the population is living in poverty. He watched them staring over at him and Aziza all serious. He actually caught himself snickering twice at their antics.

He was half way through his drink when he spotted Brenda strolling into the club with four of her girlfriends and all of them were desirable. He couldn't help but notice how different she appeared in her street clothes and with her locs down. She wore a pair of white shorts that accentuated her flaring hips with a yellow clinging shirt that revealed just how full her breast were hidden in her uniform at work. A snake tattoo extended from her left shoulder disappearing under her shirt. A decorated tramp stamp ran across the small of her back. He watched her making her way around the club greeting her acquaintances. When their eyes finally connected, she made her way towards him wearing a broad smile.

"Afrika" she smiled warmly up at them then at his date. "Is this the Sista you had waiting on you?"

"Yes, it is" he smiled down at her. "Aziza, this is Brenda. Brenda, this is Aziza."

"Glad to meet you Sista" she greeted shaking her hand while admiring her eyes.

"Me too" she replied admiring her smooth chocolate complexion and warm smile.

"How long have y'all been here?"

"Oh, about an hour and a half" he replied peeking at his watch.

"Been enjoying yourself?"

"Oh, he have definitely been enjoying himself" Aziza replied staring at a young lady that's been fixated on him since they took their seats. "The way these Sista dances and dress keep his head on a swivel" she shared staring back at the young lady then causing her and her little group to start giggling.

"We don't have the chance to interact with a lot of black males from Afrika" she shared smiling at her. "This is my sister Mable, my girls Juicy, Entice and Ecstasy."

"Sista" they greeted together smiling but peeking at Afrika.

"Glad to meet y'all" she replied slightly grinning. She had seen more than enough women being smitten by Afrika that she has never allowed jealousy to darken her heart or breed doubt in their relationship.

"Afrika let me go and see if my friend Abdullah (servant to God) is here. Most think that he is radical for his thoughts."

"I will be right here" he told her slightly smiling.

"Ladies, go do y'all and I will holla at y'all later."

"You know Dough Boy is sniffing after you" mentioned Mable causing her girls to giggle.

"He can keep on sniffing" she replied hardening her eyes. "After he fucked our cousins because I was still contemplating on him, he has nothing to discuss with me. So, drop it."

"Okay, okay" she replied giggling gripping Entice arm and leading them away dancing.

"I will be back Afrika" she told his then slowly disappearing into the crowd. As they continued to watch the party goers, the grind isn't nothing but fucking with your clothes on. All he could do was admire the brothers getting their freak on with the vibrant and eager young ladies. If the ladies say they don't get excited or catch an orgasm from their constant gyrating, they are lying. He was getting excited just watching their performances. He will definitely tell his partners what was transpiring in Barbados. Moments later, Brenda reemerged being escorted by a short muscular brother with locs extending down to his ass.

"Brothas, Sista, welcome to the island" he welcome them shaking their hands.

"Brother, Abdullah. Salaam. I'm Afrika and this is Aziza."

"Much love. Much love" he replied. "Brenda called me earlier today telling me that she stumbled upon the American that I have been privately seeking" he smiled up at him. "So, you aren't an American, huh?"

For the remainder of the night, Afrika gave him a history lesson about America that was purposely excluded from teaching. He had him pull up the American Constitution and read for himself what it say about blacks or ex slaves. The perplex expression that came upon his face was truly priceless. He had to educate him that America's whole history is one based on deception and exclusions. America claims that blacks are lazy but after building a nation, who wouldn't be lazy. From her politics to the duality of her laws to her embedded hypocrisy towards people of color, he re-educated him. With the murders of our revolutionary and nonconforming leaders in the sixties like Martin, Malcolm,

Fred Hampton, Bobby Seals, Eldridge Cleaver, and numerous others, one was actually murdered by the orders of our own alleged leader, had an adverse outcome we have never recovered. With out the directions of our leaders, America created an uneducated, uncompromising, angry, violent black man that plagues her communities today, but they act like they don't know why? What is so amazing is that Malcolm warned America about the individual that she was creating and told her that she wouldn't know what to do with them, and she doesn't. When he was finish with Abdullah, he had a whole new perspective of America and the constant duress that blacks and people of color in general endure daily between the shores of America.

Every day Abdullah and Brenda was coming to the resort to pick Afrika up then explore the uncensored Barbados. Their final night, Afrika and Aziza spent together. They had said goodbye to Abdullah and Brenda the previous night. They decided to have a candle light dinner on their balcony. They had goat, curry chicken, cabbage with potatoes and brown rice. He had brought a bottle of coconut rum from Sweet Thang and open it then filled their glasses. As they sat and ate, he realized that something was still troubling her nut she still haven't shared what? She has been like this for over four months, and he was anxious to know what, but he didn't want to be intrusive. Peeking over at her through their unnatural quietness, he spotted a tear forming in her eyes and reached to capture it before it completely fell from her eyes.

"Hey" he called softly. "What's wrong baby?" he asked staring over at her with concern in his eyes.

"Nothing really sweetheart" she replied with no conviction.

"Aziza, I have noticed that same haunting expression on your face for months. I left you alone hoping that you would work it out but enough is enough. What's going on?" he asked in a tone that she rarely heard directed at her but fully understood.

"You know I'm madly in love with you, right?" she replied softly but knowing damn well he required more than just the obvious.

"Spit it out woman" he said in that demanding tone that always sounded so sexy to her.

She sat there quiet for a moment looking over the scenery then a small smile crept to her lips. The conversation she needed to have been extremely important to her future, not so much his future. He have already assured himself of a future by owning his own successful law firm and he wasn't even thirty yet. So, she took a deep breath and slowly exhaled then stared into his eyes.

"Four years ago, I thought I lost you for good" she began while waving off his coming comment. "Na, listen baby. I have been holding this inside of me for much too long. When I secretly aborted our child, I didn't consider that I was aborting our love also. I realized much too late I wasn't considering you or your feelings and how selfish I was thinking. I wasn't ready for such a profound change in my life, and I definitely didn't want to give up my independent woman status. Life had so much to offer me, and I wanted it all. I honestly knew I was wrong for not discussing my intentions with you and all my girlfriends adamantly told me so. I was not ready for the hurt that filled your eyes that night especially witnessing your tears falling. The look of anguish in your eyes rip my heart apart. I have never witnessed such pain in your eyes before and don't ever want to see it again, ever" she reiterated. "I could have simply given our child to you to raise than abort it. When you suggested we take a step back to reevaluate our relationship, I never thought a year and a half would elapse. I slowly recognized the damage I have done and no correspondence from you assured me that I had fucked up royally. Even if I had stumbled upon you, I honestly don't know what I would have said to you or even if you would have been receptive to me."

"Time did slip past quickly I will admit that."

"Not for me, my love" she shared returning his stare with a light giggle. "For me, I was living an eternal nightmare. My girlfriends tried to console and support me, but they knew it was futile. They repeatedly told me to call you, but no, I wanted to do it my way and how foolish was that? Days turned into weeks and weeks turned into months. Before long, I was too embarrassed to call you. I was a total wreck. Ms. 9 to 5 who always had her shit in order was walking around like a damn zombie and an emotional mess. The funny thing about the whole scenario is that everybody thought that they knew why?" she shared slightly giggling. "I remember the first time I saw you. Do you remember?"

He had to reflect back then it came to him. "Yeah" he slightly smiled. "It was at Chocolate Bliss."

"Exactually" she replied with a faint smile. "You had this extremely attractive mocha complexion sister at your table. As I watched y'all, I watch you whispering in her ear and how she would blush from the erotic things that I knew you were saying. I instantly became jealous. The date that I was with notice me opening staring at you and asked if I knew you because I was definitely not concerning myself with his feelings. I inform him that you was my ex and he asked if I wanted to leave. Why would I want to leave when I haven't seen or heard from you in years? I subtly watched you for almost two hours until our eyes finally connected. When you tip your glass to me in acknowledgement, the weight of the world seems to have been lifted from my shoulder. You have forgiven me and tipping your glass to me was the significance to your toast. Although I was elated, I figure you was closing the concluding chapter to our relationship. When I received a romantic card and two dozen of Lilies two weeks later for my birthday, I knew I haven't lost you completely, but would you ever trust me again?"

"Z, that, was an extremely emotional time for me" he began while returning her stare. "I couldn't grasp why you would do something like that when it was created from our love. In my mind, what we were allegedly building was nothing more than a mirage, an illusion of my desires for us. So, I did something completely out of character. I step off from you. Although my partners wondered what had transpired, I was unable to share my pain with them. Bear was the one that eventually figured it out and started making hints about forgiveness. God and Christians can forgive, but I'm not a Christian and during those time, I wasn't forgiving anything. You slight me, I'm not turning the other cheek like Christianity advocates. If there was something that you felt you would be losing by having a child, you could have simply given it to me to raise for us, but that option was never placed on the table, and I resented you for that" he shared never averting his eyes.

"My girlfriends told me to ask you if you would raise the child, but no, I wanted to do it my way and lost you" she shared slightly shaking her head. "So, have you truly forgiven me, Afrika?" she asked wanting to know that he did and not suspect that he did.

"Yes, I have" he replied. "I didn't plan it but when I saw you at Chocolate Bliss, I suddenly forgave you especially in my heart."

"And I was glad that you did, my life was in a wreck without you."

"While I regressed similarly into a person I despised, a fake Romeo and Casanova. A sailor of love docking in strange and exotic ports. I ran though women like a junkie first-time shooting up dope for the first time, but I wasn't happy or satisfied. I was seeking that initial high of ecstasy that you induced in me, but it remained elusive" he shared with a coy smile. "It wasn't just Mona's that was detrimental to my healing process because she knows me oh so well or Bear's words that gradually healed me, it was Kimba and Tek9" he revealed slightly smiling. She knew that Mona was the one that had gotten away. When they met in Atlanta, they took a long private walk together for over two hours. While sharing blunts and over-looking the Savanna River, neither woman held their tongues. Both respected and feel in love with the other that July afternoon because of their openness concerning Afrika. "When Tek9 and Kimba told me it was time for me to come home, I knew it was time" he shared lightly snickering. "But I was still confused about my emotions."

"Confused how?"

"Did I want to experience the trials and tribulations of love again or continue too just live? A life void of love and serious conversations about the future. When we first met, I knew I had to reveal my hand to you when we were rolling for about six months and allow you to make up your own mind about messing with a drug dealer. When you step off, I was surprised but I also respected your decision and never reached out to you. So, when you returned to my arms, I was happy but apprehensive also. Will you be like a door? Opening and closing your love to me or remain faithful to the journey."

"Well, I'm glad you chose love" she replied slightly smiling. "Is that why you are still wearing a condom with me two years later?"

"Yes, Z" he replied honestly.

"Don't have any doubts about us baby, please" she requested softly gripping his fingers.

"I still do occasionally, Z" he shared surprising her. "I do sometimes still think about our child and how old it would have been. Once I accepted that it is your body and you can do whatever you want with it, I gradually made peace with your decision" he said taking his eyes off her and placing them on the Caribbean Sea. The moon was full and reflecting off the waves coming towards the shore. The warm breeze felt refreshing after a hot and humid day. He suddenly collected their disposable tray and place them in the trash receptacle. Returning to his seat, he accepted the joint that she as extending to him. They clutch fingers and cough off the potency of the weed as Caribbean music played in the background.

"So, will you please take that damn condom off so I can feel you coming again?"

"Are you sure?" he asked slightly hardening his eyes.

"Absolutely" she replied smiling. "I am taking birth control now" she reminded him.

"If you are certain, okay" he replied causing her to suddenly smile.

Returning to Justice 4 All, there appeared to be an aura or glow that surrounded them. Call it what you want but they had it. Their love was evident before the week vacation but now, it was just ridiculous. Seeing the antics that they were doing to one another had you shaking your head at them.

Thursday evening around seven o'clock, he received an unexpected call from Tek9. The information that he gave him caused him to go into lawyer mode with the numerous questions he was asking until he was satisfied then ended their conversation. He sat there for over two hours before he got to his feet and went to take a shower. A half hour later, he was walking out his front door and climbing into his car then pulled off. As he took Rt.38 towards Camden, all he could do was shake his head. He had a private conversation with Blood less than a year ago and he assured him that there wouldn't be any problems concerning the Harbor. Well, he have stepped way out of his lane concerning the Harbor and he contributed it to him not being on the scene with his partners at the exclusive parties. Tek9 had told Bear twice to step to him, but he wanted to continue using diplomacy. You can't use diplomacy against a motherfucker like Blood. He foolishly think that his shit doesn't stink until you shove his face in it. Tek didn't want to go behind Bear's back, but he was making a serious mistake with Blood. He knew Afrika would get his head back in the right state of mind.

He pulled up at Jokers on Haddon Avenue and found a parking spot across the street from the grave yard. He climbed out of his vehicle then proceed towards the club. He spoke to several people as he made his way towards the front door.

"Afrika, damn! How have you been big spender?" one of the door men asked shaking his hand.

"I've been good Dynamite" he replied returning his smile. "I hear that my partners are here?"

"Yeah, they are up in the VIP with some sisters from Philly" he informed him.

"Thanks brother" he said paying the fee then walking inside. Several women that he knew requested a dance or drink. He brought them drinks while staring up at his partners entertaining the ladies from Philly. As he made his climb to the VIP level, Tek9 was the first to see him and put everybody on point. They were noticeably surprised to see him especially Tek9 as they got to their feet smiling while watching him ascending the stairs. Tek didn't expect Afrika to get with Bear so soon. "What's up fellas?" he asked tapping their knuckles. "Queens" he greeted tipping his black New York fitted baseball cap.

"What are you doing out on a Thursday night?" inquired Bear glad to have his presence with them as they reclaimed their chairs.

"Jeans and Tim's" teased Kimba causing them to lightly snicker and the ladies to smile.

"He must have been washing that pimp of his" commented Black winking at him. "How old is she now?" he asked trying to contain his smile while maintaining his harden eyes.

"You know how old she is" he replied slightly snarling at him. "She was six this summer" he replied as they amused themselves while the ladies stared on smiling.

"You really need to upgrade to the present" suggested Murk.

"She gets me to where I need to go" he replied returning his snarl.

"Yeah, at a motherfucking crawl" replied Bear causing them to burst out laughing.

"That's why I don't hang out with y'all, I don't have to accept y'all talking about my baby" he snarled at them individually.

"That's not why" interjected Tek9 waving off his statement while grinning.

"No, why?" he venture for their amusement.

"You are just a cheap motherfucker. No, my bad" he apologized placing his hand over his heart and grinning up at him. "You aren't cheap. You are what?"

"Money conscious!" they blurted out together then burst out laughing and slapping fives or leaning on one another as the ladies enjoyed their interaction.

"Y'all are putting me on blast, damn" he replied as they wipe tears from their eyes. "Laugh at this" he stated grabbing their attention as their smiles slowly dissipated as they stared up at him. "Queens, I truly hate to disturb y'all entertainment and their amusement" he began smiling down into their eyes as staring longer into the eyes of a chocolate young lady causing her to blush.

"What's up Afrika?" Bear asked staring up at him.

"We have some business that needs to be attended" he replied brushing off his black pullover Nets sweat shirt causing them to stare at one another then at his attire again.

"You heard about Blood, huh?" Bear inquired returning his stare.

"The streets are whispering" he lied. "I need y'all to gather up y'all stuff and come with me" he instructed staring down into their eyes individually but none of them was moving. "Now, gentlemen!" he insisted starting to turn towards the stairs. As they suddenly got to their feet and collecting their stuff, Amir told the ladies that they will be back. Tek9 and

Kimba tapped knuckles as they exchanged menacing stares. As they descended the stairs under the watchful eyes of some of the patronage, North was on the move. Something was up. Once outside and away from the slight crowd that was taking a break from the heat inside, he stared at them. "It's eleven o'clock, gentlemen. Do y'all still keep that stash in y'all cars?"

"Of course," they replied together hardening their eyes.

"Then change up, gentlemen and meet be here in twenty minutes. Amir, you can step off little brother" he told him staring in his eyes.

"What? No!" he replied adamantly while hardening his eyes.

"Step off" Bear said in a soft tone that he despised then reluctantly followed his order mumbling as he headed toward Parkside Drive.

"Twenty minutes gentlemen" he told them as they disburse heading towards their respected vehicles. They open their trunks and pull out their leather bag then climbed into their vehicles and drove to an isolated spot to change out of their suits. Minutes later, Afrika was sitting in the middle of the street with his flashers on. Once everybody had arrived, he led them up Haddon Avenue then turned left on Mickle Street. Once they crossed Broadway, they turned on S 4th Street and drove down to Spruce Street then found parking spots on the darken street and exited their cars. "Where are they?" he asked chambering a round in his Glock .40.

"Near 3rd and Cherry" Bear informed him clutching his .44 Magnum.

"Tek and Kimba, you're with me. Bear, bring the brothers up Cherry Street. You have three minutes to get into position" he instructed as they peeked at their watches then split up. Bear lead them back towards 4th Street and turned the corner. Tek didn't expect Afrika to set it off tonight but then he had to laugh at his brain fart. Afrika never puts off tomorrow what can be accomplished tonight. Straight like a gangster like that and always have been since they were kids. He didn't have a problem seeking out alleged threats or going into their hood to see if the threat was sincere. For some strange reason, most were from someone saying they were joking and those that weren't found out just how prolific they were with their hands from Afrika's tutelage. He personally missed his presence.

As they casually walked down the street on the dark side, they stared up Joint Street spotting Bear with the others crossing. Checking his watch as they lean against the lean, Tek didn't have to point them out with that loud ass boom box blasting Snoop Dogg's "Dog Pound" CD across the open field. Smoking blunts and sipping on forties, Afrika was glad that no young ladies were presence, or they would have to abort their mission. As they push off the wall and approached the partying group, they never paid them any attention until it was much too late as the ten guys got on point.

"Which one of y'all is T-Bone?"

"Who the fuck is asking?" a guy in his early thirties replied pulling from a blunt while staring up at him.

"Are you T-Bone?"

"Who the fuck are you? Five-o" he snorted.

"Are you T-Bone?" he reiterated.

"And if I am?" he asked defiantly while openly flashing his canines and getting to his feet.

POW! The bullet enter his front cranium and exit through the back spattering some of his crew. By the time the shock left their eyes and began reaching while moving, the trap was already set. As they try to run up the street shooting their weapons indiscriminately, they were met by Bear. His canon erupted the semi quietness of their weapons. When the silence returned ninety-seconds later, eight were stretched out in a fifty-yard radius and two critically wounded. By the time they returned to their vehicles and pulled away from the curb, the first sounds of sirens could be heard in the distance. They hooked a U-turn then cruised up S 3rd Street and turning left on Pine Street. As they were at the light at Broadway, five-o came zooming pass with their lights flashing and sirens wailing.

After changing into their original clothes, they returned to The Jokers and the waiting young ladies within fifty-minutes. The ladies actually confessed that they thought that they wouldn't be returning. As they refreshen their drinks and continued getting acquainted, a special bulletin interrupted Sports Center to mentioned the multiple homicides on the south side of the harbor in Camden, New jersey. They never batted an eye or displace the conversation they were having, but Blood did.

He sat staring at the television in shock as he recognized some of the faces shown. Those were his men from the Harbor, and he had a damn good assumption as to who was responsible. He knew it wasn't Bear or Tek9 but Afrika and that wasn't good. T-Bone's cousin coming from out of North gave him the 411 on the clicks in North especially concerning Bear and his partners since they were always walking around the city freely. Granted, it was well known that Tek, Kimba and

Murk could be ruthless if released, but they weren't the most notorious. Afrika was and that surprised the hell out of Blood. The stories he have heard as he was growing up seems almost unbelievable but substantiated on the streets and grapevine. When he and Afrika had talked last year, he didn't see the threat that everybody had told him. In fact, he was humble and that wasn't expected by someone having his alleged status. Perhaps, no, he did ignore their conversation and didn't take it to heart but continued to walk that thin line between right and wrong. Yeah, some of his people in his circle warned him about stepping too far out of his lane and misjudging Afrika's diplomacy as being empathic. But the money he was getting from the Harbor couldn't be ignored, why didn't Bear just get frustrated and pull them out even though he said they wouldn't? Well, that motherfucking plan damn sure imploded. He knew they would be demanding another meeting and he will inform them then that he was going to shut down his business at the Harbor. All he could do was hope Bear keep those three violent psychotic motherfuckers under control. If Afrika is with them and voice his opinion, he might not want a meeting. He might demand blood. Specifically, his blood.

The next day he haven't heard from Bear as expected and that wasn't cool. So, he reached out to him and requested a meeting, but he didn't accept it without talking to his partners first especially Afrika. He was hoping that he didn't include Afrika, but he did and that made him extremely nervous. They eventually agreed to meet near Cramer Hill around nine o'clock that night. He was waiting with twelve of his soldiers. Spotting their vehicles pulling up, he suddenly became anxious as he subtly rock from side to side. As they pulled up two rolls away from him, he watched them climbing out of their vehicles and approaching. Whereas most wouldn't have taken notice of their attire, he did. Jeans, Butter Tim's, pull over hoodies and black fitted baseball caps.

"Hey, fellas" he greeted concentrating more on Tek9 than any of them.

"Apparently, you wanted to do what you wanted, huh?" Afrika stated walking up while staring him in his eyes. He peeked over at Bear. "What the fuck are you looking over at him for? I'm talking to you. You insisted on impressing your men by playing your hand, huh? Well, it's been called and by me" he snarled pulling out his Glock and chambering a round. "Since you took Bear as someone that you play, well I'm here to correct that distorted thinking."

"Wait Afrika!" he insisted putting his hands up and slightly backing into one of his men. "I'll pull my men from there for good. It's all yall's" he informed him unable to hide the panic in his eyes.

"I don't need you to give us a got damn thing motherfucker" he snarled at him. "We control the Harbor already. So, you aren't giving us shit but I have something for you" he stated watching fear grip his eyes as his peripheral vision caught Tek9 raising his hand.

POW! The Magnum 44 sounded like a cannon when it was discharged. The force of the round took him off his feet as his men leap back revealing their empty hands.

"Say something! Anything!" invited Kimba flashing his canines at them while clutching his nine-millimeter. "We will take out your whole family."

"From the roots!" included Murk.

"Wrap him up" Afrika informed them watching Blood's crew remaining perfectly still like mannequins as Kimba and Black rolled out the industrial plastic then carried his lifeless body back to Bear's SUV. "Let's bounce" he said as they turned and casually walked back towards their vehicles then climbed inside and pulled away.

"I told Blood not to fuck with them" Ice told them watching their tail lights heading towards River Road. "I'm in charge now and all the bullshit antics ceases right now. Keep your motherfuckin mouths close because y'all know, they don't make threats."

Days later, there was no mention of Blood being taken out. Not on social media and especially on the grapevine. Witnessing him being taken out in front of them assured them that the threat was as real as Ice had repeatedly and adamantly tried to warned Blood. Speculations started filtering throughout the city but that was all it was, speculations. There was no evidence to substantiate anything even when his main woman got with Ice. He looked her square in her light brown eyes and said, he was just as confused by his disappearance. All she could do was wait for homicide to contacted her, but the call she waited for never came.

Two weeks later, Afrika was sitting in his office with his eyes closed being serenade by Dinah Washington's sultry voice singing "Take All Of Me" when his phone rang. Slowly opening his eyes, he picked up the receiver and listen before placing it back into its cradle. The Hines brothers wanted to have a private conversation with him, and it perk his interest. He devilishly invited them to come to his office but they, natural declined. They couldn't face seeing some of their previous employees, especially Shakira. They had come to his building one Sunday to get a peek at his building. They thought the building would be vacant because his car wasn't park outside but it wasn't, Afrika had Aziza drop him off to pick up a file as she made a quick run. They climbed out of Robert's car and stared at the building. The conceit and arrogant disposition that usually consumed their characteristic was noticeably absent as they stared inside at the first floor ignoring the cameras. The last time he briefly saw them was almost two years ago. He was arguing the suppression of evidence by the prosecutor's office. James alcoholism had gotten noticeably worse while Robert appeared to be ten years older with the stress he was under and producing rapidly graying hairs. Now, they wanted to have lunch over in Philly at Unique. At first, he started to suggest a closer location but accepted. He could buy some new dress shirts from Shirt Corner at 3rd and Market Street. He was walking through the door around one o'clock. He spotted them at a far table nursing their drinks. He paused in the shadow to watch their interaction. It was apparent that something serious was troubling them because James was jumping all up in James ass. The look of distain was all over his face as he stared at his younger brother. He could only deduce that Robert was finally giving him a history of his conniving scandalous ways and how it had gotten them into their present predicament. During the whole tongue lashing, James never interrupted him or denounced the things his brother was saying. He would naturally be circumspective because their past dictates such apprehension. He only took the meeting out of curiosity because they no longer meant anything to him. Stepping out to make his presence known,

Robert nodded in his direction as James tried in vain to regain his composure.

"Gentlemen" he greeted standing in front of them.

"Afrika" replied Robert getting to his feet to shake his hand as James caught himself late as usual. He extend his hand for him to shake but he ignored it while snarling in his eyes. "Have a seat" Robert offer. "Are you hungry?"

"Na, I'm okay" he replied taking his seat.

"How have things been?" he asked taking a sip of his bourbon.

"Extremely busy" he replied.

"Yeah, I saw you argue a case last year. Very impressive."

"Thank you" he replied. "What's this about Robert?" he asked staring into his reddish eyes.

"Straight to the point, huh?" he slightly smiled.

"Time is money" he recited what they constantly said to him.

"I need to discuss two very serious situations with you" he shared.

"That is unusual" he replied with a coy smile. "Why me Robert?"

"Because of your natural skills" he replied honestly while returning his stare. "James had a problem with one of his mistresses" he informed him.

"If I knew this was about him, I would have declined this meeting" he let it be known while staring over into his pitiful eyes. "Being married, he shouldn't have any mistresses or side chicks" he stated watching him taking a sip from his Johnny Walker red before placing his eyes back on Robert.

"I won't argue that point" he cosigned staring over at him coldly. "The woman is making some serious allegations concerning her seventeen-year-old daughter" he shared taking a sip from his drink.

"Seventeen?" he repeated staring over at James. "What is the allegations?"

"That her daughter is pregnant by him."

"How can she make a claim like that unless he was dumb enough to have unprotected sex with her?" he asked staring at him then over into James defiant eyes and slight snarl. "And you believe what he is saying, Robert."

"I didn't fuck that bitch!" he snapped returning Afrika's cold stare.

"Afrika, he swore to me that he didn't."

"He swore, huh?" he slightly chuckled staring over at James glaring eyes while slightly shaking his head. "I hate to be the bearer of bad news" he stated then paused. "Yes, I do" he corrected himself smiling over at James. "He's been lying to you Robert. Word on the streets have been whispering about their relationship for a minute especially when they were seen at the resort in Atlantic City. How long have it been James? Five or six months, right?" he asked staring over at him but not expecting a response. "There is no doubt that she is a very promiscuous young lady and even I was impressed by her anatomy when I saw her at Eternity, but who would have conceived that she was only seventeen?"

Robert shot him a cold stare that caused him to slightly repel. If they weren't in a public place, he would have slapped the shit out of him. "Is this true?"

"I used a condom every time that I got with her and none of them had burst. I swear."

"Keep that fucking word out of your lying ass mouth" he scorned him. He wanted to reach over and snatch out his throat.

"I believe him, Robert" he couldn't believe he was saying. "She put him on blast to hide someone else" he gave his opinion.

"What?" Robert replied by his statement.

"I've seen the young lady, Robert. She might play a naïve game on a sucker like James especially since he thinks he got it going on. His arrogance made her play simple. When is your court date?"

"It is supposed to take place in August, but they are trying to settle out of court."

"Who? The mother."

"Na, her stepfather."

"Her stepfather, why?" he found himself asking then becoming quiet. They have witnessed that expression on his face before as he worked things out in his mind. So, they remained silent as he went through his process. Suddenly, clarity came to his eyes and a faint grin came to his lips. "If I were you, I wouldn't negotiate anything especially if you think you can keep it from your wife. Attacking her character isn't the problem, everybody knows that she keeps her legs open like a 7-11 except James dumb ass" he slightly smiled at his ignorance while enjoying his embarrassment. "I'm willing to bet she is pregnant by her stepfather in this torrid story. It would a safe bet that he knew about your affair and saw an easy pay day" he shared his opinion while grinning.

"If that is true, that would be some scandalous shit" mentioned Robert.

"Na, what James have been doing is some scandalous shit" he corrected him. "Now if you desired some legal advices, I would have to charge you" he stated with an unemotional stare. "What is the second situation?"

"The second situation concern our law firm" he admitted taking a big swig from his glass.

"I'm listening."

"I tried to fuck you" he began.

"No" he interjected staring over at him with menacing eyes. "If you aren't going to talk truthfully, we can cease this conversation right now. You didn't try fucking me. You fucked me" he reiterated slightly snarling.

"Yeah, you are right. I did" he openly admitted. "I should have given you the partnership that you deserved as I agreed, but I foolishly listen to my alcoholic ass brother and look at the shit we are presently in" he shared staring over at him through slightly blurring eyes.

"Well, personally I was glad that you tried to play me, or I wouldn't have venture out on my own" he shared grinning.

"With our fucked-up credit, you and I know that I couldn't barrow the money from the traditional way. I borrowed from motherfuckers that don't give a damn about the strain it place on us and the firm to repay. They just want their damn money and on time. We sold the houses that we brought and gave several lawyers their severance pay because we couldn't honor their contracts. I'm fearful that they might start getting physical to obtain their balance or worse" he shared his fear.

"They won't kill y'all, Robert" he slightly smiled at him. "There is no profit in it."

"We are considering sub-leasing."

"That would surely help your situation."

"We don't know the procedure about sub-leasing" he admitted.

"I can send one of my business lawyer over to holla at y'all tomorrow."

"For a fee, right?"

"Of course," he replied grinning as he got to his feet. "I will give you a thirty percent discount. Gentlemen" he said tipping his hat. "I appreciate the apology, Robert. James, you can continue to kiss my ass" he told him turning and walking away. Stepping out of the restaurant and feeling the light breeze, he adjusted his hat then proceeded down South Street smiling from ear to ear. He didn't have the nerve to tell them that Butch Williams now hold the note to his building and life.

Milligan and his Nextel Boys were sitting in court waiting for their corruption trial to begin. Although they were confident that they wouldn't be prosecuted, they still wonder what happen to the evidence. Was someone holding it to extort them? If they were, they would be making a grave error in judgement and get what their hand will deserve. A forty-caliber slug to the back of their scandalous head. Looking over at the prosecutor's table, he could see how anxious and irate they were as they would periodically stare over at the defense table. Something had pissed them off and they knew what it was, but their lawyers didn't. When the judge entered, the prosecutor requested an audience that included the defense lawyers. They spoke quietly for about three minutes before they returned to their respected tables.

"Apparently, the evidence associated with this case has been stolen, misplaced, or destroyed. All charges gave been drop. You and your men are excused Sgt. Mulligan."

"Thank you, your Honor" he replied getting to his feet with him men then proceeded up the isle keeping their eyes fixed on the door. Cops consumed the left side of the isle, but he refused to stare at them in their eyes. How many times is he going to escape the clutches of the law? Just as he was about to push open the double swinging doors, Commissioner Brown made her presence known.

"Watch yourself out there Mulley. You are starting to slip" she told him glaring slightly into his eyes.

He never responded just continued out the door. Once out of the courthouse and standing on the sidewalk, they proceeded towards their vehicle while unloosening their tie.

"I need a party" Mulley informed them.

"I know just who to call" Smooth assured him pulling out his cellphone smiling. "Dee-Dee and her freaks."

"Oh, yeah!" Red Neck declared enthusiastically. "They are definitely just what the doctor would prescribe" he said tapping knuckles with White Boy Mike.

A week after the mistrial, Afrika received a phone call from a former client, Santiago. He had some intriguingly interesting things to share concerning the missing evidence.

He informed him that his cousin had been in possession of the evidence and placed it in his hand for safe keeping. All he was requesting for his assistance in shutting down Mulley's illegal operation is immunity from prosecution. Afrika assured him that he had an inside track at the prosecutor's office and if he couldn't grant that immunity, he needed to hold on to the whole card and keep it in a safe place just case he ever needs it. He also said that he would like to meet with his cousin, and he said he would hook it up then get back at him. A couple of hours later he received a phone call and where the meeting will take place. Walking through Pyne Poynt Park, he had to chuckle because there was no better place for a private conversation especially from five-o and strangers. Five-o couldn't post up in an alley to do surveillance without getting put on blast from the Donks that roam through them. He was chilling at the basketball courts with three guys as he approached.

"What's up Afrika?" he asked shaking his hand.

"How have you been?" he asked smiling over at him. "Good to know you follow my instructions."

"Yeah, and my lady appreciated it too" he replied laughing at their private joke. With the money he has, he did need something to fall back on and Afrika suggested it while Maria was standing next to me. I enjoyed working on cars, so I enrolled in auto mechanic school and got certified. I am presently working for a BMW dealership in Cherry Hill. "This is my cousin Morales" he introduced. "This is Afrika, man."

"Yeah, I recognize him from the papers and from around the court house" he admitted shaking his hand. "Can you help me?"

"My job is to help those in need" he replied suddenly smiling at them.

"This is what all the noise is about" he said pulling out a video tape then stared into his eyes before surrendering it to him. "There are several mid-level drug dealers that are forced to sell the drugs that Mulley stole from stash houses while others are being extorted to rent a corner that he designate. The tape will reveal drug consumption and other illicit activities with young girls. All were given a choice of incarceration or having a private party with them that could put a couple of hundred dollars in their pockets. The majority choose freedom."

"Is there a specific place where all this takes place?"

"Yeah, I can provide you with both locations."

"Is there drugs at these locations?"

"It's like a pharmacy" he replied. "Girls have several types of drugs that gets them in a freaky mood. They especially like those damn E-pills and cocaine."

"Give me the address of both locations so I can put my people on them" he said extending a pad and pen to him. "I will reach out to my connection in the prosecutor's office and see how he will play."

"If you can help me Afrika, I will truly appreciate it" he stated sincerely while extending the pad and pen back to him.

"Don't worry about anything, Morales. I got your back" he tried to assured him. "Continue to do what you must but I will be setting something up" he said unable to contain the impish smile that creased his lips. "I will hit Santiago up when I have everything set" he said tapping Santiago's knuckles. "Morales, I got this" he said turning and walking away.

Afrika couldn't see the unconscious menacing stare that crept into his eyes, but Santiago and Morales peeked it then they peeked at one another. When he suddenly showed up at Smooth's Jazz over in Philly, Black was the first to recognize the subtle expression that was on his partner's face. He haven't seen that stare in almost four years. He became highly curious to know what plot he was about to institute and the form of justice he would administer.

"I'm in!" he announced tapping his knuckles.

"Damn!" he replied then burst out laughing.

"Who's the target?" he inquired still wearing his broad smile as their other partners caught up.

"What's up Afrika?" Bear asked with an impish smile.

"The Nextel Boys but Mulley specifically" he shared grinning.

"Oh, shit!" declared Tek9 then burst out laughing with the others.

"You are about to administer justice to five-o?" asked Murk snickering.

"Why not?" he asked peeking at them grinning. "Somebody needs to, and I honestly couldn't think of a better group of guys to do it especially since they have been sniffing around for the past two years" he shared.

"That's fucked up" stated Black laughing.

"Once I view this tape and set up surveillance."

"Surveillance?" they all said together then looked at one another and burst out laughing again.

"Wow, I would hate to have you coming for me" Tek said snickering.

"I wouldn't" he told him staring seriously into his eyes then gradually started smiling. "I'm not the prosecutor."

"Oh, yeah you aren't" he replied causing them to burst out laughing again.

"So, what do you need?" Bear asked.

"An unsuspecting, Amir" he replied causing a perplex expression to engulf their faces then they burst out laughing again.

In the weeks since their meeting, Mulley was under constant surveillance. Let me say right out the gate, night vision is a motherfucker. Bear's hired men was able to be damn near on top of them during several illegal transactions and video everything. They were standing at the mouth of any alley in Parkside when they caught White Boy and Red Neck punching a teenager in the face several times as Mulley clamp his hand on the back of a young ladies neck demanding that she shut the fuck up. Thursday, Friday, and Saturday nights, they brought several young ladies to their secret rendezvous apartment. They would party to about three or four o'clock in the morning. What really perked their interest was following them towards Cooper Hospital and meeting with someone that stayed in the shadows. Once they left and the unidentified man headed up S. 6th Street, they decided to abandon Mulley and try to get the mysterious person identity. They can always find Mulley. As they proceeded up Broadway, they turned left at Newton Street then turned the engine and lights off. As their target started crossing Pine Street, they started videoing, and the light pole suddenly illuminated his face, it was Blackout. What was Mulley doing having a private conversation with a renowned homicidal motherfucker like him? When Afrika suggested that he must be security, nobody could think otherwise because he damn sure wasn't a snitch. If he were really their security, proving it wouldn't be hard. Although they have never worked a corner, they damn sure have excellent connections, especially Afrika. Most have sought his legal representation.

In one month of surveillance, they have comprised some very damaging evidence on Mulley and his boys. Their routine vaguely waver. Some of the young ladies caught on tape were eventually pulled up and they basically gave the same story. Being extorted for sex to escape distribution charges.

"When are you going to drop the bomb on them" inquired Bear extending a blunt to him.

"Soon, brother. Very soon" he shared slightly hardening his eyes. "I need to check that back door first" he reminded him.

Afrika had chosen to meet Sullivan at Rico's in Moorestown for a late lunch. He have always liked the tranquility of the restaurant with a pond outside since stumbling upon it. The geese that reside there, year-round eggs had hatched, and their little hatchlings was free to explore their new intriguing and pristine environment under the watchful and protective eyes of their parents. He didn't know how Sullivan was going to react to the information he was willing to share. He could only hope that the perception he had of him was accurate or the lunch engagement could turn ugly and quickly. They were both seeking the same thing and didn't fore see any issues arising. Granted, he might want to know certain details, but he wouldn't be able to elaborate on certain fundamental things like where or how he was able to obtain it. If he persist in acting like a prosecutor, he will excuse himself and apologize for wasting his time while explaining that he was mistaken about his character.

Afrika enter the restaurant a little after noon. He informed the hostess that he was meeting someone, and the person was already seated inside. As a he proceeded further inside, he spotted Frank staring at him approaching. He was always dressed immaculate while his suits were brought off the rack from one of the department stores. He haven't brought himself a new pair of shoes in months and the ones he wore were scuffed up. Why would anybody become a prosecutor when the pay wasn't shit and the hours were long as hell? He was sacrificing his financial wealth for his aspiration but how much longer will he endure? He could be one of those prosecutor's making back door deals and benefiting from it monetary but then, he would be worse than the criminals they are trying to prosecute. He have to keep telling himself every few months to stay strong. Like most, he has aspirations of joining the political arena, but things were creeping along and testing his patience while the rare few actually love prosecuting criminals. Something will fall into his lap eventually and his supervisor will have to give him the promotion. If not, Afrika's offer was still on the table from two years ago. "Come work for me." What he was offering for his professionalism was thirty-thousand dollars more than what he was getting paid. Plus, he would have his own office. A very alluring offer especially with a child coming.

"Frank, glad to see you" he greeted him getting to his feet and shaking his hand.

"How have you been Afrika?" he replied smiling.

"I've been good" he replied. "Do you want a drink while our order is being prepared?"

"Sure, I'll have a gin and tonic" he informed the waitress before taking a seat.

"I'll have a glass of Moscato" he told her as she turned and left. "I'm sure you were surprised by my invitation."

"You can definitely say that. My curiosity have been skied high" he assured him while grinning.

"I kind of figure it would be considering I am paying" he replied grinning. "How is Margarette?"

"She is fine, thanks."

"She is about five months pregnant now, right?"

"Yeah" he replied surprise. "How did you know she was pregnant?"

"At the lawyers forum, I notice that she wasn't having her favorite drink."

"Very perceptive of you" he replied lightly snickering.

"Not really, that little protruding stomach is the culprit" he replied grinning. "I know you have noticed the glow around her."

"Once again, I must admit every perceptive."

"Do y'all know the gender?"

"Yes, a boy" he proudly replied smiling.

"That's good" he replied. "Now you don't have to keep her bare feet and pregnant until you get one" he shared causing him to snicker.

The waitress returned with their drinks and informed them that their orders will be done in ten minutes. They continued their casual conversation throughout their meal. Both men genuinely enjoyed the other's company. They shared small parts of their up bringing and why they chose the opposite side of the law. The little debates that they have shared revealed both gentlemen moral character. By the time their meal was over, they had mutual respect for the other and could become even closer friends if they desire. After Afrika had paid the bill and gave the waitress her tip, he stared across the table at Sullivan closely, but he was staring just as closely.

"Shall we take our drinks to the balcony?" he suggested.

"Sure" he replied getting to his feet with him and following him out onto the balcony to a table.

"I have always liked this restaurant" Afrika shared with him.

"It doesn't feel like the city is just beyond those trees" he agreed taking a sip from his second drink as he stared out at the geese. He was still curious as to why he requested this lunch, but he knew rushing him wouldn't be polite or warranted. He will inform him with a little patience. After about five minutes, Afrika took the initiative.

"Frank, I know you was disappointed in the evidence against Mulligan disappearing from the evidence cage."

"Disappointing isn't the word" he suddenly snarled. "I was piss. I know that corruption exist but when it's associated with unprofessional acts by officers is ridiculous. How can we expect citizens to assist in eliminating crime in their neighborhoods and hear evidence against officers were stolen, not misplaced as they claimed.

"You can't Frank" he tried to assure him. "You don't see what I see because you aren't from the streets. I have witnessed several cops going against the honor of the badge as I grew up. I can't tell you how many times I have been called the N word as a teenager. The relationship between blacks and cops is not one of respect. You have to give respect to receive it. You can't take it as a lot of cops try to do and it build more resentment between the two. Wearing a badge and carrying a gun doesn't get you anything, we see their true character. That word integrity that is etched in their vehicles doors need to be permanently removed. The conditions that blacks are forced to live in isn't one that they chose to live in. There are more liquor stores in our community than preachers. Do you have that where you live?" he asked with an impish smile.

"No, I don't" he replied. He have also witness officers doing deplorable things to blacks and those of color. "I have often thought about the black holocaust during their transcontinental to America" he shared surprising him. "How have y'all survived?" he softly asked then becoming quiet. He have also wondered why the commissioner board of liquors and the city council allowed such an abundance of liquor stores. He has to drive almost five miles to acquire his liquor and he better get to the store before seven o'clock or his travel distance will be substantially further. The reasoning for such a high volume wasn't hard to figure out. Keeping the residence intoxicated will assure them of possibly becoming compliance with their situation and condition.

"People actually think that we are surviving but we aren't. Look at our drop out rate in school which breeds illiteracy, our addiction rate and incarceration rate of my people, does that appeared to be a nation of people surviving or aspiring? You can be a righteous and law-abiding person, but the color of you skin can still get you murder by five-o. Howe does a simple traffic stop ends in black people being murder? Their explanation was etched into their memory bank while they were still in the academy. "I was fearful for my life." Being a cop, you chose a profession that places your life in danger every day like those that chose to become correctional officers. Psychologically, we are constantly under duress in America."

"I know" he replied averting his eyes from his and placing them on the pond.

"Frank" he called snapping him out of is daydream and staring in his brown eyes. "Supposed I was to tell you I know where the evidence is located" he blurted out.

"Huh?" he replied staring at him in shock. "You know where the evidence is?"

"Yeah, I have it" he revealed never averting his eyes.

"You have it" he replied astounded. "How in the hell did you get it?"

"Let's just say it was placed in my hands for safe keeping" he replied returning his stare.

"I'm stun" he admitted. "What are you going to do with it?"

"Give it to you" he replied with a coy smile.

"That smile indicates that you want something in returned" he informed him grinning.

"Indeed, I do. I don't want one of the officers implicated. "I'm requesting immunity for him, and he can't testify, or it will destroy his career and place his life in legitimate danger in the streets. Do we have a deal?"

"With me, yeah. Who do you want immunity for?"

"Salvatore Morales" he replied. "Word on the streets, he's an honest cop that just got caught up, but he's disappointed in Mulligan's antics."

"Good officer" he replied. "Let me get with my supervisor."

"You do that but don't mention my client's name" he told him as they laid back enjoying the slight breeze. "By the way, I have some very interesting video of Mulligan and his goons."

"Surveillance?" he mentioned lightly chuckling. "You are a P.I now too? What does it show?"

"Besides where they party at, Mulley is caught talking to a renowned murderer named Blackout."

"Blackout! Do you know his criminal history?"

"Of course, I'm checking on a rumor now."

"What rumor?"

"That he's on Mulley payroll and take care of things concerning their illegal activities."

"If you can substantiate that, I will personally place handcuffs on Mulligan" he shared with conviction in his eyes.

"Time will tell" he replied grinning.

Later that night, Afrika contacted Morales to inform him that the meeting with the prosecutor was excellent. He also inform him that Commissioner Brown will be inform and have you transferred out of the unit before anything goes down. Hearing the good news, Morales seem to relax so he naturally took advantage of the situation and asked the question that have been plaguing his mind. "Is Blackout Mulley's security?"

"Na, he's more than that. He's his personal executioner."

Afrika could believe what he just heard. Five-o was personally utilizing a renowned murderer and assassin to keep drug dealers in check. He couldn't believe his luck.

Friday morning, UPS delivered two packages to Frank Sullivan that needed his signature only. Signing for the two oblong boxes, he took them to his desk with a sinister smile on his face. The first box contained the missing evidence. He walked to an empty office to view it. He locked the door and closed the blinds. The video showed Mulley and his men smoking weed, drinking alcohol and snorting cocaine with numerous young black ladies. Morales was never at those illicit parties, at lease on tape. A broad smile engulfed his face as he turned off the video. He will have to return it to Afrika but at least he knew where it would be and more importantly, it would be secure. When he open the second box, the content made him pause as he picked it up to study it. A picture of him, Afrika, Aziza, and his wife at the Black Lawyers Convention last year. As he stared at the picture closely, he and Afrika was sharing a hearty laugh together as they leaned on one another. The picture looked that natural and their smiles were genuine. This was the first picture that he actually like and that was saying a lot. Another picture of Aziza whispering in his wife ear and the expression on her face made him suddenly burst out laughing. Aziza was saying something illicit in her ear again and she was giggling like a school girl. He picked up the phone and informed his supervisor that he needed to have a meeting with him and Commissioner Brown. He refused to disclose the content of the conversation he was seeking or the evidence he have to substantiate the accusations against Mulligan.

"Okay, Mr. Sullivan" Commissioner Brown said leaning forward with a faint smile. "What is all the mystery and secrecy?"

"I need you to assist my office in cleaning up the corruption within your ranks beginning with Sargent Mulligan."

"Many have tried Frank" she replied using his first name.

"I know Commissioner but not the streets."

"The streets?" she replied staring at him perplexed.

"Yes, ma'am. The streets" he reiterated.

"What's going on Frank?"

"I have viewed and know where that stolen evidence is located but there are few things that needs to be in place before we can institute anything."

"Are you at liberty to tell me who has this tape" she inquired.

"Naomi, you are not going to believe this, but Afrika has it."

"Afrika?" she repeated stun. "How in the hell did he get it?"

"That I don't know but he has Mulligan having a private conversation with a guy named Blackout."

"Reginald Wallace?" she stated his government name. "And you have this on tape?"

"Me, no but Afrika does. I have to conclude like him that he's the person for the string of homicides that's been occurring in certain drug areas."

"I didn't know that you and Afrika was so tight" she slightly smiled.

"We have interacted on several occasions" he smiled knowing she knew they were tight. All of them have taken pictures together at the Lawyers Forum. She was with Aziza and Margarette two weeks ago shopping for baby clothes.

"What do you need me to do?"

"First, one of the officers associated with this case is requesting immunity. This is where you come in Mr. Anderson. Would you like to be associated with cleaning up the corruption that exist in most police department or remain with blinders on?" he openly challenged him while staring in his eyes. Naomi almost broke character and burst out laughing. He was always crying about people not stepping up in investigations. Well, let's see if he steps up.

"Granted" he replied without hesitating.

"Thank you, sir" he replied slightly grinning. "Commissioner, ma'am. We need to get Officer Morales transferred out once he place is transfer papers in and no one can make it happen quicker than you. Once that occurred, we can move on Mulligan and Blackout. Do I have your permission to tell Afrika that everything is a go?"

"Once Morales papers hit my desk, I will pull him" she assured him.

"Thank you, ma'am" he smiled over at her. "I know this meeting will remain private. Afrika had an elaborate plan, and I must admit, he can be so devilish when he wants to be" he smiled directly at Naomi who couldn't contain her smile or giggle as Mr. Anderson looked on confused. When you associate the word impish or coy with Afrika, you might as well just request handcuffs. He will have immense pleasure in watching Mulligan fall from grace. He only wish that Afrika would put him in the loop. Granted, he didn't know shit about the streets and as he said, it's no place for an on-the-job training. So, he will allow the streets to reek its justice. The streets are unmerciful while the justice system is a criminal paradise and sanctuary.

As they sat at Mt. Emphraim and Sycamore Street, Morales stared over at Smooth. "I'm looking to transfer out" he blurted out.

"What? Why?" he asked surprised by his statement.

"I can't do this anymore, man" he admitted returning his stare. "I'm afraid of getting caught up in a friendly fire scenario" he expressed his concern. "I see how those three white boys are peeking at him" he said hardening his eyes.

"But where will go?" he asked denouncing his intentions.

"Put me on a corner doing traffic but I need to get away from Mulley."

"Have you submitted your letter?"

"Last month" he replied lying.

"Last month!" he repeated surprised. "Damn, man."

"I heard they need some bi-lingual officers on the east side, and I applied" he continued with his lie. "Why don't you transfer out also?"

"Na, I'll go down with the ship."

"Don't let that money become your addiction" he urged him.

"Too late" he lightly chuckled. "Plus, I love the ladies."

"Yeah, a little too much" he admitted returning his smile then becoming quiet. He wanted to plea with smooth to abandon his friends, but he knew his words would fall on deaf ears. All he could do was continue to keep him in his prays.

One week later after talking to Smooth, he was suddenly transferred to another drug squad on the east side. How fortunate was that? He didn't know how to react to the news, but he was thankful that things worked out for him. Transferring out wasn't as hard as he thought it would be it would be. They all seem pleased except Smooth. After collecting all his stuff, he shook their hands and thank Mulligan for the opportunity to obtain the experience he needed before walking out. Stepping out into the afternoon sun, he lifted his head and inhaled deeply. He was free. Starting tomorrow, he would have a new lease on life and won't venture into the corrupt side of law enforcement ever again. All can be contributed to Afrika and the work he put in for him.

Mulligan received a heads up two days later about rumors of the sudden reappearance of the video by Frank Sullivan. His informant also informed him that Frank was waiting for an appointment with Judge Taylor to present his evidence. Rumors also said several drug dealers have pass a lie detector test and will testify if necessary, in his affidavit. How Sullivan obtained that evidence doesn't matter. He won't place it back into the evidence cage that's for damn sure and where they keep evidence at the prosecutor's office was a joke. He was advised to get all his personal business in order if he couldn't obtain the evidence. If the accusations were true, he could be indicted within the next few days not weeks. A look of dread and ambivalence consumed his face as he ended his conversation and place the phone back into its cradle.

"What's wrong Mulley?" Dog asked staring over at his partner and closest friend. "You look like somebody just walked over your grave" he mentioned with a coy smile.

"Somebody did" he replied causing Dog to lose his smile and stare over at him. "They have the video."

"Who!? How!?

"The who is Frank Sullivan and the how is I don't know" he replied.

"Fuck! What are we going to do?" he asked revealing his nervousness.

"We need to contract Blackout" he found himself saying.

"Blackout! No!" he stated adamantly while shaking his head. "Are you seriously considering taking out a prosecutor?"

"Does it look like I'm fucking around" he snapped shooting him a cold stare then staring back at the corner boys selling his product.

"Mulley, we have done some scandalous shit over the years, but what you are suggesting is crazy, man."

"We won't be doing shit. Blackout will be and we will take him out if he gets that evidence."

"I don't know about this Mulley" he stated opposing him for the third time in their career.

"Okay, what do you suggest?" he asked catching his eyes. "If Sullivan submit that evidence, we are all going down. I for one don't see myself doing time with motherfuckers I put away. Do you have the vaguest idea what will happen to us?"

"Yeah" he admitted solemnly.

"I am not going to jail for the next fifteen to twenty years. After initially getting the fur tore off our assess, they will fuck us like little bitches while sucking on somebody else dick. Once they are finished with us, they will pass us around for a pack of cigarettes. I don't want to sit down to take a piss like some bitch, but that and so much more awaits us if we don't get that evidence. I know what I am suggesting is despicable but self-preservation out-weigh all logic" he said hardening his eyes with a distance stare.

"Don't Mulley."

"Listen, I'll handle this shit on my own. Get the fuck out" he ordered as he sat there glaring at him. "Get the fuck out!"

Dog opens the passenger's door and steps out. He was barely able to close the door before when Mulley suddenly pressed on the accelerator and pulling away from the curb almost initiating an accident. He watched him turn the corner of Marlton Pike heading towards Baird Boulevard heading towards Camden High. Dog stared over at the corner boys staring over at him. All he could do was turn and go in the opposite direction. He could only hope that his friend didn't do what he was threatening, or shit will get complicated and very quickly after murdering a prosecutor investigating them. Blackout is somebody that he didn't want to jump in bed with under no circumstances. He wouldn't just take out Sullivan, but his whole seed if necessary to fulfilled his mission.

"Hey, where are you?"

"In the city, what's up?"

"Meet me inside Camden High Park."

"I can be there is twenty minutes."

"I'll be waiting" he replied ending his conversation. He was enjoying the basketball game when he spotted Blackout approaching while staying in the shadows.

"Yeah, what's up?" he asked scanning the area.

"I need Frank Sullivan hit. Do you have a problem with that?"

"What are you paying?"

"Twenty-five G's."

"You need to double that for a prosecutor."

"You got it once the job is done."

"Na, half now and the balance once the job is complete."

"I'll place it in your hands tomorrow."

"Just call me" he replied retracing his steps into the shadow then mysteriously disappearing. He received his partial payment including the home address of Frank the next morning. He did his usual reconnaissance of his neighborhood during the day when most were working including distinguishing two separate routes as emergency get aways if necessary. He drove through the neighborhood at night also to get faintly familiar. While he took all of his percussions, how was he to know which cars belong to which home owner? The smoke glass Lexus and Yukon was just other vehicles to him. He never saw the heavily armed guys sitting low inside as he drove past. On the night he decided to ring Sullivans doorbell and wait for it to be answer by Frank then blow his motherfucking brains out if he didn't surrender the evidence, the moon was full and illuminating the area. As he stepped out of his car and proceeded towards his target house, two men suddenly stepped out of the Lexus and two more stepped out of the Yukon cradling street sweepers. They exchanged a long stare until the two guys holding the street sweepers chambered a round. A light chuckled escaped him as he backed up to his car then climbed inside and pulled away. The whole scenario was being recorded from the Yukon. The four men didn't climb back into the vehicles. Instead, they climbed into a Cadillac Escalade and changed position just in case he doubles back. When he informed Mulley that somebody has four street soldiers sitting on Sullivan's house, he was shocked. When he mentioned about returning the down payment, he told him he will hold on to it for the next hit he might have. Although not pleased at all, what was Mulley going to do? Insist, na, that wouldn't be healthy for his body even if he was five-o. One thing the incident affirmed in him, Blackout will be taken out if he complete the contract or not.

The next morning Afrika was casually walking into the prosecutor's office and requested a meeting with Frank.

He was surprised as hell to see him. "What's up Afrika?" he asked shaking his hand and smiling while staff member stared on. Staring in his eyes, there was a slight intensity.

"Walk with me" he instructed leading him away from the office.

"Sure, where are we headed?"

"Naomi is waiting on us."

"Naomi, what's up?"

"You will see" he replied walking on the elevator and exiting on the fifth floor. They walked into her outer office. "What's up Renee" he greeted her smiling.

"What's up Afrika?" she replied smiling. "What's up Frank?"

"What's up girlfriend?"

"Mrs. Brown is waiting on y'all."

"Thanks" he replied leading the way through the second set of doors then lightly tapping on Naomi's door.

"Come in."

Frank was surprised to see his supervisor sitting across from Naomi.

"Good morning, everybody" greeted Afrika as he and Sullivan took a seat.

"What's up Afrika?" she asked leaning slightly forward. "You don't ask for a meeting unless something came up. What is it?"

"Secrecy was needed to protect those that are associated with what we are planning, right?"

"What happen?" she asked already knowing that she wasn't going to please with what he was about to reveal.

"I got something that I need for y'all to see" he addressed her puling out a CD from his leather bag. "May I?" he asked staring over at her.

"By all means" she replied watching him getting to his feet and sliding the CD into the player then pressing play. As they focused on what was video, Frank reacted.

"That's where I live!" he announced causing Naomi to sit up.

"What?"

"That's my street, Naomi" he declared hardening his eyes. "What's this Afrika?"

"Somebody running their face" he replied staring directly at his supervisor as he and Afrika exchanged quick glances. "There is more" he said, as they focused back on the video. They watched the silhouette of a person climbing out of a car and slowly approaching his front door. When the silhouette pause with a weapon in his hand, the diminished light didn't hide his identity. There was no doubt that it was Reginald Wallace a.k.a Blackout. Four mysterious guys suddenly materialized in front of his house and two were holding AK's. You can see Blackout backing up while keeping his eyes fixed on the four strangers then pulled away.

"How did he know where I live?" he asked staring at Afrika.

"The better question is who did your supervisor confided in" he replied with a slight snarl as Naomi and Frank coldly stared at his supervisor. He would dare try to flip the script or insinuate that Naomi or Afrika was the leak. That would be very suicidal because Afrika would have beaten the shit out of him and not a smart career move because Naomi would file obstruction charges.

Walking back to his office, Frank was heated and openly shaken. His supervisor had put him, his wife and their unborn son in jeopardy. "Was that your men?"

"Some close friends looking out for you and Margarette."

"And we appreciate it" he said hardening his eyes.

"Don't share this with her. I don't need her placing unnecessary stress on y'all unborn child" he suggested.

"I won't" he replied. "I'm going to start writing charge papers on Captain Wainwright and Lt. Stone. I will also be considering your proposition, also."

"It's about time" he replied grinning.

Mulley and his squad was in Centerville making their collection when Dog spotted an awfully familiar car.

"Yo, Mulley. Do you see that white Honda?" Dog asked pointing at it while it was park in front of Joe's Barber Shop. "I continuously see that car parked in front of Bear's house.

Since we got that information from Betty Boo two months ago, I have been keeping my eyes on him. He constantly be hanging out at Bear's place, but his visits have gotten shorter.

"Do you know who owns the car?"

"Yeah, some high yellow motherfucker named Amir."

"Is he in the game?"

"We don't have a rap sheet on him, not even a parking ticket" he replied. "Although we haven't been able to connect Bear and his crew to the drug game, he's about something."

"What's his background?"

"His mother is a social worker. He's the oldest of three children. Now here's the confusing thing, the kid don't work but his car is paid in full. There is no evidence that his mother cosigned for him to obtain the car."

"How?"

"Because the piece of shit that she drives need a complete overhaul" he replied snickering. "He's a student at Rutgers University. With the price of the tuition, there is no way in the world that his mother could afford that, but somebody could. His tuition was paid in full. He is studying to become a lawyer and the kid is good at it from what I gathered. He is constantly near the top ten in his academics."

"Another damn lawyer, that's all I need" Mulley openly snarled. "What year is he in?"

"He will be graduating in August."

"Fuck that!" insisted White Boy. "Let's snatch his high yellow ass up and shake the tree to see what falls out."

"Whoa Whitey" insisted Mulley. "The last time we leaped without looking, I got burned. I know y'all don't want to go through the same bullshit that I went through, do y'all?" he asked not expecting an answer. "Where did he do his intern?"

"At Justice 4 All" Dog replied catching his eyes. "It appears that Afrika is grooming his young ass."

"Afrika?" he openly snarled again. "I can't stand his black ass. Since Shakira obtained that civil restitution, Commissioner Brown haven't been exceedingly unhappy with me" he shared. "Do you think that Afrika might have bankrolled his education?"

"I don't know Mulley" he replied honestly. "You don't know it, but Afrika does a lot for his community but undercover. He actually brought a hundred computers and distributed them to Pyne Poynt and Cooper Middle to form a computer class. Did you know that Afrika and Bear's crew goes back to elementary school together?"

"No, I didn't" he replied surprised by the revelation. "Listen" Mulley said catching their eyes. "We will start shaking that tree and see what falls. We will start by trailing him and allowing him to peek us out. We have got to see how he will react knowing that he is under surveillance.

Around six o'clock, Amir called Bear to inform him that he has been tailed by someone for about two weeks and they are back. Bear informed him not to worry and that the tail was five-o. Only then did he reveal their plan.

"What? All this time I was told to come to your house I was being set up as bait by you and Afrika."

"Yeah."

"Man, that's fuck up. Here I am thinking that you was about to bring me into the squad when y'all was actually playing me."

"First and foremost, we haven't invested in your dumb ass to follow in our tracks. Get that straight in your head" he growled. "We have greater plans for your ass. Secondly, nobody is playing you and I personally resent you implying that."

"I'm sorry" he apologize. "Y'all didn't have to keep me in the dark."

"Maybe not but we did so get the fuck over it. Afrika got Betty Boo to whisper in their ears" he revealed.

"Betty Boo, but why her?"

"You are a better man than the way you treated her, and Afrika knew she would get some delight at putting five-o on your high yellow ass for unknowingly fucking her cousin" he lightly snicker at the incident.

"But I didn't know until they were face to face."

"Yeah, we heard" he replied. "Where are you now?"

"Coming up on Camden High."

"This is what I need you to do. I need time to set this thing up. When you hit Kaighn Avenue, go to the library for a half hour. When you leave there, I need you to go to the main terminal on Broadway and walk inside. You will see somebody that you are acquainted. Once you are back in your car, hook a U-turn. If you don't see them as you drive back up Broadway, don't worry, they are there. They probably will be driving parallel to you on both sides. Retrace your route back to Parkside then go to Donkey's and get yourself something to eat. Little brother, it is extremely important for our scheme that you play things by ear and remain cool no matter what comes down" he stressed. "Do I make myself clear?"

"Yeah, I got you."

"Good, now let's set this thing off" he replied ending their conversation then putting everybody on point, especially

Afrika. If Amir play his hand, Mulley and his goon will bite their hype especially when he exit the speedline carrying a bookbag.

Amir followed Bear instructions to a T. Entering the main speedline, he notice Gabby smiling at him. She was studying studio engineering at Temple University and hooked him up for sound then extended a weightless leather book bag to him. Once she was finish, she turned to catch the next available train back to Philly. When he exit the terminal, and hooked that U-turn, his tail was gone. As he drove back up Broadway, he spotted one driving up S 6th Street and the other on S 4th Street riding parallel to him just like Bear had predicted. He lightly snicker at their antics as a tail picked him up and stayed a half a block behind him as he turned on Kaighn Avenue. As he cross Louis Street, he spotted Tek9 vehicle empty. As he near Green Street, he spotted him and Kimba standing in the shadows. Murk and Black was nonchalantly standing counter corner to Donkey's. He spotted Bear's SUV on the corner of Haddon and Kaighn Avenue.

Afrika and Frank was sitting on the Boston Cream Donut shop parking lot across the street from Donkey's. He was glad that Afrika included him in his sting operation. Parkside appears so much different to him when the sun went down. Although a beautiful area to drive through during the day, the night revealed a completely different scene. The heart beat of a community is what Afrika calls it. He took that perspective and applied it to his own community. If you didn't check the heartbeat, you wouldn't know that his community existed. Although tranquil, his coming son would haven't blinders on his eyes like he did growing up. His eyes have ignored so much thinking it didn't affect him but being a part of the human family it does affect him just like Afrika. With the bar being around the corner, those that dwell in the darkness and vehicles were constantly consuming the area. Young and middle age men were conducting business in the shadows while promiscuous young ladies and women were trying to conduct their illicit business with possible tricks while pimps and other threatening individuals was watching everything and everyone. Five-o would cruise pass occasionally but never stopping or deter what they knew what was transpiring.

"Is it like, this every night?" he asked watching a barely legal girl walking into an alley with a middle-aged man.

"Na, they respect Sundays somewhat" he replied slightly grinning.

"If I can see this, where is the cops?"

"When you figure that out, please share it with this community" he replied watching Kimba and Tek9 shooing some girls they knew away.

"This is ridiculous, Afrika" he slightly snarled.

"To live in Parkside, you have to accept certain draw backs while adopting to the norms of the community. Ask any of them would they flip their script and move their families into North" he said peeking over at him.

"I doubt that seriously" he replied having never venture into North and doesn't have any intentions either. As a white boy, they would definitely think that he has some form of mental problem casually walking through their streets and that just might get him a pass by acting psychotic. "Is Amir the young man that you are mentoring?"

"Me? Hell no" he replied laughing. "Frank, none of my other partners could have pulled off what Bear initiated. He took that little knucklehead under his wings when he was twelve. Amir was heading straight to a juvenile facility then to prison when he became an adult if not for Bear. He turned him completely around. Snatching his young butt up with one arm also assisted his development and reform" he shared snickering again. "Now, they are damn near joined at the hip. He will be graduating in August with his law degree. Just imagine, I'll have him four years before his contract is up."

"You know a lot of people are wondering about your friends."

"They are not my friends, Frank" he corrected him. "They are my family. I have never concerned myself with what anybody thinks about my family. I can only advise those wondering people to keep it a secret in their minds and make it audible. Some of them can be very emotional especially Tek9" he shared snickering.

"Tek9? He doesn't give me the impression to be the emotional type of guy" he shared his opinion. "Actually, he, Kimba and Black are somewhat menacing to be honest. If I hadn't interacted with their crazy asses over the years, I would be that white boy crossing in the middle of the street and damn near getting hit by a bus to avoid them" he shared then suddenly burst out laughing with Afrika. He personally haven't figured out which one he liked the most. Tek and Kimba had slick tongues but Black has that devilish charm. Their intellect is what shocked the hell out of him. His perception of them was completely off base and so was their respect for him. How he realized he was being accepted by them was hilarious to him but not those standing around.

When they had invaded his space a couple of years ago at a social function looking like pure gangsters as he was talking to his predominate Caucasian friends, they did excuse themselves then usher him away as his friends looked on in shock not knowing what was about to transpire or come to his assistance. They kept him entertained in a corner for two hours debating and laughing. Peeking over at Margarette walking with Aziza, Shakira, Naomi and Tweety, he blew her a kiss then continue enjoying them. Yeah, he liked all of Afrika family member and didn't care about the rumors and speculations just like Afrika and Naomi. "Substantiate your claims or shut the fuck up" he told his constitutes with slightly hardening eyes.

"Here we go" announced Afrika seeing Amir's Honda turning off of Kaighn Avenue.

Just as he was about to turn into Donkey's parking lot, Mulley and his boys pulled up and impeded him.

"Freeze motherfucker! Don't move!" order the entourage of men as spectators got out of the way seeing their guns drawn.

Bear and Afrika was in the shadow recording the entire process.

"Keep your hands on the steering wheel and don't move bitch!" order Dog snarling at him.

"What did I do officers?"

"You are guilty of being black and driving a nice car" replied Mulley sarcastically.

"Now that is an unwarranted and racist remark, sir. What is your name and badge number?"

"My name is kiss; my ass and my badge number is 187. Any more questions?"

"Just one, why did you pull me over?"

"Because I can" Mulley replied grinning. "Snatch his high yellow ass out of there."

As he opens the door, Red Neck and White Boy snatched him out and slam him on the hood of the car. "Why did you do that?" he asked staring up into Red Neck na White Boys eyes.

"You was moving too slow" Red Neck replied while they lightly patted him down.

"Place cuffs on his ass" instructed Mulley.

"Why are you placing me in handcuffs?" he asked feeling them tightening around his wrist.

"For your protection" White Boy replied.

"How does placing cuffs on me for my own protection? Unless y'all have intentions of illegally putting your hands on me then yes, putting me in cuffs would be for my protection."

"What you need to do is shut your mouth and listen" ordered Mulley looking around. "You are going to answer some questions for us, and your answers determines your fate."

"My fate" he repeated then burst out laughing. "Officer, I don't have anything to say about anything until you tell me what this shit is all about."

"During our traffic stop, the scent of marijuana was detected so we searched your car" he smiled at.

"What marijuana?" he suddenly snicker. "So, your lie is going to give you the right to search my car illegally, huh?"

"We suspect you picked something up at the main terminal down town and suspected that a drug transaction had happened" he informed him. "A jury foolishly believe everything that a cop write and reinforced under oath."

"Apparently, your oath doesn't mean shit you or your goons because that is what they are" he replied. "What is going on?"

"What is happening between you and Bear?"

"Bear? Who in the hell is Bear?"

"The motherfucker's house you where your car was parked in front of yesterday, the days before that and last week" snapped Dog snarling over at him.

"Donna might not be very attractive, but she is far from a bear" he replied slightly smiling.

Before he knew it, he was slap viciously across his face by Red Neck.

"You bitch ass motherfucker" he declared spitting out a mouth filled with blood. "You were right to place me in handcuffs for my own protection because I would be beating the shit out of your racist white ass."

"Did Bear and his crew have anything to do with the disappearance of Blood?" inquired Mulley.

"You are supposed to be five-o" he replied spitting more blood from his mouth. "Do your damn job because I don't know this Bear character you are constantly referring" he reiterated.

"Listen here, you high yellow nigger" snorted Mulley.

"Your mother is a nigger just look at you" Amir interrupted him as a blow struck him in the back of the head from Dog forcing him to stagger forward straight into a fist from White Boy.

"You are going to answer my questions or your days of seeing the sun rise is short. Where is Blood?"

"Who in the fuck is Blood!" he demanded.

"Did Bear and his crew take out Blood's crew on S.4th Street as retaliation?"

"I don't know this Bear character but what retaliation? What are you rambling about?"

"Listen, you look like a smart guy."

"Reverse psychology, huh?" he stared grinning. "I'm smart. Smart enough to know not to talk to five-o."

"We are not trying to hem you up in anything. We just need your assistance. If you cooperate with our investigation, the court will take into consideration what you tell us."

"Man, you must think I'm some kind of clown. No, that's right, I'm a nigger, right?" he stated returning Mulley's stare. "I have told you repeatedly that I don't know this Bear guy but I do know Yogi and Boo-Boo. If you are going to keep repeating questions about somebody that I don't know, we will be here all night. Either arrest me or cut me loose."

"We are just talking jig-a-boo" stated Mulley.

"If we are just talking, take these handcuffs off."

"Will it help you to remember?"

"There is nothing that I need to remember but it would be easier for me to contact my lawyer" he informed them.

"Listen, you don't know us."

"What makes you think I am unaware of you and your Nextel Boys?" he asked with an eerie smirk. "I know all of y'all names Detective Mulligan, his personal Dog, White Boy Mike, Red Neck and Smooth" he informed them. "I see Morales finally got away from y'all scandalous asses. And Smooth he said catching his eyes. "The streets have nothing but love for you and it will a damn shame when you go down with them" he informed him.

Amir knowing their names shocked the hell out of them. They all started looking around nervously. Was this a setup? Was it?

Mulley suddenly clamped his fat fingers around his throat and was about to say something to him when he noticed Amir's eyes. They were diverted and a broad smile came to his face. Mulley noticed that his squad was also staring at something. As he released his gripped and turned around, he couldn't believe his eyes. What the fuck. Bear was standing there videoing the whole incident and standing beside him was Afrika with Frank Sullivan of all motherfucking people.

"Either charge my client or release him" Afrika instructed Mulley staring into his Irish green eyes. "Did you hear what I said Detective?"

By the time Tek9 and Kimba joined them, the two-group stood staring at one another while Bear continued to video. Mulley was stun and he knew he couldn't intimidate Bear to surrender the evidence. As though he read Mulley's mind, he extended the tape to Afrika with a menacing smirk.

"What's it's going to be Detective?"

"Release his yellow ass" he instructed standing defiantly. "What do you think you got there?"

"Three cops abusing their authority" Frank replied.

"You don't know what he was saying to us, Sullivan. He was threatening our families."

"Detective, you really need to shut your mouth before you dig yourself a deeper hole" Afrika advised him.

"That punk was threatening us, and my men will attest to that" he replied confidently.

"Not if they want to perjury themselves, you should have patted my client down better" he told them as Amir pulled out a miniature mic smiling at Mulley.

"Baraka (blessing gift).

"Yeah" Bear replied never averting his eyes from Mulley.

"Take pictures of Amir mouth then take him to Copper Hospital to get a MRI of his throat and not an X-ray."

"Come on, Amir" Bear said never averting his eyes from Mulley.

"Na, big brother. You stay here. I can take myself" he said spitting out more blood before climbing back into his vehicle then staring the engine. Donny Hathaway's "The Ghetto-Live" began to play as he placed the car in gear then hooked a U-turn and proceed up Haddon Avenue towards Cooper Hospital.

"Let's bounce brothers" he said as they started to turn. "Are you coming Frank?" he asked staring at the look of disgust upon his face before he turned to join them.

Mulley watched them climbing into their respected cars then pulling away. "Those scandalous motherfucker! Fuck! Fuck! Fuck!"

Three days has elapse with no repercussion. Mulley or his men knew what to make of the silence. One thing the silence did was fuck them up psychologically and Afrika knew that it would. His partners couldn't wait for the second phase. They had a street dealer that was willing to put himself in harm's way to assist Afrika and his partners. They assured him that he could get better protection than those that will be watching his back. When Dog approached him for their weekly payoff, he buck, and it surprised the hell out of him.

"I'm not giving y'all shit anymore! Y'all been pimping us for over a year and getting paid! I rather stand like a motherfucking man then continue to be on my knees for you and your whore as master, Mulley. I rather go to jail than continue to fuck with y'all bitch asses" he told them surprising his crew. He had kept them out of the loop and in the dark.

"Are you sure this is what you want?" Dog asked returning his cold stare.

"Fuck you Dog! Go lick your master's wrinkled balls bitch!" he snarled at him while his crew burst out laughing.

"You weep what you sow" Mulligan told him slightly smiling.

"You just remember it, bitch!" he told them as they turned and walked away then climbed into their vehicles and pulled away.

Printed in the United States
by Baker & Taylor Publisher Services